TIBUF

Love, crime & rebellion
in early California

By David Caraccio

PREFACE

My journey in the saddle alongside Tiburcio Vasquez began with a thin little red book called *Crimes and Career of Tiburcio Vasquez* (reprinted by the San Benito County Historical Society). From the moment I plucked it off the shelf at the small museum gift shop in San Juan Bautista and began reading, I was hooked on the life of this prominent California bandit and determined to dig deeper into history and write a novel about him.

The more I researched and wrote, the more I became fascinated with Tiburcio's life, the times in which he lived and the rich characters he knew and confronted. I was living in the same area where he had roamed and it did not take long before this epic story began playing in my mind. I have been surprised at how many people, especially in California, do not have any idea who Tiburcio Vasquez was and how large he loomed from the years of 1854-1875.

His relative obscurity does not come from a lack of excellent research or a scarcity of recorded history. I am indebted to those who researched and wrote about my subject long before I picked up that tiny book in the gift shop. I feel obligated to specifically mention and give credit to a few of these historians and writers.

Ray Iddings of 3Rocks Research directed me to the California Digital Newspaper Collection, a vast, wonderful repository of newspapers that includes numerous articles about the events and characters in *Tiburcio!* I borrowed from 3Rocks.org's digital reproduction of Eugene Sawyer's *Life and Career of Tiburcio Vasquez,* especially to accurately describe what happened inside the courtroom at the famous bandit's murder trial.

Many other authors and their works gave me insight into Tiburcio's life and the extraordinary events that unfolded. Through their vivid accounts I gained a thorough understanding of my novel's characters and the era in which they lived. I highly recommend:

- John Boessenecker's *Bandido: the life and times of Tiburcio Vasquez* and *Lawman: the life and times of Harry Morse*
- William B. Secrest's *Dangerous men: gunfighters, lawmen & outlaws of old California*
- Adabelle Cogswell's *Tiburcio Vasquez: el bandido sin par*
- George Beers' *The California Outlaw: Tiburcio Vaquez* compiled by Robert Greenwood

Numerous other writers, stories, articles and websites guided me in each step of my journey.

DAVID CARACCIO

Tiburcio! is a fictionalized story based on true events. Historical accounts sometimes vary. When faced with discrepancies, I meshed the consistent versions. On a few occasions, I chose an account that best advanced the story line while staying true to my characters and the time in which they lived. It's worth noting that I embellished the theme of a Vasquez-led rebellion against the state. There were rumors, and I wanted to explore the plausibility of such a revolution given the bitterness and fear that existed among Californians at the time.

I must admit that during this journey, at the risk of sounding self-absorbed and a little odd, I sometimes felt Tiburcio pushing my pen and tugging my thoughts from beyond the grave, as if he also wanted his story retold.

- David Caraccio

PART I: GARCIA
Chapter 1: Jailed
Los Angeles County
May 1874

Tiburcio Vasquez lay on his back on the jail's putrid floor with a torso full of buckshot. He peered up at an old gringo doctor whose stiff whiskers protruded from his chin and cheeks like dry needle grass in the village square in August. Tiburcio squinted up at the lines deeply carved in the physician's forehead from years of concern and countless hours of contemplation of symptoms and treatments for his patients. The doctor's name was Joseph P. Widney. He propped up Tiburcio's neck in one hand and poured firewater down his throat with the other before splashing more whiskey into the dozens of small, open wounds on Tiburcio's chest and midsection. Tiburcio's body tightened and he winced as pain tore through his body straight up from his toes through his genitals and into his eyeballs. Do not cringe, the bandit admonished himself. Do not let them see you flinch. For in the end, you will stand tall and they will cower like beaten dogs.

"I don't know why we are keeping him alive," groused a deputy standing several feet behind Widney.

The deputy's words were a tinny echo in his ear. Tiburcio wondered if he was the son-of-bitch who had shot him full of lead from point-blank range. The deputy held a single-shot Remington rifle across his belt buckle, the barrel loosely but confidently settled in his left hand and his right-hand finger caressed the trigger. A nickel-plated Colt .44 was holstered on his front hip. His butterscotch trousers were tucked into large black boots, and he wore a dark-blue shirt and a broad-rimmed hat.

"He's gotta be about the last desperado left to flush out of them hills," the deputy spit out. "The law's territory is growing and these sons of bitches don't have anywhere to go. 'Cept maybe Mexico. And they can have 'em down there."

The deputy was talking to his boss, Los Angeles County Sheriff Billy Rowland, who was standing, looking over Widney's shoulder. Rowland had been watching Widney's every move. Now, with an irritating glance back at the deputy, he snapped:

"Keep your mouth shut until the doctor finishes his work. Remember this bandit's worth a whole lot more to me alive than dead."

That was the uppermost fact on Rowland's mind. Rowland, a well-fed, popular figure, a damn good peacekeeper and an even better politician, stroked his graying, trimmed goatee in one hand as he removed a gold watch on a chain from the pocket of his gray vest with the other, noting the hour. He slipped the timepiece back in its spot.

There was a lot to accomplish, Rowland reminded himself, before those meddlesome lawmen from the north come down to whisk away his prized prisoner. The thought of handing Tiburcio Vasquez over to those ineffectual deputies dampened the glee of capturing the famous outlaw now writhing on the stone floor of his jail. How cunning he, Sheriff Rowland, had been in sidestepping the hordes of officious lawmen to catch his prey. How feted he would be by citizens and historians alike. He wondered what words of praise the governor would write in his proclamation before the Assembly.

But first he had to manage this current situation. He must manipulate the entire process, while he was in control, to the utmost benefit for his city and himself. The manic, noisy Mexican crowds outside the jailhouse had to be controlled. The pushy, droll newspaper reporters clamoring to get inside had to be influenced in what they wrote. And that talkative, trigger-itching deputy standing over there had better keep his wits about him. This was Tiburcio Vasquez, for God's sake. Not just any desperado. It had taken ten years and a legislative act to capture the bastard. Shaking his head in disbelief over the furor and consternation that one Mexican can cause, Rowland looked down in contempt at the seemingly helpless man they held captive.

The doctor was running his fingers slowly along Tiburcio's skin and down his torso, all sticky with blood and whiskey. He stopped as his fingers rolled over a metal ball protruding from a tiny open wound. Furrowing his gray-haired brow, he kept a finger on the ball and snapped up a small sharp knife. He began slicing away the damaged skin around the shotgun pellet.

"God damn. Another one," the doctor exclaimed. "How close was the gunman to this bandit?"

Not waiting for or expecting an answer, Widney deftly switched tools. Wielding forceps, he extracted the pellet. Time after time, for the past hour, Rowland and his deputy had watched him do this. Time after time, the doctor dropped the lead balls into an empty metal bucket. Clank. Clank. Clank

"This man is tough," the physician said, looking up at Rowland. "No doubt about it. You best put your top deputy on watch over him, Sheriff. He's definitely more alive than dead, and I would wager to say he could still leap up and accomplish a long day's ride, if you let him."

The physician's fingers probed the prostrate prisoner's body some more, skimming over the numerous lacerations in search of pieces of lead that he might have missed.

"I am pretty certain I didn't leave any buckshot to fester in him," Widney concluded. "If those pellets go undiscovered, they can travel silently through his body straight to the heart and" - he clapped once loudly - "instantly kill him."

The doctor spilled more whiskey into the bullet holes for good measure and took a swig himself.

"OK, let's get him up on that bed."

Tiburcio gritted his teeth. Do not cower, he told himself. Talk, joke, even laugh with the surgeon – but do not show pain or fear.

The three men awkwardly and callously lifted and dragged and finally dropped Tiburcio onto the thin, straw mattress that covered the rusty, iron cot bolted to the limestone block wall. They tossed a thin wool blanket over him, and turned to leave when the prisoner spoke for the first time.

"I don't blame you boys at all for this," Tiburcio grunted, his voice strong. The men froze in their tracks. "You had a job to do. That's all."

Then his eyes rolled back into their sockets, and he was out cold.

"Damn, he talks some good English for a greaser," the deputy whistled.

"I will come back in an hour," Widney said after checking to make sure Tiburcio wasn't dead. "I don't like him slipping into unconsciousness like that. If he appears to be struggling for breath, come get me right away."

● ● ●

A cold, briny breeze sliced through the iron bars of the window and touched Tiburcio's face and flitted across his body, which was covered with only a threadbare wool blanket and shivered atop a dirty, thin, damp mattress. His eyes were closed but he knew he was alone in the dark. He had no idea where, though. So he listened carefully, the way he had paid attention to the slightest creak, quietest breath or slowest click of a gun's hammer every time he rested during his twenty years on the run or during those dangerous stints in the penitentiary. He thought he heard soft conversations and placid music in the distance. His eyes opened and the first thing he saw was a framed square of dark-gray sky illuminated softly by the moon beyond the window. His mind was fuzzy and an uneven pain throbbed up and down his left side like someone had dug out small chunks of his flesh with a dull dagger. He felt like vomiting.

Then, a noise startled him. Lie still, listen, he told himself. What do you hear? The whicker of a horse? Whose horse? A single lawman or an entire posse? Arriving or leaving? Grab your Henry rifle! Grab it, damn it! Arm yourself. Be ready. But his ravaged body refused to obey. He could not move, and it didn't matter. There was no rifle at his side.

Tiburcio glanced at the dim, yellow glow of a kerosene lamp burning in the narrow corridor, the illumination falling just short of the crosshatch metal bars of his dismal, dark jail cell. Slowly his mind lifted out of the fog like a boat suddenly thrust high on a rolling wave and caught for a moment by a lone figure from shore gazing out at the horizon. He grasped the idea of where the hell he was. He shivered again but he was beginning to piece it all together. They had done it, all right. The gringo bastards had finally won and had captured their prize. No revolt. No courageous fight. No freedom for his people. The lawmen's long hunt had ended. His dream - his people's dream - of ultimate reprisal and a long-fought-for fulfillment was over. Or was it?

He heard a horse whinny again. Now, his ears more clearly picked up the sounds in the distance: the soft plucking of a guitar braided with hopeful notes from a fiddle and a dull chattering of Spanish. Something was going on outside this jail wall, if he could only see what.

He turned his eyes upward and looked disconsolately at the iron-barred window. He breathed deeply several times, drew a loud groan and summoned the strength to roll over and struggle to his knees. He halted. The stinging pain caused him to gasp and hold still. He leaned his shoulder on the thick limestone wall for a moment. Then, slowly and painfully he hobbled to his bare feet, palms and cheek pressed against the cold stone. The cot creaked under his weight. He groaned with it. Breathing hard, he reached up and grasped the iron bars with both hands and pulled as if his life depended on it. He could just barely get his eyes level with the window. Steadying himself and gaining a toehold on an imperfection in the limestone, he heaved upward another inch and gazed out into the drifting fog and saw dozens of silhouetted figures flickering in the firelight, some sitting, some standing, some dancing. It was a beautiful, intensely encouraging sight. He was not alone. He had not been abandoned. In all his suffering, he managed a small smile.

Weakly clinging to the cold iron bars, he tried to think back to when he had last eaten. It had been a long time. He smelled a strong odor of whiskey on his tattered clothes and skin and tasted it on his breath. Why? But, of course. He remembered now. That was several hours ago, perhaps half a day, maybe even more. Tiburcio didn't really know. But he now found himself somehow clinging to the frigid metal bars and staring out of his cell window at the preternatural scene outside: a jailhouse vigil in the fog, keeping the revolutionary fire stoked.

Newly inspired by the thought of his people caring so much about this helpless prisoner and holding true to the revolution with enough fervor to spend several days and nights bivouacked outside his jail cell, Tiburcio summoned the strength and shouted: "Compadres! Amigos!"

At first, just a few heads looked up to find who had spoken. Tiburcio strained to raise his voice.

"*Aqui! Aqui!*" he cried out.

Several more people stopped what they were doing to try to locate the speaker. Determined to address his followers before the guards came running down the corridor to swoop in and beat him, he drew a deep breath and called loudly again: "Compadres! Amigos!"

He heard people hushing others in the crowd. Soon, the music and conversation died down. Tiburcio saw dozens of figures approaching the jail wall. They stopped twenty feet from his cell window.

"It's Tiburcio!" several people called out. "It's *el capitan*!

"Listen, *mi compadres*," he barked to the gathering crowd below. "Do not give up! I may be wounded. I may be caged.

TIBURCIO!

But I, Tiburcio Vasquez, am alive. I am well. And I am stirred by your love and loyalty, my countrymen. I promise that as long as you are willing, I will never let our twenty-year struggle on behalf of thousands of wronged Californios - citizens like you and me - languish and die. I know you are counting on me to lead our revolt against the Yankee invaders. And I am counting on you to keep the fire burning in each and every one of us. Are we going to let *la revolucion* die out? Hell no!"

"They said they are going to hang you!" yelled a voice, not fatalistic, not worried, but proud and defiant.

"No jailhouse has ever kept Tiburcio Vasquez locked up! And none ever will," their leader answered back. "I will soon be free! We, as a people, will soon be liberated! The time is near! Very near! Have faith - and long live the revolution!"

Tiburcio crumbled onto the cot and fell unconscious as the guards rushed into the cell. He spent the next two days confused, trembling and battling a high fever. The crowd on the free side of the limestone wall grew stronger in numbers and remained faithful to their captive leader. In his state of delirium, however, Tiburcio only saw crystal clear visions of his joyous youth and lived in the simple pleasures of a pastoral life of twenty years ago. He existed only in a dream of glorious fiestas, open land, golden palominos and, most beautiful of all, Anita.

Chapter 2: Fiesta
Salinas
1854

The young vaquero sat confidently astride his palomino under the blanched midday sun that hung and rippled over the plaza crowded with colorfully dressed men, women and children. Nearly every eye was on the teenager and his horse.

Boy and horse stood proud. They were one. Both light of limb. Both possessing shimmering eyes. The rider was festooned in a graceful blue silk *chaleco* that fit short and and tight at his chest, a crimson sash around his waist. The golden horse shined in an embossed leather saddle and silver mounting. The horseman's azure pants were snug in the seat and flared out over embroidered boots enclosed in silver stirrups. The steed's *anquera* cascaded halfway to the ground. Its neck and tail arched and flung high. Together, as one, they were ready to give the people a show.

The horseman, Tiburcio Vasquez, smiled and thrust high over his head an ivory-handled Bowie knife, its blade glinting in the sun, for the crowd to see. With a flick of the wrist, the blade sliced deep into the ground where just two inches of the handle could be seen. Tiburcio and the horse pranced a hundred paces away and waited as the audience hushed. The palomino curveted, and then became very still. Tiburcio nodded to a group of older vaqueros, who were watching their young companion on their own richly caparisoned horses. They had been friends of his father's and had known Tiburcio for over a decade. They nodded back in unison.

On either side of the plaza, two long queues of spectators, four hundred strong, eagerly waited. More people packed onto the narrow balconies of the two-story adobes that lined the square, leaning against the wood railings. The young caballero in the center looked over his captivated audience slowly, and then lowered his head and whispered in his palomino's ear: "*Arriba el Telon* !"

With that, Tiburcio spurred the mare to a full gallop, thundering toward the knife at a speed few had ever seen. Halfway there, Tiburcio threw his body over the right side of the horse, his left leg pressing hard against the saddle, his head inches from the crashing hooves. The ground blurred and his eyes strained to stay focused on the target - the knife - as the dirt and dust flew in every direction. Tiburcio labored to keep his outstretched right hand taut and steady. In a flash the knife that had lodged in the ground was gone, swept up by the handle without any slackening of speed. The onlookers gasped, then cheered.

Tiburcio halted for a brief moment, sitting back in the saddle again until he caught his breath and the festival-goers quieted.

"I need a small child, *un nino,*" he shouted out. "A boy, no older than three."

That was the age he had been the first time he sat on his papa's horse looking out at a crowd like this one. He felt his father breathing. He felt the horse breathing. Then he recognized his own heart thumping fast and in rhythm. He remembered being aware that he never wanted to leave that spot. He never wanted his father to let him go. Everybody was happy.

People looked at each other, murmuring about the gorgeous vaquero's request, and trying to find a compliant toddler. Those citizens who had seen Tiburcio ride before explained what he wanted to do and how he was carrying on his father's tradition but did not have his own child. Within a minute or two, a strong man carried his infant, two-and-a-half years old at the most, out to the vaquero and held him up. Tiburcio lovingly and confidently grabbed the child and held him strongly in the crook of one arm, fingers wrapped tight against him and his other hand holding the reins.

He turned abruptly and, clutching the child, madly galloped down one side of the plaza within a whisker of the crowd. When he rode at breakneck speed back down the other side, people asked, "where is he?" "Where did he go?" they wondered. "Is the baby all right?" They tried to get a glimpse at him, but he was completely hidden. Then someone pointed to one spurred heel - the only visible part of the rider - gripping the rear of the saddle. It was an old Comanche war stunt that Tiburcio's father had taught him many years before he died.

When he reached the end of the line of spectators, Tiburcio whipped over to the other side of the saddle and galloped in the same fashion in front of the opposite line of onlookers. The crowd was now chatting excitedly and shaking their heads in disbelieving admiration of such superb horsemanship, Tiburcio dashed diagonally across the plaza straight toward a group of revelers. They flinched and began to dart left and right to get out of the way before Tiburcio quickly reined his horse up onto its hind legs, pivoted it on one hoof and flew in the other direction, scaring another group of people across the way with same trick. He did this three or four times in lightning-quick movements before returning to the center of the square where he had begun. The child was wide-eyed but was not crying. Tiburcio kissed the young boy on the temple and the boy smiled. Everyone in the plaza whooped and roared and men flung their hats and women tossed red roses into the air. Later, the people in the plaza would contemplate and wonder if they had really seen what they witnessed, if it wasn't just some cunning act, how Tiburcio Vasquez hung onto a small child while disappearing from the saddle.

Tiburcio paused, his ensemble still looking lavish if just a little off-white from a thin coating of dust, and bowed in the saddle. He hugged the sweaty, convulsing neck of his palomino, and was done with a wave to the admiring crowd.

Tiburcio's father, Hermenegildo Vasquez, had first put him on a horse at age two. Before his tenth birthday he was breaking wild mustangs. For a decade, the father and son rode together everywhere, to the village for supplies, to hunt or out to the town's edge to watch the tall ships come into Monterey Bay, Often when they stopped, Tiburcio would catch Hermenegildo's exalted gaze upon him. The father envisioned his youngest son growing up to be a great soldier like himself, an explorer, trader and an adventurer as comfortable out at sea and in the saddle as he was on his own two feet standing on solid ground. The boy was well on his way. Hermenegildo knew he was passing on all the skills and ambition it would take for Tiburcio to succeed because this was the way his own father had taught him. But behind that proud stare he hoped he was also instilling in him forthrightness, integrity and all knightly characteristics. Those traits were more easily corrupted by outside forces. Tiburcio would then smile back and Hermenegildo would turn away satisfied.

"I remember when Spain forbid foreign traders from coming into our ports," his father said one day, gazing down at the emerald bay, busy with commerce. "It was my duty as a soldier to carry out this order. Now, Mexico is free to trade with anyone. See down there, son? That's an American ship … and those three canoes are heading out to that British clipper …"

Hermenegildo paused and observed Tiburcio before getting to his point.

"You must be ready for changes, son. Always be prepared for the unknown. I don't know how these foreigners from the east will change our landscape, or whether they will even stay long. But what I have taught you out here on these plains, on our long rides, will always serve you well - as it has served me. It is all you'll need to achieve success."

Before Tiburcio's thirteenth birthday, Hermenegildo's heart suddenly stopped. It happened in the middle of the night. When Tiburcio came to his father's death bed, he saw the same proud look frozen on his father's face, and he wondered if he had been in his last thoughts, seeing his son riding ahead of him across the open grasslands, laughing as his father pretended he could not catch the young boy on his steed.

After Tiburcio's performance, it was time to eat, drink, chat, laugh and flirt. Sitting high and comfortably in the saddle, Tiburcio slowly guided his steed through the plaza filled with chattering groups of people. Several caught Tiburcio's attention as he passed by.

"Tiburcio!" someone called. "Are you staying?"

"There will be more horsemanship, yes?" another asked, looking up at the energetic vaquero.

"Regrettably, I must soon depart. But please remember to get some rest and allow yourself plenty of time to ride into Monterey after the fiesta. There will be lots of dancing and singing this evening at my dance hall."

"*Y muchas bonitas* ?"

Tiburcio sprung out of the saddle to make his point.

"*Bonitas? Por sepuesta!* Lots and lots of beautiful women," he said. "Beautiful like this young *señorita*."

He stepped in front of the girl who happened to be walking by with a group of friends.

With one hand behind his back and the other across his sash, he faced the girl and stamped out a dance in the packed clay dirt, rhythmically accenting the steps with sharp claps. He moved with such cadence and expression it seemed as if an orchestra was playing nearby even though there was no music to be heard. A few others stopped to watch. Some men laughed and the girl obligingly smiled, then blushed and quickly stole away with her tittering friends.

"Please, come to Monterey," Tiburcio pleaded to her and to anyone within earshot as he vaulted back into the saddle. "Visit my fandango tonight."

Indeed, many folk would. Once the festival tapered off in the late afternoon, dozens planned to make the two-hour trip to the coastal city to carouse into the next day at one of any number of cheap fandangos there. But Tiburcio's dance hall was by far the most popular. Located down by the waterfront, near the little theater, it looked a bit crude, he knew, but it was known to have the best music and the best dancing and fewer brawls than all the others. These characteristics, and an energetic, convivial host, brought to his fandango a broad segment of California's population. Typically, wealthier Californio families, being proud ancestors from the best families of Spain, did not freely associate with the humbler class. But Tiburcio's unreserved friendliness, regardless of one's status, coupled with his own family's high standing in the town, made everyone feel welcome - whether they were hombres from Chile, Peru or Mexico, Spanish dons, gold-rush gringos, city officials, passionate *señoritas*, quicksilver miners or U.S. soldiers. He might not know half of the patrons at the beginning of the night, but he was friends with most of them by dawn.

At least that's how it always used to be. As he looked across the plaza from atop his palomino, Tiburcio was reminded of the day not too long ago when everyone knew everyone else. Ten years ago, the only foreigners around town might be a runaway sailor or an adventurous trader, neither of whom tended to stick around all that long anyway. Today, at a festival, strolling down a Monterey street, or taking one step inside a dance hall, one could see how times were changing. The streets were more crowded, the fiestas less intimate, neighbors less familiar. On long rides across the countryside, Tiburcio could see that the great tracts of land owned by Spanish descendants were being broken up by more settlers laying claim to the territory.

More people, more disputes, yes - but more money for the taking, too. That's how Tiburcio looked at it.

Nodding to acquaintances from the saddle as they praised his showmanship, he shouted back reminders that his fandango would open at eight sharp. They smiled or gave a whoop and a holler. Young women cast coquettish looks, and he lowered his head and touched his brim. All the while, however, Tiburcio's eyes were steadfastly searching for one person. He scoured the masses for the slender beauty whose dark eyes reflected the world right back to him; whose pupils shined in opaque ponds like faraway stars; whose long, wavy, sable hair shimmered and flowed like a moonlit river; whose full cheeks and cheerful, fleeting dimples caused him to sigh. He hunted for and craved that beauty, Anita.

They were, foremost, friends. They first met as classmates - he the handsome kid from a prominent family in the city, she the fetching daughter of a wealthy Spanish don who owned a vast stretch of land somewhere north. But most of the year she lived with her grandmother in an adobe near the mission school. Long before Tiburcio and Anita had become aware of it themselves, others knew that they were budding lovers. Their relationship had commenced with sly glances exchanged at the mission or while passing on the streets with their elders in Monterey. It progressed to a few words traded back and forth in the plaza while their mothers visited shops, or after classes when the nuns and the priests were busy with more weighty matters than making sure kids were behaving. Their conversations elevated to a banter richly punctuated with coquettishness and interspersed with thrilling touches of the hand or arm that made their hearts race and could fill an afternoon of daydreaming.

By the time she was fifteen, two years younger than Tiburcio, whenever they saw each other in public, their first gazes were those of two souls who shared a secret. Any observer could fleetingly notice that these two children shared something that no one else knew; but an instant later the piercing light that welded their souls together would soften and all that could be detected was a glow of subtle, natural flirtation between boy and girl.

The adolescent secret - the bond - they shared was forged one afternoon when they found themselves together after school with the rare occasion of having no adults around and time on their hands. It was late afternoon but there was plenty of daylight left.

TIBURCIO!

"Are you sure you want to do this?" he asked, watching the shining gems glistening in her dark eyes. "We will have to get past the eyes of the nuns."

She smiled a little mischievously. "Yes!"

"All right, then. I'll teach you," he said. "But we cannot let anyone catch us, especially your father."

"Do not worry about my father. It would be much worse if we were caught by *mi abuela*."

"I know. I know," Tiburcio sighed. "She is trying to raise a proper lady."

"And she will – but she will get much more, too."

Glancing left, right and behind for grandmothers, fathers, nuns and padres, Tiburcio led his stallion over a hill and down into a secluded gorge in back of the mission. Anita followed.

Reaching a fenced-in field used for keeping cattle in at night, Tiburcio walked Anita and the horse around for a half-hour and talked to her about stallions and riding. Only then, was he ready to put Anita up on the palomino. He made sure the girths were tight so the saddle wouldn't slip. She grabbed the reins with her right hand and grabbed the saddle horn with the other, her back to the animal as he had told her. Tiburcio stooped, and she placed a left foot on his shoulder and the right one in his clasped hands. Raising gently, he popped Anita into the saddle and adjusted her outer skirts. They were alone and free.

"Now get down," he ordered. "You don't need lessons on riding like a proper lady. You are going to ride like a vaquero!"

Tiburcio helped her down, turned and walked away, leaving Anita standing alone in the middle of the field next to the large stallion.

"Where are you going?" she snapped.

But he didn't answer. He stepped outside the gate, closed it and turned around, his arms resting on the fence.

"Let's see you get on when there's nobody here to lift you."

"Tiburcio Vasquez! Is this your idea of teaching me to ride a horse?"

"Come on. We don't have all day. *Pronto!*"

Anita took hold of the reins and the pommel.

"Don't mount like a lady!" Tiburcio shouted. She frowned back at him. "A small child can mount that horse."

Each time she tried to step into the metal loop the horse sidestepped away. After several attempts and a moment of thinking, Anita had an idea. She led the palomino over to the fence near Tiburcio. She smiled self-assuredly at him. Tiburcio grinned. She climbed up on the fence as the horse stood close by. As she prepared to swing her leg over the back of the horse, it moved just out of reach. Anita fell off the fence into the dirt.

Tiburcio doubled over laughing. She tried this method again with the same results and Tiburcio's mirth could not be contained.

Anita charged at him and playfully slapped at his arms and shoulders.

"Show me!" she shouted. "Show me!"

"OK. OK," he relented. "I will. First, mount the horse from the left side. Grab the reins and the horn, like you already know how. That's right. Tight enough so he doesn't wander off."

Anita listened but the horse started to step backward.

"Not too tight," Tiburcio told her. "He's got a heavy bit."

He moved up next to her from behind to give further directions and breathed in the sweet rosemary and aniseed smell of her hair and skin. He shadowed her movements as she performed them.

"That's why he's moving back," he told her. "Now, face the rear of the horse. Take the stirrup, turn it this way and set your foot in it. Put the ball of your foot on the bottom of the stirrup. Reach over with this hand and put it on the cantle. With a small jump, swing your right leg up over the back. There!"

She was successfully astride the horse, sitting in the saddle like a vaquero.

"Good. Put your foot in the other stirrup, sit up and grab the rein with your right hand. You look great!"

"Don't you dare let go of this horse, Tiburcio."

TIBURCIO!

"This is just the beginning, Anita. I am going to teach you to ride like a vaquero by the beginning of summer. And not just geldings. You'll be riding astride stallions. Someday you will thank me for it."

Under his tutelage, she began riding confidently in just a few weeks. Her skill impressed him. The lessons and the time spent together riding was bittersweet for Tiburcio. He didn't want to spend a second with anybody else but the days often reminded him of his time riding with his father, forever lost. Still, they stole away to ride every chance they could and their happiness could not be dampened.

"You could ride this horse into battle!" he told her.

And the summer had just begun.

On another hot July day, Tiburcio suggested they ride down to the lagoon. He often brought two horses from home now, borrowing his brother's mare. They rode off from the mission in a hurry until they reached the loamy soil near the shady lagoon. There, they slowed their horses' gait so they could wend their way through the thick manzanita shrubs on the way down to the water. At a clearing on the water's edge, they dismounted and took their boots off. Tiburcio removed the knife he always had strapped to his leg and held it in his hand as he walked cautiously out on some boulders into the cold water. Anita waded in up to her ankles. Eying a pile of driftwood stuck on a clump of willows in the middle of the lagoon, Tiburcio suggested they go farther out.

Rolling up his trousers, he gingerly stepped on the slippery stones lying deeper in the water. He looked back at Anita.

"Come on!"

"I have on a skirt," Anita said.

"No problem. I will turn around and swim out to those willows. Meanwhile, undress and come out in your singlet."

When he had reached the willows, he turned around and was pleasantly surprised to see her skirt laid out on some shoulder-high chaparral near the banks. Anita was actually paddling toward him.

"All right!" he cheered.

She finally reached him and they hung onto the willow's branches and laughed. They swam around for about a half-hour until they felt it was prudent to get out.

"We better get out and lie on those rocks in the sun. It will take some time to dry off."

Tiburcio reached the bank first and shook as much water off his body and out of his hair as possible.

"Now turn around," Anita told him. "I am getting out."

Although they talked for an hour in the sun, she did not let him look at her lying there in just her undergarment and, when it was time to go, told him to keep his eyes averted until she was dressed.

The lagoon became a frequent destination that summer. Most of the days at the water were spent in the same frolicking way. They dove. They tossed stones. They swung from branches into the lagoon. They tried to hold their breath underwater for as long as they could and swim around submerged obstacles. They talked and dreamed about the future. But there were two days in particular they would never forget and would most often reminisce about.

The first day started pretty much like any other. They were diving down into the deeper water beyond the willow clump to see who could pull up the biggest or the shiniest or the flattest rock from the bottom. The sun was nearly straight up and rays were slicing through the canopy of trees above them. Anita slipped into the dark water and disappeared below while Tiburcio counted. They were only allowed ten seconds to scour the bottom to find their stone. At the count of eight, nine, ten, Anita still hadn't surfaced. The next five seconds seemed like several minutes. He stopped counting after twenty seconds. His heart speeding, he dived in to find his friend.

He gazed out into the murky water and saw a shadow of something thrashing about. Swimming toward it, Tiburcio reached out and felt Anita's legs. She was kicking to free her foot from a thick tangle of reeds and rocks. Tiburcio, who had grabbed his knife before diving in, started cutting the water grasses around her foot and pushing aside slippery boulders until she suddenly dislodged and darted with what was left of her breath for the surface.

Afterward, they lay on the warm rocks, breathing hard but not saying a word. The sun began to dry their skin and the shadows had moved noticeably before they spoke again.

"You saved my life, Tiburcio," Anita finally whispered. "I will always remember it."

"I'm just glad you are all right," he said, smiling at her.

"I will return the favor someday," she promised, touching his wet, trembling hand. After a moment, she told him she thought something alive was down there.

"It pulled me into the reeds."

Tiburcio didn't say anything.

"You don't believe me."

"I have no reason not to," he answered. "I just don't want to stop coming here with you."

"I'll still come. I'm not scared. I sometimes wonder if I am capable of being afraid."

The second most memorable day was toward the end of last summer when the nuns finally discovered their games. It was Sunday and Anita was supposed to be studying the Bible with other classmates. Two sisters had decided to take a walk across the meadow and into the gorge to search for the missing child. There, they caught an unusual sight coming out of the woods from the direction of the lagoon. Anita was in full stride on a stallion, her long black, wet hair flailing about her and Tiburcio behind her shouting encouragement from the saddle of his own horse.

"Tiburcio Vasquez!" they shouted.

He turned to see two nuns quickly pacing out to the pasture and rode up to them.

"Is that Anita? Riding like that?" one of the sisters demanded.

"*Si*. She is good, no?" Tiburcio answered proudly. He thrust two fingers into his mouth and whistled to catch the girl's attention. Anita loped over to them. The horse snorted at the nuns.

"Young lady, you will lose all your prettiness riding like that," one nun scolded.

"You will be unable to marry!" said the other.

"I would marry her," Tiburcio stated.

"You will go see Father right away, young man! That's what you will do." the nun retorted, then turned to Anita. "When Tiburcio is long gone from your life, other men will frown upon your ways, Anita. They will not approve."

Tiburcio was lashed for his behavior, but he would gladly have done it again and again. But summer soon ended and he did not see Anita again until well into fall. And even then, he was unable to have a conversation alone with her through the entire winter. But now, it was spring - festival time - and Tiburcio was determined to find her and talk to her before he traveled back home to prepare for the fandango.

He spotted Anita standing near the fountain basin in the center of the plaza. She was laughing with a group of friends. Once she saw the young vaquero approaching, her eyes remained steady on Tiburcio. She stepped closer to the rider when he and the horse halted.

"Please, save me a dance at the fandango tonight," he pleaded, leaning toward her in the saddle.

The other girls giggled and shared a secret.

"You know I cannot come to your fandango. My father won't let me."

"Steal one of his horses," Tiburcio said with a knowing smile. "A big, fast stallion."

"Sorry. I simply won't be able to come," Anita sighed.

"That is a very big disappointment. I will have to leave my twelve-string at home. There will be no music in my heart. There will be no need for serenading."

He hung his head low, pretending to be severely jilted.

"Why must you always go off to the dance hall?" she asked, without umbrage.

TIBURCIO!

"I have told you before, beautiful Anita, I need to make as much money as I can. I save a little bit every night."

"What for?" she asked, putting her hands on her hips.

"To buy some cattle and some land."

"All you do is buy fancy clothes," Anita teased. "Fancy clothes for you and your horse."

"*No, es la verdad.* One day I will become a rancher richer than your father. And I will still be a young man when I do."

"You would be bored raising cattle, Tiburcio!"

"And you are too high-minded to come to my dance hall!" he retorted. "You know, many well-respected dons and young *señoritas* and rich merchants come through my doors."

"It's still not proper for a young girl like me. And besides, I told you my father won't let me - and for good reason. Besides, you have never even met my father. Poor manners, Mr. Vasquez!"

"Regretfully, then, I must leave you with your friends and embark for Monterey," Tiburcio said with a smile. "By the time I reach town, I will have composed a poem about you."

"What will it say?"

"Ah, you will have to come to the dance tonight to find out!"

He turned his horse gently, gave Anita a smile and loped away. He was happy. Perhaps, somehow, she would come to Monterey.

Anita watched him spur the horse and dash off into the west toward Monterey, bystanders quickly parting to make way.

Chapter 3: Friends
Monterey
1854

"My heart drops with each step farther from you, yet I hope your gentle eyes still gaze, until I return, when our hearts will beat in their own silence, and we will touch with the most delicate gesture."

Rebelde, the big golden palomino, did not like Tiburcio composing poetry in the saddle. The pace was too slow and wistful. He was hot and tired and thirsty and they were only a little more than halfway between Salinas and Monterey. The stallion knew they still had a swift hour's ride home and he let his master know his consternation by doing a little prancing and pulling at the bit until Tiburcio lost focus on his poem and sensed the horse's impatience.

"What does it matter, Rebelde? We will get there soon enough. Look at this scenery. Enjoy!"

Tiburcio's eyes fell over the vast, beautiful, rolling terrain all around him. Expansive groves of oaks shadowed parts of the golden countryside. Here and there, adobes and garden patches sprang up, but mostly there were just cattle, wild horses, deer, elk and rabbits slowly moving and grazing in the open land. An occasional coyote would appear on a distant hill of yellow, orange and purple wildflowers and quickly vanish. V-shaped flights of geese crisscrossed the blue skies above, casting fleeting shadows over the rider and his horse. Tiburcio's eyes followed the green lines of sycamores and willow that signaled unseen streams and swampy areas. These natural markings told him where he was.

"Ah, Don Cervantes," he alerted Rebelde as they approached the tract of the long-time family friend.

Tiburcio had been lost in poetry for most of the journey, but now that his mind had stopped turning the words over and over he realized he was hungry and thirsty. The Cervantes' home would be an excellent place to stop to rest his horse and get a bite to eat. He thought he could faintly smell the familiar aroma of spicy beef, chili and corn tortillas coming from Señora Cervantes' kitchen.

If he ate at the Cervantes', he told Rebelde - since no one else was there to listen - he could quickly wash up at home and sooner be on his way to prepare the dance hall. He would only have to change clothes and gather his two companions, Anastacio Garcia and Jose Higuera, who were expected to be waiting for him in Monterey, before heading to the western end of town to begin the fandango.

Rebelde heard excitement in his master's voice and picked up the pace.

"You know this place, don't you, old boy?" Tiburcio said, patting the horse's lathered neck. "Doña Cervantes always has something good cooking. You're a smart one!"

But as Tiburcio got closer to the Cervantes' property, something didn't seem right. The westernmost boundary of Cervantes' land ran along the creek as far south as the manzanita and mahogany grove that lay ahead. Yet, a segment of fence that wasn't there at his last visit had been erected clearly inside the Cervantes' property line. The fence enclosed several head of cattle, and a crude hut that had never been there before either.

Riding a bit farther, Tiburcio came upon a white man in a floppy hat mending some post. A rifle leaned against the railing next to him and a six-shooter was at his side.

"Hello? Who are you?" Tiburcio yelled as he slowed Rebelde nearly to a standstill.

"Who wants to know?"

"My name is Tiburcio Vasquez. This is not your property."

27

"Sure it is," the man answered. "I got my deed last week, signed by the judge and everything."

The man said something else, but Tiburcio had already hurried on and didn't hear. He would get the true story from Don Cervantes. As he approached the stucco adobe, he saw five unfamiliar horses hitched outside. By the looks of their saddles and bags, they belonged to a group of yanquis of some official status and rank. He felt a twinge of trepidation as he leaped off his horse and hitched it to a post under a tree near a water trough. He jumped onto the wooden porch with a loud thump of his boots and purposefully stomped through the open doorway with a great deal of spur-jingling and flourish.

It took only a quick glimpse inside to realize all was not well at his friends' house. Señora Cervantes was kneeling on the floor over a small leather trunk that had been dragged from its hiding place to the middle of the room. She was frantically removing its contents - loose paper documents, a dried ink well and pen, tin cups, two small knives, some soap - and setting them on the floor around her.

"I can't find the original grant," she cried, setting the items on the floor all around her. "We've lived here for twenty years. Why don't you believe us? We've never had to show our petition to anyone."

Three men stood over Señora Cervantes and two sat in wooden chairs at a heavy block table near the open fire. At their hips were .36-caliber Remingtons. They all turned to look at the visitor making the loud entrance. Tiburcio saw that these men were U.S. government officials. Land Commission officials, he assumed. Or perhaps from the Surveyor General's Office. They turned their attention back to the woman on her knees, except for one man at the table who sized up Tiburcio a while longer from the table.

"We have no recording of the title," an official told her as another translated the words into Spanish. "And since a dispute over the property has arisen and another party has entered his name in the register for this parcel, you will need to submit a boundary description. Something official. Not vague. No natural or geographic markers. A judge in a court of law will determine who owns this piece of land."

"Look," said another of the officials who was standing over Señora Cervantes. "We can give you two weeks to find evidence of the original transaction. Barring that, you will need to assemble friends and relatives and bring them forth to testify before the commission in San Francisco."

"Two weeks?" Señora Cervantes wailed. "It might as well be two days. Or two years. We have no petition. We have only our word!"

Don Cervantes, who had been standing quietly near the door, spoke next, calmly and deliberately.

"Sir, we have seen many of our friends overrun by squatters. Two weeks? Ten weeks? Six months? A year? What is the difference? Thousands of squatters are swarming all over the region, from Sacramento to San Francisco. We need our claim title approved immediately. Or we stand to lose everything."

"Perhaps I can help," Tiburcio interjected in his perfect English. "I can affirm these people live here."

The group of men laughed, except for the one who had been watching Tiburcio closely from the table.

"Well, that settles it," the translator said sarcastically. "The boy confirms it. We can go home now."

The others stopped chuckling when they noticed the man at the table hadn't laughed. He was looking Tiburcio up and down.

"You are an articulate young man, and apparently of some means," he said. "What is your name?"

"Tiburcio Vasquez."

"Yes. Of course," the official said, nodding his head, proud of his power of recollection and knowledge of his area of expertise. "Vasquez. Of the Cantua land grant, I believe."

He turned to the others to explain.

"He is the young owner of the popular dance hall down by the theater in Monterey, where my brother-in-law is a constable," he said, before turning his eyes back to Tiburcio. "You speak English very well. You are well-educated. And your family is well respected."

"Then please allow me to help my friends," Tiburcio pleaded.

"Nevertheless, I am afraid we need a little more evidence than just your words and your honorable status. The Cervantes know what they must do."

"I will pay whatever is necessary on behalf of my friends. How much will it take."

"Bribery, son?"

"A payment to guarantee a delay in the proceedings."

"Your friends need a good lawyer. Spend your money on that."

Hat in hand, he started to move toward the door, but paused at the threshold.

"I hear you have been running around with your cousin, Anastacio, a lot since your father's death. He's been kind of a mentor to you, my brother-in-law told me."

"We are cousins. That's all."

"Be careful about who you are willing to help and who is willing to help you," the official said, tossing his felt hat onto his head, signaling that their official visit was finished, and the other men followed him outside.

The man was right. After his father's death, Tiburcio did not stop riding and hunting in the vast plains all around Monterey. But he had gained a new companion, a young, unbridled family friend named Anastacio Garcia. In Hermenegildo's absence, Anastacio, who was four years older than Tiburcio, soon became his mentor and a fatherlike figure. The pair would often be in the saddle from dawn until dusk at Garcia's ranch in the golden hills above Monterey. Anastacio, like Hermenegildo, preached the virtues of horsemanship and marksmanship. But the similarities ended there. Anastacio held a much bleaker view of the changes that were coming to California.

TIBURCIO!

In the past two years, Tiburcio had heard a growing number of stories like this one. They all began the same, and all ended in favor of the English-speaking settlers. Now he was witnessing it first hand and still was at a loss to know what to do, if anything. He imagined Land Commission officials had started their jobs with good intentions, sorting out issues based on federal law passed three years ago. When they accepted their appointments, he presumed government employees did their work diligently and performed their duties in a generally fair-minded way. But California land issues had spun out of their control. Out of everybody's control.

The yanqui flood simply could not be held back. At least not by legal means, Garcia often groused. Anastacio told Tiburcio he could count a dozen friends and relatives living between the emerald forest and the azure ocean who had been chased from their property by the squatters - *gabachos* as he called them - who helped themselves to the land whether it was claimed or not.

"The only way we can stop these *gabachos* from stealing our land is through the only way they understand anything," Garcia seethed. "With guts, gunpowder, lead and sharp steel."

With Anastacio's words burning in his ear, Tiburcio ran outside after the government men. He stomped onto the porch as they were mounting their horses. The leader halted and stared back at the young man with the furrowed brow and clenched fists. He eyed a shotgun leaning against the adobe just behind Tiburcio. This could turn bad, he thought.

"Why do you need more evidence?" Tiburcio challenged loudly.

The head official narrowed his eyes and peered at Tiburcio. Then he smiled devilishly.

"It's demanded by law," he said authoritatively in English. "If everything is in order, your friends will find the proper documentation in the archives in San Francisco. There are lawyers who can help navigate the process."

"Are you blind? They don't have the money to travel to San Francisco. And they can't afford your American lawyers!"

"If it's important, they will find a way," the lead official remarked, throwing his leg over the saddle of his horse as Don Cervantes and his wife shuffled out of the house and stood next to Tiburcio. "We'll send a post in a week with a time and date for you to appear before the board to review your claim, authorize any documentary evidence and hear testimony. Don't miss it."

There was silence except for hammering in the distance. Tiburcio inadvertently glanced at the shotgun against the wall.

"Let's stay calm," the official said.

More silence. The air was strained. Hands slid almost imperceptibly closer to holsters.

"You're not thinking about doing anything crazy, are you son?"

Tiburcio didn't know what he was thinking, his mind was so jumbled. Anastacio would know what to do, he thought. He was certain he didn't want his friends, the Cervantes, punished on account of his actions or words, and, at any rate, he could see the officials were done with their business here.

"Wait! I will pay two thousand dollars to you to get the hearing postponed, to buy the Cervantes more time."

"No, Tiburcio!" Don Cervantes protested.

"We will see you in two weeks," the land commissioner said. "Have the money here, Mr. Vasquez, or be in San Francisco with a very good lawyer next to you."

With a kick to his horse, the official rode off and the others followed.

Tiburcio turned away and sat dejectedly on a wooden bench on the porch. Don Cervantes stood next to him.

Don Cervantes, a strong man in his sixties with deep lines across his square, dark brown face, a wide nose and thick, gray hair parted to the left, sat down next to Tiburcio and watched the riders until they were out of sight. Doña Cervantes joined them on the porch, but stood with her arms folded across her bosom. Don Cervantes, in an unhurried fashion, folded a corn husk lengthwise across his lap and set it on his knee. He then opened a silver box of tobacco and spread two pinches of leaves evenly along the crease. Nobody uttered a word until he finished rolling the cigarillo and licked its edge.

"Why are we ruled by a force so many legions away?" Tiburcio burst out as if the words could not be restrained in his throat for a second longer.

Cervantes stood and slowly walked inside to the stove to light his cigarillo. When he sat back down outside, he still didn't say a word. So Tiburcio continued with the same urgency.

"We are always under oppression. First, we were ruled by a despot across the ocean; now we are controlled by pale conquerors from across an entire continent."

"We lost the war," Cervantes said, self-composed. "That's the way it is."

"Maybe some of us are still fighting the war."

The old man exhaled a swirl of smoke out of his nose and mouth and answered.

"Then you accept the consequences. Who is still fighting the war, Tiburcio? You are sounding more and more like your fiery friend, Anastacio. Doña Cervantes and I received our land grants from the government and moved here from Mexico just like your mother's family, the Cantuas. This is part of the consequences of that decision. We all must live with the results of our actions."

"So you are willing to let the gringos delay your claim for years and years, while the squatters infest your land? How many neighbors have you lost in the last five years to the invaders? Who is that man hammering at the fence? Is he the one who is going to take over your home? Who is going to fight for our rights?"

Cervantes didn't answer. He looked at Tiburcio and noticed the resemblance to his father. Since Hermenegildo's death, he had seen Tiburcio becoming more and more of a young firebrand. Hermenegildo was a fighter, too, a government soldier. Maybe it was in his blood, Cervantes thought. Maybe it was just his age. Still, there was a sharper edge to Tiburcio's vehemence than anything he remembered in Hermenegildo. He knew the reason: Anastacio Garcia.

Garcia had married Tiburcio's cousin, Lupe, and in the absence of Tiburcio's father, he had taken it upon himself to tutor the boy. At El Tuche, Garcia's ranch in the hills just north of the wide-mouthed bay, he taught Tiburcio how to ride like a Comanche, throw a sixty-foot riata, drive a herd across all types of terrain and shoot a rifle and pistol with unbelievable precision from both a standing position and in the saddle.

Yes, El Tuche. What a fitting place to fuel the fire in Garcia, Cervantes thought as he blew smoke rings into the clear, late-afternoon air. In 1846, Alta California history had marched right up to the edge of El Tuche and looked young Anastacio in the eye. Neither blinked. But Anastacio would forever remember the exact moment U.S. warships churned into Monterey Bay under the leadership of Commodore John Drake Sloat. Anastacio had been galloping freely, as he had done a thousand times, across the wide, grassy meadows of El Tuche when he saw Lupe calling to him in the distance. She told him something significant was happening in town, so he rode as fast as he could down the hills and into the capital of Alta California. Within hours of the gringo ships' landing, the streets teemed with scores of yanquis shooting their rifles in the air. Anastacio and hundreds of other Californios could do nothing but gaze unbelievingly at the sight of foreigners suddenly running amok in their quiet seaside town.

He stood there feverishly wondering what would happen to the small city next to the placid ensenada. The answer came later that day in a final, stabbing statement. The yanquis hoisted their red-and-white striped flag up over the Custom House. The city, indeed all of California, was declared a part of the United States. Garcia was seventeen. Tiburcio was not yet a teenager.

"You have been hanging around Anastacio too much, Tiburcio," Cervantes finally said. "He's bitter, and he thinks robbing a few Americans traveling alone along the highway is a way to get back at all the gringos for stealing California. Don't look at me like that, Tiburcio. I have heard these stories. He flaunts his ill-gotten money from cattle thievery and highway robbery. He may be older than you, and he may be married to Lupe, but you do not have to follow in his footsteps. It will lead to trouble."

Señor Cervantes took a deep suck on his cigarillo as if it were part of his speech, blew the smoke out, and continued: "You'll soon grow up, Tiburcio. Your education and your parents' strong upbringing will lift you past the bitterness that is consuming Anastacio and so many other Mexicans that is the result of the war. Of losing the war."

"How is your mother, Tiburcio?" Señora Cervantes asked when she felt her husband had finished. She was composed now, and Tiburcio could tell the strong woman was embarrassed that he had seen her weep in front of the government officials.

The young man grinned, thinking of his doting but headstrong mother.

"She is feisty and completely in charge, as always," he answered.

"Will you see her tonight?"

"Yes. I must stop home before going to the fandango."

"Oh, the girls talk so much about your dancing and guitar strumming, Tiburcio," Señora Cervantes teased. "I hear it every time I go into town."

"Yes, my boots and my twelve-string do my bidding for me."

"Your home is still over an hour away. You must be hungry from your horsemanship at the fiesta. Why don't you supper here, wash up and go to the dance full and fresh?"

"Dinner sounds wonderful, Señora Cervantes. But I'm afraid I'd have to leave right after I eat. Anastacio and our friend, Jose Higuera, are waiting for me at my mother's house. We are going to the dance hall together."

"We don't mind, Tiburcio. Stay and eat. Then you can go." Don Cervantes said.

"Your mother is working so hard these days, Tiburcio, with the vegetable crops and the restaurant and the cattle. Please send her our greetings."

Tiburcio nodded.

They ate outside at a sturdy wood table. When the plates had been taken in, Tiburcio stepped off the porch to leave, but stopped a few feet away and turned around.

"I thought I could help," Tiburcio called out earnestly to both of them. "I hope I did not get you in deeper trouble. But once we buy time and get the local officials off your back, you can get the proper paperwork from San Francisco. I can give you some more money. If you need to hire a lawyer, I can help pay. I have two thousand dollars in a strongbox at home. I've been saving ever since I began operating the dance hall. I slip a coin or two in there every Saturday night. I'll let you have it all or some of it. Whatever you need to keep your property. I know you're proud people, but I offer it with an open heart, no conditions and no judgment. I will bring it all tomorrow."

Chapter 4: Home
Monterey County
1854

Tiburcio approached his family's property from the west, the setting sun at his back. He rode up a dirt and pebble pathway that cut through a three-acre field of tomato, pepper, cilantro and chili plants not more than a foot high. The bed of shiny, dark and pale green hues spread up to the patio area of his stone-walled, white-tiled adobe, where he lived with his mother, two brothers, two sisters, a pair of field workers and a housekeeper.

As beautiful as it was to sit on the wide, shaded patio and look out at the vegetable field soaking up the sun, the house's real character was found in the front. If a person started walking south from the once-bustling waterfront for nearly three-quarters of a mile, before he reached the Vasquez adobe, he would first stumble upon a two-story, white-stone building with a portico in front: Monterey's town hall. Upstairs in a long narrow room in the town hall, official city business and public assemblies took place; downstairs, schoolchildren did math and sang verses. Next-door to the town hall and classroom, drunkards, thieves and indebted gamblers came and went from an eight-cell county jail. Behind this hall and this jail stood the clean Vasquez adobe.

Two towering, twisting Monterey pines kept the Vasquez home and patio shaded and cool and provided an uninterrupted birds-eye view of the jail and town hall. Seven years ago, Tiburcio and his siblings sat high in one of the pine's sturdy branches and watched the convicts build the town hall.

Tiburcio still would often find his younger sister up there when she wanted to be alone and undisturbed.

As Rebelde clopped up to the house, Tiburcio nodded to two Indians leaning against a wheel on the shady side of a wooden ox cart, done with their work for the day. He was close enough now to hear a cacophony of English being spoken on the patio. He counted roughly fifteen blue-uniformed, fair-skinned American sailors and soldiers sitting at long tables on the patio, eating enchiladas and tamales and drinking beer.

There must be a thousand ways to take yanquis' money, he thought, and his mother had stumbled upon a good one. It wasn't long after Hermenegildo's death that she turned the Vasquez adobe into a restaurant in order to supplement her income from growing and selling vegetables. Her cantina was so successful that she had branched out and begun shipping meals by horse and wagon over to San Juan Bautista to feed the teamsters. Tiburcio was proud of her.

Angling his horse toward the adjacent stable, he more closely looked over the white patrons. So many gringos these days. Ten years ago, you hardly ever saw a white man. Year after year, more and more gringos everywhere. You take their money but you give up the pastoral life.

His eyes then settled on a small table in the back corner that wasn't occupied by Americans. He saw Anastacio tilting back in his chair against the white adobe wall, waving a whiskey bottle in one hand while he talked to Higuera.

There was no mistaking Anastacio Garcia in a crowd. His thick, curly, ebony hair plunged from under a black beaver-felt hat to well past his shoulders. This low-brimmed hat, which hardly ever left his head, and his burnished dark mane, were his trademark. Although Tiburcio could not see it, a Colt .44 was shoved into his waistband and a carved wood-handled poniard was strapped to his bootleg. Anastacio's sheer black eyes fixed on Tiburcio.

"Amigo!" Anastacio called out loudly to get Tiburcio's attention. "Aqui!"

TIBURCIO!

Anastacio was muscular and handsome and witty. But he had a legendary temper. He could be smiling one moment and reaching for his gun the next. When angered, the veins in his forehead and thick neck visibly throbbed. He was intimidating when mad. And he usually got mad when he was drunk. And he was usually drunk.

Tiburcio nodded to his friends, acknowledging their presence, but dismounted and walked his horse to the stalls to give Rebelde rest and feed. He emerged from the stable about ten minutes later, and waved again to Garcia and Higuera, before crossing the patio in his brisk and energetic way. Anastacio could wait. He needed to see his family. He slipped through the open kitchen door to greet his mother.

He heard Guadalupe commanding her crew of three children and two female Indian helpers from the back of the snug *cocina*. Sunlight filtered from the patio into the front part of the kitchen but it was quite dark toward the rear. A dizzying aroma of garlic, onion and roasting meat filled the room. In front of Tiburcio, three plates of steaming food waited on a blue and white tile countertop next to a grinding stone and pestle. A copper kettle of frijoles and a pot of *pozoles* bubbled on the stove. Pork sizzled in a pan. Roasted deep-red anchos chilies crackled on another plate. Most of the rest of the counter space was taken up with tortillas, bags of rice, garlic, tomatillos, herbs, eggs, *nopales*, knives and colorful clay bowls filled with salsa.

Tiburcio listened for a moment to his mother's instructions and incessant chatter. She hadn't seen her youngest son enter the kitchen.

"Dice the carnitas," she ordered excitedly, followed by a staccato of questions: "Where is that pot that always disappears? Have you peeled the chilies yet?"

Tiburcio watched his ten-year-old sister, Maria, the youngest, clatter some dry beans onto the counter and spread them into a single layer. Maria did not see her brother, either, as her tender fingers flitted over the speckled seeds. Loose strands of thick black hair fell over one of her eyes and shaded her face as she intently followed through with her chore. She always made him smile by just looking at her. She worshipped Tiburcio.

His brothers did not, however, especially Francisco, the eldest. Francisco always had to keep his hands busy, and was presently cutting the roasted pork in thin slices. He and Tiburcio tolerated each other but shared few close moments. Antonio, on the other hand, was hard-working but saw more of life's gentler moments and rolled better with its vicissitudes. He liked to good-naturedly bait his younger, wilder brother. Antonio was standing near the steaming plates on the countertop that would soon be taken out to the guests.

"Look who has come to help?" he exclaimed in a mocking tone. "Tiburcio is here to help serve the yanqui patrons!"

"Let them get their own food," Tiburcio answered tersely, the incident at the Cervantes' home fresh in his mind.

"Why are you home from the fiesta so early?" Francisco chimed in. "You usually return after all the work is finished and everything is cleaned up. Was the fiesta boring?"

"No."

"Were the crowds too small?"

"Of course not. There were hundreds of people lining the plaza from end to end."

"Well, that's good. Otherwise, it would have been a terrible waste of your valuable time and effort not to mention those fancy clothes!"

"*Yo sabe*," Francisco said, turning to Antonio. "I know why he is back so soon. There were not enough beautiful women in the crowd."

"You are right, Francisco. It would be a shame for Tiburcio to dress up so handsomely for nothing but vaqueros and *abuelas*."

Antonio could joke and laugh but he understood his young brother's interest didn't lie in farming the land, driving cattle or even feeding gringos, and that was all right with him. He understood his younger brother's proclivities better than their

40

father ever would have and much more than their assiduous older brother did.

Tiburcio patted Antonio on the shoulder as he walked by.

"It would do you well, Antonio – and you too, Francisco – to enjoy some dancing and music once in a while. There is a big world to discover outside mother's adobe. There are so many beautiful señoritas at the rodeos and fiestas and fandangos, but they won't be interested in you until you actually stop working for a few hours and pay attention to them. And stop smelling of chilies."

Tiburcio jerked his thumb toward the patio and continued.

"Believe me, *mi hermanos*, the señoritas at the fiesta look a whole lot better than the drunken soldiers I see out there. And, Francisco, the women there look much, much better than the cattle you spend so much time with, running them up and down the hills."

Even Maria was laughing now. But Francisco retorted.

"You might do better in the long haul to stay closer to home, Tiburcio, and forget about those romantic dreams of yours. Women like to look at the fancy vaqueros but they go home with *el hombre de negocios*. I know the young woman to whom you are trying to make love. Don't look surprised. Everyone knows. Anita will only break your heart. It will be her father who decides whom she marries. She will have no say in the matter. Everybody knows her husband will be a rich, white landowner so Don Constanza can be sure his estate is not only preserved but grows and grows and grows. He's not going to let you get in the way. I don't care how handsome you look up on your palomino, or how skilled you are at riding tricks. That will not win over Anita's father."

Tiburcio winced at his brother's statement.

"You know so little of the way of women's hearts, brother," Tiburcio sighed. "Anita and I are still young. I still have a few years left to convince her father before she is betrothed."

"*Hola, m'hijo*," called his mother, who was now placing rice and beans on a platter of steamed tamales near the stove.

Tiburcio walked into the galley and gave her a hug and a kiss on the cheek. She looked him over. "Look at you. You are dressed like Don Pio Pico. Where do you get these clothes? They are not found on the shelves down at Señor Boston's store!"

Tiburcio laughed heartedly.

"Your friends are waiting for you on the patio," she dryly informed him.

"How long have they been here?"

"Long enough to get very drunk," Francisco interjected. "Garcia is drinking aguardiente by the liter and getting that fire in his eyes. He's been showing off all day by spending lots of money all over Monterey - money I am sure he stole somewhere between El Tuche and here."

Tiburcio defended his friend adamantly.

"In all my time spent in the company of Anastacio, I have never seen him rob a single soul or commit any violence, except to a stubborn mule. He works for an honest living, just like you and Antonio, on ranches around here – in addition to keeping up his own homestead. His money is unblemished. Since when is spending money a crime?"

"Why is he drinking and carousing here? He should be home at his ranch with Lupe. Don't they have a newborn daughter?"

"If you think he does not adore his children and our cousin, then you are mistaken, Francisco. He would never let harm come to them. He's in town on some business and is visiting friends along the way, including us. Where is the crime?"

A moment of silence, except for the clattering of pots and plates, filled the kitchen, then Tiburcio changed the subject of conversation.

"Anyway, I'll take Anastacio and Higuera with me when I go to set up the ballroom. The fandango is going to be big tonight. Many people are coming down from the fiesta."

"But Tiburcio," Guadalupe interrupted, "I need to talk with you. I need your help."

TIBURCIO!

"You don't need me around here, mother. You'll be closing soon and the soldiers will leave and go staggering around the streets until it's dark and the dance halls open."

"I don't mean right at this moment, Tiburcio. You see, I have bought some cattle. It's a large herd and your brothers could use your help getting them over from Salinas."

"You bought cattle? How large of a herd?"

"One-hundred and fifty head."

"Business is very good, no?"

"I have a little extra money, that's all. It's an investment"

"You would not believe the *Americano* appetite for beef, Tiburcio," Antonio jumped in. "It's astonishing. Prices start at seventy-five dollars a head. To raise a steer and drive it to market costs less than twenty dollars. So we're going to raise our own supply, clear fifty dollars per head of cattle. Ranchers have become richer than all those foolish gold seekers."

Tiburcio whistled.

"With that much profit, you might convince me to go into the ranching business."

"Now that would be something for Anita's father to see!" Francisco said. "Hell, I would like to see that."

"'Might,' I said. But not quite." Tiburcio added, smiling. "Running a fandango is more suited to my tastes. It's more entertaining. It's still more lucrative. Nevertheless, *por mi madre,* I will help you drive them over the hill. When?"

"In three days," Guadalupe said. "Right now, I must get these plates out to the customers. I will talk to you about all this business in the morning, *si*? Don't stay out all night."

Guadalupe tenderly patted Tiburcio's cheek and hurried outside with two plates. Maria followed her, carrying two more.

"If you were a ranch owner, Tiburcio," Francisco continued as he moved on to the chore of sharpening a knife, "you would be doing something legitimate to make money. That's what will win over that young girl's father."

"There are many, many ranch barons, my brother. It's my tender side - my poetry and songs - that appeals to Anita. That is all that matters to her. Not property."

"Poetry and songs won't put food on the table and clothes on her children's back."

Tiburcio took a warm tortilla off a stack, ripped it in half and dipped it into a bowl of salsa. With a full mouth, he added: "First I win her over. Then, her father."

At that instant, a gunshot rang out from the patio.

Tiburcio was the first to get outside and see Garcia standing defiantly on a chair, the sun glinting off the smoking revolver he waved above his head. Garcia was shouting at several soldiers, who stood at a cautious distance and angrily shouted back at him.

"Get down and fight like a decent man, greaser," yelled a golden-haired man of about nineteen, who was being physically restrained by his comrades. His face was red and contorted with fear, inebriation and rage.

Tiburcio's mother and sister scurried toward the house. Tiburcio stepped in front of Guadalupe, holding her still by cupping her shoulders with his strong hands.

"Are you all right? What happened?"

"You get your friends out of here, Tiburcio. This is a respectable business. The *alcalde* is right next door and I am certain he heard the gunshots."

"To hell with the mayor. What offended you?"

"No. You obey me, Tiburcio. Your father and I didn't raise a hellcat."

She twisted away and stormed inside.

Tiburcio stepped quickly between the group of *Americanos* and Garcia.

"What's happening?" he yelled at Garcia, repeatedly looking back over his shoulder at the furious gringos.

"That gringo," Garcia snapped, the veins in his neck and temple pulsating as he pointed the barrel of the pistol down at his foe, "showed disrespect for your sister. So I knocked him down and gave a warning shot. The next one is right between his eyes."

The soldier being restrained took a swipe at Tiburcio, catching hold of his collar and jerking the Californio toward him. Tiburcio jerked away and bore his light gray eyes into him. He managed to remain level-headed. The other Americans pulled the soldier back. Tiburcio turned again to Garcia.

"Put the pistol away and get down!" he demanded. "This has to cease. Have you forgotten the mayor's office and a classroom full of children are right there?"

Garcia seethed, pumping the Peacemaker up and down in the air.

"Forgotten? How can I forget? How can I forget the shame of you residing next to the very town hall where the foreign land grabbers forged a constitution. And now, you are more concerned about the *gabacho* mayor than your own sister being mistreated by these jackass imperialists."

"*Pendejo!*" Tiburcio screamed.

He had never shouted a harsh word to Garcia in his life. The surprise of it made his raging friend momentarily, almost imperceptibly, pause, then smirk. Higuera, all the while, sat calmly and amusedly at the table with his hand on his own revolver. He softly laughed when he saw Garcia's reaction to being called an idiot by his protégé.

"Come on, friend," Tiburcio said flatly to Garcia, changing to English so the soldiers could hear his words and his tone. "I'll buy you a drink tonight at the dance hall. I have lots of work to do before then. Let's leave this episode behind us."

Garcia suddenly leaped down from the chair, his boots landing with a loud clap. The sudden move made his antagonists jump back.

"Tell that gringo to watch his stinking mouth around the ladies, Tiburcio, or I'll fill him full of holes. *El burro!*" Garcia bellowed in Spanish, pointing his gun straight at the soldier's face.

45

Perhaps unwisely, Tiburcio completely turned his back to the mob of gringos and looked at his friend face to face. His hands were on each of Garcia's shoulders and he penetrated Garcia's eyes with his glare. Garcia kept his gun and an eye steadily aimed at his enemies.

"Anastacio! Listen! This is a place of business. My family's business. Put that gun away. You're not going to ruin my family's reputation and standing in this community with your drunkenness and wanton shooting. My mother has worked too hard to get this far without a husband at her side. It's not easy. You owe it to her. Come on, it's time to go."

Garcia let Tiburcio's words settle in, and his focus slowly turned away from the group to the boy he had helped raise in absence of a father. His voice was low and steady but the words hissed and cracked between gritted teeth.

"What do you think is going on all around you? *Que*? You think you, your mother, your family, your friends, our people, can keep making a living among these thieves, rapists, pillagers and lynchers? You don't think they want to take your mother's business for their own? The *gabachos* won't stop until they own all of our businesses, Tiburcio. You think they are content in letting you and your mother take their money? You don't think they want your home, too? Your property? Ah, even your women? Even Anita? Everything? Sooner or later, they will get everything. They already have their American mayor seated in Monterey. And their American governor in Sacramento. That didn't take long, did it? Yes, they'll take everything – unless we fight back and not back down for anything."

Garcia shoved the weapon back into his belt. He glared long and steady over Tiburcio's shoulder at the Americanos. Then, he looked down at Higuera, who had stopped grinning.

"*Vamonos*!" Garcia said to him with a demented half-smile.

Putting his arm around Jose's shoulder, he brushed Tiburcio aside with an outstretched, sturdy forearm. Garcia and Higuera walked silently past the sailors and soldiers to the stable. Tiburcio followed his friends to their horses, which were

46

tethered and waiting by the outbuilding. Garcia and Higuera unhitched the steeds from the post and mounted.

"I'll see you in town, *mi amigo* ," Garcia called out as they trotted past the county jail and town hall toward the waterfront. "You owe me a drink for letting the gringos off the hook. This is going to be a night to remember."

And the pair galloped down the street.

Chapter 5: Jailed (2)
Los Angeles County
1874

The jailhouse guard waited a long time for Tiburcio to stir. He had been assigned to watch him ever since the prisoner tried to provoke a riot from the window of his cell and then collapsed. The guard had closely observed him through most of his bouts of illusion and high fever over the past two days. Then, last night, the guard finally got the chance to talk to the infamous bandit. And, much to his surprise, he rather enjoyed his company. Tiburcio talked freely, graciously, and was polite and charming. So much so, the deputy was a little saddened when their conversation waned and then ended altogether as Tiburcio rolled over onto his right side and, facing the cold granite wall, pulled his wool blanket over his ears.

However, early the next morning, the guard snapped out of his slumber to find Tiburcio's close-set, gray eyes open and watching him. It was 4:00 a.m.

"I never asked you, what is your name?" Tiburcio said to the guard

"Frank Schilling," the guard answered, sitting up straight and looking around to make sure nothing had gone wrong while he had nodded off.

"Are you supposed to be dozing while you are watching over me?"

"I dozed off for only a moment," Schilling lied, his slightly high-pitched voice piercing the quiet, chilly air.

He tilted back in his chair again and touched the Colt single-action revolver lodged safely in the holster at his hip, then changed the subject.

"It's going to be a busy day, Mr. Vasquez."

"Why do you say that?"

"Are you aware of what is going on outside this jailhouse?"

"I remember some singing and shouting."

"That's not the least of it," Schilling said. "Everybody wants to visit you. Scores of reporters are clamoring to interview you. Dozens of ladies from town are asking to check on you personally to make sure you are comfortable and not being mistreated. A bunch of people claiming to be relatives and friends wish to see you as well. Hell, there was even a playwright from Merced who asked to visit so he can write a script. It's very chaotic out there."

Tiburcio smiled bemusedly as Schilling reached over and grabbed a piece of paper off a stool.

"My guest list from the sheriff here must have one hundred names on it. That's a lot of visitors … for a murdering thief."

He added the last phrase condescendingly, just to show the killer that he knew with whom he was dealing. In his jail sat no celebrity, no star prisoner – as many of those camped outside might believe – just a despicable human being, a Californio, a cold-blooded murderer headed for a quick trial and the gallows.

Still, Schilling kept repeating to himself: "I ain't ever had anyone this famous in my jailhouse."

He quickly shook that thought away. Thinking about the prisoner's fame only led to the next, almost paralyzing thought that if something should happen – an escape, a suicide, a hostage-taking, even a lynching – he, Frank Schilling, would either die humiliated or live only to be ridiculed and his family shamed. Hell, he might even end up at the end of a rope himself. Thankfully, Schilling concluded, the bandit would soon get a doctor's approval to be transferred up to San

Francisco and his burden, as exciting as it had, been would be lifted.

"So, who are you going to escort in first?" Tiburcio suddenly asked, turning his lively eyes to the guard.

The guard glanced at the prisoner's sunken right eye and scar on his neck. They were obviously gunshot wounds. He had never heard that Tiburcio Vasquez was ever shot. He's definitely more than a lover-bandit, as the papers said, - this son-of-a-bitch is hardened, Schilling thought. Handsome but hardened.

"I asked, Who are you going to bring in first?" Tiburcio repeated.

"Not so fast," Schilling answered abruptly, his mind back on his duty. "First, we eat some breakfast. Then, Sheriff Rowland wants to see you. After that, I don't know who will be allowed to see you. The sheriff will arrange the visitors to suit his interests."

"What are the sheriff's interests?"

"Publicity. He likes to control things. He wants to be in the cell when the reporters are doing their interviews. He needs to make sure the story is told properly."

"I will try to oblige him."

"As for me," the guard said, leaning forward conspiratorially and chuckling, as he ran his finger along the handwritten list of names, "I wouldn't mind getting some of these pretty dames in here. I've seen a few of them waiting outside under their umbrellas. Some of them are pretty high society, too."

"I wouldn't know," Tiburcio said, with sudden disdain in his voice.

This abrupt change in the prisoner's demeanor surprised Schilling. But Tiburcio's vituperation was directed at Sheriff Rowland – that cunning, portly bastard. Hate surged up in the bandit's gut. He grimaced and turned away so the guard couldn't see his face.

"Them wounds hurting you bad, eh?" Schilling said.

Tiburcio grunted. He was furious only because he had underestimated the sheriff and wound up behind these bars. Hell, wasn't that his own fault? Why hate the sheriff? He only had himself to blame for not having his revolvers on him and his rifle at his side when the posse showed up. But he never told anybody where he was hiding. Who could have betrayed him?

It didn't matter. Rowland, seemingly indifferent and merciless, had played it careful and cool. And it paid off. The sheriff had caught his bandit unarmed as he ate breakfast. And his men put a charge of buckshot into him just for good measure.

"It's not over yet, sheriff," Tiburcio muttered loud enough to catch Schilling's attention. "I didn't fear you, so I didn't keep my eyes on you. But I've killed no one, and therefore I will not hang."

"Whaddya say?" Schilling asked.

"Nothing. I need to see a lawyer. I need to get out of here."

"Gotta go by the list."

"Who's on that list?" Tiburcio demanded. "Give me their names."

"I can't give you that information. It could be dangerous."

"All right. All right," Tiburcio capitulated. "Just tell me if a woman named Anita is on the list."

"No."

"Come on, Frank, at least tell me who my first visitor might be? Besides *el jefe gordo*."

"I'll tell you this: There's a reporter for the *Los Angeles Herald* and an editor for the *Star* high on the list. The sheriff will likely let them see you."

Tiburcio swung his feet off the bed, sitting upright. He was now eager.

"*Arriba el Telon!*" he snapped. "*Guardia*, if I'm going to talk to reporters, I need to get ready. They're going to want me to pose for some photographs. I need some fresh, cool water and a towel. And a comb and a mirror."

Tiburcio looked down at the dirty, blood-stained undergarments he was wearing and shook his head woefully.

"I need some new duds. These bloody garments, won't do. The sheriff doesn't want me to look like I'm being abused in here, does he?"

"He said there were some clothes left in here from some other prisoner. You can wear them."

"Anything decent?"

"Hell, yeah. He was a high-rolling gambler. Very fashionable."

"What happened to him?"

"He was shot to death trying to escape."

"Damn it, Schilling. I don't want a suit with a hole in it."

"Oh, the suit's fine. He was shot in the head."

"Fine. I need a vest, a tie and shined boots, too. Come on, Frank, fetch 'em for me. If you cooperate with me, I'll cooperate with you and we'll see about getting some of those classy ladies in here to keep us company for part of the night. What do you say?"

Tiburcio got out of his blood-stained clothes. He washed up from a bucket of water and, despite the constant, throbbing pain throughout his body, felt healthier than he had for two days. He combed his thick, raven black hair and parted it to the right. He brushed his profuse mustache down toward his goatee beard and stepped into his new, clean garments. He put on a white shirt with a short tie, a gray vest and jacket. He pulled on some short ankle boots with blunt, square toes. He looked nothing like the ferocious criminal of his reputation. He was comely and dressed like a fine gent. By 7:30 a.m. he had eaten a breakfast of runny eggs, hard bread and a potato, and stood at the bars ready to meet the public.

"Sit down, *bandido*," Schilling told Tiburcio. "Nothing can happen until Rowland shows up."

After several minutes, the bandit broke the silence.

"Is Anita on that list, *hombre*? I need to know. I did not believe you before."

"No, Mexicano," Schilling relented. "There is no one named Anita on the list."

"Very well," Tiburcio said, shrugging his shoulders. "Let the parade of people in, then, whoever they might be. I hope I get to see her before I am hanged, though."

Tiburcio decided, now that he was behind bars, it served no purpose to thwart Rowland. He would cooperate to a certain extent. But if he were going to enlighten the public on some of his life, exploits and career, he knew enough not to give the prosecutors anything that would make their case easier.

"If I have reporters clamoring to talk to me," he said to Schilling, eying some newspapers on Schilling's desk. "I first want to see what they have already printed about this entire affair. I want to know what the world outside the jailhouse is saying about my capture."

Schilling agreed and slid three newspapers he had been reading through the rails.

The first one Tiburcio opened up was the *Los Angeles Herald*. The headline screamed:

Vasquez Captured

The robber severely but not

fatally wounded

Party of Los Angeles men reap the

honor of the capture

The story began: "If an earthquake had shaken the foundation of our city and swallowed up one-half of our places, scarcely more excitement would have ensued than that which followed the announcement of the capture of Vasquez on yesterday afternoon."

Tiburcio smiled as he read, very much amused. The article went on to describe the capture in detail – not much of it the way Tiburcio recalled but the important thing, the bandit thought, was it was flattering to him nonetheless. *The Herald* reporter said he was amazed Vasquez lived through all the gunshots, so many that the bandit had been weakened from the loss of blood to the point of near death.

The posse was given ample credit for the capture, and the newspaper declared it a great day for Southern California, "a day in which the majesty of the law was vindicated and an effectual check placed upon outlawry in this part of the country forever."

Tiburcio looked up at Schilling.

"That's not bad," he said.

He folded the newspaper back to the editorial page and read: "The captured robber has defied pursuit, mocked all strategy, and eluded for months the skill of the bravest and most celebrated detectives on the coast."

"I like this guy. Is this editor, Ben Truman of *The Star*, outside?" Tiburcio asked. "I want to talk to him first."

Around noon, Schilling was called to the jailhouse entrance. Tiburcio heard a commotion as Schilling opened the tall, heavy door a crack. Several men began shouting at Schilling but the guard stood firm in the doorway to bar their passage.

"Get back, get back!" he demanded.

Sheriff Rowland then pushed through the crowd and slipped into the jailhouse. Nobody tried to gain entry past the rotund sheriff. Rowland whispered something to Schilling, who answered back into his ear.

"Stand back!" Schilling shouted. "I will call out one by one names on the list. If you hear your name, come forward. Everybody is limited to a half-hour with the prisoner. OK. Ben Truman."

Somebody in the middle of the throng cried out and a man began shoving his way toward the jailhouse door.

"Let him through," the sheriff shouted.

"Come on, Ben," a man in a bowler hat yelled as Truman passed by. "Be fair. No exclusive deals."

"Yeah, Truman. Don't take all day. We have deadlines," yelled another man who had been barred from entering.

Ben Truman stepped into the jail and the door slammed shut, muffling more shouting from the crowd. Schilling escorted the editor to Tiburcio's cell.

"I am Major Truman," the editor declared, thrusting an open hand through the bars.

"Glad to meet you."

Truman, a short man, about five-foot-four inches tall, bald and round in face and body, sized Tiburcio up. Then he shook his head in disbelief.

"That damned *Herald*. They are a bunch of liars. You ain't no more hurt than I am. 'Weak from the loss of blood,' my ass. Come on, Tiburcio. Give it to me straight."

Sheriff Rowland cleared his throat from behind the reporter.

"Go ahead, bandit, tell him about the capture," Rowland said, goading Tiburcio. "And tell him the truth, because I don't like reading lies in the newspaper and I just might cut off all visitors if your tale ventures too far from the truth."

Tiburcio didn't see any harm in being gracious and obliging his visitors. It might make his incarceration and the entire trial process a whole lot easier.

"Well, Major," he began. "Of Sheriff Rowland and all the gentlemen who captured me. I will say they are all brave men. They took desperate chances, and it was one in a million that they succeeded. They could have killed me, but did not, and they have treated me in the kindest manner."

Once he got the particulars of the capture, the editor wanted to know more about Tiburcio's early life. Tiburcio avoided detail. He had not yet heard from any public defenders and guarded against giving too much evidence, especially with Rowland in the room.

He looked at the sheriff. He appeared to be bored now that he wasn't a part of the story. But Tiburcio could tell he was listening to every word.

"The first years of my life were spent in the county of my birth in the usual manner of my life and class. My first difficulty occurred in Monterey, in a ball room, when I was fifteen years of age. I was engaged in a fight, but no blood was shed."

"A constable was killed!" Rowland yelled. "What do you mean, no blood was shed?"

"This is my interview, sheriff," Truman replied irascibly.

"I was innocent, but forced to flee from the officers," Tiburcio continued, ignoring Rowland's groan and cautionary glare.

"After your escape from the officers in Monterey, where did you go?" Truman asked.

"I gathered together a small band of cattle and went into Mendocino County. I resolved to begin a new, lawful life as a legitimate rancher. At length, I determined to leave the thickly settled portions of the country, and did so."

"How did that go? How was Mendocino County, and ranching and all that?"

"It certainly didn't go as planned."

"Do you want to tell me more?" Truman asked.

Tiburcio laughed disdainfully.

And so the interviews dragged on. Tiburcio met with a half-dozen reporters and editors. By suppertime he was worn out, hungry and beginning to get irritated with the persistent questions. The answers brought back too many painful emotions and memories of a life that went by too fast. After the last newspaperman left, he fell back on his cot and closed his eyes. He did not know what the reporters would conclude or how they would write their stories, but he remembered the early days as if it was yesterday. He knew exactly when and what had gone terribly wrong.

Chapter 6: Trouble
Monterey County
1854

It was 7:00 p.m. by the time most of the Americans had departed from Guadalupe's cantina following the trouble on the patio. Tiburcio was back in his small bedroom off the *sale* getting ready for the long night ahead. He washed his torso, face and arms at a basin on a small round table. A small square mirror was nailed on the wall above the table. His eyes slipped down from his own image in the mirror to a Daguerreotype lying on the table. The slip of silver was framed with a mat and pressed into an embossed leather case. He had posed for the picture six months ago at a local studio for the rather handsome sum of five dollars. But he felt it had been worth it in time and money. In the image he was sharply dressed in a vest, jacket and tie. His eyes were fixed, shoulders square, confidence captured. His left hand grasped his lapel and his right hand held a round, black felt dress hat.

Tiburcio pulled up his tight satin *pantalones* and slipped on a red *sarape* and embroidered *bolero*. He grabbed his guitar out of habit and thought of Anita, then gently leaned the instrument back against the wall. For some reason he picked up the photograph off the table instead, and stuck it in his inside his jacket pocket before walking out of the bedroom and bidding his family farewell.

As he left the stable on his horse, he saw a soldier lingering on the shadowy street. As he approached the man, he thought he heard him say something derogatory, but Tiburcio ignored him. Then the soldier reached out and slapped the rump of his horse.

" No toques ese caballo!" Tiburcio barked.

He continued on, listening to the soldier's laugh fade into the distance.

Tiburcio arrived at his dance hall feeling a bit more anxious than usual. A stitch of sadness weaved through the edges of his consciousness. He tried to forget what had happened at the Cervantes' home, then his mother's house and with the lone soldier on the street. Something didn't feel right, but he pressed on, because there was a lot of work to be done before the first patrons began arriving in a little over an hour. After the floor was swept, the tables wiped clean, the bar stocked, and the orchestra members started tuning their instruments on the stage, Tiburcio's spirits changed for the better. A palpable energy was in the air. He always thrived on the power of an approaching night.

Tiburcio walked outside into the warm night and stood on the boardwalk in front of his establishment. He looked up at the cavernous building he rented. It was indistinguishable from the other wood buildings on the edge of this unsavory part of town. Set between the whaling station and the theater-saloon, his fandango stood west of the Custom House, where traders paid duties and stored their boxes of tallow, cowhides and edible goods. Years ago, his father would often be found at the Custom House in the course of his work, making sure commerce was being done in a fair, orderly fashion.

Tiburcio watched a few couples hurry arm-in-arm past him on their way back home for a quiet evening. The first few intermittent patrons soon gave way to a steady stream of guests. More and more people began parking their horses and carts, hopping up off the dirt-packed street onto the wooden plank walkway and gliding through the doors behind him.

"It looks like it's going to be a big crowd tonight, Tiburcio," said a young woman who had joined him outside.

He nodded.

"You look tired," she observed.

"It's been a long day. *Es bueno.*"

TIBURCIO!

The señorita was one of the girls he paid to stand around to try to coax patrons into the hall at the beginning of the evening. Dance halls typically drew bigger, more diverse crowds after a large fiesta. This night was no exception. Dons and grand dames. Store clerks and Indians. Thieves and merchants. Servants and laborers. Lawmen and gold miners. Yankees and native Californians. Tiburcio and the young lady greeted them all.

"Are all the tables set up and the liquor bottles put out behind the bar?" he asked the girl.

"Yes."

"Is Rico behind the card tables, watching?"

"Yes."

"And we have two at the bar?"

"Yes. Everything is ready. Would you like to go inside? I will be fine out here by myself."

"No. It is a nice night. I think I will wait out here for a while longer."

"Don't worry, Tiburcio," the pretty worker said, sensing his unease. "Everything will be fine tonight."

He heard the music start up and turned to go inside. But first he assayed the weathered wood structure and admired the sturdy, large, rough-hewed exterior trusses. The color and richness of his fandango was derived from the people and the music not the appearance of the place. That's for sure, he mused.

Tiburcio walked straight into a boisterous swirl. His eyes had to adjust to the yellow glow of kerosene lamps and he breathed in the overly perfumed air, which smelled richly of gardenias, roses, talcum powder and closely packed humanity. The orchestra's guitars and accordions filled the room with music clear up to the wood rafters. Women carried brocaded fans and waltzed in costly silks. Dons in rich waistcoats whirled beautiful girls around the room. The Americans stood around in frilly shirts, frock coats and gilt-buttoned swallowtails.

The young proprietor was always ready to accept a request to kick the celebration up a notch with his singing and dancing. But that would not be necessary tonight. Nor would he have the time. For the next two hours, he spent his time keeping an eye on the liquor, because that is what kept the night alive and the money flowing. He kept another eye on the gamblers, because one feud over a card game could empty the place in a hurry. He also remained vigilant over Garcia, who was swilling brandy across the hall.

When Tiburcio's fandango sprung into action like tonight's, other dance halls around town usually closed early. The owners - some new and unestablished and others lacking his eclectic collection of characters for guests - had no choice but to shut down and join in the frivolity at Tiburcio's place, reluctantly spending money instead of making it.

Tiburcio knew jealous enemies lurked under his own roof. Tonight, however, he felt trouble would not come from any sore competitors, nor from card players who perceived they had been cheated, nor from the boorish Americans who, as Tiburcio would tell newspaper reporters twenty years later, often tried to push the native men aside and monopolize the women and the dancing. No, if any trouble arose tonight, Tiburcio suspected, it would come in the form of a friend. And so he made sure he kept a tight surveillance, especially on Anastacio.

Tiburcio walked through the main hall to check on the two side rooms, where the card games were taking place.

"I have not seen the constable all night," he yelled to Rico even though he was standing next to him. "How is everything?"

"I've never seen it this busy! But the games are honest and the players' suspicions are under control."

Convinced that this was true, Tiburcio returned to the main hall and drew a deep breath. The crowd may be more than I bargained for, he thought. At least he had decided to bring in several extra thick, flat boards and set them on sawhorses - every one of these makeshift tables was now being used.

"What are you thinking about?" said a sultry voice next to him that somehow rose above the noise and confusion. "Or should I say, who are you thinking about?"

Tiburcio knew before he turned around that it was Antonia Romero, a slender, tall, coquettish woman of about twenty with an alluring grin. He smiled back at her.

"You look so solemn and worried, Tiburcio. Are you not having fun? Are you not going to dance?"

"I guess I'm not in the mood," Tiburcio said.

"Oh," Antonia bemoaned, resting her head on his shoulder. "Won't you reconsider?"

He took a close look at Antonia and his face beamed. He couldn't resist.

"That is, Antonia, I wasn't in mood until I saw you. Allow me to reconsider. Of course, I would be delighted to dance with you. I think it is just what I need to do."

"*Si*, Tiburcio," she agreed. "Have fun!"

Tiburcio glanced over at Garcia one more time to make sure he wasn't causing trouble. Higuera appeared to be behaving respectably, too. Antonia saw him look across the room.

"So you are worried about your drunk friends, Tiburcio? How cute. You are like a mother. *Usted es la gallina.*"

He laughed.

"I am just a businessman," he told her. "I told the constable yesterday to stay close to my dance hall tonight, but I haven't seen him. You can see there's a larger crowd than usual. So many people are already drunk. Already once today, I had to talk Anastacio into keeping his Peacemaker holstered."

"Then, you have done all you can. You have plenty of good, reliable people helping you."

"Yes, you are right. I should not worry."

Antonia peered again over at Garcia and Higuera.

"Perhaps they would like to join us. Let's go over there. We'll dance the *jarabe*!"

Tiburcio and Antonia walked over to his friends' table. Garcia and Higuera politely greeted her. Tiburcio caught the eye of the band leader and yelled some directions to him. A syncopated rhythm began. Tiburcio started stepping slowly to the beat and Antonia began to move her hips and head to the syrupy rhythm. She wore a glittering red skirt and white blouse with red, white and green ribbons in her reddish-brown hair. She danced mostly on her toes, but the heels of her boots would come down hard on certain beats.

Antonia pulsated as the rhythm picked up. Tiburcio backed away to watch. It was her turn to act out the thrill of the chase in dance. This was now Antonia's performance.

Several men surrounded the dancer, catching on to her flirtatious movements. They began to whistle and hoot. Catching her stride, she bent at the waist as she moved past each man, putting her head tantalizingly close to his face and then whipping it away before he could place his hat on her.

"I will capture you!" yelled Garcia with a guttural laugh.

He took another gulp from the bottle of fiery alcohol and banged it down on the table. Taking his hat in his hand, he stood up to catch Antonia's attention. Just when he did, a whole bunch of Americans pushed their way past him into the inner circle to watch the beautiful dancer and see what was happening.

More and more of the dance-hall attendees gathered to admire Antonia's skilled improvisation of the popular ballroom dance. She kept evading being "captured" by the young men trying to set their hats on her head. As the beat quickened, the crowd stomped their feet and clapped their hands in rhythm. The floorboards shook.

Tiburcio leaped out of his chair and led Antonia backward in a fast and fluid dance step until she was up against a wall of spectators. He spun her around and she moved away from him like poetry. Tiburcio slipped into the crowd, laughing hard and clapping. He watched Antonia expertly whirl back to where Garcia and Higuera had been seated. The circle of patrons closed ranks and he could not see Antonia, Garcia or Higuera anymore.

Standing alone, smiling and catching his breath, Tiburcio felt a presence at his side. Its silent pull was stronger than all the music and dancing and hollering. He jerked his head to see who it was and looked directly into the pair of the most mesmerizing black eyes he had ever seen. He swallowed hard. Anita was standing right here. Right next to him. She wore a black silk dress with ruffles at the hem, cuffs and neck.

"You... You... You ... You're here," he stammered.

"Ah, Tiburcio the Poet," she teased.

"Anita," he exclaimed, taking hold of her hands. "I want to shut the hall down. I will kick everyone out instantly and we'll be together, just us. Forget all these people and their shallow entertainment. They can go somewhere else, for all I care. I want to talk and sing and play guitar only for you."

"Oh, so you did you bring your guitar?"

"No, but I will find one," Tiburcio said.

Without taking his eyes off her, he reached over and tapped one of his helpers.

"Quick, fetch me a guitar."

"I'm not sure if the mood is right for a serenade, Tiburcio," Anita said, glancing with a wry smile at the raucous stomping, clapping and dancing going on just a few yards away.

"Oh, I know a quieter place. A place much more appropriate for a proper, young lady like yourself. By the way, what is a proper, young lady doing at a fandango. I thought you told me ..."

"A wealthy friend of my father said he was going to attend a fandango in town, so father became curious. I told father that his friend was likely talking about your dance hall, and my father, much to my surprise, said perhaps it wouldn't hurt to see what goes on at the Monterey fandangos and what kind of business a young man like yourself might be running. Still, he is allowing me to stay only an hour."

"Seconds ago I would have given everything for a just minute with you. Now I get an entire hour!"

Thirty feet away, Antonia's dance was reaching a crescendo. She skipped past Garcia and Higuera as if they weren't there. Higuera laughed at the small snub, but bitterness tightened in on Garcia. Someone accidentally struck him with their elbow. Humiliation stabbed at his chest.

"What are you laughing at?" he snarled at Higuera. "It will be her last dance if she let's these gringos have their way!"

Across the hall, Tiburcio gazed into Anita's eyes, afraid that should he look away she would vanish as quickly as she had arrived.

"I wrote a poem for you on my ride home," he said.

"Did you put it down in writing? In your beautiful penmanship?"

"No. I have it right here," he said, tapping his temple with a finger.

Anita started to say something else but shouting from across the room distracted her. Tiburcio tried to ignore the interruption.

"Let's dance, Anita!" Tiburcio exclaimed, grabbing her attention again.

"Oh, I will be the envy of everyone in your fancy fandango, Tiburcio," she teased.

He led her by the hand to the edge of the dance floor as the lively number was finishing up. The ravishing Antonia had plopped a sailor's hat on her own crown and the crowd was tossing coins at her feet. As the sailor stood in front of her and great applause filled the hall, she tossed the hat on the floor and stepped toe and heel around it. The tempo picked up and her legs and arms were a blur of motion. As the last beat struck and faded, the musicians raised their instruments in congratulations.

In the dim torchlight and commotion of the hall, Garcia tried to shake into focus the hatless man who had his arm around Antonia, smiling at his prize. Garcia recognized the golden-haired boy. He was astounded.

The sailor shrugged at Garcia and kissed Antonia.

"*Hijo de puta.* You are going to pay for this!" Garcia shouted in rage and charged at the sailor. Higuera followed.

The sailor had no time to react. Garcia's right fist caught him square in the temple and he crumbled to his knees. A fellow sailor raised a half-full whiskey bottle and was ready to crash it down on Garcia's skull, but Higuera's hands locked onto the *yanqui's* arm and forced the limb down onto his bent knee. The ulna shattered and the bone's crunch and the man's wail crackled above the commotion. Garcia finished off his nemesis with a boot-kick in the face. The sailor lay motionless on his back.

The Mexicans, however, quickly found themselves outnumbered. Several Americans closed in on them until their backs brushed up against the wall.

Tiburcio never got his guitar. Nor his dance. His eyes remained transfixed on Anita, unwilling to believe what was happening just a few yards away. His dream was blowing apart. Anita looked in horror at the growing brawl.

"Tiburcio," she urgently whispered. "You must get out of here! Go!"

"I don't want to. I want to stay with you."

"Don't be foolish! You must! I am afraid for you!"

"I can handle this."

Tiburcio slowly turned his attention to the ruckus. He saw Garcia and Higuera swinging away at eight or nine gringos as dozens of guests scattered in the confusion. The *gente da razon* quickly vanished and Tiburcio saw several of his countrymen and workers scurry out of the hall as if a bull were loose inside.

"Go now, darling," Anita implored. "Leave!"

"I have to get Anastacio and Higuera out of here. I have to calm everyone down."

Tiburcio ran straight into the fracas. People were yelling and cursing from the fringes of the fistfight where a dozen people were now caught in a cyclone of punches and kicks. Someone tossed a bottle and it shattered at Tiburcio's boots. A chair flew into the fray and crashed to the floor, spraying splinters. Miraculously, no weapons had been drawn yet.

Tiburcio grabbed a dazed man who was on his hands and knees and pulled him aside so he wouldn't get trampled by the other fighters. Trying to reach his friends, he pushed another gringo out of the way. Garcia was crouching at his right, ready to spring. Higuera was bent like a wild animal to his left, panting and spitting and ready to swing away again. There was a momentary pause in the fighting but a dozen *yanqui* fighters began closing in on the three Mexicans.

"If anything happens," Garcia yelled to the others in Spanish, "and we have to split up, meet at the eucalyptus grove by the water."

Higuera and Garcia bent low with their arms out and ready for action. They lunged in unison at the throng, which surged back. This bought them a little time and space, so they shifted along the wall toward the entrance, their only getaway. The doorway was about fifty feet away.

They never saw Constable William Hardmount enter the room. The officer charged in from their blind side. He knocked Higuera hard to the floor with a club and whipped his huge forearm around Tiburcio's neck, choking him. Garcia saw just a blur dashing at them from the side and suddenly saw someone manhandling his partners. He pulled his revolver out of his waistband and pistol-whipped the large figure in the head with the ivory handle. The constable's knees buckled and Tiburcio pulled free from his grasp. Tiburcio looked up just in time to see Garcia take aim at the lawman's heart and pull the trigger.

Everything froze for an instant. Hardmount collapsed onto his stomach and blood oozed from underneath his body onto the dirty wood floor.

As the officer lay dying, Garcia snapped into action, showing no effects from the aguardiente .

"Tiburcio. Follow me! Let's go!" he yelled on the run, the revolver still smoking in his hand. He darted swiftly and agilely right and left around stunned patrons and slipped out the front door.

Higuera, dazed from the blow to his head, was not so quick. Still, he fought out of the grasp of two Americans who had snagged him and stumbled out of the room.

"Stop him!" someone yelled.

A merchant who lived above Tiburcio's business and owned the neighboring general store ran into the dance hall armed with a shotgun. Hearing the call, he spun back out the door to give chase to Higuera.

Higuera was not yet twenty yards down the street when the merchant raised the shotgun and fired. A charge of buckshot smacked Higuera in the backside and sent him sprawling face first onto the gravelly street.

Inside the hall, Tiburcio caught Anita's teary, frightened eyes across the floor. He had frozen upon seeing her again and it was about to cost him his life. He followed her eyes to the front door where ten or fifteen bloodthirsty men had sealed off that exit. She pointed with two quick nods of her pretty head to the back door.

"Go! Hurry!" she silently yelled.

Tiburcio turned and raced toward the rear of the hall.

"There goes the last one!" someone shouted. "Get that murderer!"

When Tiburcio was a few feet from the back door, a cowboy stepped into the doorway, blocking his escape. The massive figure filled the entire door frame and he passed a large Bowie knife from hand to hand as he stepped toward Tiburcio. Tiburcio skirted around a long, sturdy, wood table littered with empty glasses and liquor bottles as angry men closed in on him from behind. He had one chance to escape and little time. He wedged his shoulder under the table and lunged it with such force that it bounced and skidded at the cowboy who sidestepped to get out of the way. The glasses and bottles shattered on the ground. Tiburcio leaped onto the sawhorse that had supported the upended table and he soared out the back patio.

The patio had a twelve-foot adobe wall around it. Tiburcio saw an ancient, soaring olive tree stretching its branches over the top as if it were reaching out to help him. Praying the branches were sturdy, he sprinted at full speed and leaped. He got a toehold on the wall and grabbed a bough and, with a grunt and a heave, hoisted himself over the enclosure, dropping into the serene darkness on the other side.

Tiburcio went flat with his back against the cold stone. He heard the cowboy's boots scraping to get over on the other side of the wall. He listened to every sound from every direction. Whipping his head back and forth to make sure no one was coming around either corner of the building, he darted away and ducked into a row of massive oak trees. The night was moonless. Fog was rolling inland from the bay. He waited in the dark, scheming how he would retrieve his horse from the front of the hall and make it to the eucalyptus grove. He had little time to devise a plan.

He saw shadows of frantic men coming and going from the building. Getting to his horse hitched in front and mounting a getaway was insane. It would be easier to get to the horses and *carretas* at the far side of the building. Still, the odds of stealing one of those and escaping were only slightly better than going for his own horse. He didn't know how long Garcia would wait for him at the grove but he knew he had to act fast.

He pondered using the opaque night to move stealthily on foot from one building to the next until he reached the main road out of town. Impossible. He would eventually have to cross a wide thoroughfare in the open. Even if no one saw him attempting that, he would next have to get across the tidal flat in plain view from the main road before finally reaching the shielded woods. It would be a half-hour by foot to the grove. With each breath, time closed in on him. He stepped from tree to tree, uncertain of the best escape route. Suddenly, his heart skipped a beat and his throat constricted. He felt and heard the beat of hooves crashing toward him. A rider and horse was descending on him at full gallop. Tiburcio reached down and pulled the knife from his boot. He crouched, prepared to leap at the attacker and defend himself.

He couldn't believe his eyes. He stood straight up and dropped his hands to his side. It was his own palomino bolting towards him. And Anita was in the saddle.

Just inches in front of him, she pulled up on the reins and the horse reared high on its hind legs. She leapt off the animal nearly in the same motion that Tiburcio mounted. The lovers did not spare a second on dialogue. Looking down at Anita, his eyes spoke of all the passion of every unspoken word he felt for her at that moment. She smiled as if they were simply passing each other in the sunny plaza. Tiburcio reached into his jacket and pulled out a leather case, dropping it into her hands. A second later he lunged out of the trees, turned sharply right and galloped in the direction of the ocean. He was out of sight within moments.

Anita stayed hidden for a few minutes as she heard people shouting in the direction of Tiburcio's furious dash. There was a gun shot, but it sounded as if it came from up the street in the direction opposite of Tiburcio. Waiting another moment, she brushed the front of her skirt and smoothed out the pleats and walked the long way back to the hall, gaining her composure with each step before suddenly showing up in front of the building, where she saw her worried father looking for her in the commotion. She touched the case to her breast, but would have to gaze later at the encased photograph of Tiburcio. It was safe in her corset for the time being.

Inside the hall, a volatile band of citizens gathered over the dead body of Hardmount. Sheriff Ned Lyons walked in, kicking strewn bottles and glass out of his way. The cursing citizens looked at the sheriff.

"What the hell is going on?" Lyons asked.

"The proprietor of this hall and his greaser friends killed Hardmount."

Lyons looked down at his officer's body.

"You sure he's dead?"

"Shot clean through the heart."

"Are you positive Tiburcio had something to do with this?" asked the sheriff. "Where is he?"

"Hell yes, he had everything to do with this. He and that highway man who's married to his cousin."

"And a third one," someone added.

The sheriff slowly looked around the hall. His calm demeanor was not quelling the fomenting vigilantism among the citizens. In fact, the sheriff seemed oblivious to their frenzy and that made them even angrier. There was a thump at the entrance and two men dragged the wounded Higuera by the feet into the hall and lay him next to the dead constable.

A vengeful cheer erupted.

"If we don't make an example out of these miscreants, sheriff, there will be hell to pay," the first man told Lyons. His name was Dee Sturgis, a local hotel and saloon owner. "Hell to pay for you, for the mayor, for the town, for Americans and Mexicans. Hardmount here wasn't your typical officer. He was a generous citizen who went beyond his duty as a lawman to keep the peace and prosperity going around here."

They all heartily cheered Sturgis.

"Hold on!" shouted Lyons. "I need to know some facts here. First, is there a doctor who can tend to this fellow?"

"Tend to that fellow?" fumed Sturgis, pointing to Higuera. "Hardmount never got no tending to. The only tending that greaser needs is a hanging!"

This tirade sent the group into a higher state of agitation, and a trio of men split away and left out the front in a hurry.

"This town is not some lawless mining outpost," the sheriff harangued. "This was the first capital of the state of California. I am in charge here and I want some answers in this investigation."

"We need to mete out quick justice, sheriff. Those men are headed into the hills. There are two dozen witnesses who will tell you the three of them acted in concert in the death of an officer of law."

TIBURCIO!

"I want to say something," interjected a distinguished-sounding voice near the back wall of the hall.

It wasn't loud, but something in the easy inflection demanded respect. Its calmness was in great contrast to the mob's frenzy. Every head turned to the speaker, an older, well-educated man with a slight but distinct Spanish accent. He was a wealthy landowner whose rancho, handed down by the Spanish government, was one of the oldest and largest in the area. He didn't particularly like or dislike the gringo government now in charge nor was he proudly loyal to the Mexican leadership. He simply preferred to be left alone to live his rural life and, above all, keep his rich land.

"Don Constanza," the sheriff greeted. "I'm surprised to see you here. You are a long way from home. Did you witness the murder?"

"I brought my daughter, Anita, here for just a short time so she might speak with a friend, the young vaquero, Tiburcio Vasquez. She was so headstrong and, well, daughters have a way, you know, so I gave in. Of course, I regret the decision tenfold now."

For the first time the vigilantes saw the girl behind Don Constanza.

"*En todo caso*," he continued. "She saw the violent episode with her own eyes, and she can tell you exactly what occurred and how we got to this hopeless state of affairs."

With some gentle coaxing from the sheriff and her father, and with the crowd's energy in abeyance, Anita wiped away her tears and explained what she saw. She fearlessly defended Tiburcio, saying he was merely trying to stop the fight. Her testimony ended with a damning statement: "Garcia pulled the trigger of the gun that killed Constable Hardmount."

"Thank you, Don Constanza, and thank you, Anita. I'm sorry this had to happen with you present tonight," the sheriff replied.

"My daughter tore away and fled from my arms she was so frightened, sheriff," Don Constanza continued. "But when I

71

found her after a few minutes she was poised again. So I wanted you to hear what she had told me. She has never lied and has always done the proper thing."

"Again, I'm sorry," the sheriff said as father and daughter left the hall.

"There's the most powerful statement yet," Lyons continued. "I will establish a committee to investigate the affair before I am finished here. At eight in the morning, at my office, we will examine the facts, decide the guilty parties and take measures to hunt down the fugitives and bring them to justice."

The sheriff called to a deputy who had accompanied him into the dance hall.

"Take this wounded suspect to jail for the night. Get a doctor and dress his wounds," he directed. He pointed at two other men. "You and you, help me put the constable's body on one of the wagons outside. We'll take him to the priests at the mission."

The deputy removed Higuera with the help of some other men. With the sheriff gone, it didn't take long for the same men to agitate for more immediate recompense.

"We don't need an investigation. These men took flight together! A smitten little girl's opinion on the matter is worth no more than a pile of horse shit. They are all guilty."

"If they aren't all guilty of murder," another man added, "and I ain't saying they aren't, then at the very least they are guilty of resisting arrest."

"At any rate," another citizen reasoned, "we need to get outfitted to hunt them down. That takes some financing and preparation. It will be done easier tomorrow morning once we convince the sheriff and other town leaders."

"Look," Sturgis yelled, "the sheriff is scared of Garcia. Anyone can see that. This delay gives Garcia time to escape and set up a base in the hills, where he will continue to terrorize our citizens."

"And what if the sheriff doesn't put much credence in the preponderance of evidence!" another man demanded of his peers.

"Yeah," shouted several others, pumping their fists. One of the three men who had left the room after the sheriff arrived now stepped forward and held up a thick rope in his hand.

"I grabbed this rope off the greaser's own horse. Who is going to follow me to the jailhouse and hang him with his own riata? I know at least one greaser who won't get away with this brazen killing! Let's get him."

Their fury swept them out of the building and down the street toward the jail.

The men assigned to take care of Higuera hadn't quite reached the jail when they heard the mob coming fast on their heels. The deputy and the doctor, who were now carrying a nearly lifeless Higuera with one arm around his waist and his arms draped over their shoulders, looked at each other hopelessly. They laid Higuera down on his back on the street and ran away. Higuera's eyes opened and the stars above witnessed his silent fear, confusion and pain.

The mob violently grabbed the suffering victim and hoisted him up, loudly declaring to several residents who had come out of their homes that this man would serve as an example to other lawless creatures in Monterey and all of the state of California.

Then, the hateful assemblage retraced their steps back to the dance hall.

In front of the great front entrance, where Tiburcio had proudly stood just a few hours ago, the vigilantes slipped the thickly knotted hemp snare around Higuera's neck. The end of the rope was swung over a large beam above the doors leading into the hall and every man who could get a handle on the rawhide, grabbed it and pulled the slack tighter and tighter.

"We will hang this man in front of this heinous establishment," Sturgis declared. "But what about the murderer who owns the place? He has taken our money in numerous ways, over and over, night after night, and how does he thank us for doing business with him? By participating in the killing of one of our finest citizens, Constable Hardmount. Why should his business remain standing? Let's teach him a lesson he'll never forget."

"Burn it down! Burn it down!" the mob chanted.

A half-dozen men ran into the fandango, grabbed the torches that lit the hall and touched them to the whiskey soaked tables and chairs.

Outside, Higuera's feet were hoisted off the wood-plank walkway and soon his body swung limply from the rope in front of the blazing structure.

Chapter 7: Fleeing
Monterey County
1854

Tiburcio arrived at the grove like crashing thunder. He dropped from his fatigued horse and led it to the watering hole. Rebelde's chest heaved. Garcia's horse grazed nearby, its thirst already slaked.

"I think the sheriff saw me galloping in this direction," Tiburcio huffed.

"Did he follow you?" Garcia asked, tossing Tiburcio a canteen of water.

"No. He looked confused. I think he was on his way to the dance hall."

Garcia studied the marine layer of fog spreading inland from the bay. It was beginning to creep through the tops of the trees in the grove and settle closer to the earth. An owl cried out from a tree. High eucalyptus branches rubbed together, squeaking like notes from an untuned violin.

"Good," Garcia said, looking up and all around. "We should have cover for a while. We have a long ways to go, though. There is no telling if a scouting party is going to band together tonight or in the morning, but we need lots of distance between us and them. The fog will hide us until we're about twenty miles from the coast, and the stars and moon will help light the way through the mountains."

After a moment, he added, "Damn, I wish I could light a cigarette."

"Where's Higuera?" Tiburcio asked forebodingly. "I heard shots."

"*No sabe,*" Garcia answered quietly.

"Where are we going?"

"To a secure place in the Panoche range. There are lots of compadres there, plenty of grass for the horses and shelter. A white man cannot get there without an expert guide. The mountains are almost inaccessible. But I know this terrain as if it were my second home. Its streams and canyons will buy us our lives, *mi amigo*. We will ride all night and most of the day. We'll need fresh horses somewhere along the way. That means you may have to say goodbye to your beloved palomino, Tiburcio."

"She can make it through anything."

"It is time to grow up, Tiburcio."

"You are not my father."

A crooked smile crept onto Garcia's face.

"Ha! Just think, your brothers thought we were wasting our time in the hills at the ranch. Well, now you will need every ounce of my tutelage if you are to survive. Well, enough chatting as if we are visiting on a Sunday on your mother's patio. The horses are rested and I feel danger approaching. Let's go."

Garcia put a spur to his horse and galloped northeast out of Monterey. Tiburcio followed. An hour later, they were climbing the rugged hills of southern Santa Clara County. They crossed and re-crossed countless cattle trails to throw off any pursuers. They crunched straight through thick chaparral and splashed across numerous streams. In the moonlit darkness, the trees cast sharply defined shadows on the hard bare ground. The purplish red bark and crooked branches of manzanitas appeared like terrified ghosts reaching out for help. Tiburcio tried to note landmarks and switchbacks so he could remember the route back to Monterey, if he needed to return alone, but it was useless.

Garcia guided them clear of the towns of San Juan Bautista and Hollister. And he avoided the well-traveled trails. Too often, these routes traversed over a hill where they could have been seen from miles around. As swiftly as possible they journeyed deep into the Panoche mountain range, stopping for just a few short intervals to rest and drink.

They didn't sleep all night. Near daylight, their pace slowed and they descended out of the foothills and trotted along a bank of a stream. Tall red alder shot up around them and thick crooked sycamores and willows thrived along the waterway. Hundreds of noisy birds flashed about overhead and warbled in the trees in the fresh morning. Duck and geese incessantly criss-crossed the skies above the waterside canopy.

Early in the morning, Garcia caught sight of a solo traveler and they scurried up a rock without being seen. They surreptitiously observed the man, who turned out to be a hunter returning to town with several grizzly, deer and mountain lion pelts. They let him pass without molestation.

"Easy pickings," Garcia said after the hunter was out of sight. "But we'll let him go this time."

Midday, deep in the uninhabitable land south of Hollister, the companions stopped one last time to slake the thirst of their horses. The sun was high and the day was going to be warm. They were resting on a sycamore trunk that stretched out over the middle of the purling creek.

"We are about to make a final mountain ascent," Garcia said. "But your horse is slowing."

Tiburcio was fatigued and hungry, but he tried to put up a protest.

"Rebelde is fine," he muttered.

"There is a ranch with a herd of mustangs about an hour from here. It's the last homestead before our destination. With a couple of fresh steeds we can outdistance any posse that might be following us."

"Jesus, Anastacio. How much longer?"

"By noon, we'll be at our hiding place, safe from everyone except fellow *pistoleros*. Come on, we'll begin leisurely."

Garcia took the lead position again. Tiburcio followed single-file. Garcia held the reins in his right hand above the raw-hide riata coiled on the horn of the Spanish saddle. His left hand rested on a rolled blanket on the horse's rump. He often glanced back at Tiburcio.

"Your horse's step is slowing, Tiburcio. Even at this slow of a pace, I can see his leg is injured and his muscles are tightening. We need to start picking up the pace. We might have to ride double until we can find another horse."

"We have outdistanced by sixty miles any gringo who would be crazy enough to try to follow us. You aren't thinking straight, Anastacio."

Garcia stopped abruptly and glared. Tiburcio knew better than to speak anymore. Garcia then looked over the terrain in every direction.

"This is where the ranch is located," Garcia said. "Get off your lame steed."

"He is not lame. I'm better on this horse than any other we can find. I can ride him like a Comanche."

"Get down, now!" Garcia bellowed. Tiburcio obeyed. "Get your rope, your saddle bag and blanket and your bridle off the horse and unsaddle him."

"No."

"Do as I say!" Garcia hissed. "Out here you are lost, Tiburcio. Even if your steed can stumble out of this terrain, he will perish when we reach the wastelands. Then we'll be easy targets. If you ever want to return to Monterey and see your mother - and Anita - again, it would do you well to listen to me."

Tiburcio's young mind was in a haze, his body ached and he was shaky from hunger. He had no choice but to obey.

The horse, despite being unburdened of his load, buckled and started to go down on its front legs. It struggled to stand erect, and finally did.

"We can't leave him on the trail. He might wander and give us away," Garcia warned. He pulled his pistol out.

"What are you doing?"

"We have to kill it."

"*Estás loco*? You're not killing my horse. He is like a good friend who knows my every thought."

"I will leave you with your lame horse to be caught and hung by the lawmen, if you prefer," Garcia threatened. "Three choices, Tiburcio. Kill your horse, stay and perish with him or have me shoot you both."

"I will tie him some distance from the trail where he can't be observed. I will return tomorrow and guide him back to camp."

"No! You are not coming back here for a long, long while."

Garcia jerked the horse's reins and led him deep into the thicket.

"This horse is fine!" Tiburcio called out, following Garcia through the dense brush. "You got us into this mess, Anastacio! Not me. And not Rebelde! I will handle my stallion!"

But he saw Garcia put the gun up against his favorite horse's head. A shiver ran through him and he could not bear to watch what happened next. He closed his eyes tightly, turned around and started walking briskly away. At the edge of the thicket, he froze as the sound of the shot rang out and he felt it sting his heart. He let out a cry and tears flooded his eyes. He heard the horribly clear but flat sound of the large animal falling into the thicket and he fell onto his knees, crying. The gunshot echo stopped and everything was deadly silent for a moment. Tiburcio wiped his eyes and fought back more tears.

Garcia walked out of the thicket, but before he could say anything, they both heard a horse utter a neigh from up the trail where the path turned and disappeared behind brush and trees.

"Stay here!" Garcia ordered and leaped on his steed.

Tiburcio was left standing alone, feeling vulnerable without a horse. He looked into the thicket and could not see the dead animal.

Several minutes later, Tiburcio heard two shots, the first from a rifle and the second from a pistol. Fifteen minutes later, Garcia was back. He rode up with a buck-skin belt in his teeth and the reins of a new, saddled horse in his grip . A sorrel with a white main and tail, it fought against its new master's will. Tiburcio noticed a new Colt revolver in Garcia's belt.

Dismounting, Garcia asked through clenched teeth: "What was that gringo doing up here?"

He flung the buckskin belt over his horse's saddle.

"I got you a new ride, Tiburcio. He's spirited. Cost someone his life, too, so be appreciative."

Garcia guided the new horse over to Tiburcio and tossed him the reins.

"Now, let's see what our deceased traveler was burdened with carrying."

In the various belt pockets Garcia discovered fifteen hundred dollars in gold and silver coins. He walked over to the horse and tossed open one of the saddle bags. Before examining what was inside, he looked at his shocked companion.

"Whatever is in here is yours. To make up for losing a good horse."

Garcia rummaged in the saddle bag and counted another eight hundred dollars in gold and silver.

"I'll leave it in here, since it's yours. Now, we must fly. This stop has cost us a lot of time. There's another thirty five miles to go."

Up the trail a ways, Tiburcio noticed there was no sign of Garcia's bloody work. Neither of them spoke for the rest of the journey.

For the next three hours, the two Californios rode over a rocky, barren terrain with the high sun beating down on them. There was scarcely a shrub for shade or so much as a squirrel or rabbit to be seen. Tiburcio savagely shook the water canteen for a last drop of water. Just when he was about to explode with all the hunger, dehydration, frustration, rage, regret and resentment built up inside, Garcia stopped ahead.

"Here we are!"

They trotted between two sheer outcrops into the mouth of a great canyon. Past this narrow opening, the scenery suddenly and drastically changed. The dry landscape unfolded into a wide, lush basin spotted with oak trees and carpeted with luxuriant grass and wildflowers. A lazy stream lined with willow brush and sycamores cut through the valley floor. Hungry and exhausted, the two vaqueros had finally arrived at the hiding place.

Garcia looked at his young pupil and perceived that Tiburcio, in spite of his fatigue and sorrow, was in awe. He could not believe there could be such a paradise beyond the lonely, wild and inhospitable plain they had just crossed.

"Welcome to Cantua Canyon!" Garcia announced. "It's perfect. *Es como el cielo*. Look back at that entrance. It is so narrow that two or three men supplied with ample weapons and ammunition could hide behind those rocks and hold off an entire Army regiment."

Tiburcio had expected to see a half-dozen scraggly outlaws subsisting on nearly nothing. To his surprise, people and animals were up and about, and he heard uplifted voices of men and women, the jabbering of children, the shrill of jaybirds, the yelping of dogs. In the sun-filled valley, dozens of horses grazed on an abundance of clover in a large pasture. Along the edge of a clearing, men groomed horses, split logs and sharpened knives, while groups of women in the center of the camp cut and salted meat or squatted at fire pits cooking beef and tortillas in pans over open flames. Down at a creek in the distance, women were washing clothes.

About one thousand feet beyond the clearing, Tiburcio saw several adobe buildings about a half-acre apart from each other. In front of some of these, old men were smoking cigarillos, gazing out at the activity. These houses had been given up by luckless miners and then used by followers of the famous bandit Joaquin Murrieta, who had discovered the perfect spot to evade pursuers and recruit outlaws. The newcomers had erected several tents between the adobes.

Garcia seemed comfortable and familiar with the people and the setting as he walked his companion around the land.

"These are displaced Californios, Tiburcio," he said with a sweep of his hand. "Displaced by war. Displaced by gold. Displaced by manifestos. They are defeated soldiers ready to rise again. They are safe here. This is where our liberation begins."

Garcia summoned an Indian over and told him to take their worn-out horses to water and picket them in the field. A pair of women, who hadn't even spoken to the new arrivals, brought them a hearty, simple meal of meat, tortillas and *pinole*. Tiburcio and Garcia ate alone by the campfire and washed the food down with water and *aguardiente*.

After the meal, Garcia took Tiburcio to one of the buildings. Their blankets were already unrolled on the ground inside. Tiburcio looked around and saw belongings from at least two other desperadoes who had made quarters in the building but were not present. The fugitives lay down and pulled their mantas over their heads and fell into a deep slumber.

Sixteen hours later, Tiburcio awoke. He remembered where he was – that much was clear. He remembered getting here. But he was uncertain about how long he had been here and what time it was. There was a waning chill in the air, so he assumed it was morning. Beyond this uncertainty, he felt a pervasive uneasiness. He sensed a distinct animal ferocity in the room. God, he prayed, not a bear.

It was not a bear. It was a man. At least he believed it was a man. Its large body and coarse features sat in the gloom on a low stool near the wall. The figure's nose was wide and triangular and its thick, black hair was matted. Its mustache and beard were as unclean and neglected as its clothes. It didn't move, but closely watched Tiburcio as if it were ready to bound toward him at the slightest provocation. It stared angrily at the boy out of yellow eyes set back under a protruding brow. To Tiburcio's further astonishment, he noticed the pupils in these sunken orbs moved independently of one another. At the moment, the beast's right eye seemed to be regarding Tiburcio, while its left eye gazed up at its own thick eyebrows. Then his left eye dropped and his right eye twitched as it tried to gain focus.

TIBURCIO!

The savage stood up, and he kept rising. Nearly six and one-half feet tall, all of its two hundred and fifty pounds pounds of muscle moved slightly toward Tiburcio, who cried out "El Diablo!" in all the force of a whisper.

But it wasn't the devil. It was Juan Soto, known to the yanquis as the "Human Wildcat." His reputation for murdering, sometimes for no apparent reason, inspired terror even among his own people. Soto was one of the state's most dreaded outlaws. When he finally spoke to Tiburcio, though, his voice was low and smooth and strangely soothing.

"You look shocked, Tiburcio," stated Soto, knowing his effect on people. "No. Frightened is a better description."

"How do you know who I am?" Tiburcio asked.

This sent Soto into sardonic laughter. After a minute, he abruptly stopped laughing.

"I know everything within one hundred miles of this hiding place. The closer you get to this camp, the more I know about you. If I don't know enough about you to satisfy me, I kill you. It is that simple. In your case, I want to know where you got that horse you were riding?"

"Garcia gave it to me."

"I see. Do you know whose horse it is?"

"No. Garcia shot my palomino. It was the best mount I ever had, and he shot it in the head. It could have made it the rest of the way easily. I was left without a horse when Garcia went up the trail. I couldn't see what he was doing. He came back with that one."

"What happened up the trail?"

"I saw nothing."

"Did he come back with anything else, besides the horse?"

"A money belt."

Soto stared at Tiburcio for a long while. The boy felt uncomfortable under his repulsive gaze.

"I hope you didn't bring bad luck to our camp," Soto finally said. "Garcia speaks highly of you. And for you, our newest recruit, it's good to have at least one friend in this camp."

"Recruit?"

"Yes - recruit," said another voice from the doorway. It was Garcia. "It's about time you woke up. I have everyone gathered by the fire so we can lay out our plans."

Soto lumbered toward the door.

"Just a moment, Soto. I want to ask you something. You stay here, too, Tiburcio."

"What is the mood up here at Cantua?" Garcia asked the giant man.

"Suitable at the moment, but bleakness is in the air. The men believe we will not have enough money and supplies to get through winter, let alone sustain any type of revolution."

"They have been grumbling?"

"I have not heard them directly. But in your absence, yes. In my absence, yes."

"Perhaps they would prefer to go back to eking out whatever living they can manage - without land, without cattle, without a prayer."

"They know things are changing rapidly. They have seen enough to know. They do not want to go back. Not yet."

"But they want progress? Now?"

"Yes."

"Then, our timing could not be better," Garcia said, suddenly cheerful. "Progress they shall have. Tell the men I will be out in a moment. First, I want to say a few words to my friend, Tiburcio."

The teenage boy avoided his mentor's stare in the dim light.

"You look angry, Tiburcio. What is wrong?"

"What is wrong? What is wrong? Twenty-four hours ago, I was pocketing hundreds of dollars on a Saturday night at the dance hall. I lived in the house of one of the most respected families in Monterey. I owned an excellent horse that was the envy of vaqueros everywhere. I was free to visit the loveliest girls in the county, attend the grandest festivals, thrill hundreds with with riding stunts. Now, I am isolated deep in the mountains with a bunch of hard-cases, I am innocent yet hunted by the law and my closest friend is a cold-blooded murderer. A mass murderer."

"Your life was a house of cards," Garcia answered. "This is where you belong. It is not so bleak as all that, Tiburcio. These people need you. You will be famous and loved by many. You will see."

"I just want to go back down the mountain and return to Monterey. I want to profess my innocence."

Garcia laughed derisively. But he figured the young man might just have to come to certain realizations by his own accord. I can't beat everything into him, he thought. For the moment, however, he tried to be empathetic.

"I have not been home for a very long time, either, Tiburcio. I cannot tell you how much I miss Lupe and the children. *Los ninos* follow me around at the ranch like a bunch of ducklings as I do my chores. My oldest is beginning to ride a horse. His brother is trying to keep up, even though he's two years younger. Lupe is knitting clothes for the newborn, Rosa, who I probably won't recognize next time I see her. And little Dominga just started walking. She's thirteen months old. She took her first steps while I was up here in Cantua Canyon the last time. You should have seen Lupe. She was so furious that I missed that milestone. And El Tuche is beautiful at this time of year, Tiburcio. You remember? After summer, when some rain has fallen and the hillsides are green all the way down to the ocean. It is a beautiful time of year. I miss a lot, too."

"Why don't you go home, then? Why all of this?"

"I will soon."

"When?"

"We must grow out our hair and beards. Disguise ourselves. Ay, you have been here only one day!"

"I have seen enough already."

"I need to take care of some business here. You can help me, Tiburcio. The men and women out there need money and supplies. I cannot let them think it would be wiser to return to the towns and countryside where they came from than stay in Cantua, where we can make a difference in the course of history, reestablish our culture, which, I suspect you are finally beginning to acknowledge, is under assault and is quickly being buried."

"When, Anastacio?"

"Give me two weeks. Perhaps three. The posses will have combed the entire area from the Panoche range to the ocean. They will have paid a visit to El Tuche and realized I have not been there for a long time. Things will settle down in a few weeks, at least a bit. Then you can go do what you have to do, and I will go and visit and comfort Lupe and the children. But I must come back here before long. Soto and Carabajal and Molina and the others can only take care of things for so long at Cantua in my absence."

Garcia became lost in thought. Then, he told his protégé to get up and join him at the campfire.

Tiburcio remained sitting up on his blanket.

"I had nothing to do with that constable's murder, Anastacio. You must understand: I need to go back and defend my name, and not hide up here like a criminal."

"*Bueno. Bueno.* You do that, Tiburcio. I do not advise it, but I will not hold it against you."

Two dozen, long-haired Mexican bandits mingled around the campfire. Some stood poking the embers with sticks; others reposed with their backs against their Spanish saddles. Every one of them had side arms or a Henry rifle within reach. Tiburcio joined the ring of bandits and former soldiers. They were a hardened group, some with pock-marked faces, many with visible scars.

Garcia wasted no time informing the group that it was time to begin accumulating the necessary wealth and assembling warriors willing to fight the intruders. He quickly began talking to the men about robbing a stagecoach near Hollister. Tiburcio watched his friend command the attention of the outlaws. He heard him plotting in detail when the coach was expected, how much loot he surmised would be available, how many passengers it would be carrying and who they were, what time it was expected, where the men would attack it, how they should act, how they should dress, which words they would use, what might happen if they had to speak English, who would survey the road to the south and who to the north, and finally how the escape would unfold.

The more Tiburcio listened the more he grasped how evil Garcia had become. In less than twenty-four hours, Garcia had murdered two men on impulse, one of them an officer of the law. He had committed highway robbery without so much as a second thought. He was, it was now clear, the de facto leader of a large band of outlaws, including one of the most notorious ever, Juan Soto. And Tiburcio could not be so sure the state of affairs would not get more strange and wanton.

In the middle of this mess stood he - a member of the respected Cantua family, whose great grandfather accompanied the grandest explorer ever, Juan Bautista de Anza, on the high seas; whose grandfather helped establish the mission at Santa Clara; and whose father had been an alderman in San Jose. He was being swept along by events like debris in a rushing river that is tossed onto the shore at the feet of criminals.

"Tiburcio," he heard Garcia call. "You will accompany me, and help me communicate with and subdue the driver, the shotgun messenger and passengers."

"Why don't we just shoot them all dead?" Tiburcio asked sarcastically.

The words pealed like a bell, heard long after they were spoken. Every head turned toward the newcomer. But he and Garcia were longtime friends, they were family, and that should account for something, so Tiburcio continued his jaundiced interjection.

"A mass killing shouldn't raise too much suspicion, *si*? What is another murder, done at the hands of our leader, Anastacio Garcia, going to hurt? What does it matter that more vigilantes are on our trail, stalking us right up to the mouth of this hideout."

As the men stirred, Garcia fumed inwardly, silently, wondering where the boy was going with this insolent interruption. His eye twitched and his neck veins pulsated. He swallowed hard. Tiburcio didn't let up.

"Is he insane? Is he hoping that, by terrorizing innocent citizens, the sheriff and all these gringos will just slink away? You wantonly killed a constable two nights ago in front of a hundred witnesses. Yesterday, you ambushed and murdered a lone rancher on the very trail that leads straight to where we stand right now. Hell, we will probably run right into the posse on our way down the mountain to rob the stagecoach. I'm certain, as you have told me, that they are hunting for us all over the hills at this moment. Are you not dancing with danger by committing these senseless acts? Are you not putting us all at risk? Jeopardizing your so-called revolution?"

Tiburcio saw his friend flinch. The others listened carefully to the bold, young man, with his eloquent speaking and big words. They saw he was well-educated, unlike most of them. Was Garcia leading them all to an early grave for no reason at all? Had they followed the wrong general into the tip of a bayonet? How would Garcia respond?

"I hope you are finished with your bluster, Tiburcio," Garcia grunted loudly through gritted teeth. "It's time you realize something, my pupil. It's time you take the blinders off. I planned the shooting of that constable – at your nightclub – down to the last detail. I dragged you into this mess to do you a favor, *carajo*! You see, we up here don't take kindly to the stars and stripes. I don't know how you became so blind as to not see the brutal acts being committed against your own countrymen, on their own soil. We all see it! Our brothers are being cheated out of their land and their possessions stolen, and what are you doing about it? Showing the thieves a good time at your fandango. And even there, they push us aside, debauch our women, call us damned greasers, assault us. And what do you do? Ask them if they would like more food and drink. Do you not feel their hot breath on your collar, boy? Is it because your skin is lighter than these dark-skinned brothers around you? Does your light skin blind you to what is happening, Tiburcio? I have never done, nor will I ever knowingly do anything that will bring danger to my own neck or to the neck of anyone here. This I guarantee."

Garcia paused, taking time to look into each man's set of eyes.

"But we need to eat, we need to survive, and we need horses, cattle and money to do so! Unfortunately, there's a price to pay!"

Tiburcio saw a few people nodding their head. Others stood motionless. Soto looked amused, a wide, repulsive grin on his face.

"I saved you while you still have a chance to do your countrymen some good," Garcia continued, gaining steam. "I didn't see any Americans waiting to sort out the details of the constable's murder. No, they just wanted to lynch a Mexican. I saved you before it was too late, Tiburcio! The Americanos would have just as soon driven you from your business like dogs at a fox's tail. I'll bet you that your cheap dance hall isn't even standing as we speak. They've burned it to the ground, because it's owned by a Mexican. And to them, that's a sin. But even if you could have stuck around without getting your neck caught in a noose, Tiburcio, you would have eventually seen such wrath come down on you that you would have had to flee your beautiful Monterey anyway. For there is not chance in hell for a Californio to succeed unless he obeys every last word of the gringo. No chance. Not when they are finished with you giving them what they want and can just as easily take it themselves. I am giving you a chance. I am giving us all dignity and a chance to survive and prosper!"

Tiburcio looked at the faces of the men. They supported this man as their leader. The leader who used to terrorize these parts, the legendary Joaquin Murrieta, had been gone and not seen for so long that no one was sure if he was still alive or not.

Rumors that Murrieta's head had been carried by Captain Love and the Rangers into Stockton and put on public display were beginning to ring true. And into this void, Anastacio Garcia stepped, persuading men with his vehemence. Tiburcio could see his friend controlled and led this band through fervor, fear and intimidation – and because these men could not function without a master.

"And besides that, Tiburcio," Garcia raged on, "these fellow countrymen you see around this fire need you more than you need the white man. You owe them more than you owe the *yanqui* invaders. But they have already realized the truth to which you remain blind. We are not here to enrich ourselves. We are here to survive. And if we survive long enough, we will fight back with a statewide revolution. Whether you like it or not, Tiburcio, you are now part of our revolution."

Tiburcio felt like he was standing on uneven ground. He had to speak again.

"I understand what is happening to our country with these invaders. But I am still innocent of murder. I am determined to return to Monterey to clear my name. Despite what you think, Garcia, I can do more for our cause as a free man, lawfully taking and accumulating the Americans' money, than I can up here in the hills with you. But do not fear, my countrymen, I will never give you away. That I promise. You are noble. Your cause is noble. Your leader is noble."

"Yes, I know you, Tiburcio," Garcia said in a low, fatherly tone. "You are intelligent and that can serve our people well. You have your own strong will, too, that's for sure. The heat of vigilantism will dissipate, and you will do what you feel you must. Go back down into Monterey and find out for yourself how things are, and how they have changed. I guarantee you will return to these mountains once you see how short the rope of their justice really is. We will be here for you, brother. You will return."

Chapter 8: Grief
Casa Vasquez, Monterey
1854

Guadalupe Vasquez heard the mob coming down Main Street as she lay awake in bed. She threw a shawl over her shoulder and lit the candle next to her bed. As the voices outside grew louder, panic struck her.

Antonio knocked on her door.

"What is it?"

"A mob is coming down the street toward the jail. They are following a deputy and another man carrying a wounded person."

Francisco came striding down the hallway with more news.

"They just dropped the wounded man and the mob is spiriting him off down the street, away from the jail, in the direction of the waterfront."

"What is going on?" asked a young girl's sleepy voice in the darkness.

"Nothing, Maria. Go back to bed."

"Where is Tiburcio?" the girl asked.

"Yes, where is Tiburcio?" Guadalupe asked her sons. "This doesn't have anything to do with the fandango, does it?"

"Do not overreact, mother," Francisco stated. "I am sure he is fine."

Guadalupe rushed down the narrow corridor and slipped outside into the night. Her children pursued her. In their haste, the candles they were holding blew out and the only light on the street was from the moon. Guadalupe took off running in the direction of the mob. They hurried past Casa Serrano and

Casa Soberanes. Little Maria trudged along, too, keeping up with them.

Behind the theater, the night sky was lit up in a hazy orange, yellow and brown. They could smell cinders, and past the theater they saw the flames.

"It's the dance hall!" she cried. "It's the dance hall. Oh, it's not Tiburcio, is it?"

The Vasquez brothers turned and shielded from their little sister the sight of a dangling body illuminated by the conflagration.

Francisco carried Maria back home as Guadalupe began beseeching anyone on the streets for the whereabouts of her youngest son and other incomprehensible answers. Was he inside the burning building? Who had been hung? Why did a mob torch the dance hall?

Scores of people loitered in the streets, many of them American sailors and soldiers. Guadalupe saw the sheriff exchanging words with several men. She was a prominent citizen and that, along with her desperate plea to find answers in the chaos, gave her the right to approach and interrupt the group no matter what its earnest business.

"Sheriff! Where is Tiburcio? What has happened?"

"So you're the mother of that greaser!" Sturgis hissed, but the sheriff and others hushed him up.

Lyons apologized and led Guadalupe several feet away to speak privately.

"Your home should burn, too!" she heard Sturgis shouting at her as he was pushed back by Lyons' deputies.

"There was a shooting, Doña Vasquez, a fatal shooting, at the fandango. From what I can tell, your son's friend pulled the trigger, but there is evidence that Tiburcio also took part in the melee that led to the murder."

"Whose murder?"

"Constable Hardmount."

"Oh, Mother of Mercy! But Tiburcio loved that good man. He would never harm the constable."

"Things got out of hand."

"Tiburcio is innocent, sheriff. You have to believe me. I will prove it."

"There will be time for that later. We are forming a posse to search for Garcia, who we believe pulled the trigger, but also for Tiburcio, who has fled the city with him."

"You are not taking that man on the posse, are you?" Guadalupe asked, pointing in the direction of Sturgis.

"He has volunteered. I will make sure he obeys the order that Tiburcio is to be brought back alive for questioning only."

"Tiburcio is incapable of murder, sheriff. He is being wrongly accused and his life is at risk. I am going straight to the alcalde."

"I would not advise that, Guadalupe," Lyons said earnestly. "A weapon was discharged on your patio, next to the mayor's office, earlier today. I had reports of a fracas at your cantina. I know all about that. It did not please the alcalde. So I don't think the mayor will be favorable to your opinion if you wake him at this hour. I have a job to do. One of them is to get the facts – before the alcalde is brought into the mess."

"And what about, Anastacio? He is my niece's husband. What guarantees have you made that he will be brought back alive?"

"I have made it clear to everyone that he is to return to face trial. However, ..." the sheriff said, his voice trailing off. "Guadalupe, I must clear the streets now. People are inflamed. There is a structure still burning. Go home, and I will inform you of everything in the morning."

● ● ●

Garcia thought it unwise, but two weeks after Constable Hardmount's death, he and Tiburcio left the isolation of Cantua Canyon and under starlight entered the fringes of Monterey County. They dressed commonly, like lower-class Mexicans, and rode horses of no great stature in order to avoid detection.

Tiburcio had grown a stubble beard and tilted his sombrero forward to shadow his face.

Garcia, who could not, despite his efforts, persuade his protégé to be more prudent, escorted him as far as Hollister. Garcia planned to skirt the town of Monterey altogether and swing wide north to his ranch at El Tuche. Tiburcio, however, was determined to go to his mother's house in Monterey.

"Lupe will not take the news well that my freedom and life is in danger," Garcia said.

"Tell her and the children hello for me. I hope to see her soon."

"I cannot stay long at El Tuche," Garcia reminded Tiburcio. "And you will not be able to stay in Monterey, I am afraid."

"We will see what happens."

"Before we part ways, Tiburcio, let me give you some advice. If you get in trouble and can't make it up the mountain to the Cantua retreat, your next best bet is to get to San Juan Bautista. It is populated and controlled by our people and the white citizenship is mostly sympathetic. The gringo lawmen usually stay clear from there. And if they don't, we at least know when they're coming. In San Juan, there's a man named Salazar. Go to his house and tell him you are like a son to me. He and his beautiful new wife will treat you like family."

Tiburcio nodded.

"Stay off the road and travel along the river as much as possible," Garcia added as Tiburcio started off alone without a word.

Two hours later, Tiburcio approached the Cervantes' property, where he had visited on the fateful day of the constable's murder. Tiburcio hitched his horse to an oak tree about one hundred yards from the house and slowly walked toward their patio. In case they didn't recognize him, he kept his arms up and away so they could see he wasn't about to grab the gun strapped in the shoulder holster under his poncho. Halfway to the house, he heard an angry growl.

TIBURCIO!

"Halt! Don't take another step," a familiar voice called out in English from the dark porch. The shotgun glinted in the thin moonlight as it was raised. "Who are you?"

"It's me. Tiburcio."

"Tiburcio Vasquez?"

"Yes. If I am causing any danger to you I will leave immediately."

"No. Come up here quickly and let's go around to the shadowy side of the house to talk."

As Señor Cervantes smoked a cigarillo, Tiburcio told him his version of the episode that the whole county was talking about. He explained how he had been hiding out in one of Murrieta's old headquarters until it might be safe to come back to Monterey.

"It's good to hear the truth, Tiburcio. So much rumor and speculation are swirling around these parts. If it weren't so serious, I would have laughed at how young Tiburcio had stirred up an entire county. But it is not safe yet. Why in God's name did you come back?"

"It's my home, señor. I've done nothing wrong."

"I don't know much, Tiburcio, and I have my own problems, as you know. But people say the vigilante committee pronounced its sentence equally against all three of you: Death. I do not think the town folk are likely to give you much of a chance to tell your side of the story."

"That's unfair! I have never done anything to put me on the wrong side of the law."

"It doesn't matter. Few Americans in the city would make the distinction between your being in the wrong place at the wrong time and the actual deed. The vigilantes formed three scouting parties that combed the hills for two weeks in every direction in search of you and Garcia. I believe they are still banded together. Do you know what happened to Higuera?"

"No."

"Higuera was hung by a mob not an hour after the murder. That anger has not died down."

After a moment of silence, Cervantes tapped Tiburcio's knee and added lightheartedly, "I'm glad to see you are safe, though. Your mother will be happy, too."

"Yes," Tiburcio answered. "How is mother?"

"I have heard she is devastated but is trying to live as normal a life as possible. Yet, her business has suffered greatly. The soldiers are avoiding the cantina. But she continues to serve a few natives and travelers passing through. I think that's good because working helps take her mind off of everything. Just like when your father died."

"I am on my way to visit her."

"Do not surprise her in the night, Tiburcio. Let her get whatever rest she can. Stay here, and in the morning I will put you in the back of the horse cart and take you down there."

Tiburcio considered the offer. He looked at his friend's face. It seemed to have aged many years in just a fortnight. Then he asked, "How about you? Have you heard from the Land Commission. I hope you have not forgotten my offer."

"I think we are doomed, Tiburcio. We cannot find proof of our possessions to show the authorities. Señora and I are simply waiting it out, like a couple of cornered wolves. We hear stories of Mexicans being pushed off their land and being hung when they object. The sheriff tries to keep the peace but too often is either unwilling or unable. That's why I spend many sleepless nights on the patio with this gun and this dog, waiting for I don't know who or what. But I have nowhere to go, and no money to get there, so I will defend my house with my life."

The fugitive and the homebound prisoner didn't say anything for a long time. A night owl called out in the clear night. A raccoon or a possum thrashed through some brush, perking up the dog's ears.

"They say a young girl addressed the sheriff on the night of the murder," Cervantes said, breaking their silence. "Strangest thing people ever saw."

Tiburcio grabbed the old man and gently shook him for more information. Cervantes saw his eyes get bigger. Tiburcio was leaning so far out of his chair Cervantes thought the boy would fall into his lap. He laughed. It was the first time in a long time.

"Anita? Was it Anita?"

"Yes, the daughter of Don Constanza."

"What did she say?"

"She said it was Garcia who had shot Constable Hardmount through the heart. Brave girl. Are you two in love?"

"I don't know. I think we might be."

"That would seem about right. They say the poor girl is not doing so well. People around town are saying that the violent episode was almost too much for her young heart. She is filled with grief. She remains in bed, unable to overcome the depths of despair. And her poor father, one of the finest rancheros in the state, got into a pushing and shoving brawl outside a general store when he heard people talking."

"What happened?"

"He had to defend his daughter's honor after some miscreants suggested she was in love with a murderer and a coward. Such foreboding drove her to infirmity, and she's been in bed for two weeks. They say she is a mere shadow of herself."

"I must see her!" Tiburcio exclaimed and leaped to his feet.

"No!" Cervantes ordered. He stood up. His suffering eyes bore into Tiburcio. "You go see your mother, if you must. But let the poor girl recover. You two are not destined for each other."

"What do you suggest I do, then?" he answered impudently. "Have you forgotten how your heart was once young and filled with passion?"

"Write to her, instead. You are a marvelous poet. It will be easier on her heart and safer for everybody."

"Perhaps that does make sense," Tiburcio said after a moment. "But how do I get her the note?"

"Your mother, after you speak with her, can tell you where Anita's dearest friend lives. Her name is Margarita. Nobody would ever suspect she had received a note from you."

Tiburcio's chest relaxed, and Cervantes could see his tension ease.

"First, you must take care of your mother and yourself. Or, you will never see Anita … or any other woman … again."

"I must go."

"Are you sure you don't want to stay here until morning."

"It's better not to burden you. And better to travel in the few hours left of darkness."

Tiburcio started to walk away, then looked back at the old man on the bench.

"What will happen with you?"

"I will be fine."

Cervantes's dog followed Tiburcio. The visitor tried to shoo him back to the house.

"Let him accompany you to the horse," Cervantes said. "He will sniff out any danger, if there is any. When you reach your horse, whistle twice, and I will call him back."

Tiburcio and the dog cautiously made their way to the horse. Tiburcio mounted and was about to whistle when he remembered something and leaped back to the ground. He opened up the saddlebag and took out the ill-gotten money belt that Garcia had tossed him. It had the original eight hundred dollars in it, plus another two hundred dollars Garcia had given him for his travels. Tiburcio grabbed hold of the dog and cinched the belt tight around its girth.

"This is for your master. He needs the loot. But perhaps he will share a trifle with you."

Tiburcio whistled two times and started for his mother's house as the dog ran back to his master.

• • •

TIBURCIO!

Every night since her brother's abrupt departure, Tiburcio's sister, Maria, had sat up in the enormous Monterey pine, perched in the same spot where she and her brother watched the convicts build Colton Hall five years ago. One night her mother discovered her hiding spot and made her come inside and sleep next to her. But Guadalupe was usually too tired and distraught to check on her daughter's late whereabouts. At last, her nightly treetop vigil was about to pay off.

About three miles from home, Tiburcio abandoned his horse. Before forging a river that was as deep as the mare's neck, he detached his belongings from the saddle and held them over his head as they plunged in. Near shore, Tiburcio slipped into the shallower water and bobbed and waded onto the sand bank. The horse made a splashing dash out of the river and up the bank a little ways before stopping and wandering riderless among some sycamore and alder trees. Tiburcio shooed him off.

Dawn was still a couple hours away when Tiburcio reached his Monterey home. He moved stealthily about the perimeter of the property to make sure nobody was lurking. That's when Maria scared the devil out of him.

"I cannot believe you avoided capture," she quipped from above. Of all the things to do, she laughed. "You need to be more careful, brother. Don't you ever look up?"

Tiburcio had drawn his gun, but now he stared upward with his arms limp at his sides.

"You better stay up there, because after the fright you gave me I am going to whip you when you come down," he joked. "You could have been killed."

Maria climbed down quietly.

"I would have warned you, somehow, if I had seen you were in danger. The only person who has come around tonight is the jail guard, and that was hours ago. Let's hurry inside."

Maria rousted her mother out of bed and told her to close her eyes as she guided her down the sturdy hallway.

"Maria, I do not have time for your games."

In an instant, Guadalupe's deep, suppressed sorrow lifted. She stood motionless for a few seconds unbelieving that it was her son she saw standing there in the dark. She pulled him close and hugged him so tightly tears spilled from her closed eyes.

"Did you not think I would return?" Tiburcio asked her when she released her grip around him.

"Of course. … Some day."

"Do you think I had a hand in killing the lawman?"

"No," she answered without hesitation. "Nevertheless, I have made plans for you."

"Plans? To leave here? So it's true I am not welcome in Monterey anymore?"

"That is the sad truth, son. I believe with all my heart that you will be able to return without prejudice in the near future. For now, it's not safe. That is why your brothers and I have made arrangements. That is why they are not here."

"I not only risked my life coming here, then. I am risking yours and everyone in our family. I am sorry. I have been selfish in coming home. They tried to warn me."

Guadalupe wiped the blur of the tears away with her sleeve so she could clearly see her boy. She smiled.

"Since when did you become able to grow hair on your face?" she teased.

Her effort to be lighthearted was fleeting, though.

"Mother," Tiburcio said, the words gushing forth. "I will go stand before father's grave and swear to his spirit and to you and God that I am innocent. I am innocent of any crime. I was only standing next to Anastacio, trying to control the madness. But in an instant the mood of the crowd changed. Suddenly, none of our countrymen were there, and the Americans turned vicious. I was acting on instinct. I knew my life could be sacrificed at any moment so I fled. Now, I have returned against better judgment to see if the excitement and anger had cooled. I now know it has not. But I am glad I came for one reason: to look into your eyes and see for myself that you believe I am innocent."

"Of course, I do. There will be a time when you can return and profess your innocence before a judge and the entire city, if you need to. But that is for later. I must tell you of the arrangements your brothers and I have made for you."

She explained how the Cantua family owned a small tract of land in Mendocino County, north of San Francisco. His brothers, Antonio and Francisco, were already on their way now to Ukiah with a herd she had bought in Salinas.

"Like the land, these cattle will be yours," she explained to her curious, bewildered son. "You have learned enough from your father and from Anastacio – God bless his soul – to be a good rancher. There are enough head of cattle to start a respectable business. You will need to hire at least one hand to help you, but I will leave that to your discretion."

Tiburcio glanced at Maria, who had not stopped grinning since she discovered her brother was safe.

"I will write you often," Guadalupe said, speaking with urgency. "I have names of good people in those parts. But my son, heed my instructions: Avoid evil companions and their evil ways. Let God show you the way. You have been given a second chance. What happened has broken my heart with grief, but if you leave your burden at this door and follow the righteous path, I will survive. Do as I say."

"I will do what you have arranged. I am thankful for my family, and I am ashamed to have tainted our name. As I will follow your directions, I ask a favor from you, now. There is a young woman in town named Margarita, who knows I am in love with her dearest friend, Anita. Through her, I want to deliver a message to this friend. Señor Cervantes says you know where I can find Margarita."

"I do. I will deliver the letter, but you must leave for Ukiah immediately."

"I will need a horse."

"One is already saddled and fed in the stable ... in case you returned."

As Guadalupe packed her son food and water, Tiburcio wrote on parchment in large and gracefully flowing letters:

"Dearest Anita:

Forgive me for the long silence between us. I was compelled to flee for my life. The picture in my mind of your sweet, innocent face on the night of the tragedy has sustained me through the past several weeks. When the excitement surrounding that terrible event subsides, I will be able to profess my innocence to the world. For now, I must tell you that I am innocent of any crime and slander that you have heard associated with my name. I can only hope you believe me. You have always had a natural way of knowing exactly how I feel in my heart; I know you will look into your own heart to judge me. I have plans for us in the future. I will settle down on some land up north. When I am established and have saved enough money, I will send for you. If you love me, be patient. We will be together soon, and I will play my guitar sweetly for you.

Love, Tiburcio

Chapter 9: Whipped
North of San Francisco
1854

After four days and nights of riding hard on the northern trail, Tiburcio finally caught up to his brothers before they and their small herd of forty head crossed the Carquinez Strait between Suisun Bay and San Pablo Bay.

"Let's get them across, then. The sun will soon set," Antonio said.

Whooping and hollering, the three vaqueros plunged the herd into the cold water. Some of the beeves tried to turn back, but the strong water current, splashing horses and frantic rush of the heifers from the rear forced them back into the channel. Deep, loud drones of protest from the cows carried over the countryside until the cattle became hushed as they united in a massive, tense, determined propulsion to the other side. The leaders of the herd sensed the shallower water and once their hooves touched solid ground they came stampeding onto the shore, the rest following.

"Keep them in the canyon!" Tiburcio called out from behind the last of the emerging cattle to Antonio and Francisco, who were already on dry land. "Don't let them ride up the walls!"

After quieting the bulk of the herd, the Vasquez boys spent the next few hours rounding up scattered strays. Around sunset they found a spot where the cattle could graze and built a fire.

The days became mostly monotonous. But that was about to end. They had not seen another soul for twenty-four hours and, on the final leg of the trip, trouble came.

Six horsemen with guns drawn rode up over a hill to the north. Francisco was riding point, Antonio flank and Tiburcio, being the youngest, was in the dusty rear. The strangers rode up close to Francisco and told him to halt. Tiburcio peered through the dust into the distance to see what was happening.

Suddenly, two of the men fired their guns and the herd panicked. Two other men began flapping colorful blankets and the cattle started into a full-scale stampede. When Francisco and Antonio looked at the men to find a sign of explanation for what they were doing they realized they were being held at gunpoint.

Tiburcio rode up and three men closed in on him.

"What the hell is going on?" Antonio asked.

"We are seizing your herd. Dismount and toss your firearms to the side."

The brothers slowly stepped off their horses and flung their pistols away.

"Where are you mother-fucking greasers going?"

"Ukiah," Antonio answered.

"I got news for you. They don't want you or your herd up there."

"What are you talking about?" Francisco said incredulously. "We own land near Fallis Valley and our herd is properly branded. You have no right to stop us like this."

"Listen here, cocksucker. We have been following you since you crossed the county line. We have Wanted posters with us, and we are certain that that man over there, with the light skin and gray eyes, is wanted by the law for killing a constable in Monterey County. That leads us to reasonable suspicion that this herd was acquired by illegal means or may be intended for ill-gotten gains. Therefore, we will confiscate it."

"Are you with the law?" Francisco demanded.

"I'll tell you who we are, greaser! We are a vigilante committee! We have the sheriff's authority in this county to keep the peace!"

"But foremost, we are reasonable folks," said another man with small eyes and a face with thin lips and a sharp nose who put a hand up to silence his partner and spoke more calmly. "We have a deal that may be advantageous to everybody. It works like this: you give us your cattle and horses and we allow you turn around and go on your way unpunished. That gets you criminals away from our peaceful, thriving, lawful community and makes you somebody else's problem. That way, there is no need to involve the sheriff - and that saves that fella there from getting hung."

"To hell with you," Tiburcio cursed. "Whether you think I am guilty of murdering the constable doesn't have anything to do with my brothers or their herd. Take me, but let them pass or allow them to return to Monterey with this herd."

Francisco and Antonio looked at their troubled, young brother. Tiburcio spoke to them in Spanish.

"Brothers. I am sorry. The unfortunate incident at the fandango will not fade away. I will go on my way and not burden you anymore."

Tiburcio turned to look at each one of the gringos, who were laughing disdainfully.

"You are not in a position to negotiate," the narrow-faced man said, first pointing at Tiburcio then moving a bony finger to Francisco and Antonio. "Whatever you two boys can pack off your horses and carry you may keep. But such display of generosity on our part will cost you something extra. Just to keep the deal fair."

"What?" Francisco asked.

The man nodded to his three companions next to Tiburcio. They dismounted and grabbed Tiburcio by the arms and dragged him to a nearby oak tree. Another man carried a rope over to the tree.

Antonio and Francisco were paralyzed with uncertainty and fear.

"You are committing a grievous crime!" Francisco blurted out.

Nobody uttered a response. One of the men pulled a hickory branch from the back of his saddle and walked over to Tiburcio.

"What are you going to do to him?" Antonio demanded, stepping forward to the sound of clicking revolver hammers.

"Go, brothers. Go," Tiburcio yelled in Spanish. "They only want me. Don't tell mother. And don't worry, I will survive!"

"Do you really want to see what happens next?" the bony man said in a wicked voice and a smile that showed small, rotting teeth. He stepped within inches of Antonio's face. "If you start walking now, we won't whip him until you descend that distant hill and are out of earshot."

"Let him go, you son of a bitch. You don't know what you're doing," Antonio shouted.

"I know we are done negotiating. I know that much. I also know if you say another word, or attempt to fight your way out of this mess, or otherwise interrupt justice in any fashion, we will kill him right before your eyes, fucking greaser. Get going. Don't turn around."

"Go, brothers!" shouted Tiburcio. "Go now!"

The men ripped Tiburcio's shirt off his back as the brothers started to walk away. His hands were pulled around the trunk of the tree and tied tightly. As the whip struck his skin, he gritted his teeth and closed his eyes. Tears squeezed out and ran down his cheeks. He grunted loudly with each strike and counted the number of times he was lashed. Despite the searing pain, he kept counting - ... forty-eight, forty-nine, fifty. His back was hot and he could feel blood leaking out of the wounds. Then it stopped. When he opened his eyes, he saw the gaunt man's face close to his own.

"We done with you, greaser. You in the Lord's hands now. If He feels a reason to send somebody kind your way before the sun and the wind or wild animals kill you, then that's His business. But we ain't the killing type, per se. We mete out justice and leave the rest up to God. Either way, do not let us catch you in these parts again. If you survive, I suggest you keep your nose clean."

• • •

Tiburcio lifted his head and squinted into the sunlight. His neck was sore. His back stung like a million wasp bites. He shivered but wasn't cold. He had gone unconscious, and now that he was awake he did not know what time of day it was. Ten in the morning? Two in the afternoon? He closed his eyes tightly and reopened them. He couldn't believe what he saw.

A young girl, eight years old at the most, was looking at him inquisitively. He looked at her freckled face and red hair. She stared back at a dirty face lined with cleanish streaks from tears and sweat. Tiburcio's red eyes strained to focus on her.

"Who are you? Are you bad?" she asked.

Tiburcio was surprised he could talk but his speech was labored and his voice hoarse.

"To you … I suppose … I am … the devil."

The girl stepped back.

"You know what they say about … the devil?" Tiburcio asked, resting the side of his head against the oak to which he was still tied. "If you … set the devil free … he no longer will trouble you."

"How do I set him free?"

"First .. tell me… where do you live? … Are you alone out here?"

"My property is right over there. My daddy is chopping wood."

Tiburcio could hear an ax striking wood in the distance.

"Good. Here's what you do, then. … Reach in my boot and pull out that big knife in there."

The girl did as she was told.

"Now, start sawing at those ropes holding my devil hands. Don't be scared."

Surprisingly, it did not take the girl long to slice through the ropes. Tiburcio wiggled his fingers and turned his wrists.

He could feel the rope's grip. He snatched the knife out of the girls hands and put it back in his boot.

"Mister? Why were you tied to that tree?"

"The Lord works in mysterious ways. Now that you've freed the devil, you run back to your house. But don't tell anybody. Don't ever mention what you did. You freed me. You freed the devil. You can't be taken by evil. Everything is fine now."

Chapter 10: Work
Ukiah, Mendocino County
1854

Tiburcio had no place to call home. He had lost his cattle, his property and his pride. He had packed only a tent, a blanket and the Bowie knife. He still owned the knife. He had only brought along the clothes he was wearing. He now did not even have a shirt. Less than a month ago, he possessed more than any man his age. Yet, the gringos kept taking from him. His dance hall, his freedom, his cattle, his guns, his land, even his flesh and nearly his life.

As he stumbled away from the tree where he had been tied, he thought about returning south, perhaps to Cantua where the disillusioned were huddled. Instead, he decided to go north, farther away from his trouble. He no longer held out hope that his family's land in Fallis Valley remained uninhabited and, besides, he had no means to make a living there, so he simply plodded north, farther from his past life.

Tiburcio traveled alone in the mountains, hardly seeing a soul. The only time he came close to another living person was when he ventured into a valley and stole a shirt from a clothes line at a ranch house. From the high trail upon which he journeyed he overlooked vast plains and watched herds of cattle and wild horses moving freely. He camped near rivers and gulches and listened vigilantly to the night sounds until he fell asleep. He ate berries and nuts and an occasional fish, rabbit, rat or possum that he might catch if he were patient.

After five days on the trail, he ascended into the tall redwood forests. He guessed he was east of Ukiah and turned westward. He soon found himself on a busy road, where he learned from some travelers in a wagon that it indeed led to Ukiah.

Tiburcio, penniless and disheveled, was walking toward the bustling town when he came to a gateway along the roadside with a painted sign that read: Circle J Ranch/Workers Wanted. Though tired, he briskly walked up the lane to an elevated ranch house that overlooked a wide stretch of country from all sides. The house was unadorned, plain. A kitchen was attached to the main building and a stable was set off about thirty yards from the house. He saw a large group of men talking near some white-fenced paddocks. Tiburcio noticed that most of the dozen or so ranch hands were Mexicans.

"Hello," he said in English.

A rangy white man with a large belt buckle, bow legs, barrel chest, cowboy hat and bandana and a stubble beard stepped forward and sized up Tiburcio.

"Howdy. My name is Ian Forester. I own this ranch. What can I do for you?"

"I've been traveling a long way ..."

"By the looks of things, son, you've traveled to hell and back."

"... all the way from Monterey. I have no money, no horse and have eaten very little in two weeks. Your sign says you need workers. I need a job."

"Yeah. But what can you do?"

"Just about anything on a horse."

"What else?"

"I can play the guitar."

"Anything else?"

"Nothing else that you would be interested in, mister."

"How good of a rider, are you?"

"The best."

The men looked at each other.

"What's your name?"

"Tiburcio Vasquez."

"Well, Vasquez, we were all looking up at that bull feeding himself on that steep hill. We were trying to decide who should go get him and take him to the lower pastures where he belongs. And that's when you walked up."

Tiburcio peered into the distance at the bull on the hill.

"That's an exceedingly quick drop," he noted.

"Damn near perpendicular," Forester acknowledged. "But if you can lasso him and drive him down to the valley below, you got yourself a job."

The men smiled and snickered and poked each other with elbows.

"Get me a horse," Tiburcio said.

Tiburcio rode over to the top of the precipice as the rest of the men watched. He gave them a nod and started cautiously down the steep grade. The bull began moving away in an uninterested way. As Tiburcio neared the massive animal, it started running and quickly picked up so much speed it appeared as if he would soon tumble end over end. Tiburcio bumped along after the bull, trying to keep up with it, fighting against going over the neck of his horse. If any of them - bull, horse or rider - fell, they'd be dead.

The bull slowed and began traversing the hill, giving Tiburcio time to grab the coiled hemp rope from the saddle bow. Holding tight to the rein with his free hand, he came up behind and slightly to the side of the animal. He swung the lariat into a blur above his head then let it fly.

He lassoed the bull on the first toss and it started across the hill at such a fast clip it quickly lost its footing and rolled, turning end over end as huge clods of dirt and heaps of grass flew everywhere. Tiburcio pressed his knees hard against the saddle, slackening and tightening the riata as the animal bounced toward the bottom of the precipice, finally coming to a standstill.

In a flash, Tiburcio leaped out of the saddle and cut the rope with his Bowie knife. The bull came to its feet, swung around and charged at him with a good head of steam. The young vaquero nimbly leaped back into the saddle and steered his horse up the hill until the bull snorting at his tail grew tired of the slope and gave up the pursuit. It returned to the lower pasture and Tiburcio rode the rest of the way to the top.

"That wasn't the most elegant work I've ever seen but a damn gutsy effort and you got the job done. Payday is Friday," Forester called out as Tiburcio, sweating and panting, approached the owner and the ranch hands.

The other ranch hands congratulated him.

"You sleep in the bunkhouse with the other workers," Forester continued. "It's got a good floor. Coffee is served up at the house at 4:00 a.m. We start work at 5:00. Breakfast is between 8:00 and 9:00. You get Sunday off."

The daily work on the hundreds of acres of Forester's property seemed to never end. There were herds to move, cattle to round up, horses to break, fences to fix, tools to mend, fields of grain crops to work, the occasional fox or uninvited traveler to chase off the property and, twice, the killing of a trespassing bear. The workers told Tiburcio to be vigilant for Indian intruders coming out of the forest to steal horses, but he never saw any evidence of that.

At night, Tiburcio and the others reenergized. They soon discovered Tiburcio could play guitar brilliantly and dance like they had only fantasized. Before long he was teaching the dozen or so men steps to the *Jarabe* and other folk dances.

"I'm tired of playing the role of the señorita," he chastised his bunkmates when they didn't get the steps right. "You are all too lonely for this to go on much longer without the most dire of outcomes."

But the newcomer did persevere and make dancers out of them.

"No more standing with your backs to the wall while the women dance," Tiburcio told his students.

On many occasions, Ian Forester, his wife, young daughters, brother and sister-in-law would come out on the wrap-around porch of their house in the evening and see the bunkhouse lit up, music, whooping and stomping rising out. Forester would smile and trade curious glances with his family. He liked to leave the men alone after the work day and not interfere with their small amount of leisure time. However, he was beginning to wonder more and more about exactly what was happening in that little building down from his home. He had heard music coming from the little house before the new worker's arrival, but it had taken on a richer quality and tone, and lasted longer now, sometimes well past midnight. The strumming of the guitar seemed now to be connected to a soul. The sound was not solitary – it was united with the flow of life, sweeping up everything around it, perhaps more like a soul in search of another soul. Forester sometimes sat on his patio listening past midnight, thinking about his own life and the legacy he would pass on.

The ranch owner noticed the quiet, new Mexican laborer had quickly assumed the role of a leader among the workers. Tiburcio's educated manners, handsome looks, boundless energy and intoxicating charm naturally made him rise in their esteem. But under the surface Forester saw deep pain and restlessness. Indeed, Tiburcio never stopped thinking about Anita and planning how to knit their future together again.

Tiburcio's time at the ranch went by quickly. He worked through the slaughter season, and the leisure of winter, until it was spring time again. It was now May 1855.

One night Forester decided to walk down to the festive bunkhouse. His loud knock abruptly silenced the music and celebration. But his pleasant and humble smile put the men at ease. They welcomed him inside.

"Please, please continue," Forester implored. "I want to hear who's playing that beautiful guitar."

All the men glanced at Tiburcio, who had placed the instrument against the wall.

"Welcome to our *fiestita*!" Tiburcio exclaimed.

Soon, the house was again filled with music, singing, clapping and dancing. At a break in one of the tunes, well after 1:00 a.m., Forester stood up and announced he must go. At the door, he looked back into the room. He motioned for Tiburcio to come over and spoke to him confidentially.

"I would like to invite you to perform at my own *fiestita* on Saturday night two weeks from now. I am entertaining about a hundred guests, friends and acquaintances, and it would be great to have you play your guitar for us. It would make it most festive."

"Absolutely, boss."

"Around 5:00 then. Guests will arrive at 6:00."

Tiburcio was not overwhelmed entering Forester's spacious ranch house, but he much admired the show of good taste and luxurious furnishings in nearly every room. Beautiful frescoes adorned the wall, large bouquets of flowers perfumed the air. Artificial, mechanical birds that bobbed and whistled were being wound up like a clocks by the housekeepers. The apartment where supper was going to be served featured six different wine glasses for each table, silver napkin rings and the best china plates.

Forester showed Tiburcio where he would be stationed to play at various intervals, such as the guests' arrival and mingling before dinner.

"I have hired a band to play at dinner. You may take a break then. Also, they will play, along with you, for the after-supper dancing. It's important to play something with a lively tempo, something welcoming, as many of our guests will be coming from as far away as San Francisco. They will be escorted upstairs to dressing rooms and then descend again for the reception. I am so happy you agreed to play."

Tiburcio, however, did not hear those last words. He was stunned into deafness and muteness by Forester's beautiful daughter, a girl of about sixteen, who had entered the room believing her father was alone. Their eyes met and locked on one another's for a long, meaningful moment.

"Ah, Tiburcio, meet my daughter Alana. Alana, Tiburcio will be playing his guitar for guests throughout the evening."

"My pleasure," she greeted, holding out her hand for the musician to take.

"It was a pleasure to be asked by your father to entertain the guests. It's doubly so now."

TIBURCIO!

For the remainder of the evening, Alana made sure she did not stay a stranger to Tiburcio. He would catch her green eyes watching him play from across the room. More often than not, however, she would have to turn away as a young man interested in her company would make his way over and compete for her attention. When the guests were seated for dinner, Tiburcio walked out onto the side patio for a break and stared out into the cool night.

He felt Alana's presence before she said a word or touched his arm above the elbow.

"Nobody plays the guitar like you do. It has quite a hold on my heart."

If Alana's eyes were beautiful in the house, out here in the dark, with just the moonlight, they were as passionate, brilliant, captivating and bewitching as the stars above.

"I try to find one person in the audience to play directly to," Tiburcio told her softly. They were very close to one another. "It makes my music *mucho más fervoroso.*"

She leaned closer and their lips met, softly once, twice. A door slammed and they drew back. There were footsteps and then one of the men infatuated with Alana appeared.

"What are you doing out here?" he asked her.

"I was offering a refreshment to one of our musicians."

"The ranch hand?"

"Tiburcio. I'd like to introduce you to Virgil."

He left Tiburcio's hand hanging in midair.

"Well?" Virgil inquired.

"Yes?" Alana replied.

"Did he want a drink?"

"No," she said.

"Yes," Tiburcio said at the same time.

"Go get him some water," Virgil ordered.

"A shot of whiskey will do, please," Tiburcio corrected.

When Alana left the porch, he turned to Tiburcio.

"I know Mr. Forester enjoys helping out our native Californians. But if you are thinking about taking advantage of your employer's generosity - which does not in any way, shape or form extend to his oldest daughter - you better just go back to where you came from, greaser. ... And where is that place? I heard Monterey."

"I'm glad Mr. Forester had guests check their guns at the door," Tiburcio responded. "Too bad he didn't have them check their arrogance and stupidity, as well. Excuse me, I need to prepare for the dancing. I may even be called upon to step out on the floor myself. Poetry wins a woman's mind, strings capture her heart, but dancing, Virgil, dancing brings them right into my arms."

"I know people in Monterey," Virgil said. "When was the last time you were there?"

"It's been a year."

"Why did you leave?"

"It's a dull town."

"That's not what I have heard," Virgil concluded, briskly walking away.

Tiburcio played intensely and danced feverishly until after midnight. He tried to slip away alone and safely to the bunkhouse, but somewhere between the ranch house and his home, Alana caught up to him. They didn't say a word, but walked hand in hand away from the house party. Tiburcio finally walked in the front door of the bunkhouse at 3:30 a.m.

He worked harder than ever that week so he wouldn't have to talk much. And when Forester banged on the door after the work day on Friday, he froze. The boss never came around at that time.

"There's a fiesta in Ukiah on Saturday night," he told the workers looking them up and down. "I want you all to work a half-day tomorrow and go into town. That is, if you'd like."

When Saturday came, the men prepared for the trip into town. They noticed Tiburcio hanging back, reticent, and not getting ready.

"Tiburcio! We can't go without you. We're bringing our own entertainment. You! The women will take a special liking to us once they hear your guitar."

TIBURCIO!

"We need you to start the dancing!"

Their pleading and Tiburcio's natural attraction to entertaining others led him around to joining his new friends, and they soon were on their horses, waving to the Foresters as they rode out the ranch's gateway.

He and his new friends didn't make it back to Forester's property until sunrise.

As he rode home, Tiburcio realized he hadn't enjoyed an evening that much since leaving Monterey.

Sunday was usually quiet around the bunkhouse and ranch, but Forester noticed today it was like a graveyard. The men had had a wild time and were sleeping off their revelry. He made sure he didn't disturb them.

But come Monday, the workers were at the breakfast table at 5:00 a.m. sharp and working by 6:00. At mid-afternoon, the ranch hands were taking a break, standing around the stable with Forester, who was, like a couple of the others, smoking a cigarette. Someone caught the sight of a group of about five riders coming up the pathway from the gate. The visitors wore revolvers at their sides and Henry rifles on their saddles. As they approached, Forester cautioned his men to stay back and stepped forward to meet the posse.

"We're looking for one of your workers," an officer with a badge said to Forester. The officials fanned out. "His name is Tiburcio. Tiburcio Vasquez."

"What's the meaning of this?" Forester asked.

"You have a ranch hand who is wanted in Monterey, Mr. Forester. An officer was killed in this man's place of business about a year ago. The fugitives, a couple greasers, have split up since the murder. We believe one of them is here."

"I read about that incident. You should be looking for that murdering thief, Anastacio Garcia, not Tiburcio. And at any rate, you have no business here. Unless I get the word directly from the judge, I don't want you coming on my property in search of Tiburcio Vasquez or anyone else. I want you off my ranch."

"We gave you a chance to cooperate, Mr. Forester. If you want us to return with the judge, we will do that. But I can't promise things will stay as peaceful as we would like."

The posse left in a hurry, stirring up dust all the way down to the gate and into the road. Tiburcio walked up to Forester.

"I'm sorry about the officers," he apologized. "I just want you to know I'm innocent."

"I know."

"But one thing I can't stand is suspicion," Tiburcio said. "I don't want to bring any of this trouble to your family or your business. I will leave here by nightfall."

Chapter 11: Consent
New Almaden, Santa Clara County,
Spring 1855

There was only one direction to go now: south. There was only one safe place to go: Cantua Canyon.

Tiburcio had left the Circle J ranch four days ago, and each morning signaled a warmer spring day than the last. Summer was around the corner, but Tiburcio was as dark and cold as the dead of winter night. He traveled toward an unknown fate. Thoughts of death and loneliness devoured his mind.

Forester had given him one of his horses, a handgun and the rest of his wages for the week. He rode along a ridge where brown sagebrush grew down the hillside and crackled with hopping quail. He approached a wide gulch and came to the brink. He looked down the ravine, across a slow-running creek and up the hill on the other side. As he surveyed the trail he would ride down to get to the creek, Tiburcio saw several figures below encamped in the shadows under some cottonwood. About seven horses were hitched close to the stream. Blankets were spread in the grass in the tree shade. A half-dozen men lay on them in an easy manner. Some used saddles for back rests or rolled blankets for pillows. Even though they appeared to be lazily enjoying the summer-like day, rifles were within reach of everyone in the party and handles of large hunting knives and revolvers could be seen sticking out of their belts and pants.

Tiburcio pulled his horse back away from the hill's edge and out of sight. He dismounted and crawled on his belly to the bluff to spy on the party. Tiburcio's alarm eased a little when he realized the group was composed of Californios. Still, they could be dangerous. He crawled away from the ledge and stood up again when he was out of their line of sight, not taking any chances. He was about to climb back into the saddle when he heard the click of a gun's hammer at the back of his head.

"Put your hands in the air," the armed man said in Spanish.

When Tiburcio lifted his arms, the man seized his revolver and knife and tossed it behind him. Tiburcio heard the rustling of another man picking up the weapons.

"Get back in your saddle and follow me down on your horse. Don't try anything. Don't look back. '*El Halcon*' has a rifle pointed at your back, and he's a dead aim."

As the three riders approached the camp, Tiburcio saw a muscular man standing next to a horse at the base of the hillside, his curly black hair coming down out of a stiff Peruvian vicuna hat. Anastacio Garcia smiled at his protégé. Tiburcio recognized the mammoth figure with the coarse hair and errant eye who stood next to Garcia: the half-Indian, half-Mexican, Juan Soto.

Tiburcio's abductors still had their weapons pointed at him when they halted the horses in front of the camp site.

"Tiburcio!" Garcia called out, laughing. "Don't you know it's dangerous to travel alone in these hills."

"What the hell do I have to fear?"

"Nobody. Except us, the '*Manilas*,' " Garcia answered as he made a sweeping gesture with his hand toward Soto and the other men. "Meet my new band of Mexican revolutionaries. Your escort there is Felipe Carabajal. The pock-mark faced man with your weapons is Ramon Molina. Felipe and Molina were keeping an eye on the hills behind us and saw you approaching an hour ago. You shouldn't be so careless. Even if you are not a white man, I know some Mexican bandits in these hills who might not care one way or another about that small detail and kill you instantly. But since you are alive, let's go under the trees and talk. It's been six months at least, and a couple of seasons, since we parted ways, no?"

Garcia ordered one of his men to fetch some water in a bladder and bring it to his young friend.

"How are Lupe and the children, Anastacio?" Tiburcio asked.

"*Muy, muy bien, gracias*. She sends her love."

Garcia asked about his friend's adventure since they had departed ways.

"I assume you did not spend much time in Monterey," Garcia said.

Tiburcio told him everything: how Maria had been waiting up in the tree for his return; the tearful reunion with his mother; her ill-fated plans for him and her benediction.

Garcia interjected: "Ah, you never were cut out for the quiet and secluded life of ranching."

Tiburcio continued his tale: how he encountered his brothers on the trail and the ambush, the whipping and his journey by foot to Ukiah. Garcia listened like a devoted father. Tiburcio told about the pain of having his mother's cattle stolen without a fight. He explained how he tried to find honest work, only to be forced by the authorities to flee again. Despite his friend's calamity, Garcia smiled with satisfaction when he heard that his repute had reached all the way to Ukiah. But he offered a bit of solace, too.

"Your tale does not surprise me, Tiburcio, as awful as it sounds. I have seen this coming. However, you are safe here, with us. From Livermore to Mount Diablo and over to Sunol, no one dares disturb us. We have made it so no white man is safe to venture over this terrain unarmed. And if he does, he better think twice about it. We, Mexican confederates, can move safely about here, strike when we want to or when we need supplies or money or cattle. We are recruiting more and more rebels as we reclaim more and more of the land we've lost. To hell with your land in Fallis Valley, if it still exists. We have land here now."

Chuckling, Garcia added, thinking back to his friend's story, "Your presence up there in Mendocino County must have worried the law quite a bit. They must have thought we had expanded our territory into the all-white, civilized areas of their great state."

One of the band of men came up to Garcia and spoke in his ear.

"We've cooked the last of our meat?" Garcia repeated. "None is left? Let's pull up camp. We need to hunt for something."

When they were alone again, and the men were busy decamping, Garcia bore into Tiburcio with a serious glare.

"I must tell you something. I will be giving up El Tuche."

"Give up El Tuche? No!"

"Yes. It is for a greater cause. I will relocate to the southern part of the state, near the pueblo of Los Angeles. The men around here are getting restive, so we need to get them some money and begin our revolt against the invaders. For six weeks, we - the *manilas* - are going to split up into three groups and plunder a dozen stagecoaches and ranches. After, we will meet back at Cantua Canyon with enough horses, cattle, money and recruits to raise hell. Before the lawmen can organize, we will have moved to Los Angeles to prepare our southern front."

"Southern front?"

"In the war to recapture the state."

"The entire state?"

"Yes. But it may not need to be a war of complete subjugation. With a few well-placed victories, we can win over the government, and through conciliation regain our place in society. But make no mistake, Tiburcio, it is still revolution. If we must kill every white man in California, then we will."

"What about Lupe and the children?" Tiburcio asked.

"I will summon them before going south. If I can't make it to El Tuche, Lupe knows the plan. She knows to leave and relocate down near Los Angeles."

"She will never leave El Tuche," Tiburcio declared.

"I know. That's why I had to tell her I was giving up this reckless life to settle down and be an honest vaquero at La Brea Rancho, near Los Angeles. I told her I needed to go away and make a little more money working some herds so I could buy my own cattle. Then, I told her I would be done. Done with the life of a bandit."

"She doesn't suspect your revolution?"

"*Our* revolution! The fewer people outside of our band who know we are plotting the better. I am unconcerned about my family's well-being. They will be well-provided for. I am more concerned about you. It's time for you to commence a different life, my friend. You tried to be honest. You tried to live and work by the gringos' rules. Now you see it's a complete falsehood. Like I told you, they only take and take and take. What they don't take of our culture, they dilute through marriage and the strong arm of their law. Everything changed in 1848, Tiburcio. Our past lifestyle is getting us nowhere. And it is getting our fellow countrymen nowhere. You need to be a part of the revolt. We need you, Tiburcio."

Tiburcio mulled over his words. Then Garcia continued.

"Let's be honest, my friend. The quiet, pastoral life is not for you." He laughed, and Tiburcio smiled. "You are more cut out for the life of a liberator. It's lucrative. You are a born leader. You can still be a true vaquero. And, at the same time, you can be a beloved hero to thousands of your countrymen."

"But when I left Monterey, I gave my mother my sworn word that I would resist evil," Tiburcio told his friend, staring directly into his black eyes. "I cannot bear to bring any more disgrace upon her or my family. She has been a good mother to me."

"Then you must return to Monterey and obtain her blessing. If you are determined to follow this course, you must look honestly into her eyes and obtain her blessing to commence the career of an outlaw, a hero outlaw. Only then can you be free. Truly free. When you hear the encouragement from your own mother's heart and love-filled words, you may return to us to carry on the revolution. This much I understand. There is no doubt she has heard of your travails and is saddened. She must understand, however, that you will be no ordinary highway robber. If you choose this life, you will gain a financial status that cannot be disputed. But to your people, you are not merely an outlaw. You are joining an army of your countrymen, for your countrymen. If you must be called an outlaw, it is only because your sole purpose is to rise up against the yankee laws and yankee invaders for the betterment of the lives of our own people. If that makes you an outlaw, so be it. Is this what you want, Tiburcio? We need moral, patient, brave men like you, Tiburcio. We need you!"

They hit the trail with the noon sun straight above them and a strong, warm breeze coming off the bay and blowing in the face of the party. A little north of Oakland, they came around a hill of chaparral and were about to descend onto a grassy plain. Garcia was in front of the pack. He reined in his horse and made a gesture for the others to be still and silent. A dozen antelope were making their way across the plain and would pass within a rifle's shot of them. The wind was blowing the men's scent down the trail, away from the animals, and did not give away the hunters' presence.

Garcia and Soto dismounted and bent low as they cautiously moved forward to position themselves for a good shot. As the animals approached the trail, the men fired. One of the antelope fell to the ground as the others bounded into the brush and up the hill. The one that had fallen, sprang up and it too darted out of sight.

"Let's go after the wounded beast," Soto said. "It will be lying not a quarter of a mile into the brush."

"No," Garcia said. "We should have killed it forthright. We will push on."

"That is foolish. I will take *El Halcon* and retrieve the antelope. In a half an hour, we'll have it flayed and the meat in our saddles."

"We are sitting ducks if we wait here. What if a posse heard our shots? If you break off, you could be ambushed. We should have been a better shot. We will push on."

"We will catch up. Come on, *El Halcon*," Soto said and impudently left.

TIBURCIO!

As the rest of the band continued the journey, Garcia was visibly upset over Soto's disrespectful confrontation. But a tantalizing sight on the main trail below caught his eye and diverted his attention. He made a gesture for the riders to stop.

"Tiburcio," he called in a raspy, low voice. "Did you see that wagon? It's a butcher's wagon filled to the hilt. The driver appears to be solo and unarmed. I assume you are still skillful with the lasso. Go down the trail and stop that driver."

"I will not, Anastacio. You understood the deal. I must have my mother's benediction."

Garcia pulled his revolver from his belt and fanned it across the remaining *bandidos*.

"Christ! Does anyone else want to disobey my command? It will be the last time, I swear to it!"

The other men were silent.

"Felipe," Garcia said. "We need to get that driver and take his goods. You and Ponce, tie him up and take the wagon. We'll meet at the river."

"Wait," Tiburcio commanded, knowing he would rely on these men's protection and support. "I am the best with the *riata*. I'll go with Felipe."

Carabajal and Tiburcio rode up behind the wagon driver, who, already alarmed by the gunshot he had heard, had opened up the reins. He whipped the horse hard and the wagon flew around a turn. On a straightaway, Carabajal nodded for Tiburcio to grab the rope. The rangy wagon driver quickly glanced back at his attackers and saw Tiburcio let the lasso fly. He jerked the reins and the wagon lurched right, avoiding the rope. His eyes met Tiburcio's for an instant – a moment neither would ever forget.

But the driver's attention quickly turned to his perilous task. He had tugged the wagon so violently to avoid the lasso that it was now careening down the hillside out of control. Tiburcio, Carabajal and Ponce watched the wagon miraculously bounce out of sight without busting a wagon wheel or axle or losing any of his merchandise out the back.

"That is one lucky man," Carabajal said.

Garcia could not believe what he heard when they returned: an unarmed man in a horse-drawn wagon had gotten away from the most feared band of bandits in Northern California without so much as a scrape and a holler.

"Is this driver charmed, rides with an angel or something?"

His mood darkened even more.

"We should have just shot him dead!"

That evening the party camped under a copse of live oaks near a spring. They ate antelope, and Garcia washed it down with an ample amount of aguardiente.

They rode all of the next day, crossing the Soledad River into San Juan Bautista, where Garcia, Soto and Tiburcio spent the night in the homes of two friendly and prominent Mexican families. Carabajal, Molino, El Halcon, Ponce and the rest of the confederates camped in the hills beyond the city. They had agreed to rendezvous at the Cantua hideaway in six weeks.

In the morning the three horseman rode slowly down the center of the dirt road in San Juan Bautista – open, free and unmolested. It was mostly a Mexican town, sympathetic to Californios and barely tolerant of visits from the white sheriff and any of his deputies. Garcia pointed to a large, brick, two-story rectangle building to his left and his companions turned to look.

"That's the Breen residence. He was a member of a party that got caught in an early snowstorm in the Sierra. Bought the adobe from General Castro."

As the riders passed the residence and then a building that housed Mexican soldiers, they caught the attention of a bespectacled schoolteacher named Tom Clay. He had been reading *Harper's New Monthly Magazine* at a small kitchen table next to the window of his cabin house. As Garcia and Soto passed his small, modest home at the end of the street, Clay lowered the magazine and watched them through an opening in the gossamer curtain.

What a sinister threesome, he thought. He had not encountered any bandits since his arrival a few weeks ago from

Texas, but this group looked like the trouble he had been warned about. Clay wiped his blond, oily, short, straight hair down above his ear as he had a habit of doing when he was thinking about a particular subject. If he were a lawman, or even looked the part, he might saunter out and demand to know who these men were and what business they had in town. But he was rail thin, a mere one-hundred-sixty pounds and nearly six-foot-one. He saw that the rider with the coarse black hair and no hat was nearly a foot taller than himself and twice as heavy. His only chance if he ever had a quarrel with these men would be his intelligence and cunning, he thought. He set his round-lens glasses down on his book and rubbed the bridge of his nose.

He liked to read about spies, typically British spies. These stories, like the one he had been studying in Harper's, fueled his sense of adventure. But since settling down to teach at the schoolhouse these imaginary accounts provided the extent of his derring-do.

He peered out the window again and noticed the riders had stopped. A boy of about seven years had been facing the other direction in the middle of the street watching a teamsters wagon leave town and, mesmerized as young boys are apt to be, had not heard the riders approach. The boy turned around to find one of the men, the muscular, smaller one in the hat, yelling something at him. The disturbance made Clay sit up straight. He recognized the boy as George Redford, whose family was from Gilroy. George would often accompany his father on the teamster wagon so he could visit his grandparents, who lived outside of San Juan Bautista. George was deaf.

Clay did not know what the rider was saying to the child in his silent world, but from his saddle the large man shoved him into the dirt with his boot. Clay ran outside to help the crying boy up off the ground and wipe his tears. He watched the men reach the fork in the road at the edge of town and spur their horses into flight, hurrying off in the direction of Monterey.

Later that day, for the second time since Hardmount's death, Tiburcio again sneaked into Monterey. Inside his childhood home, his mother looked him over: He had grown a bushy mustache and a full goatee since his last visit. He looked a few years older, more handsome than ever, his eyes still youthful and lively.

Tiburcio breathed in the familiar scents that spilled out from the kitchen and enveloped the home. He could smell the *albahaca, tomillo chepil,* cilantro, *epazote, maza* and beans. A slight candle wax smell also permeated the *vestibulo* where he stood.

Guadalupe sat on the sofa, and Tiburcio bent onto one knee before her as he tried to explain his difficulties.

"In the past year, Mother, I have seen more than I ever wanted to. So much is out of my control. I am going to go out in the world and take my chances, and likely suffer at its hands. But I need to find my own destiny. And I need your blessing." he told her.

"Do not worry yourself over me, Tiburcio," Guadalupe said, knowingly. "You must lead the life you feel is best – and you must live it in the way you believe you should, the way I believe you have been taught. I have never seen you reckless or treat anyone unkindly. I know you will protect the less fortunate, even as you must protect yourself. I know, even under the most difficult circumstances, you will do what's right, what's honorable. And I am confident, and you can leave here confident, in knowing there is nothing that you could do to disgrace me or our family."

Tiburcio squeezed his mother's hand and put his forehead to hers, until she broke away after a few moments.

"Listen, son," she said softly in his ear. "You may not know if you have the courage to face what you find out there in the world. But face your fears in the present, only in the present. Do not turn away from them and the answers will become clear. The bravest people do not lack fear. Rather, they face and know their fear intimately."

She stood up and gently pulled Tiburcio to his feet. She changed the subject.

"A letter has arrived for you. Margarita delivered it here a couple months ago for her friend, Anita. Wait here."

Tiburcio's heart pounded and raced as his mother retrieved the note from his bedroom. When she brought it to him, it smelled of sweet rose perfume. He tore into it.

It read:

"Dearest Tiburcio:

A great weight was lifted from my shoulders when Margarita read your letter to me. You are alive and safe! And I already feel better knowing it. You may profess your innocence to the world, but there is no need to do so on my part. I know you are innocent. My heart and everything I have ever witnessed in your presence tells me so. I do love you, and I will be patient. I hope everything is going well up north. By the time you read this letter, perhaps you will be settled and I can show my father what a hard-working, honest and prosperous man you are. Remember, our situation may seem bleak now but I have just seen the sunshine of the future break through. I have not been this elated since I saw you on the night of the fandango. Play your guitar as if I were next to you. I know I will be soon.

Love, Anita

Tiburcio rode away from his mother's property with a leaden heart. His mare's slow gait eventually led him to a fork in the road outside town. Here he faced a dilemma. If he turned his horse east, he would be on his way to where he had agreed to meet Garcia and Soto. If he reined the horse north, he would be on the long road to Don Constanza's ranchero, Anita's home. It was a false dilemma. He really had no choice.

Under other circumstances he might have been more cheered by Anita's letter, but it reminded him of his every misstep since the constable's death and reinforced two bald facts: it would be a very long time before they saw each other again face to face; and he was far from settled down anywhere, let alone on his own property up north. He was disenchanted, wrathful. He owned no land, no money and no cattle. He was a fugitive from murder, and a deserter of the wishes and dreams he had shared with Anita. Yes, his only option was to go east and find Garcia. Anything else was fantasy and didn't exist, never had.

Garcia and Soto came riding up on the boy from behind as he stood frozen in his thoughts.

"Jesus. Where did you come from?" Tiburcio asked, trying to regain his composure after being startled.

"I have unfinished business in these parts, as you did," Garcia said. "Now, we have tracked a man looking to buy sheep from some of the ranches along the river. I have word he will be coming through here, loaded with money. We need to get up the main road about a half-mile."

They scooted into the dense foliage along the roadside and made their way on foot up a hidden deer path. They did not have long to wait before they spied a lone, wizened figure riding along where the trail jogged toward them.

"Jesus, Garcia. He's an old man," Tiburcio whispered urgently.

"Shut up," Garcia quipped. "He's got money, doesn't he?"

He and Soto examined their revolvers and checked the chambers.

Garcia stepped out into the trail and shouted in Spanish: "Halt and dismount."

As if he had suspected an ambush the sheep buyer immediately went for his pistol. Tiburcio heard a loud pop next to him that left his ear ringing. The man never saw Soto. The giant's bullet slammed into the old man's temple and he dropped stiffly from his horse, which vaulted into the thicket.

Garcia grabbed its bridle and led the horse back to the road. Soto searched the old man's clothes for money while Garcia examined the saddle pouch. They stood over the dead man and counted about two hundred dollars in coins and another two hundred dollars in gold and silver. They exchanged disappointed glances.

TIBURCIO!

The murderers communicated mostly in silence, each seeming to know their roles. Soto carried the body in his big arms to a flooded part of the riverbed about fifty yards off the road. Garcia unsaddled the dead man's horse. Tiburcio stood frozen, stunned.

"Tiburcio!" he called. "Take this horse up the hill about a hundred yards and let it go. I'm going to dispose of the saddle and bags over here. When you get back, go to the river and help Soto bury the body."

Tiburcio didn't move.

"What is wrong with you?"

"Less than two hours ago, I made a promise to my mother that I would act honorably. You just killed an old sheepherder for four hundred dollars. What the hell does that have to do with liberating our people?"

"*Cabron*!" Garcia seethed, pointing to his temple. "What do you think it will take to defeat the enemy? It will take intimidation! Sometimes we will have to be ruthless! And it will take money! Lots of money! There are arms to buy and comrades to lure off white-owned ranches and out of the mines. You can't beg for guns and you can't use soft soap to get men to abandon their livelihood. Now get rid of this horse and help Soto dispose of the sheepherder."

After finishing their deeds, they rode off one at a time along a cattle trail above the main road, keeping about one hundred feet between the nuzzle of one horse and the tail of the other. Soto was in the lead, followed by Garcia and lastly Tiburcio.

In the early evening, Soto stopped and waited for the other men. Together, they climbed farther up the hill through the brush. They picketed their horses in silence, laid out some blankets and rested.

"A little higher up there are caves," Garcia said. "We can sleep with shelter over our heads tonight. It feels like the dew will be thick in the morning. But while there is still some daylight, let us discuss the stage coming from Gilroy to

Hollister. It will be arriving midmorning down on the main road."

He stood up, walked over to a manzanita and cracked off a branch to sketch the plan in the dirt. He scratched out what looked like two roads and scraped away a circle of dirt to represent towns.

"Right around here, about ten miles out of Gilroy, where the road runs along the river, it gets kind of chopped up and sandy from the silt spilling over. The stage ride is always bumpy and slow-going from about this point for a half-mile to here. This is where we'll rob it."

He looked into the men's eyes, then back down at the explaining end of his stick.

"This is a passenger stage with a treasure box full of workers' wages on its way to a Hollister hotel. What lies between us and that treasure is a shotgun messenger. He'll be armed with that bastard of a gun and some six-shooters. Pretty God-damned formidable. He can shower plenty of lead in our direction. So here's where it gets good, because you two are probably the best men I could want for a robbery like this."

Garcia smiled, then continued, using his stick to illustrate all the points of his plan: "We'll be behind some brush – it grows pretty thick down there by the river – and jump out when the coach gets in our range, about here, thirty yards from us. Tiburcio and I will be on the right side; Juan, you'll be on the left. There's a hill on the right side, and over that hill will be our horses. Now, we can't let this stage get away from us, because we don't want to be drawn too far from our horses. If that driver doesn't want to heed our call to halt, I will take his life. Soto, you'll take down the shotgun messenger – he'll be sitting on your side watching every shadow in the chaparral. I am counting on your dead aim, because we can't have the messenger blasting away at us. And Tiburcio, you need to be prepared to shoot the horses, if necessary. It should not be difficult, because the coach can't go fast anyway in this soggy part of the road. But only shoot the horses if the driver doesn't halt and they start galloping away."

TIBURCIO!

Garcia looked at Tiburcio as if he were only speaking to him now.

"My friend, it's your first holdup. I cannot accurately describe to you how fast these events will unfold in reality. One after another in quick succession. You must be prepared. I will do the talking. If the stage driver and his guard cooperate, this will go smoothly. If they don't then, well, we have our assignments, *si*? If we need to improvise, you follow my directions without fail or hesitation. *Comprende*? Good. It may save your life."

The men settled into the caves for the night. Tiburcio took a smaller opening in the mountainside while the other two men occupied a larger cave.

When the sun went down, Tiburcio could not see a thing in the dark. He was not sleepy, so he fumbled around for three candles in his saddle bag and lit them. After a few moments, he heard a rustle in the corner of the cave. Even in the darkness he knew it was a rattlesnake. It was staring at him, slowly shaking its tail. Tiburcio was too afraid to move and for a long time he alertly watched the rattler. Soon, the last candle went out and Tiburcio could not help crying. He hadn't cried for many years.

As he wept he tried to remember his mother's words. Slowly, they came back to him: "Face your fears in the present. Do not turn away from them and the answers will become clear. The bravest people know fear intimately."

He struggled with his fear for a long time in the dark cave until he stopped fighting against it, stopped denying it and stopped desiring it to be gone. He now accepted the fact that he was dead scared. He felt the raw terror in his body, especially deep and wide in his chest, and how it mixed with other anxieties like several raging fires becoming one big inferno. But no matter how strong the panic became he did not try to alter what he was experiencing in any way. He did not try to push it away or conquer it. He tried not to think about why he was scared and how he could make himself unfrightened. Instead, he merely sensed the fear, without judgment, and observed it strengthening and weakening moment to moment. The fright shined crystal clear but no longer was alarming. It had transformed into a distinct and separate entity from his body until, finally, Tiburcio stood up, walked over to the snake and stared down at it. After a couple minutes, he calmly returned to his blanket, pulled his covers over his ears and fell sound asleep. In the morning, the snake - if it had been there at all - was gone. So was his fear.

The next day, as he crouched in the thicket near the road with his hands gripping the Henry rifle, his throat tightened, his chest ached and his heart beat wildly. Although he again was gripped by terror, his mind and thoughts - just like when he had stood over the snake in the cave - seemed to be vast and lucid. His fear present but separate. He heard Garcia urgently calling his name from a few feet away.

"Here she comes!" Garcia said, revolvers ready in both hands.

He hoped Soto, on the other side of the road and hiding behind some boulders, was ready, too.

There was a sound of wood wheels scraping the road and the rattle and squeaking of shaking metal and lumber as the stage slowly labored over the rough section of road. Sixty yards. Fifty yards. Forty yards.

"Let's go!"

Garcia and Tiburcio bounded out of the brush in two hops. Soto had come out of hiding a few seconds faster, by mistake, so the shotgun messenger bolted upright and lifted his gun with intention to shoot the Human Wildcat with one barrel of twenty-one buckshot, the other barrel for the rest of the bandits.

"Halt there!" Garcia shouted, but the sound of gunfire drowned out his words.

The guard had gotten a shot off but the charge emptied harmlessly up into the deep blue sky. He lurched forward and fell under the wheels. Soto's bullet had struck him in his throat.

"Halt!" Garcia shouted again.

TIBURCIO!

The driver pulled the lines and the brake as the bandits closed in on the stage. The messenger lay under the carriage between the two axles with his throat gurgling. He went to draw a revolver but could not lift his hand before Soto crashed another bullet into his forehead.

Inside the wagon, the passengers stifled their screams and wept. Garcia ordered them out of the carriage, explaining in English that there were two heavily armed men outside so they would be wise to exit with their hands in the air. His young friend, Garcia told them, would help the women with the step.

There were five passengers: four women and an elderly man. They stood, along with the driver, on the side of the road until their raised arms ached. Soto took over the duty of guarding the travelers with his two six-shooters as Tiburcio stripped them of anything of value: watches, wallets, rings, necklaces. Garcia cautiously entered the carriage and combed through it.

When he stepped back out, he glared at Tiburcio, who was standing idly.

"Did you search them?" he demanded in Spanish.

"No. They have their hands up."

"Check them all – the ladies, too – to make sure they aren't hiding a gun or something. Pat their waists, their boots, even their bosoms. God damn it, don't let us get taken by surprise!"

Garcia grabbed the strong box under the driver's seat and tossed it onto the ground. He took two steps back and fired three shots at its lock. The box splintered open. He scooped up the coins, silver and gold and put the loot into the bag he was holding.

The final job was to get rid of the horses so the victims couldn't go anywhere very fast, let alone follow the bandits. Garcia unbridled the horses and scurried them off down the road with a slap and a gunshot.

After seeing the horses turn out of sight, he ordered the victims to turn around, lie face down on the ground and keep their hands and legs stretched out. Tiburcio, Soto and Garcia sprinted up over the hill to their horses.

They lashed their steeds on at top speed.

"Where are we going?" Tiburcio shouted.

"On a wild ride!" called out a madly grinning Soto.

"To the quicksilver mines!" yelled Garcia.

They covered more than sixty miles without stopping, riding high into the hot Diablo Mountain range. The air was dry, much different than Monterey's climate. About halfway to the mines, they exchanged their horses for fresh ones at a friendly Mexican-owned ranchero. The landscape did not get any more cheery. Few trees existed except for clusters of sycamores near a few water sites. The only signs of life were insects, thick in the air and on the ground. The bandits rested at nightfall, but Garcia again urged them on under a full moon after midnight.

By midmorning, they descended into a crusty, barren patch of earth and rode onto a rough road that stretched as far as the eye could see. Garcia stopped and gestured for the other riders to halt.

"We can take it easy. We are in friendly country, Tiburcio," he said.

Tiburcio looked around at the harsh, arid scenery. A few live oaks dotted the flat, brown earth.

"Is this a joke? Friendly to the devil!"

"It doesn't look like much, but down this road we will enter New Idria. There are few Americans at the mines, except for the superintendent, but he must protect us if he wants to keep his job, his life and his family. We will be welcomed like conquering warriors, and we will be able to buy anything we want: liquor, large stacks of chips at the gambling tables, women, a bath. This is where the life of an outlaw pays off. Right, Soto? That stage was carrying loads of gold and coin. And, in a day or so, we will be able to ride off with ten more recruits desperate for such money and action."

The mining town of New Idria rose out of the parched earth. Along one main street, six or seven one- and two-story buildings jutted up. Off the main street, a few crude, wood homes existed in random order among a vast village of tents. The tents had thin canvas sides and roofs tacked to light frames. There were no windows – light and air passed through the fabric. Above the tent village, large gouges defaced the mountains and the smell of sulfur was in the air.

"Let's make our entrance known!" Garcia yelled and he and Soto lashed their foaming-mouthed horses toward the town at dizzying speeds.

The main street was alive. Dozens of men – Chileans, Peruvians, Mexicans, Indians, Spaniards and a few Irish and Cornish miners passed each other, laughing and talking among themselves. Dozens more milled around in front of the structures or atop horses or along the wooden sidewalks. When some of the crowd saw the riders tumultuously approaching they shouted and hurrahed. Garcia and Soto answered with ear-piercing Comanche hollering.

They galloped past a post office, a bank and a store and halted in front of a large hotel and saloon. It had a white colonnade in front and numerous windows on the second level. Its grandeur appeared misplaced in the rugged mining town of twelve hundred people. As they noisily dismounted, several men, mostly rough and dirty, and a couple of disheveled women poured out of the barroom, smiling and welcoming and slapping the threesome on their backs as they sprung from their horses.

A large group of people followed the newcomers from the bright, warm sun into the dark, musky saloon. Garcia led his posse past a lengthy bar. Shelves of short- and long-necked liquor bottles were displayed behind it . The visitors walked over to an empty corner table in front of a raised stage.

"*Mira, hombre. Ven aca,*" Garcia yelled to the barkeeper as he took a seat.

The man rushed over.

"Bring us a bottle. No, two. One brandy and one gin. Tonight, Tiburcio, we'll push back the tables and dance. I know you miss the fandango. But, you just wait. We'll find some maidens born without virtue and raised without modesty!"

When the bottle arrived with three small glasses, Garcia took several coins out of his pocket and slammed them on the table.

"No, no," the barkeeper said. "*Ninguno*."

"You are a good a man. I accept. But I insist on paying for a round of drinks for everyone else, though," Garcia replied.

The patrons cheered as he filled his pals' glasses to the rim and then passed the bottle into the crowd. Several men and women swarmed around Garcia's table. A dozen miners and cowboys also stood at the bar. Soto lifted a young woman onto his lap.

Garcia smiled at his young friend.

"How do you feel?"

"Alive!" Tiburcio answered, and was surprised to hear excitement in his voice. "Alive. Yes, alive!"

He did not know where feelings of remorse might be hiding in his heart, but they did not make themselves heard. Like the scars from where his skin was torn away by the vigilante's whip, those feelings were numb. Perhaps later he might have empathy; perhaps after everything was set right again.

Tiburcio had not finished even a glass of liquor to Garcia and Soto's five. And they were busy playing cards and merry-making while he merely sat and observed.

"I am going to step outside for a minute," he announced.

"Fine. Soto and I will try to drum up a little more excitement for you," Garcia laughed sarcastically. "I know you are used to a little more action."

Outside the saloon, Tiburcio came upon a group of Mexican teenagers mulling around the three of their horses. They all froze except for one boy with his hand in Soto's saddlebag. The startled boys' eyes grew into big circles, and finally the culprit looked up. Tiburcio grabbed his Colt out of his belt and strode up to the kid whose hand was in the bag. The others stepped back. Tiburcio put his gun to the head of the thief, who was a few years younger than himself but nearly the same size. He grabbed the youngster's throat and led him to an alley between the saloon and the bank next door. The boy's friends dispersed in all directions. Tiburcio pinned the boy against the wall.

"Have you lost your mind, kid? I ought to blow your brains out just for your being so God-damned stupid. Do you know you are stealing from the most desperate outlaws in the state?"

Tiburcio saw fear in the boy's eyes.

"But we don't know each other, right? Right! So I will tell you how this is going to work out. If I catch you stealing from me or any other Mexican in New Idria - ever - I will gun you down right on the spot. I don't care how old you are!"

The boy swallowed hard, tears welled in his eyes.

"However," Tiburcio continued through gritted teeth albeit in a bit softer tone, "if you ever need money, you just ask me for it. Don't ask anybody else. Don't steal it. Don't borrow it. Don't beg for it. Ask me. Here is twenty-five dollars. Next time I see you I might ask you for it. Or maybe the second time I see you I will ask for the money. The point is, don't spend foolishly. Don't act foolishly. You will always carry this twenty-five of my money as a reminder of how stupid your actions were, a reminder of our little conversation here - an unspoken agreement that you understood every single one of my words. Got it?"

"Yes, sir."

"Of course, if you can't produce my money when I ask, you will be killed."

"Yes, sir."

The barrel of Tiburcio's gun left a red and white welt on the temple of the boy, who slumped to the ground in the alley and wept after the bandit walked away.

Tiburcio did not go back to the saloon. Instead, he walked around the town for a long while, wending his way around the tents. He thought about the group of teenagers who were trying to take Soto's possessions. They were nowhere to be seen. His euphoria upon arriving in New Idria and his truculence over the confrontation with the boys subsided with each step. He walked past the fringes of the tent city where cattle and sheep were being butchered in the slaughter corral, their hides stretched out to dry on the hillside. He made his way up over the hill thick with chaparral and along the banks of the San Carlos River until he came upon a large, two-story building that looked like it belonged in San Francisco. It was the mine superintendent's residence.

He stared up at the structure and thought nobody was home because it was so quiet. As he was about to turn to leave, he thought he caught a glimpse of a figure through a window upstairs. The sash moved but he didn't see who it was. Anita? He was embarrassed by the ridiculous thought. A few paces away he turned back to the house and wondered if he had really seen a pretty, young girl in the window with a corner of the curtain pulled back.

On his way back to the saloon, he resolved again to write to Anita but decided not to make mention of settling down on a ranch. He would merely keep her knowing that he was constantly thinking of her and hold out the possibility of meeting someday, hopefully soon.

Two hours later, Tiburcio returned to the saloon and was hit by a loud wave of shouting, laughing, glass jingling and coins rattling. Two dozen people were gathered around a large table in the center of the room. As Tiburcio inched closer, he saw Garcia and Soto sitting around it with six other men. They were playing Faro. The same girl from earlier was sitting on Soto's knee and now another stood behind him with her arms draped over his huge chest. Garcia also shared his seat with a fair-looking woman. They were boisterously laughing and leaning back and forth in their seats.

Some of the card players looked more anxious than others, tapping their buckskin bags of coins against the table or massaging red and white round wood chips from stacks of assorted heights as if trying to rub the pain off of them. At one end of the table was a well-dressed man, the dealer, standing in front of a wood box with cards in the middle of it. Just to the left of him was a croupier, who stood over a pile of Mexican silver pieces and dollar and half-dollar heaps of U.S. coins; he manipulated several red and white markers on an abacus-like device.

The dealer looked down at thirteen cards, all spades, in two rows of six. One card was set off to the side. The first row of cards escalated from the ace, to his left, up to the six card; the card off to the side was the seven and the next row went from eight to king. There was a flurry of bets being placed on the cards. Then, the dealer turned over a card and placed it to his right. Next, he placed a card from a second stack to his left and this ignited a furious amount of elation and yelling. The croupier raked away the losses and paid the winnings.

The dealer cast a furtive glance at the cards, then at the players' money and finally their glasses.

"Barkeeper, anyone?"

One man with a low pile of coins and an empty buckskin pouch called out his order and the barkeeper quickly set down a glass and filled it. He tossed the whiskey back and was ready for another round.

"Make your bets, gentlemen!" the dealer said. "All down?"

"Hold on!" Garcia barked as Tiburcio crowded into the motley group. "Put your bet on a card or two, Tiburcio. Where the hell have you been?"

Tiburcio leaned over to tell him something confidentially.

"I don't know how to play very well."

This sent Garcia into a loud guffaw.

"Sure you do. It is just like we were playing at El Tuche!" Garcia bellowed. "But you are right - you are terrible - even my wife and children take money from you at cards."

Garcia wailed again in laughter.

Tiburcio put coins on and between several cards.

After the dealer had placed the losing and winning cards, Tiburcio's money still sat untouched. But one of the other players had come to the end of his purse.

"I am out," he told the dealer and stood up to leave.

" *Espera*! I will make you a deal," Garcia replied. "I will give you - not loan you - but give you two-hundred dollars if you stay in the game."

"That is too kind. What are the conditions?"

"You must ride with us tomorrow."

"Ride with you?"

"Yes. Ride with the revolutionaries. We could use your help on a little business we have to take care of. Do you understand?"

"Count me in."

Tiburcio kept playing, too, and was up four-hundred dollars. He was enjoying the attention and admiration of the room, especially the young girl who had left Soto's side to sidle up to the handsome young man.

"Bar the door!" Garcia shouted, laughing and pointing at Tiburcio. "This boy is taking our money! And our women!"

Several musicians had taken up positions on the stage. The barkeeper had begun to push back all the tables and chairs to create an open dancing area in the saloon. Garcia's table remained where it was.

Two fiddlers and guitar players along with a pair of accordion players started to warm up.

"This is going to get good," Garcia shouted to Tiburcio.

The festive music started and Tiburcio watched as some of the vaqueros didn't bother with formalities. They pushed their sombreros back on their heads at a forty-five degree angle, grabbed a prostitute and plunged into dance, swinging their partners with their spurs clicking against the floor, their revolvers flapping at their sides. A frequent whoop rose up over the music.

Tiburcio danced nearly every number, and once even got up on stage to play his guitar. Many women waited for him to finish his song and put down the guitar so they could dance with the new, welcome face at the camp. Tiburcio appeared to be enjoying himself, and others basked in his gaiety. However, sadness over the absence of Anita crept into his heart despite - or perhaps because of - the presence of music and dancing.

It was well after midnight when Garcia and Soto disappeared upstairs with their women and he was left with a few late revelers. The saloon owner, who had kept watch on his investment all night, told Tiburcio his room upstairs was already paid for, and showed him the way.

Tiburcio went to bed alone, but having the room between Garcia and Soto didn't do much for his sleeping. Eventually, however, the giggling and bedpost-banging and moans and groans ceased and he drifted off. Completely fatigued, with a roof over his head, a soft mattress under his back and clean bedding wrapped around him, he slept until late morning. He awoke in reverie. Anita filled his mind like a river in spring. He threw off the covers and found his pen and paper in his jacket. He had to write down his thoughts; he would worry later about how to get the letter to her.

Dearest Anita,

As a boy, I would think of the perfect woman. Not any woman, a particular woman. A friend. A lover. There are many distractions as a boy, but the thoughts of this woman were strong. She had long, wavy black hair, dark eyes that sparkled like deep water, a voice as soft as a cloud. Her hands were delicate; her ideas and actions strong.

She is you.

Our exchanges have been brief but filled with all of past time and future time. Everything you do stirs me, elates me, is perfect.

You are with me even when you are far away. Take a green leaf from a tree before the summer ends, and I will be with you before its color fades.

Love, Tiburcio

By the time he finished the letter, pulled his pants on and went downstairs, it was nearly noon and Garcia and Soto were already playing cards and drinking. Several men and women lingered around the table. The room was boisterous again. Garcia saw his friend walking down the stairs.

"Lazy!" he shouted, rising out of his seat and meeting Tiburcio halfway across the floor. "These men want to join our liberating regiment, disciplined and at the ready – and it's a little difficult to persuade them of the gravity of our cause when you amble down here after half the day is spent! I ought to send you back to Monterey!"

Garcia stepped a little unsteadily back to his chair, with several people parting to make way for the desperado. He grabbed the neck of a quart bottle of aguardiente and took a swill.

"Give the boy some room," Garcia commanded, sweeping his arm across the table. "Pull up a chair, Tiburcio. I am going to deal you in!"

Tiburcio glanced at Juan Soto, who sat at the chair to his right. He couldn't see Soto's eyes under his bushy eyebrows but the terrifying outlaw appeared sullen and withdrawn. He hardly looked up through several hands of poker.

"You are the worst card player I have ever sat across from," Garcia laughed at Tiburcio. "You better stick to banditry. Soto, on the other hand, he could make a living at cards. He's just not much of a conversationalist, which takes most of the fun out of it. If you are going to take someone's money, Soto, at least give him the pleasure of colloquy!"

After several more hands, in which Garcia finished off his bottle of whiskey, the letter in Tiburcio's pocket seemed to be getting heavier and heavier. His fingers incessantly tapped over it. Finally, he excused himself and went outside to look for a reliable messenger who could surreptitiously deliver his missive. The U.S. post would not do.

There were many poor, mining families at New Idria who relied on the youthful vigor of their children to bring in some extra money. And since Tiburcio was willing to pay handsomely for the errand to be carried out, it would not take long to find the right person.

By the time the boy saw him he was already starting to run away.

"No! Wait!" Tiburcio called.

The boy - it certainly was the same kid Tiburcio had caught stealing from Soto - must have suddenly realized running was the wrong thing to do and stopped. As Tiburcio approached, he was already fumbling around to find the money in his pocket .

"No, no. Put it back. That's all right. I have something else to ask you."

After Tiburcio explained the mission, the boy agreed to do it. He was paid half of the delivery fee up front and promised the rest upon a successful return.

Feeling much lighter now that he was unburdened of the letter, Tiburcio walked with a spring in his step back toward the hotel-saloon. He turned a corner where a dentist had set up shop and ran into the chest of Juan Soto.

"*Cabron*! You scared the hell out of me," Tiburcio exclaimed. "What are you doing? Following me?"

"Looking for you," Soto corrected, his gargantuan figure practically pinning Tiburcio to the wood wall. He was speaking quietly. "Garcia got word of a stagecoach filled with thousands of dollars traveling tomorrow morning."

"You came after me to tell me that? Couldn't that wait?"

"Robbing another stagecoach is madness," Soto said. "Word has spread about the dangers on the highway throughout Panoche and it won't be so easy."

His wayward eye tried to align with the straight one to no avail.

"Why tell me?" Tiburcio asked.

"Your friend is drinking a lot. I cannot remember the last day he was sober. I want to make sure he isn't going to do something dangerous, and get us all killed or captured."

"You didn't seem to be concerned about all this last night."

"Last night was not the time. I needed to stay close to Anastacio. He may get a little too bold. Strike the wrong target.

Or be a little too quick on the trigger. Or, worst of all, continue boasting. That is my biggest fear. I cannot always be around."

"Anastacio is the leader. He knows what he's doing."

"He is. He is the leader. But I was there when you spoke about your concerns to the refugees at Cantua. Your words got me thinking. Now you know my concerns … in case you begin to have doubts about Anastacio again. In case there comes a need for you to make these important decisions. Instead of him."

That night, in a private back room of the saloon, Garcia - a bottle in his hand - argued for one last highway grab before going separate ways and lying low. Tiburcio, Soto and a dozen new recruits all listened to Garcia's plan to use Indian tactics to waylay the coach.

"This one, my friends, is loaded with cash," he grinned. "*Esta es 'El Grande.'* We have enough men to do it right."

Four robbers, he explained, on one side of the road would keep pace with the coach at fifty yards' distance. Four others would be riding parallel on the other side. With their Henrys and Winchesters, they would take shot after shot at the coach, breaking up its wood frame and fraying the nerves of the passengers. The horses and the shotgun messenger would also be targets, but nothing else directly. The guard's shotgun would be ineffective at the range at which the bandits would be firing, Garcia explained.

Two other men were necessary for the plan to work: one a sentry stationed about a mile behind the bandits; the other a mile ahead.

"We need more men and better tactics because the law is beginning to wake up," Garcia said. "And that makes it all the more fun."

He concluded: "We set out tomorrow morning, 4:00 a.m. from the livery."

Then Garcia walked back into the saloon to drink and gamble some more.

The next day the plan started exactly the way Garcia had planned. Passengers shrieked as the wagon splintered with every gunshot. Realizing they were well outnumbered, the guard finally ordered the driver to stop the coach. He flung his shotgun off to the side of the road and put up his hands, waiting for the robbers to descend upon them.

But the bandits hesitated. Garcia did not give the sign to swoop down on the stage. Instead, he was looking at his forward sentry racing full speed toward him. Garcia held up his hand to motion to everyone to wait for the next order before acting. The stage driver and shotgun messenger looked around confused in the sudden silence. Across the road, Soto held up an open palm to signal that he understood Garcia.

The sentry pulled back hard on his horse's reins, bringing the mare to a hard, dust-whirling stop in front of Garcia. He was so out of breath it was difficult to speak. His sentences were short but to the point.

"Another stage. That direction. Don't know who. Or from where. But a well-armed posse is with them. Possibly lawmen."

"In a stage? Where are they?"

"A mile back."

"You!" Garcia said, pointing to the third man. "Go with him and stop or slow down that coach. I'll send Soto and another man."

Garcia slapped Tiburcio in the chest to tell him to follow him and lunged toward the halted coach. Soto saw the leader's actions and followed. Tiburcio and Soto trained their guns on the messenger and the driver. But Garcia ordered Soto and a recruit to head up the road and help the others.

"Delay or kill whoever is in the other coach. I don't care," he told Soto.

Garcia knew he had to act fast. He dismounted and shoved the stage hands off the coach and into the brush. Tiburcio and another man went about their work inside the coach. Tiburcio's companion led the four passengers, three women and a man, out at gunpoint while Tiburcio checked the contents inside. He froze. A strongbox sat on the floorboard labeled: "New Idria Mine wages."

"Oh, shit!" he cursed, scrambling out of the coach. "*Amigo. Ven aqui!*"

By the time Anastacio got over to the coach, gunshots from down the road were echoing in the canyons. Tiburcio pointed to the strongbox.

"We can't steal from our own people. They are giving us protection," Tiburcio said.

"How did you get so smart?" Garcia quipped.

He headed back to the brush and hurried the two stage hands to the coach with his pistol drawn. Then, he addressed the victims.

"Sorry for the inconvenience. We wanted to make sure everything was secure. There have been so many holdups on this road. You are free to proceed to New Idria," he told them. "Again, I am so sorry for the way you were treated.."

The bewildered passengers looked up the road to where a gun battle was raging.

"Hear those shots?" Garcia continued. "That's probably the bandits we were looking for. They were coming upon you so it's a good thing we intervened. We want to do all we can to protect our miners and their wages. Again, sorry for the inconvenience. Be on your way."

As the splintered stage rumbled up the road with its passengers, Garcia dumped several gunny sacks from his saddlebag and flung them to Tiburcio. "Quickly tie these around our horses' hoofs."

They had just finished tying the last gunny sack, when Soto came galloping up. He was alone.

"Three lawmen are still pursuing us," he said, huffing.

"Are you the only survivor?"

"Yes. Your recruits were worthless. We'll have to go in different directions."

The lawmen approached taking wild shots at the bandits. Garcia and Tiburcio wheeled their horses into the manzanita chaparral and lashed them. Soto dashed across the road and up the opposite side. Two lawmen went after Garcia and Tiburcio and a third companion chased Soto. After a few miles of hard riding, the sacks had worn off, but they appeared to have done their job. The lawmen were off their trail for now.

Their ride back to New Idria didn't let up. They arrived at the mining town in the evening. As word spread, several mine inhabitants came out of their businesses to lend a hand to the bandits. The horses were whisked away to the livery and the bandits were herded upstairs to hotel rooms that looked down onto the main street. From this vantage point, the entrance to the town could be watched.

The innkeeper brought some beans and tortillas with a bottle of brandy and two glasses up to their rooms. They sat at a table near the window, ate and kept an eye on the road. Neither said anything for about twenty minutes. Then, Garcia looked up at Tiburcio.

"Where is our money?"

"Right there," Tiburcio said, pointing to saddle bag on the bed.

"Take five hundred dollars to the innkeeper for his inconvenience. We'll grease the superintendent later."

When Tiburcio returned he noticed Garcia intently looking out the window into the dim evening.

"See anything?"

"Just some miners and some women standing around. A few prostitutes, too."

Tiburcio took a swig of whiskey. As he set the glass down, Garcia knit his brow and his eyes narrowed at something happening outside.

"What is it?"

"They are scattering! Everyone is scattering like mad."

"Must be the posse coming," Tiburcio said, his whiskey-warm throat tightening. "Can you see up the road?"

"No. Not far enough. Wait! There's a large, slow, shadowy figure coming – and it isn't Soto."

Tiburcio chuckled, always flabbergasted at the way his friend could muster a joke in the midst of a crisis.

"Let me see."

"Oh, *mi Dio*. It's a bear! One hell of a big bear!"

"What can we do?"

"Let's go kill it."

"You are crazy. Let it go. It will wander right through town."

"Do you know the havoc a bear can wreak?"

Garcia took a shot of liquor and quickly bounded down the wooden staircase. Tiburcio followed, their boots making thunderous footsteps throughout the inn.

"Don't go out there," said the saloon keeper.

Dozens of people had taken refuge inside the barroom.

"There is a thousand-pound bear out there. The best marksman couldn't take him down."

When the two desperadoes didn't stop, the keeper called out: "At least let me get you a couple horses."

The horses were ready behind the saloon, riatas coiled at the horns. Tiburcio was the first to ride out in front of the bear.

"Is it Saturday?" Garcia asked. "He must be heading for the refuse pit near the slaughter-corral."

As the bear got closer, Garcia was shocked at its size. He had never seen one that large. He suddenly realized trying to handle the animal was insane – and he was about to warn his partner that their plan was entirely too ambitious, a complete misjudgment, and call the whole thing off when Tiburcio, his adrenaline racing, let the rope fly and lassoed the beast. That's when his troubles began.

The bear started tugging both the horse and the rider down the street and then lumbered into a jog. Tiburcio strained at the riata. His wild-eyed mount foamed at the mouth. Garcia, on foot, followed his protégé and the animals, finding the entire matter increasingly humorous.

The bear violently pulled rider and horse to the end of the main street and unexpectedly stopped. Tiburcio couldn't believe his luck. He pulled in the slack on the rope and turned the horse sidelong, putting solid equine girth between him and the bear. Making the horse sidestep, Tiburcio crept closer and closer to the bear until he looked the animal straight in the eyes. Garcia watched curiously, wondering what his friend had planned, as Tiburcio gripped the riata with all his might and bore his inner thighs into the horse for stability.

"OK, *el oso*, let's go for a nice, little walk."

"Bravo!" Garcia mocked, asking: "Now what?"

The entire town seemed to have come out of every building, house and tent, peering down the street in the twilight at the strange scene. Suddenly, the bear had thoughts other than a leisurely stroll on a leash. From an awkward gait, it opened into a four-legged sprint toward a long, deep, watery ravine that ran parallel to the town with Tiburcio and his horse in tow and completely at its mercy. Down the bank the beast fled. Tiburcio let out the rope as fast as he could, but it wasn't enough. At the swampy water's edge, Tiburcio and the horse hurled and crashed onto the bear and all three fell in a furious tangle. Mud and water and fur flew. Tiburcio thrashed wildly to extricate himself from the horse and beast. He could smell the animal's warm breath on his face and feel its angry grumble. Frantically, he grabbed his knife and cut the rawhide in one swift movement. Sputtering and spitting blood, he sprinted, with a limp, up the bank. The horse struggled onto its legs and dashed away, too.

Believing he was at a safe distance, Tiburcio turned around to keep an eye on the bear but kept briskly walking backward. Finding itself alone in the water, the bear stood to its full height and growled long and loud in the direction of Tiburcio. Then it swiftly turned and ran in the direction it had always intended to go.

"Go!" Tiburcio shouted at the bear, his heart racing. He had cuts and welts on his bloody, muddy face and his right leg ached. "Go! I've freed you! You son of a bitch!"

Garcia didn't stop laughing until they got past the astonished, jabbering crowd and were back inside the hotel room. Workers at the hotel filled a large basin with water and brought dressing to the room and asked if they could summon the doctor. Tiburcio refused the professional medical help, but he allowed one of the prostitutes, at Garcia's insistence, to help nurse his cuts and scrapes. His chest was bare and she gently washed the dirt and scrapes on his shoulders and arms, then his torso.

It had been an hour since the incident with the bear when there was a knock at the door.

"*Qui vas?*" Garcia asked.

The innkeeper answered. A man was here to see him. Yes, he was alone. No, he did not have a gun.

Nonetheless, Garcia put down his drinking glass and picked up his revolver.

"Enter."

A rather tall fellow in a bowler hat, suit and pocket watch and chain took a few steps inside and introduced himself.

"My name is Belcher. Lewis Belcher."

"Why do I care?"

"I happened to be on the stage that you came across earlier today – the stage carrying the miners' wages. We are staying in New Idria for the night. Quite an exciting place, I might say. Much more so than I had ever imagined."

"It can be," Garcia said, casting a glance at the shirtless Tiburcio and his female attendant. "But I still don't know why you are calling. Or who you are."

"Again, I am Lewis Belcher. I was born in New York but came to Monterey in 1847."

"I would know you if you spent any time in Monterey," Garcia said dubiously.

"Yes, well, I got caught up in gold fever and worked the gold fields in Tuolumne. I was gone for a few years upon arriving. I returned to Monterey three years ago. I own large herds of cattle and have a fair amount of property."

Garcia again looked at Tiburcio to get a hint of whether the young man had heard of the Belcher name, but Tiburcio was talking privately with the woman sponging his wounds and was not paying attention to the guest. Belcher continued talking.

"I've inquired and have learned who you are and I am impressed by the way you operate. Handling two stages at one time, when one is loaded with men trying to kill you, is extremely impressive. May we speak in private, Mr. Garcia?"

"Tiburcio is my captain. He knows everything that I know," Garcia replied, but he asked the woman to leave the room. "OK, we're alone. What is your business, Mr. Belcher?"

"I am sure you have heard about the protracted legal battle over the estate of a land owner named Jose Maria Sanchez," Belcher began.

Tiburcio and Garcia nodded knowingly at one another. Belcher was not surprised that they had heard of the case.

"Then you know who William Roach is?" Belcher asked.

"Of course, he is the former sheriff," Tiburcio said, pulling on an undershirt over his bandaged wounds. "He is a very prominent white man. He gave up the top law position to be guardian of the Sanchez children. Lyons took over for him. Why do I get the feeling this has to do with the rumors and suspicions of buried gold stolen from the Sanchez estate?"

"Yes, young man, you are on the right trail. Well, Judge Creaner in Stockton appointed me receiver of the estate and ordered me to go and demand repayment of the seventy-five thousand dollars, plus interest, and other property Roach has embezzled from the estate. As guardian, Roach had never taken care of the needs of the Sanchez children. He did not invest any of their money safely, and he loaned much of it at high rates of interest."

Belcher took a seat across the table from Garcia, who still gripped his pistol, and wiped his brow with a handkerchief he had extracted from his pocket. Garcia poured a shot of brandy. Belcher continued.

"Roach and his cronies did not take kindly to my demand for the return of the money. Roach's defiance got him tossed in jail for contempt of court. He rotted there through a trial and many attempts to get free. I am just returning from Stockton, where I learned Roach has escaped from custody. Some say he has gone to the East Coast, but if there is still seventy-five thousand dollars in gold lying somewhere, I know he is not far from Monterey."

Belcher wiped his glistening forehead again.

"Let me get to the point. I am a respected businessman. I don't go around waving pistols like some bounty hunter. But I cannot let this man or his friends, who are swarming Monterey, get this money. Have you been in Monterey recently? No? It is swirling with speculation that Roach is back and will unearth the money soon. I must find him before he gets to the money. I need the best bodyguard I can find. And I think I ran into him today. The way I saw you secure the stage this morning and fight off that pursuing posse ..."

Belcher ended the sentence abruptly.

"Is it possible that posse was after you? And not us? Perhaps some of Roach's friends?"

"That is possible, Mr. Garcia. I do not know. And that is why I need protection. There is a lot of money at stake here."

"I am busy in other pursuits," Garcia said dismissively, but was curious nonetheless. "What do you see my time as being worth?"

"Twenty percent of the seventy-five thousand."

"Fifteen thousand?" Garcia replied, unimpressed. "What exactly would I do in your employment?"

"Simply put, you would protect me everywhere I go until we either find Roach or the money or both."

"This employment will take me away from other lucrative endeavors. It will also expose me to more danger – I am not welcome in Monterey."

"I can offer you twenty thousand dollars. If the cash we find is more than seventy-five thousand – and some people, including the courts, say it could be hundred thousand dollars – I will offer you twenty-five thousand dollars."

Garcia took the offer and Belcher sealed the deal with the outlaw in a handshake. They agreed to leave as business partners tomorrow morning. After the businessman left the room, Garcia asked Tiburcio how his wounds were feeling.

"Imagine. Wrestling with a bear," Garcia chortled.

He was in high spirits and couldn't believe his luck of running into Belcher. Tiburcio saw the deal otherwise.

"That bear is nothing compared to what you are getting mixed up in," Tiburcio said. "Battling a sheriff and his cronies for a small stake in some buried gold? And returning to Monterey where a mob wants to lynch you. I will take a fight with a bear any day."

This made Garcia heartily laugh for a long time.

"Oh, Tiburcio, you idiot," Garcia admonished him. "It's all so perfect. I am going to steal the money myself. To hell with both of them. By the time the mess is sorted out I will be in Southern California, with Lupe, the children and enough money to liberate the entire state. While I set up the southern regiment in Los Angeles, you, as my captain in Northern California, will be in charge of Carabajal, El Halcon, Ponce, Molina and Soto – if he is still alive – and any new recruits. Your band will continue raiding ranch operations up here until we signal the beginning of the war. Sometimes I can't believe my luck! Good fortune walked right into our hotel room and handed us seventy-five thousand dollars. The gringos will pay for crossing one another and seeking my help!"

Another set of knuckles rapped at the door.

"Christ, this is a busy room," Garcia cursed. "Come in, with your back to me and your hands in the air."

Tiburcio opened the door and the superintendent of the mines stepped awkwardly into the room. He was not used to walking into a room backward. He kicked the door shut.

"May I turn around?"

"Yes, majordomo. What's your business?"

"I want to know what is going on? I have sent a group of lawmen from Monterey back down the hill. They were looking for you."

"Perhaps, they were. We will be following them out of here in the morning."

"And they were looking for another group of guests in this hotel. It's becoming hard to keep track of everyone's comings and goings and what side of the law they are on."

Garcia stood, a bit wobbly at first, and walked over to the bed.

"That is true, majordomo. That's why there's something extra in it for you."

He tossed the superintendent a bag of money.

"Five years without any problem among the miners," the superintendent boasted. "That's better than any other operation of this type in California. If I weren't risking my freedom, not to mention my life, I would thank you and your friends for it. But we know where we stand. I take your money quietly."

"We have a mutually agreeable arrangement," Garcia reminded him. "I seem to attract these types of relationships."

Tiburcio watched the superintendent walk back to the door.

"Do you have a daughter, sir? If you don't mind my asking?"

The boss bristled and turned to glare at Tiburcio. Garcia guffawed, spitting up a swallow of brandy.

"Yes. And that's all you will ever know about her. Her life is tough enough already out here in isolation. Deal or no deal with you bandits - don't ever speak to her without my permission, young man."

Chapter 12: The Washington
Monterey
Nov. 6, 1856

For months, rumors had spread around town that the outlaw wanted for murdering Constable Hardmount was back. In many instances it was more than hearsay. A large number of residents claimed to have shared a whiskey at the bar with Garcia or that they had seen him on the streets or in a carriage in the company of Lewis Belcher.

"Ahh," the listener would say knowingly and disdainfully after catching wind of the news. "Must have something to do with the Sanchez affair and the hidden seventy-five thousand dollars."

Upon his return to Monterey, Garcia's appearance bore little resemblance to the night he fled. His curly black hair was much shorter, cut around his ears. His black vicuna hat was gone. And he adorned himself in all the finery of a wealthy, respected man about town. Over time, however, his hair again grew out from under his shader and he began to walk around confidently and comfortably in the open as if ancient grudges had been put aside. He still carried two single-action revolvers everywhere he went.

There were reasons for his audaciousness. The new sheriff hadn't put a high priority on arresting the highwayman. After Sheriff Lyons was quickly driven from office following the mob's hanging of Higuera, his successor, John Keating, figured as long as the city was safe and quiet there was no need for aggressive law enforcement. And Monterey had been that way for a while. Furthermore, Garcia was bored with his employment as Belcher's body guard. It wasn't lucrative – at least not until he came into possession of the missing seventy-five grand – and it wasn't exciting. No dashing escapes, no hidden identities, no posse chases, no attentive whores at the end of the day. In addition, Belcher was always telling Garcia to put away the bottle before he was half way through it. Each time Garcia grudgingly obliged, but only because if he were to be fired for drinking on the job then his chance at obtaining the huge cash amount would be remote.

It was under these mixed circumstances that an intoxicated Anastacio Garcia entered the luxurious Washington Hotel at 10:00 a.m. He had left a note at Belcher's room upstairs that explained he had come across some important information and they needed to rendezvous downstairs immediately. He saw his boss sitting in the far corner of the hotel saloon with a drink in his hand and back to the wall. Garcia had looked there first, knowing that Belcher feared planting himself anywhere else in the room in case someone might shoot him from behind. Garcia took a seat next to Belcher at the table. They both had sight of the entrance.

"It has come to my attention," Garcia said, not looking at Belcher, his eyes scanning the barroom, "that Roach is back in town and will be making his appearance at this hotel today."

"It's the first word I've heard on his whereabouts since he was mysteriously sprung from jail. I thought he was recovering in Stockton from some kind of illness," Belcher replied.

"Yeah, well, anyway, I am pretty certain that he – or some of his hordes of friends – has dug up the gold."

"He has the gold? We need to find him!"

"Will you shut up?"

"Don't speak to me like that! I will fire you and call off the entire deal."

Garcia caught the barkeeper's eye.

"One bottle of wine over here!" he called.

"You bastard. You are not going to get drunk," Belcher cursed, grabbing Garcia's arm. "We are this close to getting that money, if what you say is accurate!"

"I am surprised a judge ever ruled in favor of you. You are such a stupid, incompetent man."

"Listen here, Garcia…"

"No! You listen. A former state senator, Isaac Wall, and a constable named Tom Williamson, are leaving town by pack train in a couple hours. They are going to meet Roach at some undisclosed location where he has been hiding. They will no doubt take their share and give Roach the rest."

"How do you know this?"

"Roach told me."

"Roach?" Belcher yelped. "You double-crossed me!"

The barkeeper, with a sidelong glance at Belcher, put the open wine bottle and a glass in front of Garcia, who stood up to pour himself a swallow. He tossed the liquid back and set the glass down hard. He picked up the bottle by the neck with his left hand and drew his pistol with his right.

"I cannot say it has been a pleasure doing business with you," he told Belcher, stepping around the table.

He raised the gun, leveled it at Belcher's chest and shot him through.

Garcia casually walked out of the bar into the drizzly, cold late afternoon. He headed for the southern hills above the main road out of town. He had somebody to stalk.

• • •

Twenty-four hours after Belcher was shot dead, Sheriff Keating stood in a ravine on the banks of the Salinas River with his boots buried in an inch of mud. Rain furiously tapped on his wide brim and ran down the shoulders and back of his long, brown leather overcoat. A deputy peered down at him from his position on the ridge overlooking the ravine. Another deputy and several residents were searching the area thirty yards south of Keating. The sheriff was looking down at the body of Isaac Wall, who lay face down in the muck. Marks were still visible in the mud that showed he had been dragged to the ravine and tossed down the side. Keating could see where a bullet had entered the back of his head.

Keating leaned down and with a great heave turned the body over. He saw the ball had passed through the back of Wall's head and come out his right eye. His clothing was mostly undisturbed except for being pulled through the mud. His pistol and spurs were gone and the ring on his finger had been forcibly removed.

"Looks like it was a bullet from a Minnie rifle," Keating called up to the deputy. "Wait. Another ball passed through his left wrist. With that bullet we found in the horse's back, I'd say three shots were fired at Wall."

"Hey, sheriff!" called a lawman standing downriver. He was Undersheriff Joaquin de la Torre, a battle-hardened Mexican war veteran and an ambitious lawman. "I think we've found Williamson."

Keating slogged downstream to examine the second body. He surmised from the bruises on Williamson's forehead, cheeks, nose and chin that the murderer had dragged the constable face down and had halfheartedly attempted to hide the body in the bushes. The sheriff kneeled over the corpse to examine it more closely. Keating ran his fingers over the back side of the head. Under the hair he could feel a hard lump; Williamson had been shot in the thick part of the skull.

"I feel a ball, but this didn't kill him," Keating said dryly, looking up at de la Torre. He turned Williamson's head to the side. "A point-blank shot tore his ear right off."

Keating furrowed his brow and rubbed his forehead. He looked up at the thick gray and whitish clouds roiling above. The rain had stopped.

"Wall still had one thousand dollars in his money belt," Keating said, thinking aloud. "There was another two hundred dollars in Williamson's saddle bag when that frightened horse showed up at the ranch without its rider."

"Our highwaymen must have gotten alarmed and took off in a haste without the money," de la Torre said.

Keating pondered this, but shook his head.

"No, this campsite and all of their belongings have been ransacked but nothing taken. I think our villain was looking for a lot more than a few hundred dollars."

"Garcia?"

"Yes. A half-dozen witnesses saw Garcia shoot Belcher back at the hotel. Wall and Williamson are friends of Belcher's enemy, Roach. And then there is the seventy-five thousand dollars buried somewhere. Garcia is going after the money himself, eliminating anyone else on the trail."

"What's next?"

"The wagon is on the way to bring the bodies back to town. Let's return to Monterey and gather the best posse we can. We need to stop Garcia."

• • •

Ever since Tom Clay picked George Redford up off the ground in San Juan Bautista as those nasty greasers rode off, he had felt a fatherly and sympathetic heart-tug for the deaf boy. Clay had worked extensively with the deaf, but he was more interested in giving the boy some of his childhood back than providing any assistance because of his disability. Day after day he watched the boy drifting around town trying to entertain himself, usually shunned by the other children. George was either walking around in his silent world alone or working on a teamster's load with his father's crew as it rolled in San Juan Bautista.

"Next time your father leaves you here, maybe we can go to the rodeo in Salinas," Clay told George, speaking in gestures and finger spelling.

The next time didn't occur until late in the year.

"It's not the best weather, but at least it's cleared up a bit from yesterday," Clay told George, who was sitting in front of him in the saddle. "These days, they run cattle all year round, though."

And that's when he encountered Anastacio Garcia for the second time. Clay and George were sitting on a corral railing watching a parade of livestock coming through when the school teacher couldn't ignore the growing commotion behind him. At first he had barely noticed the men talking, but slowly their conversation grabbed his attention. He turned and his eyes went straight to the black figure in the middle of a dozen vaqueros. Garcia had a bottle of brandy by the neck and was talking so animatedly that the liquor was splashing out.

"I was so angry when I didn't find the seventy-five thousand dollars that I left the little amount those boys had in their possession untouched in their money belt. Not that they will be using it anytime soon. Hah!. If you boys are a little short on cash, I will tell you where I left the bodies and you can help yourselves!" Garcia guffawed and swallowed four or five gulps before the bottle left his lips. "Hell, I will tell you where I left a dozen bodies around ranges north, east and south of here!"

He turned and caught Tom Clay's resentful gaze.

"What the hell are you looking at, gringo? I'll shoot your head off, too! What's another dead yanqui?"

• • •

Keating had his posse. And he had his destination. There would be no slow prying of information and sleuthing in the mountain ranges. He would go directly north to El Tuche with the most hard-nosed posse he could assemble: Undersheriff de la Torre, a lover of conflict who badly wanted credit for capturing or killing Garcia because he was hell bent on earning the distinction of first Mexican sheriff under United States law; Captain Jim Beckwith, a civilian whose military background was shady but who had proven himself worthy of a good fight in several other posses, including the one that captured

Murrieta; another civilian, Charles Layton, the keeper of the new Point Pinos lighthouse who often became bored at his outpost off the rocky, pine-covered Monterey peninsula and would leave his wife and four children on adventures of pursuing outlaws; and four of his best deputies.

They planned to ride to El Tuche before sunrise. The early morning was dark and foggy. Keating grabbed his hat off the standing rack near the front door of his office at the jailhouse. He was feeling confident that by nightfall the county would be rid of the fear of Anastacio Garcia. Keating was relaxed yet energetic and bounded out of the building, nearly running over Tom Clay coming up the steps.

The sheriff looked up into the tall teacher's glasses in the darkness. Clay wiped down his oily hair above his ears and prepared his declaration.

"I must go with your posse to catch Anastacio Garcia," Clay announced, his breath showing in the cold air.

"We have our posse assembled already," Keating said and tried to scoot past. He didn't want his ebullient mood to wane.

"I can help. I have been in some adventures. In Kentucky and Texas. I am new here but I can prove to you, sheriff, that I am needed on your posse."

Keating again looked at the thin, scholarly features of Tom Clay.

"Why do you want to come along? What do you do for a living?"

"I am a school teacher in San Juan Bautista."

"Then why are you here, in Monterey, wanting to hunt down an outlaw?"

"I have twice encountered this miserable beast, and on both occasions he made my blood boil. The last time was two days ago at a rodeo in Salinas. He confessed to killing more than a dozen men."

Keating grew interested.

"Did he mention a man named Wall and another named Williamson?"

"Yes."

"Listen, Mister ..."

"... Clay. Tom Clay."

"Mr. Clay, my men have their horses saddled and packed. We have discussed our plan in great detail. You are simply too late, regardless of your vigilant desire. Besides, your schoolchildren need you more than we do. But there is a way you can help. I would like you to stay in Monterey until we return. I will need you here when I get back more than I need you with me during the capture. As a witness, you can help with the trial rather than the capture. Understand?"

Clay agreed and let the sheriff go on his way.

Keating was not disappointed when he arrived at the Custom House to meet his posse. A large crowd of dozens of citizens had gathered. Several held torches and candles. They applauded and whooped when they saw the sheriff coming down Main Street. Before the eight posse members departed, he addressed the vigilantes of the town.

"Dead or alive, my friends," he shouted in conclusion. "Anastacio Garcia comes back here to answer for his life of crime - dead or alive!"

• • •

Garcia was always prepared for a raid at his ranch house. He sat at a rough wooden table in the middle of the room with two revolvers in his belt. A loaded Spencer repeating carbine and a Henry rifle leaned against the edge of the table. Other firearms were stashed at every window and door in the cabin. He had enough ammunition to supply an entire Army regiment. The heavy, oak front door, the side entrances and the window covers were bolted shut. The four children were asleep in a high loft, away from any spaces between boards that might allow stray bullets to find their way into the house.

The posse, for its part, was counting on arriving early enough to catch Garcia sleeping off a night of heavy drinking.

They would be disappointed. He had seen the looks cast his way at the rodeo, and when he stopped drinking, on the ride home, it became clear that he had said too much, too loud. The bandit knew that the time had come for him to sober up and face the law – no matter how many men the law sent at him.

Within a mile of the house, Keating divided the posse into three groups. Baldwin would take three men and swing to the rear. De la Torre and Layton would pursue a direct path to the west and the sheriff and another deputy headed east to watch over the front of the cabin.

"Wait further orders when you get to your positions," Keating told them.

"Wait? Why wait?" Layton protested. "He's outnumbered eight to one. His escape is impossible!"

"If we wait," the sheriff explained, "we can fire forty-eight conical bullets into his fortress before having to reload. He could maybe get off twelve rounds, if he's good. Understand the arithmetic, Layton? I like them odds. Good, let's go."

A half an hour later, Garcia heard his dogs rustling out from under the porch where they slept. They gave sharp, quick barks of warning. Garcia smiled, knowing his instincts had been correct. Those dogs had sniffed out the bodies. The vigilantes were coming.

Layton and de la Torre reached the property first. They were both overzealous. One wanted, entirely too much, a lifetime story to tell; the other envisioned hastening an ambitious career in law enforcement. They also thought it was insane to lose precious minutes before daybreak. Layton quickly attacked the front door with an ax and de la Torre rushed the side door. As Layton hastily hacked away at the entrance with the ax and the butt of his rifle, Garcia lifted his carbine and pointed it at the side door.

"Who is there?" he called out.

"Joaquin de la Torre! Come out and surrender to the sheriff!"

165

"Go away, now, Joaquin. You are a traitor. Go away or I will kill you!"

"You are surrounded, Garcia. We are a dozen strong. Give yourself up and spare your children the horror!"

"You are a brother, de la Torre. You are a Mexican. I don't want to shoot you. I am giving you a chance to walk away."

Layton continued ripping at the front door and had nearly busted through. De la Torre began kicking at the side door.

"I will teach you to betray your countrymen, de la Torre!" Garcia screamed, marching straight for the side door. Two feet away from the door he raised the rifle, pointed it at a small crack in one of the wood panels and fired. De la Torre fell dead, shot in the heart.

"That is what happens to traitors!" Garcia spit.

He turned toward the front door, where Lupe was suddenly standing as if reading her husband's mind. Upstairs, the children had begun screaming.

"Silence!" Garcia commanded.

He then nodded knowingly to his wife.

Lupe threw the door open hard and stood aside as Garcia emptied a revolver, dropping Layton dead.

And that's when the sheriff reached his position in front. Cursing at what he saw, two of his men lying dead, he now realized he had no choice but to fire at once on the cabin. His party took aim at the doors and windows and fired away. Garcia rapidly returned the volley of lead as the children screamed over and over again. Lupe tried to calm the kids but had her hands full tending to her husband.

"Stay upstairs!" she told the terrorized children.

As Garcia dashed from window to window, Lupe reloaded for him and tossed him weapons. Garcia ordered her to take down the ladder so the children would not be tempted to come down in the middle of the battle.

Under a renewed fusillade of bullets from the house, the sheriff told his assistant that he did not feel it wise to approach the quarters.

"Twelve rounds, eh sheriff?" his deputy grumbled.

166

"He must have some of his confederates with him. I was given false information that he was alone," Keating shouted, then barked orders. "Listen up! Every time their shots subside, we will unload on them."

By this time, Beckwith had arrived at the rear of the house. He saw and heard the commotion and all four of his party opened fire. Garcia, his hands full in front of the house, could not immediately return any of the shots at the back of the property. Several minutes later, the gunfire from both ends diminished. In the calm, he spied through a space in the boards one of Beckwith's men sprinting in a wide berth to the front, where the sheriff was positioned. Then another. A few more minutes ticked away before another wicked storm of gunfire tattered the cabin. Two members of the posse snuck up under the cover of a brisk barrage and took away their fallen comrades.

Throughout the morning, Garcia would start a lively blast from the house and the posse would shoot back with an intensity three times as severe. He persuaded his wife to take up a gun on occasion so it would appear that he was not a lone gunman. Keating believed the bandit was not alone but he could not say for certain how many men were inside. Outside in the timber, the sheriff analyzed the situation. He first cursed the fact that he hadn't brought more men to sufficiently cordon off the house and maintain a vigil on all four walls to make sure Garcia didn't slip away unnoticed. As it was, Garcia definitely enjoyed certain tactical advantages. He occupied a fortified position, and the sheriff and his men would have to eventually enter the house to get him. Furthermore, now that morning light had long since broken, the lawmen were clearer targets than he. If Garcia practiced an ounce of stealth, he could see them but they could not see him.

"If this keeps up," the sheriff told his men, "we'll set the roof ablaze and smoke them out of there."

Around midday, Garcia thought it was too silent for comfort. He tried to listen for any movements outside. Then he heard a rustling from one side of the house. Unknown to the bandit, Keating's men had spent the past hour tossing dry hay on the rooftop. Garcia heard something solid strike above.

"Children?" he called. "Are you safe?"

"Yes, daddy," the oldest replied.

"What was that sound I heard up there?"

"It was something on the roof."

"Maybe a squirrel."

Garcia took a furtive glance out the window and saw no shadows. Minutes later, he looked again. A small trail of black smoke drifted from the house.

"Daddy, I smell smoke."

Garcia shouted out the window in the direction of the sheriff. "You bastard. You are trying to burn children alive? They are in the attic!"

No response. As Garcia was about to leave his post near a supply of arms and a pile of ammunition to get to the children, the sheriff's answer came in a hail of bullets.

"Children! Come to the ledge," the bandit shouted.

He heard nothing from upstairs. Lupe whimpered.

"Stay here. I'll check on them."

Garcia ran toward the stairs in a low, crouched position, but halted. His wife let out a piercing yell. A bullet had sliced right through her hand. Garcia tore down one of the window curtains and bounded back to Lupe. He wrapped up the bleeding flesh after making sure the bullet was not embedded.

Lupe's peal had caught the children's attention and when Garcia looked back at the loft they were all peering over the side with wild looks on their faces. Then he remembered. It had rained last night. The thatched roof could not be put ablaze so easily.

Nevertheless, the thought of the sheriff's evil plan, with no regard for the lives of children, to drive him from the adobe enraged him. He stood up in plain view in front of a shattered window and rapidly unloaded four revolvers and several barrels of twenty-one buckshot into the willows and thicket in front of the house.

"Anastacio?" Lupe said weakly, her back against the wall. "You are running low on ammunition."

Garcia looked around. It was true.

"What is that phrase, darling," he asked his wife gently with a wink, "that Tiburcio always whispers in his horse's ear before he performs a stunt."

"*Arriba el telon.*"

"Of course! *Arriba el telon!*"

He swiftly tossed two bandoliers across his chest, stuffed a Colt in his belt and grabbed two more revolvers in each hand.

"Lupe? Do you remember our plan? The one we discussed about me settling down and becoming an honest rancher. About living peacefully in Los Angeles, away from here."

She nodded.

"That is still the plan. *Si?* Nothing has changed. Just like we discussed, you will arrange the voyage for you and the kids after I get down there. Give lots of time for things to die down around here. In, say, three months, we will meet at La Brea Rancho. *Si ?*"

"Yes."

Garcia kissed Lupe, then took a deep breath and tried to peer out the window without being seen.

"I hope that steed is still tethered in the woods out there," he prayed aloud.

"Run hard, Anastacio! Run your fastest!"

"*Arriba el telon !*"

Lupe threw open the front door. In a blur, Garcia sprung from the house in a lightning-like salvo aimed at the posse in the thicket. Keating's hat flew off as a steel ball ripped it from his head. Beckwith dropped to his knees with a bullet in his throat. Confusion swirled among the law officers. Garcia's flight covered over fifty yards but he finally reached his saddled mare unharmed. Regaining his composure, Keating finally realized Garcia had been the only outlaw in the house. And now he had fled right under his nose. He ordered two men to the house.

"Remain there until you hear from me again! Watch the property day and night in case Garcia reappears. But do not arrest or in any way molest Garcia's wife," he commanded.

Taking the three remaining lawmen, he raced off in pursuit of the heartless outlaw.

Chapter 13: Deceit
Monterey County
January 1857

Keating sat despondently at the cherry wood roll-top desk in his office. Once again, for the thousandth time, head in hands, he judged his own actions. The past several weeks had been the worst of his life. Day and night, he mulled over the events and re-evaluated all the steps he had taken and played out the scenarios over and over again in his mind, trying to figure out what had gone so dreadfully wrong. No matter what, rehashing that day never made anything better or made any answers clearer.

As if living with the responsibility of having three men under his command dead and a serial killer at large wasn't horrifying enough, there were the rumors on the streets and in the saloons that the sheriff was scared of Garcia. He was blamed for not going after the bandit sooner. Some whispered he may have been in partnership with Roach and Garcia all along, and all three were going to split the seventy-five thousand.

If it were just the rumors, Keating might find peace. He could take solace in friends and ignore the talk. But his reputation, livelihood - even his life - were in jeopardy. Since Garcia's inexplicable escape, he had to constantly be on guard against citizen insurrections. As soon as there was so much as a hint, he had to move to quell them. Countless times, he had had to calm vigilante violence with pleas for patience and respect for the memory of Wall and Williamson, two men who believed in order and lived their lives by example. Luckily, he had Roach, the town's leading citizen, to thank for stepping up to his defense in the face of the mob and imploring the town folks to give the sheriff time to get his man, to give the law one more chance.

When that opportunity might come, he had no idea. And since he had no idea, Keating had too much time on his hands to rehash over and over again the escape and pursuit of Garcia. Did he not have a choice but to turn back and give up pursuing Garcia into the mountains? Wouldn't anybody? Garcia knew the twisting trails high above more-traveled roads much better than he, much better than anyone. The lawmen hadn't even gotten a bead on Garcia, let alone seen any signs of his travels, even though they searched the mountains well into the following evening. And this is where Keating preferred to let the issue lie. He had tried. He had done everything he could.

By the time he returned to Monterey on that fateful day, every resident had heard about how the fearless lone bandit had escaped from a cabin surrounded by eight well-armed lawmen. Three of those men were now dead, yet their enemy - a single man - was unscathed and on the run.

The sheriff was desperate. He knew that few lawmen get a second chance. And in his desperation he came up with a new plan of attack. Slowly his thoughts turned away from what had happened at El Tuche and started to wrap themselves around this new idea, this new plot.

Keating dispensed of the town's vicious talk in his mind so it would not get in the way of his evolving strategy to capture Anastacio Garcia. Let the mobs think he was floundering in self-doubt without a clue as to how to bring the notorious resident to justice – if he stayed true to this new plan and kept faith in his ability to get the job done, Garcia would be jailed before springtime. And the sheriff's legacy would be sealed. He just needed patience.

Keating bet his life that the desperado would not return to Monterey. He also strongly believed Garcia would remain in territories untouched by his violent acts. Therefore, foremost, he took actions to ensure the killer would not strike again.

Keating telegraphed authorities in Fresno, Tulare, San Luis Obispo and Los Angeles descriptions of the outlaw and his most outrageous crimes and asked them to keep a careful watch. Next, he staged deputies near the roads in and out of El Tuche and informed every merchant in Monterey to keep an eye out for Garcia's wife, who might visit town to get some food and supplies for her husband. Indeed, that was why he did not arrest Lupe, even though he was positive she had in some way abetted her husband during the gun battle. It was one act he had gotten right. Her actions from here on out might give him clues to the fugitive's next move.

The Christmas season passed and weeks went by without any sign or word of Garcia or his wife. Threats to remove the sheriff from office grew even louder in the new year. With his new plan hatched, Keating remained stoic and confident and, miraculously, in a job.

He caught a break in the second week in January. Five bundled figures – an adult carrying an infant and three young children in descending order of height crossed the bridge over the estuary, turned toward the bay on Alvarado Street, passed the large two-story adobe that stored U.S. military supplies and soon arrived at the Pacific Coast Shipping Company office.

The agent at the window recognized the cousin of Tiburcio Vasquez and wife of Anastacio Garcia. Like everyone, he too had heard about the battle at El Tuche. He looked at Lupe's right hand, which was stiff and covered with a glove as he handed her four tickets.

"Here you go, Mrs. Garcia," the agent said, trying to remain focused on the business at hand. His heart was beating fast. He so desperately wanted to run to tell the sheriff. "Passage for four on the steamer for the port of San Pedro."

Lupe gave the man the exact fare in silver dollars. She used her left hand.

"The ship will anchor here in four days for you to board," he said with a smile. "Where is your final destination?"

"Mexico," Lupe answered quietly. "I am leaving California forever with my four children and am going to live with relatives in Mexico. I think it's the best thing for us. All things considered."

"I wish you the best, señora."

The agent watched the family cross back over the bridge and then closed his ticket window and hurried down the street. He found Keating at his office with his head in his hands.

"Perhaps this will cheer you, Sheriff. I just sold Lupe Garcia passage on the Yerba Buena. It will anchor here in four days and then travel south. She said she is leaving California forever with her children to live in Mexico."

"Where is the steamer's final port of call?"

"San Pedro."

"She will lead us to Garcia," Keating stated as an indisputable fact. "Thank you, sir."

Before the agent closed the door, Keating added sternly: "And please don't tell anybody else about this episode."

Alone once again, Keating raised his arms in triumph. He felt exceedingly self-assured. But he reminded himself that his task, the most important one of his life, was not finished. Who should he send on that ship to follow Lupe, he pondered. He could not send one of his deputies. Garcia might meet the ship in San Pedro and recognize one of his men. Even Lupe might become suspicious if a lawman was aboard. He needed someone who would never be suspected. Someone less rugged, less intimidating, less authoritative than any lawman or member of a posse. Yet, someone who could be trusted and willing to get the job done at any cost.

"I know!" Keating declared aloud. "That school teacher. He's perfect."

He had little time to spare. Keating immediately dispatched a deputy to San Juan Bautista to find that adventurous teacher, Tom Clay.

Chapter 14: Voyage
Destination: San Pedro
January 1857

"Here we are again, Tom," Keating said, sitting across from the school teacher. "Why are you interested in this escapade? We are talking about pursuing a cold-blooded murderer."

"It's all those spy novels, I suppose," Clay said. "They've sparked my inner adventurer."

"I see. Well, as I told you, we need to escort you up to San Francisco tonight, where you will sail off on the Yerba Buena tomorrow. You understand everything? Befriend Lupe and find out whatever you can about her and her plans. She will be easy to spot from the photograph I gave you and her four children in tow. If she asks, you are a school teacher in San Francisco. Upon docking in San Pedro, get to the local authorities immediately. Don't do anything foolish on your own, Mr. Clay – no matter what you have read in those silly books of yours."

The ferry boat's arrival in Monterey Bay drew dozens of people to the docks. The modern, double-ended Yerba Buena was a thirteen-hundred-ton vessel, three hundred feet from bow to stern with twin smoke stacks and a blue and white hull that was twenty-one feet high to the wheelhouse. An open deckhouse wrapped around the boat and most of the lodgings as well as a saloon stood below. The incoming ship not only carried loved ones to and from the town, but also contained letter mail and large quantities of newspapers from San Francisco and the East Coast. The Yerba Buena was bringing news of the world to the sleepy harbor city.

A dozen people debarked the ferry, then a couple dozen more walked across the plank to board, the Garcia family among them.

Lupe Garcia did not join the wall of passengers at the rail waving goodbye to loved ones until long after the anchor had been pulled up. She sat back on the cabin deck and watched the Monterey Peninsula shrink smaller and smaller until it was just a dot. Lupe then gathered her four children and told the two older ones they had to carry their own suitcases to their cabin. Lupe hoisted little Rosa into her arms and picked up her large bag.

At the stairs, however, she lost her footing and stumbled, dropping her luggage. The bag cracked open and garments and stationery spilled out. A watchful Tom Clay scrambled to help. He awkwardly introduced himself as he bent on one knee gathering up Lupe's things and securely shutting the valise. After insisting on carrying her luggage to their cabin door, he dismissed himself cordially, saying he hoped to meet again.

Later that evening, they did. The family and Clay chatted on the chilly deck.

"To where are you traveling?" he asked.

"Los Angeles."

"Oh, I know the pueblo very well. I taught school there for two years when I first arrived in California from Texas."

"That must have been wonderful. I have not been there for a very long time. Perhaps you can point me in the right direction when we get there."

"Certainly. So you are not continuing to Mexico?"

"No. I am meeting someone in Sonora and they are to take me to La Brea Rancho. That's where my husband is."

"It would be my pleasure to help you secure a coach to Sonora as soon as we dock in San Pedro."

Lupe looked away, out into the black sea.

"I can't help noticing you are a little melancholy," Clay asked. "I hope I am not being meddlesome, but I like to help people if I can. Is there anything I can do?"

"No. It's just that, well, I am leaving a family home that I have loved for many years for a life of uncertainty. I will never see El Tuche, my home, again. I had so many dreams for our family there."

"I know the feeling. When I left Texas, I wasn't certain that I was making the right move. But I told myself I was merely trading one set of dreams for another. You can do that, you know. After all, they are dreams. They can change."

She smiled at the thin, blond man, thinking of a safer life away from Sheriff Keating and a suspicious city.

"Some things can't change ..." She let her voice trail off into the night breeze.

Her older children were playing tag. Lupe's baby was a wrapped bundle held close to her bosom. Clay was immediately fond of the well-behaved, good-looking kids, who mostly shared Lupe's soft appearance, but his emotions were mixed. He suppressed an intense hatred that they were bred from that killer, Anastacio Garcia.

Clay wiped his oily hair at his temples.

"Why is your husband not accompanying you on this trip? If you don't mind my prying," he asked.

"Too busy getting our new home ready."

"What does he do to make a living?"

She hesitated, then stammered that he was a cattle rancher.

At that moment, Hector, the five-year-old, came hopping and limping up to his mother, tears in his eyes. He had fallen and scraped his hands on the deck. At the same time, Dominga, the three-year-old began complaining about how cold it was and how far they still had to go. As Clay watched, Lupe tried to no avail to offer solace to the children. Then he tried. He got the children's attention and produced two silver dollar pieces from his pocket and showed them to the children. Suddenly, he looked behind and all around. The coins were gone.

"They must have flown into the sea," he said, revealing his empty hands.

"Maybe you dropped them," the oldest by a year, Carlotta, suggested.

The children began looking around the deck.

"Wait, Dominga, I see a glimmering object in your ear."

Clay cupped his hand and magically grabbed a piece from her ears.

He did the same to Hector.

"Well, I am not completely sure these are mine, since they were found in your ears. Here, you keep them."

The children looked for approval from their mother.

"You are a good, new friend, Mr. Clay," Lupe said. "It makes me sad …"

"What does?"

"Oh, it seems I am either alone with children or around rough men. My world is either tough vaqueros or small kids. I haven't spoken to, oh, somebody like you, someone different, in a very long time. Someone gentle, like my cousin, Tiburcio."

"You say you have relatives in Mexico. Why don't you continue south and live with them?"

"And abandon my husband?"

"Well, no …" Clay hesitated.

He had nearly slipped. He reminded himself that he was here not to save her life, or even give her comfort, but to help catch a bandit and killer.

"I just hope your new dreams work out, that's all," he added.

They spent most of the next two days together during meals, walks on the deck and for games to pass the time. Then they came to San Pedro and it was time for Lupe, the children and their new friend Tom Clay to take one of the small passenger boats ashore. Reaching the dock, Clay helped the family get settled on dry land. He inconspicuously looked around for any sign of lawmen, but the dock was quiet. The Yerba Buena was the only ship to have anchored at the port in some time. Clay told Lupe he would go inside the customs building to arrange for transportation to Sonora.

He entered and ran into a posse of lawmen.

"Are you Tom Clay?" asked a burly man in a vest fastened only at the top button, a short necktie and a flat, wide-brimmed hat. A five-shot revolver was holstered at his side.

Clay looked over the seven other men with him, all with rifles, some with pocket watches, most with round, low-crowned hats. His eyes finally settled on the two hounds lying at their feet.

"Yes, I am."

"Were you able to chat with the greaser's soon-to-be widow?"

Clay filled with consternation over the sheriff's harsh tone.

"Please watch how you refer to her," he answered. "She's done nothing wrong."

"Ah. You took a fancy to the greaser's wife, did you?"

The sheriff looked at his men, who laughed.

"Li … Li.. Listen …" Clay stuttered.

"Sir," the sheriff boomed. "You have done your duty. We thank you. Now, tell us where we can find that son-of-a-bitch Garcia so we can hogtie him and ship him the hell out of our county so you northern boys can administer your justice."

All eight pairs of eyes bore into Clay, who felt much less important than any spy he had ever read about. He felt meager next to these lawmen, unarmed and no longer useful. Still, he mustered up the strength to convey what Keating had told him.

"Sheriff Keating asked me to tell you to proceed with extreme caution in approaching and apprehending Garcia. He is extremely dangerous, and is now believed to have dozens of trained bandits with him. He is sophisticated in surveillance and knowledgeable of this mountainous terrain. Furthermore, he has no remorse…"

"Does your sheriff think we're stupid down here?" the sheriff interrupted.

"He just wants you to know with whom you are dealing."

"OK, Mr. Clay. I have heard enough. The bandit and his men are not near. We checked that out. But I am sure he suspects someone might be tailing his wife. So, where is Mrs. Garcia going?"

"She has asked me to arrange a stage to Sonora. She is supposed to contact someone there and then go on to La Brea. Garcia has a forty-acre ranch somewhere up there and is expecting her arrival any day."

"We can't go into Sonora," the sheriff said. "That's strictly a Mexican town. We would stand out like George Washington himself among all the greasers. But if we let her vanish into those streets we'll lose her."

"Why doesn't Mr. Clay offer to drive her to Sonora?" suggested a deputy. "He could say there were no available drivers. We can make sure there are no drivers."

The sheriff mulled this plan over in his mind. Time was getting short.

"Does she trust you?" he asked Clay.

"Yes."

"Does she know the way to the ranch?"

"She has not been there for a very long time."

"Ok, we will take our chances. When you get back out there, Mr. Clay, you need to compose yourself, despite your obvious fondness for the soon-to-be widow."

"I resent your insinuation. Sheriff Keating chose me for this job, did he not?"

"He did, indeed," the sheriff responded, soliciting more chuckles from his posse, although the import was lost on Clay.

He continued, "You must talk her into getting on a wagon with you and driving straight to the ranch, not Sonora. Tell her you will be escorting her since no driver is available, and besides, none want to venture into Sonora. We will have the mules hitched and ready for the Garcia family on the other side of the building. Next to the stable. The ruse should put you right on the property and under the bastard's nose."

"Then what do I do?"

"Get back here and give us details on the trail - were there outlaws watching the road, are there any other houses or ranches along the way, how many armed men are at Garcia's gate and on his property? And pay attention to the exact directions to the ranch. Your information needs to be air-tight. We'll move in on him when the time is right."

Clay returned to Lupe and her children and told them the make-believe predicament.

"By the time we get to Sonora we could be halfway to La Brea," he explained.

"Anastacio really wanted me to go to Sonora first. But I suppose under the circumstances it's the best thing to do. I'm certain my husband will understand. I do hate to impose on you, though, Mr. Clay."

"Nonsense," he answered, gathering their baggage. "The wagon is all set, just around the corner."

"At least let me pay for the transportation, Mr. Clay," Lupe said.

"No, no, no. You may, however, invite me someday to a nice supper at the ranch."

With Lupe next to him up front and the children leaning on their valises in the back, the stage squeaked down the street and onto a rutted trail leading up into the brown hills beyond San Pedro. The sheriff and his deputies were nowhere in sight.

From the moment they left the dock, Clay felt sadness and emptiness deep in his stomach. He did not feel the sense of pride and accomplishment and justice he had thought he might when he left Monterey on his mission. There were too many loose ends. In fact, the mission was entirely unsettled and was even becoming more dangerous with every step the six mules took. If only there had been a quick arrest at the dock, he thought. Then he could have celebrated a job well done. Instead, as the wagon lumbered up the La Brea trail, he began wondering who would take care of Lupe and the innocent children once Garcia was handcuffed and hung.

From a hillside vantage point, the Los Angeles County sheriff watched the wagon begin its journey and thought about how that school teacher was either the bravest or the most idiotic man he had ever laid eyes on. Keating must have warned him how violent Garcia and his gang could be. In the two months since the Monterey sheriff's telegraph to other officers, there had been an unprecedented spate of cattle rustling and reports of savage robberies on the highway and at mercantile stores in the region.

The sheriff had only recently begun to get an understanding of how cohesive of an operation Garcia was running. The members of Garcia's gang dutifully carried out their orders and attacks with precision and in perfect unison. They seemed to have an elaborate checkpoint system monitoring all the trails leading to the La Brea ranch. And their numbers were growing right under the sheriff's nose. He suddenly regretted sending the naive school teacher into the lair.

In the weeks since Garcia had fled for his life from El Tuche, he, Tiburcio and Soto had reunited and were cleaning out local ranchers of horses and cattle. They had recruited dozens of bandits and were making a small fortune in the enterprise of selling ill-gotten property to any of several markets for a substantial price reduction. They were fast-becoming heroes in those quarters of Los Angeles solely occupied by residents of their own nationality. They could freely move about in these parts, spending lots of money in the saloons and stores and in turn receive important information about the activity of the sheriff and various stages. So it was with great surprise that Garcia's minions caught sight of the shabby, mule-driven wagon coming up the road with a gringo at the reins and a Mexican family aboard.

When Lupe's stage arrived in late afternoon, La Brea Rancho appeared to be a camp freshly deserted. Signs of recent activity were all around the property but not a soul could be seen or heard. Sunlight cut sideways through the trees but did not offer much warmth. The property stretched over forty acres along several miles of a bending creek. There was a main house, a kitchen shack attached to it, and even a bathhouse equipped with a spring-fed tank over a grate where the water could be heated. There was a shed for cows, a horse barn and fattening pens for hogs. Long rows of stalls and corrals stood in the back.

Someone had recently felled an oak and split the logs. Mist rose from the warm ax blade. A line of gray smoke wafted out of chimney. The pigs were in a state of agitation.

The wagon driver and its occupants stared into the quiet surroundings, each with their own thoughts. Lupe breathed deeply and happily and thought that it already felt like home. Clay breathed for what felt like the first time since departing the port. He had expected to encounter resistance from the outlaws somewhere along the trail but had not. It seemed odd that he had slipped all the way into the outlaws' headquarters without a hint of suspicion. Now he stood in the silent, eerie pall. He might have preferred to have encountered some of the gang to this stillness. But he had done his job. He knew the location and setup of the getaway.

He carried her bags to the door and she thanked him for getting her and the children safely up the mountain. He hesitated.

"I could stay around until your, uh, husband shows up."

"That's quite all right, Mr. Clay. Thank you, very much."

"Yes. I 'spose you'll be wanting to get settled in. It's been a great pleasure traveling with you."

The family watched their new friend leave from the porch, then walked in and found a small fire at the hearth and a kettle of soup warming. A black-hatted man with black, hair coiling down to his shoulders was sitting in a rocker in front of the fire with his back to the door. He was leaning forward, stirring the kettle. One hand gripped a whiskey bottle.

"Close the door, Hector," he said, without taking his eyes off the flames.

"Anastacio!"

Garcia stood and turned around. Lupe ran into his arms. The bandit hugged his children. He showed them their room and told them to go explore outside – within sight of the house.

Lupe watched her husband and noticed something unusual in his behavior.

Alone with Anastacio, Lupe looked closely at him. He was wild eyed and jittery.

"How did you get here?" he asked. "You were supposed to go to Sonora, where it would be safe until I received word of your arrival. How did you get here?"

"A young man, a nice schoolteacher from Texas who I met on the ship offered me a ride since there was no transportation to Sonora."

"I told you to speak to no one."

"He was harmless. You should have seen him."

"Here? To the ranch? This schoolteacher escorted you?" Garcia raged. "I told you to go to Sonora and not to talk to anyone until you got there!"

Garcia rushed outside and sprinted nearly an eighth-mile down the dirt road, Lupe following. But the wagon was out of sight. He stood a long while thinking in the middle of the trail in the woods. Branches crackled and leaves crunched. He drew his revolver and let out a bird call. Somebody returned the call and in a few moments several members of the bandit's band were standing next to him.

Lupe was out of breath when she reached her husband.

"Did you see that wagon?" he asked his men.

"Yes. Of course. We watched it the entire way. There was only one other person in it besides your family. He was unarmed and not suspicious."

"Was it being followed?"

"No."

"Are you certain?"

"Yes."

"Are we trailing it back down?"

"There are still men posted along the way, watching."

"Go kill the driver. Now! Bring me back the horses and the wagon."

"No!" cried Lupe.

TIBURCIO!

The three men who had started sprinting to the stable for horses stopped.

"He is an innocent man!" she protested.

"A couple months ago you saw eight gringos try to kill me," Garcia admonished. "You helped me escape. Why do you suddenly want to protect a white man?"

"I've seen too much maiming and killing. I want it all to stop," she cried. "He's an innocent man. Just a school teacher! A boring, quiet school teacher."

Garcia thought about this for a moment, then asked her: "Did he board the ship with you in Monterey?"

"No. He had already taken passage in San Francisco."

"Listen," Garcia shouted to the men. "Follow this gringo all the way down the mountain and everywhere he goes until he leaves Los Angeles. If he goes to the sheriff, or the sheriff approaches him, ride back immediately and inform me."

Two days later, Garcia left La Brea to rendezvous with Tiburcio and Soto. He found them at a designated spot as they were packing up camp under several wide live oaks. Tiburcio was a bit more lively this afternoon than his counterpart since it had been Soto's turn to spend the night wide awake watching for suspicious signs. A magpie was screeching loudly from a nearby tree.

"God almighty, I'll shoot that damn thing, if I get a look at it!" Soto exclaimed, unholstering his revolver.

His eye caught Tiburcio's glance.

"What are you staring at?"

"I … I've just been wanting to ask you ever since we held up that first stage how you can be such a dead shot … with that eye moving all about, and raising the gun up and down like you do. It's damnedest thing I've ever seen. It defies all logic. All that eye and hand movement."

Garcia descended upon them in the middle of their conversation.

"Don't you see, Tiburcio?" he interjected. "That damn, noisy bird - and you and me for that matter - isn't safe now that

Juan has drawn his weapon. Once he draws, you're as good as dead. Go ahead, Soto, show him. Shoot that magpie."

Soto raised his arm straight up, well above his target. Then he brought it down until the gun was level, and the bird directly in his sight, and fired. The magpie fell from the branch.

"He shoots like he's swinging an ax, raising his arm up and then down and then - whack - nails the target. I don't get it!"

"But he can't draw to save his life, Tiburcio," Garcia laughed. "Soto would not enjoy such a sterling reputation if he had to draw every time. Go ahead, Soto. Try to hit that bird over there with your gun holstered."

Soto rapidly drew but missed the bird by five feet.

As little sleep as Soto had, Garcia was in the worst shape of the three. Tiburcio and Soto quickly saw that he had finished a good share of an aguardiente bottle on the way down the hill.

"Are you finished packing up yet?" Garcia asked, tossing the empty bottle into some bushes. "Good. Then let's pay a visit to some of the finer establishments of Los Angeles. I have five more mouths to feed up at La Brea!"

"Five mouths?"

"Lupe and the kids showed up. Just like that."

"I thought we were meeting Lupe in Sonora," Soto said.

"It turns out that there was no stage willing to take her there, so she came straight to the ranch."

Tiburcio looked at Soto with alarm.

"Everything is fine," Garcia assured them. "Some schoolteacher took a fancy to her on the ship and drove the family up. We tried to trail him back down but lost him. It's not important. He was no threat."

"*Bueno*. So here's the plan, Anastacio," Tiburcio said. "We will split up in Sonora and familiarize ourselves with the streets. When we are finished, we will compare notes this evening by the camp fire. In the morning we will clean out the best businesses on the American side of town. We won't touch any Mexican establishments."

"I know the God damned plan, *puta*! I am in charge of this operation!"

"I just want to be certain we all are on the same page," Tiburcio explained impatiently. "Perhaps you should sleep off your journey. You are not fit to be seen on the streets."

"Listen, Tiburcio. I am our elected general. You are my lieutenant and will take orders from me. Do you understand?"

After a silent glare, Tiburcio realized there was no way to persuade Garcia to hold back. He changed the subject and asked how Lupe and the children were and whether they had arrived safely.

"They had an uneventful journey and are in good hands now," Garcia answered. "Let's get into town. I am thirsty!"

The three separated and moved from tavern to store, getting acquainted with other Mexicans and Indians. Two hours later, around 4:00 p.m., Soto and Vasquez casually met up on the street and looked up and down for Garcia so they could depart back to their camp.

An hour later, they still hadn't found Garcia. Visits to several general stores and saloons turned up nothing. About to give up waiting, Tiburcio grabbed Soto's arm and pointed in the distance. Garcia was staggering into a saloon on the American side of town.

They walked briskly in that direction to steer him out of trouble. When they were within five storefronts of the saloon, they saw a group of five officers hastily exit the Court House building ahead of them and cross the road. Tiburcio and Soto picked up their pace just behind the officers. They abruptly stopped when the officers entered the saloon. Tiburcio and Soto were paralyzed over what to do next.

As they stood outside, Soto tapping his holstered revolver with his hand, the officers came crashing out of the saloon, dragging Garcia. Garcia thrashed and cursed in their clutches as he was roughly pulled across the street and up the steps of the Court House to the jail inside.

"Christ!" Tiburcio exclaimed. "What do we do now?"

"We cannot risk our own lives," Soto said. "If we get caught, our whole band - and the revolution - is finished. We must hurry back to La Brea."

Soto was pushing and pulling Tiburcio, who had become incapacitated with doubt and fear, in a retreat down the street.

"We have been betrayed!" Soto said as they retreated down the street. "As soon as the sheriff hears Garcia has been arrested he will send an army up to La Brea. Lupe and the children are in immediate danger. So is everything we have accomplished so far. The people who have entrusted us to fight on their behalf, the scores of compadres up at Cantua, the Mexican ranchers who aid us - they will become disheartened, crushed if we fail now. Their faith in the revolution will dissolve. Come on, Tiburcio! We may have time to alert the men, gather Garcia's family and get the hell out!"

Chapter 15: Lynched
Monterey Jail
February 1857

Garcia's wrists and ankles were shackled and three deputies watched his every movement from the moment the iron jail door first clanged shut. Two days later, he was tossed on a steamship and hauled up to Monterey under close guard as word of his capture traveled quickly up the coast.

In Monterey, he was trailed by a bloodthirsty mob from the ship all the way to Monterey County jail, not a half block from Tiburcio Vasquez's family home. Guadalupe Vasquez had heard he was coming, but she stayed inside weeping and wondering if her son was next. Maria, now a teenager, took her familiar post in the pine tree overlooking the jail.

Garcia knew his fate was in the hands of the vigilantes. Lying sheetless on the bug-infested cot, Garcia shivered more from fear than from cold. No longer did two or three deputies watch over him. Only the jail registrar was on duty, and he remained outside the cell block. Every Monterey business shut down, and upstairs at Colton Hall an angry mob argued over what course justice should take.

"A fair trial, sentencing and execution would be the most beneficial outcome for our community and our young statehood," stated one of only a handful of people who shared this view. "Vindictive and swift vengeance by an illegal mob is for a less civilized era!"

"Hold your tongue," shouted another man, standing on a chair. "What if we cannot convict Garcia of the constable's murder or the death of Mr. Williamson? What kind of fuel would we be throwing on the simmering embers of revolution that we keep hearing of? What kind of example would we be setting for other thieving, murderous desperadoes? How could anyone in this county and surrounding communities feel safe from lawbreaking greasers and malcontents who refuse to become part of our new, vibrant and growing state?"

Another man in the minority shouted: "But do we have positive proof of his guilt?"

That set off an explosive rebuttal filled with vitriol.

"Nobody can doubt his guilt. He is a robber and an assassin. It's more than his profession. Murder is his nature!"

At that moment, Sheriff John Keating entered the room. All eyes turned to him and everyone was quiet.

"I am on my way to visit Anastacio Garcia. I will secure his waiver of a trial and will offer a priest, as my duties warrant."

There was a grumbling of approval. His mission clear, Keating exited. Below the great hall, he found the outlaw quietly sitting in his cell, knowing his fate was sealed. Nonetheless, Garcia opposed Keating and asked for a proper trial.

"None of your victims had a trial, Mr. Garcia," Keating told him from outside of the cell. "I'd say you are getting the better end of the deal. A chance for redemption in the eyes of God."

"Where are the guards, Keating? I have a right to protection! You must protect me!"

"I will send two guards with orders to protect you. But you better be prepared. There is nothing I can do to weaken the resolve of that mob. If they want to, they'll find a way to lynch you. Even some of our most respected citizens are in favor of a summary hanging."

Later that evening, two hundred dark, seething figures stood outside the jailhouse door. A guard sat on either side of the entrance. Looking into the face of the mob, the guards stood up, dropped the cell keys into the dirt and parted ways. A dozen of the most irate citizens kicked open the front door on the cell block and found themselves peering in at the prisoner.

A sinister smile from the prisoner greeted his peers.

TIBURCIO!

"So you've come to free me, eh?" Garcia shrugged in the darkness.

They unlocked the cell door and closed in around the Mexican. Garcia remained sitting calmly on his cot.

"We are not even going to honor you with a last breath of fresh air. You will die here in this cage, like an animal!"

One of the vigilantes pulled the looped end of a lariat over Garcia's head, allowing for a moment his thick black hair to fall over the rope. Several men savagely pushed him onto his back as others firmly bound the bandit's stocking feet to a heavy iron ring attached to the wall. Garcia mumbled something to himself and looked up at the ceiling. The vigilantes pulled the noose tight and in a heave of inhuman fury stretched the bound prisoner to his physical limit until his vertebrae snapped. On a pine tree branch above the jail, a young girl watched, listened and wept.

• • •

From Sonora, on the day Garcia was apprehended, Tiburcio and Soto stampeded up the mountain, calling all the sentries out of their hiding spots along the trail. Their haste stirred up the camp at La Brea. As they dismounted they were surrounded by two dozen men demanding to know what was happening. Lupe, in the distance, stepped out on the porch to listen. She scurried the children inside, although they still listened from the windows.

"Garcia has been captured and we can expect a massive raid by the sheriff at any moment," Tiburcio explained, now that he had regained his wits. "I do not fear Garcia betrayed our hiding place, but you can bet it has been compromised by someone, somewhere. The law will be coming to round up the rest of us. We have no choice but to flee or hunker down in a epic gun battle. And I do not believe the time has come for a last stand ... not yet."

He glanced at Lupe, whose face told of deceit and guilt and worry and disbelief. She had only wanted to put trust in another person.

"So, Juan and I will get Garcia's family to safety. The rest of you must leave in small groups, taking the side trails. Eventually, in perhaps two weeks or more, we will regroup up north at Cantua."

He looked over the group for any sign of disagreement.

"Let's get out of here. I will see you in a while. Make haste for Cantua."

Many men had already abandoned the ranch when Tiburcio sat Lupe down in front of the hearth where she had first seen Anastacio just a few days ago.

"The best place for you, Lupe, and the children is Mexico. Go stay with your family."

"And leave my husband to rot in jail?"

"I wish it weren't so, Lupe, but it's over."

"What do you mean, it's over?"

"Anastacio merely bought some time when he battled the law at El Tuche. He bought time to get his family away safely. He bought time to fuel the revolution. Now, he must await his fate. You must go to Mexico, while I will try to get back to Monterey to find out what kind of justice they will mete out. I will let you know in person or by letter what is happening in the court of law with Anastacio. But you must go as soon as possible. Your children depend on it. Anastacio would want this. He has told me so."

"I have no money. How am I going to get to Mexico?"

"Do not concern yourself with that. I will give you money. More than enough for you and your children's needs. But we have a long journey ahead. You will not be able to catch the steamer at San Pedro. We must go by land."

As he let this news settle uncomfortably, Tiburcio walked to the open window, where the massive Soto was packing the mules while the Garcia children flitted around below his waist, unaware that they would never see their father again and how far their mother was taking them.

"Juan," Tiburcio called. "How much longer?"

"We can depart in a half-hour."

"Make it twenty minutes. And don't let me forget my guitar in our haste."

They decided to drop down the steep back side of the mountain by pack mules via the deer and cattle trails. Once they reached the foothills, Tiburcio could furtively make his way into one of the inland pueblos and hire a guide to help them skirt the wintry mountains and stay on track through the deserts into Mexico.

The descent was difficult and longer than expected. It took two days to get four young ones, a mother and luggage down the mountain. After two more days, they found a horseman who knew the land and was willing, at a pretty price, to take a family and two men with secrets to hide two hundred miles across the border. They arrived in Mexicali in two weeks. Soto and Tiburcio escorted Lupe and her children to their family village.

Before departing, Tiburcio gave Lupe all of the money he possessed, about fifteen hundred dollars, and hugged her as if he would never let her go. When he finally did, he never looked back.

● ● ●

"We need money and food," Soto said.

It was the first time they had spoken in hours. The sun was setting on the other side of the San Diegueto River, orange and white clouds frozen in the sky. A fire burned between them in a pit surrounded by rocks. Tiburcio rested his boots on a boulder and his back against his saddle.

"Maybe I should go to Monterey. Maybe he needs us…"

"Shut up! Don't start making things up, Tiburcio! You know he's dead. I know he's dead. I'm certain the word has spread through towns. But Lupe is gone, and won't hear about it. We did everything we could."

"We didn't do anything."

"You saved his family."

"He would expect more."

"He would. He would expect you to be a river to his people, the ones who wait at Cantua. The ones relying on you. Let the riches flow to them and show them the way."

"I feel lost."

"Get your guitar. Play something."

Tiburcio walked over to his bed, picked up the twelve-string lying on the blanket and carried it back to the fire. Soto watched him lift the instrument by the neck with two hands over his head and bring it down on a large rock, smashing it again and again until he held only the head stock and a small piece of the neck.

"You will see her some day soon, Tiburcio," Soto said quietly.

They didn't speak about Anastacio, Lupe or Anita ever again. For the next six months they calculatedly raided cattle ranches, hoarding money and working their way north. They hit quickly and disappeared to hidden adobes scattered in the vast hills separating the valley from the ocean. Sometimes they sold the animals right away. Other times they paid someone to drive them up to Cantua so the cattle could feed until they were ready to sell or butcher. Cantua did not lack for meat or money.

On a dry mid-July day in 1857, the two bandits descended upon Luis Francisco's corral along the Santa Clara River and drove dozens of cows, nine horses and a mule off the land, leaving Francisco with just a few yearlings, colts and older mares. Little did they know that the patience of the law officers was about to pay off. Francisco's herd was being reconnoitered.

The bandits decided to get rid of the cattle quickly so they returned to Sonora for the first time since Garcia was captured.

They parked the herd at a friendly Spanish residence they knew and slipped into town to find a buyer. They were directed to a butcher who told them he was willing to buy the meat.

"We are compadres," Tiburcio told the butcher. "Sonora has always been friendly to us. That is why I will sell you the meat for a price of four hundred and thirty-five dollars."

"This is not the same place it was when you left, amigo," answered the butcher, an older man with tight but smooth mahogany skin and wrinkles just around the eyes and mouth.

"What is this riddle, man? I am trying to sell you some beef for a good price, and you insist on being insolent. Tell me what time you want me here, and I will be here."

"Noon, tomorrow."

That gave the lawmen barely enough time to get an arrest warrant. The next day, the sheriff shoved aside the butcher and placed a deputy in the back of the shop. Other deputies outside watched for the other bandit, Soto.

Just before noon, Tiburcio left Soto on the streets to signal if any trouble arose and approached the shop alone. Tiburcio looked up and down the street, saw nothing but normal activity, then entered.

"I have come to collect the money," Tiburcio announced to the butcher. "The herd is delivered at a spot where you can easily round them up to be slaughtered."

Tiburcio looked closely at the man's face.

"Are you nervous about something? I will not deceive you. You are a brother. So where is the money?"

"Come in the back. Away from the door in case my customers get suspicious."

As Tiburcio stepped one foot inside the back room, a deputy jabbed a pistol barrel into his forehead and told him to put his hands up. Tiburcio stared in disbelief at the deputy.

"You are mine, bandit."

Three days later, the judge looked at the handsome, well-dressed horse thief standing calmly in his courtroom. Tiburcio Vasquez had just pleaded guilty to grand larceny.

"The judgment of the court is that you, Tiburcio Vasquez, be imprisoned in the State Prison of the State of California, for a full term of five years, now ensuing from this day. You are remanded to the custody of the sheriff."

Chapter 16: San Quentin
Marin County
1859

Most of Doña Guadalupe's days were spent in darkness and grief. She had lost her restaurant and had moved out of Monterey. Now settled in San Juan Bautista, she sold Mexican food to teamsters hauling their loads from the New Idria mines. She raised enough money to buy a few gifts and afford travel to the prison north of San Francisco to visit her boy. She lived constantly fearful for the lives of Tiburcio and all the other unfortunate sons locked up among thieves and murderers and gamblers in that fortress of vice and crime. Kneeling and praying for all of them at her bedroom window in the moonlight is how she ended her long days.

Her only solace came in the long trips she made every two or three months to the gates of San Quentin to visit Tiburcio. Every time she let go of her son's hands and got up to leave the waiting room, she felt less apprehensive about his plight, and her spirits were lifted a little. It's how he wanted it. Mother and son talked mostly about ordinary subjects, news from Monterey and stories about their relatives. She always asked about his well-being. And he assured her she had nothing to fear.

"Don't you worry about me, mother. I am being treated very well," he lied, holding and caressing her hands. "Because of our family's position, they make sure I am taken care of. The food is pretty good. We work hard during the day, but the beds are comfortable and everything is quiet at night."

Guadalupe smiled and did not seem to notice the bleak surroundings, the shackles at her son's ankles, the number on his clothing and his long, gritty hair and neglected beard. She would not have gazed upon a saint any differently.

For Tiburcio, on the other hand, it was a good thing the visits were short. He could not have kept up the deception much longer; the hardening of his soul would have shown.

San Quentin was a brutal place. Tiburcio arrived just after the state government was forced to wrest control from a private contractor running the prison. The state was compelled to stop the outrageous treatment of inmates. But the prison guards' behavior was too ingrained. Abuses at their hands continued unabated. Gambling was rampant. Fights broke out frequently. Stealing carried on endlessly. The work - making bricks, chopping wood, or being hired out as a laborer to build roads and buildings, usually from sunup until sundown - was dangerously rigorous. The leg irons were heavy. The cells remained cold, dank, bug-infested, small and overcrowded. Disease spread frequently. Prisoner floggings did not cease. Killings were not uncommon. Inmates survived as they had always survived, by forming confederacies and obeying the hegemony behind the bars.

The state's reformers earnestly tried to carry out their ideals of rehabilitation. They attempted to eradicate idleness through hard work. But inside the stone walls of San Quentin, the prisoners, when they had time to themselves, did everything in their power to thwart prison officials' designs and evade penitentiary discipline. Locked together tightly, they shared criminal customs and secrets.

"If we give them the habits of industry," the prison warden said in a speech to state legislators in Sacramento, "they will overcome the indolence that led them to their lives of crimes in the first place."

For some prisoners, such "habits of industry" meant illicitly manufacturing alcohol and clothing and weapons for trade. Bartering was alive and well within the prison walls. The liquor, the cons soon discovered, could be used to bribe some guards into time off from work or protection. These were the prisoners' habits of industry.

TIBURCIO!

As Tiburcio observed from his first week of incarceration, however, the majority of the prisoners were not nearly shrewd or smart enough to profit from such ingenuity. This was left to just a couple dozen men. For every one educated prisoner, twenty-five were ignorant or simply lacked the ability to think independently. While the policymakers liked these odds and believed the dangerous, intelligent thinkers would sooner or later be dominated by the brutes, in reality the opposite occurred.

The majority of Tiburcio's fellow convicts were Mexican, and most of them rough, bitter and homicidal. They answered to some of the most feared names among Californians: Carabajal. Red-Handed Dick. Juan Soto. Ramon Molina. Ramon Romero. Eduardo Gallegos. Yet it was Tiburcio - forever linked as the close associate of Anastacio Garcia - who saw his status rise quickly among the inmates. He was superiorly educated, charming, seemingly fearless, and enjoyed by association a reputation of being a brutal outlaw and defender of his people. He gambled with the best of them and took their money. Yet, their losses came back to them in one form or another as Tiburcio gave away the gifts and the goods his mother and sister brought on their prison visits; or he might write love notes to the wives and girlfriends of these illiterate thugs. In addition, he took the prison population's demands for extra privileges - longer visitations, more recreational time, pens, ink, paper, newspapers and books - to the authorities. Sometimes he even succeeded.

He gave the ignorant brutes encouragement that life would improve once they were freed. He tirelessly preached that revolution was at hand, slowly rolling and gaining energy like a gigantic wave approaching shore. For those whose prison terms seemingly would never end, Tiburcio assured each one of them that they would not have to serve the length of their sentences, if they trusted him. He kept his eyes open for an opportunity to escape.

That opportunity came a day after his mother's last visit.

Tiburcio had noticed that the gate where the inmates re-entered the prison after working in the brickyard was obscured from the heavily armed guard towers. The lower guard post jutted out from the high, thick wall, but as they walked past the gatekeeper's shack below, none of the gun-toting watch guards could see them.

Nearly forty inmates limped back from their hard shift at the brickyard that day. Tiburcio was in the middle of the pack. The group clogged up near the wall, as they always did, waiting for the gatekeeper, John Spell, to open the barrier. Two guards stood at the back of the gang of prisoners and another one on each side toward the middle of the pack. When Spell turned his back to the wall of inmates to open the gate, Tiburcio stole a glance at the watch tower to make certain, for the hundredth time, that no guards could see him. He could not see the guards in the back on the line or those on the side so he knew they couldn't see him either. In an instant, he slammed Spell into the solid iron gate. Another con punched Spell in the kidneys while a third pressed Spell's arm up high on the gate and pulled his fingers back until they snapped and he dropped the key. There was a rumbling on the other side of the gate as the guards wondered why the portal hadn't opened yet.

Tiburcio tossed the prison keys away and yelled for the inmates to make a break. The mass of prisoners overpowered the guards to the rear, trampling them. Prisoners scattered in all directions. Looking down on the fleeing mass, the tower guards opened fire . A man next to Tiburcio screamed in agony and fell to the ground. In step with Tiburcio was another inmate, Jesus Mendoza.

Some of the guards outside the prison walls seized several inmates quickly. But there were simply too many convicts running in too many directions to apprehend all of them. Their freedom was a matter of chance now. A dozen were pursued into the foothills at the base of Mount Tamalpais.

Tiburcio and Mendoza fled to the waterfront and slipped into the icy bay. They slogged in the shallow water along the narrow shoreline until they were about three hundred yards south of the prison. Tiburcio asked Mendoza if he could swim. Yes, he answered.

"That's a good thing," Tiburcio replied.

He motioned for him to follow as they glided out toward an abandoned boat.

"What do we do now?" Mendoza asked as they lay prone on the shabby hull.

"We wait here and pray the guards overlooked us. At dark, when things have quieted, we will paddle toward San Francisco Bay."

And that's what they did. In the morning, they reached the tip of Marin, where there was another matter of business to take care of. Tiburcio entered a small shop owned by a Mexican, a distant relative of Anastacio Garcia.

"We need clothes," he told the merchant.

"I do not sell clothes."

"Good. Because I have no money. But we need clothes."

"No money. Definitely no clothes."

"I am a liberator. Sent by Anastacio Garcia, the husband of my cousin. I will repay you many times the amount of any articles with which you can part."

"Why didn't you say so? Let me see what I have in the back."

The merchant's eyes darted around the shop as he hustled Tiburcio away.

After changing their attire, they snuck on the ferry and crossed San Francisco Bay. It was easy to steal two horses in the big city. They escaped into Contra Costa County, riding a winding trail among oaks and manzanitas and through buckeye and poison oak. They went around hills, across ravines and up steep ascents. They came to some rolling hills with spots of clover untouched by cattle.

"This is where we must split up," Tiburcio told his companion. Mendoza looked at him with surprise. "I will meet you in three weeks in Jackson, in Amador County."

"What will you do?"

"I must find someone."

"I understand. Does she live around here?"

Tiburcio smiled.

"Close, my friend. Very close. Her father is a wealthy ranchero who moved up to these parts from Salinas. He bought some vast land somewhere around Livermore."

Mendoza looked over the sparse rolling land.

"Good luck finding your lover. I will see you in Jackson!"

Tiburcio rode alone along a cattle trail on the fringe of Mount Diablo. The air was hot and dusty. He and his horse needed a taste of cool water, so he started down the rocky descent. Suddenly, his horse stumbled and fell, and Tiburcio tumbled out of the saddle, falling hard and awkwardly on his shoulder. His head struck the mountain's bedrock. The horse galloped out of sight and Tiburcio lay momentarily unconscious on his back. When his head cleared, he tried to get up but fell back down, because the pain in his shoulder and around the collarbone was so strong and deep it took his breath away, and when he moved he felt nauseous.

"I'm sure a mountain lion will find me before a man does," he thought after a half-hour of not moving in the sun.

He was wrong. A rancher and his foreman came riding up on beautiful horses of dapple-gray and chestnut. They were dumbstruck at what they saw. Sitting high in the saddle over Tiburcio, they looked down and asked him his name in Spanish.

"Rafael Moreno," Tiburcio answered.

The rancher was a distinguished-looking older man, slightly graying, thin-faced and wearing a gold watch and chain even out in the wild. He was dressed well for riding in a short graceful embroidered jacket, trousers snug in the seat and high *botas*. He carried a musket and a tinderbox.

"Tell me, *cojo*, what are you doing on my land?"

"I am traveling from Mexico across California," the injured trespasser said, squinting up at his new companions, the older of whom now looked very familiar.

"You don't look like you're doing much traveling," the rancher said.

As they looked down upon him, Tiburcio didn't realize what an astounding sight he must be to eyes used to seeing nothing but rolling land, herds of mustangs and cattle. He had lost a lot of weight in prison, enough to be considered *muy delgado*. But his hair had grown amply: a thick bush on top of a rail-thin body. His well-groomed goatee now a full, ragged beard, he looked much older than he did five years ago.

"My horse threw me and I fear I have injured my shoulder. I can't move it without severe pain. And it hurts to breathe."

"It is critical to have a good horse. Nevertheless, Señor Moreno, you are lucky. My adobe is nearby. I can get a doctor by this evening. First we'll fetch a *carreta*. At the house, we will get you a hot bath and a shave. Perhaps when you are healthier, in a week or two, we can find you a better horse and you can continue on your way. Where were you going, anyway?"

"Amador County."

It was mid-afternoon by the time the ranch owner got the cart, with Tiburcio sitting in the back feeling every bump, and four hands alongside in saddles, to his hacienda. It was Friday, and, like most days around the ranch, the hours had been uneventful. Then came the news of the wounded traveler. The rancher's daughter, a slim girl of eighteen years with black eyes and wavy hair, stood on the broad porch and watched the *carreta* slowly make its way. She could not see the man who was the cause of all the excitement.

"How dreadfully boring it is around here that the simple arrival of an injured Mexican traveler sparks such great interest," she said to her mother.

"When you are married in a few weeks and living in your own adobe and keeping up your own home, you will find new meaning in life. And then there will be children to keep you busy."

"It's drudgery now. It will be drudgery then," she said.

"Then you won't mind going to your room when they arrive. The guest may need some privacy, and not want a lot of strangers milling about."

"Mother, I am eighteen years old. I do not have to go to my room!"

"Perhaps not. But do not interfere."

The daughter slipped inside and watched the activity through the window sash. She could now see the traveler protesting at one of the ranch worker's offer to lend him a hand. The traveler - she could already see he was full of himself - insisted on debarking the cart without anyone's help and walking unassisted on his own two legs. He stood and took some steps with an air of confidence, although he was supporting his right shoulder by holding his elbow with his other hand. His shirt sleeve had been torn off and his shoulder was bandaged to his body. He slowly walked toward the colonnaded front porch and up the stairs. Then, for the first time, he looked up. Anita turned pale and let the sash fall and turned away. She had seen his clear, lively light-gray eyes.

"It can't be!" she panted.

"*Que? Caro?*" her mother asked. "You look like you've seen a ghost."

"Nothing, Mother. I will be in my room if you need me."

Anita went directly to her chest of drawers and pulled out the Daguerreotype that she had kept for the past four years. She ran her fingers along the familiar features of the man in the picture and slipped it back under her sashes and undergarments next to several fading letters.

The main house on the rancho was five thousand square feet with a dining room, study, parlor, kitchen and eight bedrooms. Tiburcio was guided into the parlor and told to sit in a brocaded chair that looked out over the porch and held commanding views of the land. The house was lavishly furnished, including an inlaid mahogany piano imported from Europe. The walls displayed several oil paintings and family portraits. A polished crystal chandelier hanging overhead brightened the room without a single candle on it being lit.

"Did you not have any bags for traveling?" Señor Constanza asked his guest.

"My sorry horse took off with all my possessions."

"I see. Well, I have sent a worker to summon the nearest doctor. In the meantime, I have the bath being filled with warm water. You may sit in there a while."

"I am sorry to be an inconvenience."

"Nonsense. Out here along the Stockton Road, we are often an overnight stopping place for travelers on their way to San Jose and San Francisco. We are used to company. I just don't usually find them lying flat on their backs on the outer reaches of my land."

Tiburcio laughed, then groaned from the pain.

"I will stop talking," Constanza said. "But when you are feeling better I would like to hear about your travels and from where you are coming."

Less than seventy-two hours after breaking out of prison, and for the first time in two years, Tiburcio was clean-shaven on his neck and cheeks, well-fed and lying on a soft bed. The physician had come and gone and Tiburcio was trying to avoid talking to anyone - it could only lead to suspicions. Instead, he focused on what he had begun to realize. This was Anita's home, or at least it was her father's. Tiburcio had sent her a dozen letters from different towns across the state, but he wasn't sure if they had ever reached her or if she had simply ignored them. She may have gotten married by now. She may have started a new life, on a new ranch, with her own family.

But if she were still here … he could not believe his luck. He had wondered many times over the past year how he would approach her house, who he would encounter there, what he would say, how he would feel. It had been providence that he was bucked off that horse and was now lying in comfort possibly under the same roof as his lover.

Tiburcio might have dozed off in his reverie under the satin sheets if he hadn't heard a young woman's voice in the parlor off the bedroom. It was late evening. The voice was familiar.

"Who is he?" the young woman asked her mother. "Are you sure he is just some traveler?"

"Quiet. Father told you not to disturb the guest."

"Then I will go out on the porch and ask father."

"You have been quite agitated since our guest arrived. Are you all right?"

"Did the stranger get his hair cut?"

"What kind of question is that?"

"It doesn't matter. I am just making conversation."

"Yes, Beatrice trimmed his hair and beard after his bath. Father insisted on it if the man is going to be traveling again."

"Will he be leaving soon?"

"I suspect in a week."

"What is wrong with him?"

"His shoulder is injured. He also suffered a bad blow to the skull and may have bruised or cracked a rib and possibly his collarbone."

"Does he have a name?"

"Rafael."

Tiburcio recognized the voice. He smiled into the dark and slept without stirring for the next twelve hours.

In the morning the house and its outside gardens were hushed, except for the sounds of birds and one young admirer. Anita was spending time in the flower garden next to the hacienda, smelling the Castilian roses and examining the hollyhocks, white lilies and nasturtiums. The quiet of the garden was good for her restless soul. She hadn't slept despite the strain of affecting that she was as bored as always and was not intensely interested in their guest. She had stayed up late reading his letters by candlelight. The morning breeze in the garden was very slight but inside her head chaos swirled like the wind.

Her meanderings had taken her behind the room where Tiburcio was staying. The room had a small, uncovered window just above her. She could not reach it even on the tips of her toes. But she heard the slow, divine strumming of an old guitar that was stored in the guest room. His fingers had not lost their passionate touch on the strings. She sighed and her back fell against the wall just when she heard her name being called from the front of the hacienda.

When Tiburcio heard the call he stopped playing. He cracked the door open and peered out. The front door to the house was ajar and he could see some type of departure taking place at the porch. Servants were loading a wagon and people were hugging. He prayed Anita was not leaving.

He heard her mother and father giving orders to servants and then saying farewell. Their voices sounded somber and he caught snippets of an argument between father and daughter. He stepped out of the room to get a better view and saw the horses and wagon departing. Anita was half-heartedly waving good-bye from the porch.

Then, fear set in. Were they leaving to alert the sheriff that they had a runaway under their roof? Had they tracked down his horse and learned that it was stolen and he had no traveling bags? Even if they were just going into the city to get food and supplies, they would certainly hear the news that there had been a breakout and some inmates were still on the run.

"You should be happy, Anita," a house servant said as she and the daughter walked inside. "Your parents are going to talk to the mission priests to make the last arrangements. There is not a better, richer man in all of Contra Costa."

Hearing this, Tiburcio snuck back into his room. He eased back into the bed and sat against the bed board. He pondered his next move for a long time until there was a soft knock at the bedroom door. The door opened and Anita stepped inside. She held a tray in her hands.

She shut the door with her back and leaned against it. They stared at each other a long time before saying anything. Anita spoke first.

"I brought you breakfast, Rafael."

"I am not Rafael."

"Sure you are. I heard you playing the guitar, and I knew beyond a doubt it was you."

"I was having trouble playing. My shoulder … It wasn't very good, I'm afraid."

Anita took a deep breath and came over to the bedside. She placed the tray on the night stand and looked closely at him.

"You look better," she said, smiling.

"I have had a shave, a long sleep and some hot food," he answered.

Her hand grasped his lower arm.

"I knew it was you the moment I saw your eyes," she said quickly as if trying to get it out in one short breath. "But tell me, is this a miracle that you fell off your horse practically at my doorstep? Or were you trying to find me?"

"I was looking for you. I have been trying to get back to you for four years. "

"It is about time. It is almost too late."

"Too late?"

"My father and my suitor have just left to finalize our wedding plans. There is a lot involved, especially on the business side. I am to wed a very wealthy landowner. An American."

His chest tightened.

"Do you love him?"

She knelt at his knee and began crying. He stroked her soft and gorgeous black hair in one hand and held her other hand in his. She looked up.

"Tiburcio," she blurted. "You were not supposed to leave me for so long."

"It was not supposed to be this way. So much has happened that was not supposed to happen. So much has turned out wrong. But I have not changed, Anita. Even though I have been most cruelly treated. Even though I feel I was born on this earth just to suffer. I have not changed. Yet, so much around me has changed."

"Can it be the same, Tiburcio? The same between you and me?"

"I don't know. I do not want you to suffer, too, Anita. I did not come here expecting your companionship, even though to spend the rest of my days with you is my deepest desire. I came to tell you I am sorry for the life I must lead. I have no choice anymore. I have been imprisoned and beaten and so loaded down with iron that it would make you weep. And for what? One unfortunate incident four years ago.

"Still, if the manhunts, the chains, the beatings were all the suffering I would have to endure, I would still be the happiest man on earth. But to suffer without the sight of your beautiful eyes or the touch of your soft hands and cheeks or the sound of your gentle laugh - that is too much for even me to handle. I have prayed to the Supreme Being that you will somehow not forget me or my promise to make you the happiest woman in California. I can still do that. I beseeched God to somehow make the years seem like seconds in your mind so that I would not lose you. I was afraid of His answer. I broke through a prison wall just to see you one more time."

"I know what life is like here, without you, Tiburcio. I do not like it. Tell me what life will be like with you."

"We will be wealthy, but we will give most of our riches back to our people. We will stay in the finest hotels, but we will be free from any walls that could bind us. We will be alone, sometimes with just each other to hold, but we will have many admirers and we will feel the people's respect everywhere we go. We will be loved - but, unfortunately, hated by many, too. Most of all, Anita, we will not be afraid of dying because we will have learned to live without regret, and for the greatest reason. And with each other."

Anita leaned toward him, their eyes dancing inches apart, and said: "There have been times, Tiburcio, that I have wanted to give up. I have told myself again and again that now is the time to move on so that I might enjoy a moment in the present. But it was always too difficult. Your letters would come every now and then and I would burst open like a lily. Then I would close and fade again. Now I am nearly taken, and my life will be comfortable, safe and serene. My mother and father will be happy and rich beyond imagination. And I? I will pay with my soul."

"But you cannot leave here with me, Anita. You asked me what life will be like: in the end, there will be torment."

"Never! Not if we are together!"

"I am an outlaw, Anita. I cannot go back. I can only go deeper to the other side. I must save my fellow countrymen from the anguish I have met. Even if it means I will die."

"What you are willing to fight for is what forced us apart. I hate the way the land, the people and our lives have changed, Tiburcio. Don't leave me here!"

She looked down and wept. When she looked up again, their lips neared, hesitated, touched and lingered. Tiburcio lunged to embrace her and cried in pain. Anita jumped back. Then they both laughed.

After drying their eyes, they talked about mundane things, such as their childhood, school days and Anita's daily life around the ranch, and how the small gardens are all hers to care for. Well past the time it would have been considered safe to remain in a traveling guest's room, Anita stood to leave.

"So, you will come with me?" Tiburcio inquired.

"Yes. Next Sunday. It's always quiet here on Sunday. And very predictable. Father and mother will likely go into town."

"Remember, until then, I am Rafael Moreno. I will communicate through letters under your pillow, OK?"

She smiled and skipped out of the room into the curious stares of the servants. She was thankful her younger sisters had all married before her and had long been out of the house. They could never understand thoughts of eloping.

The Constanzas returned to the hacienda in late evening. Supper had been put on hold until their return, but now Señor and Señora Constanza, the ranch foreman, Anita and Tiburcio sat at the long mahogany table and talked about the trip into town.

"We heard news of a breakout at San Quentin," Constanza told them. "It seems the prisons are not run any better under the state's jurisdiction than by private enterprise."

"How many escaped?" Tiburcio asked.

Anita stared at him in horror. He was calm, picking apart a pheasant bone in search of meat.

"There were three dozen inmates who fled the prison grounds. Several were shot instantly. They captured about twenty at the base of Mount Tamalpais. Two are still at large."

"Do they know where they are roaming?" the foreman asked.

"The sheriff asked us if we've seen anybody ..."

Anita choked on a drink of water and coughed wildly. When she had been calmed, Constanza continued.

"I told him we've only seen a lone traveler from Mexico but he is welcome to come look around the property."

"Will he?" Tiburcio inquired, trying to make the words not appear to be caught in his constricted throat.

"He believes the men have split up and have journeyed much farther than these parts by now. Regardless, he is coming to look around the property the day after tomorrow. You may accompany us, Rafael, on the ride-along."

"In Mexico," Tiburcio quickly added, with a hearty gulp of red wine, "we don't have prison breaks. The threat of death is enough. They need to teach outlaws here a little more fear, I think."

"Apparently so," Constanza replied.

That night, Anita found a note under her pillow. It detailed their escape. Tiburcio wrote that they must depart in the middle of the night. He had stolen a loaded rifle and pistol from her father and stashed it outside the property in a citrus grove. He had appraised Anita's father's prized stallions on his walks around the ranch and knew which ones he would take. They'd have to ride bareback. Tiburcio could not go to Anita's room to get her. The wooden floor of the hacienda creaked too much and everyone's sleeping quarters were too close for any privacy. The only way was to call to her from outside her window.

Anita went to bed in her nightgown but changed under the covers into an old dress and laced leather ankle boots. She waited under her bedsheets for his prearranged signal. When she heard the bird call, she tossed off the covers and threw open the window. Tiburcio held her waist as she dropped from the window to the ground. Then he clutched her hand as they dashed around the back of the house to the stable. As he was about to mount one of the horses, he saw Anita staring blankly at him.

"What's wrong?" he asked.

"These are not the best horses father owns. We'll be at a disadvantage if we're pursued."

"Sure, they are. I looked them over myself. Let's go."

"No, they aren't."

"Well, they'll have to do," he replied impatiently. "They seem to be fine stallions. Jump on. I need to grab the guns at the ravine."

"Guns?"

"Don't be naïve, Anita. We don't exactly have the blessing of your father, the Church or the State of California on the matter. There may be trouble."

As they rode off the property, a servant stepped away from the outhouse. He saw movement in the dark and watched two figures on horseback stop for a brief moment near the road to pick something up and then gallop south toward Livermore. Walking back to the servants quarters, he thought about this sight. Just before entering the house, he had the intuition to go check the stable. The gate was open and at least two animals were gone. His hunch was correct. Horse thieves.

The servant ran to the main house and knocked at the porch door. The housekeeper answered after what seemed to be a very long time.

"I must talk to Señor."

"What's wrong?"

"Bandits!"

Soon the house came alive. Servants lit candles and one by one the family emerged from their rooms. As Señor Cervantes grabbed his rifle and started out the door, he stopped. Two doors were still closed despite the commotion. Everyone followed his eyes.

"Anita!" he called.

No answer.

"Rafael!"

No answer.

He marched to Anita's door and turned the knob, but it was locked. He pounded. Then he stepped back and aimed his muzzle at the door.

"Stop!" the housekeeper yelled, running over with a ring of keys held up in her hands.

The door flew open. The bed was empty. The window open.

" *Mi Dio*! She's been kidnapped by the traveler. I need two more men, Arturo! Quickly. Meet me at the private stable."

Constanza and Arturo stood in front of the private stable. Arturo tossed open the large wood doors. Two massive stallions, dapple-gray and chestnut, stood bridled and saddled in a pair of large stalls.

"Our guest didn't know we had these animals, did he?" Constanza proclaimed, with a confident smile. Indeed, Tiburcio had thought the stable was a small chapel by its appearance and never thought to look inside. "We can catch up to them before sunrise."

They vaulted into the saddles and rode to the other stable to give directions to the other pair of riders, one of them a superb game tracker. Then they whipped the reins and bolted into the night in pursuit of the elopers.

Tiburcio and Anita skirted Livermore to the north and rode east for most of the early morning hours. Before daybreak their horses were exhausted, but they had reached well into the Sunol valley. Tiburcio guided them along the bed of a shallow stream where the sycamores, willows and alder bushes were thick enough to hide amongst. The stream wound downhill through the arroyo for several miles until it fed into the larger Calavaras Creek. This would be their route.

"I am fatigued, Tiburcio," Anita told him.

He halted the horses and looked around.

"We are shielded. We can rest. It's not quite daylight so I doubt they have had time to realize we are gone."

He unsaddled the horses and picketed them where they could eat. He rolled out a blanket and prepared a meal of bread, meat and some milk. When they finished eating he suggested she get a little sleep. But she did not want to close her eyes. They embraced and made love as wildly as their mad dash from the ranch. Afterward, Anita dozed off.

But her awakening was startling, frightening. Tiburcio swept her off the ground and tossed her onto his horse's flank. She held his waist tightly and leaned forward with him. They cantered in and out of the sycamore and willows, bowing their heads to avoid plunging branches. He soon found a clear opening into a V-shaped valley and picked up the pace.

He kept thinking how thunderstruck he had been when he heard Don Constanza yell his daughter's name just as morning light was breaking. How did they find them? He was somewhat thankful, too, for at least her father's shouts had given him a chance to mount and escape. Now, flabbergasted again, he heard more shouting and the calling of Anita.

"How are they keeping up?" he shouted.

"It's the horses I told you about. We should have taken those," Anita screamed back over the din of the chase.

Judging from the echo, Tiburcio guessed Constanza and his men were no more than one hundred yards to the north. He spurred his tired horse as fast as it could run. He glanced back and spied four riders on splendid, massive stallions coming up from behind. The pursuers took to the hurst above and to the right so he galloped up the bank to the left.

A fifty-yard-wide chasm and a large tangle of trees provided the only barrier between the riders. There were no clear trails ahead and little solid ground. Tiburcio cursed under his breath at his laboring horse, which was slowing with every step. He hated to alarm Anita, but he pulled a revolver out of his waistband.

Tiburcio fled down the bank where the landscape turned flat and opened up for a few hundred feet. He violently kicked the horse's side and gained a little more swiftness from the animal. It wouldn't be enough. He stole a look behind and saw two of the riders gaining ground.

"Anita?" he shouted. "Are you all right?"

"Yes."

"Hold on tight. I need to get over that knoll in a hurry!"

That's where he would make a stand against the horsemen, from a higher vantage point.

With the crest just yards away, gunfire crackled all around Anita and him. Jesus, he thought, does he want to kill his daughter? A bullet ripped into his shoulder. Anita shrieked as Tiburcio fell out of the saddle. She could not reach the bridle and, just a few feet from the hilltop, Anita leapt off the horse as well.

"We still have to make it over the crest," Tiburcio groaned, his pistol remaining in his grip, waving for Anita to continue a few more feet over the hill.

Tiburcio stood to make the final run for cover but lost his footing. His boots kicked loose rocks and dirt as he clambered up a few more feet. Anita looked down at their pursuers, who were less than forty yards away. One of them drew a bead on her stumbling, wounded lover, and in desperation she bounded downhill toward him.

Anita threw her arms around Tiburcio to help him climb and a bullet struck her temple. She fell stiffly backward, sliding down a sloping carpet of clover and grass and leaves. Tiburcio turned and unloaded his chamber at the hunters. The men fell flat as the bandit's bullets whistled over their heads.

Anita's father, stunned at what he had witnessed, told his men to hold their fire. In a stupor, he watched Tiburcio crawl on his stomach over to his motionless daughter.

Her eyes were closed and bright red blood streamed down her face from the side of her head. Tiburcio could not feel her pulse. He could not feel her breath. The men were approaching steadily but were cautious. In a panic, Tiburcio hopped up and scrambled over the crest of the hill, reloading his gun on the way. Another barrage of bullets snapped into the ground and whizzed past him.

His options were poor. Wounded and low on ammunition, he could not survive a gun battle with four men. If Anita were alive and he tried to escape with her, he would be caught. If she were dead, was it not meaningless to stick around and risk his own life for nothing? He had no choice. Tiburcio bolted for the wooded area below.

By great providence, the horse he had abandoned had not trotted far. Tiburcio bounded onto the weary animal and coaxed it into another sprint just as the four men reached Anita. He did not look back. Tears blinded him and his wailing was louder than the thunderous sound of hooves and cracking branches all around him.

• • •

It did not take long for the law to catch up to Tiburcio in Jackson. They discovered his stolen horse outside the saloon in broad daylight, calling out to the law officers like a beacon. He was nabbed while sitting at a saloon table, staring blankly ahead, unaware of the six lawmen standing behind him with their guns drawn.

His sleeve torn and arm bloody and dangling at his side, Tiburcio was incoherent from hunger, pain, fatigue and, most of all, heartache. There was no fight left in him. Part of him had died. He finally looked up, and the lawmen saw a humiliated, defeated, hopeless fugitive.

"Let's go, bandit," the sheriff said.

"Yeah. Let's go," he repeated, indifferently.

TIBURCIO!

Back at San Quentin, he was flogged and tossed into a dungeon for solitary confinement. He was denied food for several days. An extra year was tagged onto his sentence. The other prisoners could see that none of the punishment mattered to Tiburcio.

He walked silently. If he ate, he ate silently. He worked silently. He preferred to be alone. He did not wash, he did not shave.

He watched two cellmates, Carabajal and Procopio, also known as Red-handed Dick, become free men. They whispered to him that they would see him and Soto in a year at Cantua Canyon. Tiburcio managed a single nod, then flopped down again onto his cot.

In late September, just a few weeks since his last escape, Tiburcio and sixty other inmates were assigned to unload clay blocks from the San Quentin brickyard onto the three-masted schooner Bolinas.

The sixty men worked within gunshot range of the heavily armed prison watch towers. Also, two armed watchmen on the barge guarded the cons. At precisely noon, they were called to supper. There, inside the eating hall one day, Tiburcio looked up and down the bench at his fellow inmates.

"Enjoy your last meal in here, gentlemen. And say goodbye to this place when you clean your plate."

It was the most Tiburcio had said since his return to prison.

"What do you mean, Tiburcio?"

"The ship we're loading is tied to the dock. We are going to take over that schooner, and when we do we are one rope line away from freedom. We must act fast. We can overpower the guards on the barges, take them hostage and toss the schooner's crew into the water. We cut the tie, haul the hostages below deck, hide on starboard away from the guard tower's guns and sail away from this miserable place."

"And who will sail the schooner?" an inmate asked.

"These schooners are easy to sail. I just need two of you to help me with the masts. It will take no time at all, especially in this windy bay, to run out of the range of their big guns. Besides, they won't shoot if we have hostages."

Tiburcio got his volunteers. He assigned them each to a task.

In leg and wrist irons, they were marched back out to the wharf. Once their manacles were detached, the convicts began loading the Bolinas with the bricks. The men kept glancing at Tiburcio for the signal. They would have to do it soon, before the schooner became too heavy with its load.

"*Arriba el Telon!*" Tiburcio shouted.

Twenty men leaped into the water and charged the barges. They punched and kicked and subdued the two guards, and then climbed onto the schooner with their hostages before a single shot was fired. Twenty other men, including Tiburcio, hurled the schooner's crew into the frigid bay. One inmate stole a crew member's knife and tossed it to Tiburcio, who in one stroke cut the ship loose from the dock.

The watch tower guards saw the jailbreak, but were unable to respond. They could not fire away because of the two captured officers. Within moments, forty prisoners crowded to the starboard side out of sight. Several pushed the two guard hostages below deck. The tower sentries cursed but kept an intent watch, waiting for a chance to do something, anything to stop the escape.

Then they got their break. The ship's sails fully caught the breeze, but instead of coasting far out into the bay, the starboard side rapidly swung in the other direction. Within seconds, the schooner was broadside to the prison and three dozen inmates suddenly exposed and unprotected from the massive artillery of the guard towers. Tiburcio had not seen the underwater hawser that moored the ship to a buoy. The inmates stared dumbfounded for a split second at the Gatling guns before the guards unleashed a barrage of firepower at the Bolinas .

"Oh, Jesus!" Tiburcio cried as he realized his fatal mistake.

Men quickly dropped all around him. First three, then seven, then twelve and more. The schooner splintered and its deck turned red with blood. Inmates wailed and collapsed.

"You fucking gringos!" Tiburcio yelled as he scrambled to find a white shirt or towel.

He waved the towel frantically from behind the bulwarks. The gunfire waned to a few pops, then stopped. Tiburcio kept waving the flag. He looked around the deck at several groaning, dying men. Others were silent, contorted figures with gaping wounds.

The final toll was seven dead, twelve wounded, none escaped. Tiburcio was again severely beaten and for several months segregated from the rest of the prison population. He was punished with another year in the fortress. By the time he was released from solitary confinement, many more of his fellow bandits, some of the most villainous and insolent characters to ever roam California, had been freed.

From outside of the prison, Procopio, Carabajal and the others managed to keep him abreast of their conquests. They solicited the help of Tiburcio's sister, Maria, to get information inside the prison. During her visits, which came as frequently as monthly now, she smuggled in notes and letters that told of the increasing terror brought on by the desperadoes in the hills of Alameda and Santa Clara counties. The letters described how the Mexican bandits could brazenly ride into towns, armed to the teeth, and strike businesses almost at will.

"No one is interested in hunting us down," wrote Eduardo Gallegos. "The settlers are at our mercy, just glad we spare them their lives. Meanwhile, they watch their horses and cattle get driven off in droves. It is unbelievable and we are encouraged. Make haste when you have served your time!"

Except for a stretch of road from Stockton to Hayward, Maria told Tiburcio, the cutthroats had made the region unsafe for white travelers and businessmen to pass through. They lived in remote *jacales*, alone or in pairs, and planned their conquests in dark cantinas and loud fandangos filled with brigands like themselves. Their wives and children hid out at Cantua, waiting for the revolution.

"And the most amusing part of the whole affair are the so-called lawmen who are supposed to protect the citizens," Procopio wrote. "The citizens have put their faith in and elected a beardless, boyish sheriff in Oakland who prefers to fight anti-Union gringos with his fists rather than battle us with horses and guns. While gangs of us fugitives, horse thieves, highwaymen and killers live recklessly in the surrounding mountains and canyons of the Coast Range, this sheriff, *El Muchacho* we call him, is the top law enforcement official."

"Are you not encouraged by their stories, Tiburcio?" Maria asked.

"I will be in here for eternity," Tiburcio said. "It doesn't matter. I have nothing outside these prison walls."

"Yes, you do. Let me tell you what else *nuestros amigos* are saying. They believe the time and circumstances are nearly ripe for liberation. They say they can strike freely at stores, ranches and coaches from Alameda to Hollister and all the way down into Fresno County and Los Angeles.

"Soto says the best thing the law did for us is throw all of the revolutionaries into this cauldron together. The wounds we have suffered only festered, and we have grown stronger and more united. Having survived their floggings and miserable conditions, the bandits say they are even more determined to bring down this government. When you leave here, Tiburcio, you are going to lead this revolution. You are going to be greater and more famous than Joaquin Murrieta."

"Me? It won't be me. I have failed everybody. Even the women I have loved. I am far too bitter to lead these men."

"No, Tiburcio," gentle Maria said. "You still have hope. Deep down. You give the men hope. And you never give up. That's what's important. Murrieta - he was too bitter over the rape of his wife. His anger and personal vendetta did him in. You are smarter than that. You are better than that. You are stronger than that."

"What about Procopio? He is Murrieta's nephew. He has the bloodline to lead the liberation. Let him carry the revolution."

"Soto says prison has broken him down. He couldn't lead a pack of dogs. He will not last long."

"Tiburcio," Maria whispered. "All through the hills, from Alameda to New Idria, the Mexicans travel free and the white man's law is too timid to do anything to stop them. You will inherit an army of rebels, Tiburcio. I will see you soon. Free and determined.

"*Vaya con Dio!*" she said.

Quickly, Maria was ushered away by the guards.

On August 13, 1863, Tiburcio, having exchanged his wool striped prison suit for civilian clothes, watched the heavy iron doors open. He walked several steps out into the sunshine and heard the metal clanging of the cellblock door shutting behind him. He was a free man once again.

PART II: Morse
Chapter 1: El Muchacho
Oakland, Calif.
September 1863

Harry N. Morse, the smooth-faced candidate for Sheriff's Office of Oakland, California, sat at his office desk and wondered where the energy and excitement in his life had gone. Just outside his door, an unmistakeable vitality pulsed through the streets of downtown. Oakland had tripled in population to nearly twenty-four hundred people in the past decade and he felt that every one of them, except himself, was bustling around with grand plans. He had hit a lull at age twenty six and now sat reflecting on what he should be doing with his life and why he wasn't. Morse was unaware, however, that he was about to hear the news that would forever alter the direction of his life.

Before that moment, he did not feel history tugging at his collar. He knew what the tug of history felt like. History's pull was like your father taking you by the nape of your neck without a word and leading you either to the shed for a whipping or to the general store for some candy - you never knew which until the yanking stopped and you found yourself staring straight at your destiny.

That first tug came at age at age ten when he determined that he would be a seaman. Harry was the descendant of founding puritans who came to the eastern shores two hundred years earlier. He was born in New York City to a father who was a fine tailor and a mother who was a proper English wife. But Harry's young imagination was stoked by the tall ships from Europe and California that he saw lined up on the East

River to trade cowhides and herbs for fine clothing. He stared long and hard at the strong, rugged sailors who were so heartily welcomed by every riverside business. Who were they? They had no time to sit around. They worked doggedly until every last crate, sack and barrel was unloaded, and then they loaded more onto the vessels. Within days of their joyful arrival at the docks, the sailors were gone again, sent off by weeping young ladies. These proud seamen trod back onto their ships, leaped into action and sailed away to their next great experience.

To where? Harry wondered. The sailors' unbelievable and boisterous tales filled the pubs and stores for days. What else could a boy so inspired by the sea spirit do? He signed on to sail between New York and California.

Four years later, Harry's fellow crewmen, drawn by gold, all signed up for vessels on a one-way trip to California. At age fourteen, he followed, ready for his chance to extract enough yellow nuggets from a sluice box or a trenched hill to fill his duffel bag. But when he got to the West Coast, he was dead broke and couldn't go anywhere. So he took a job in the big town of San Francisco, cooking for sailors. After only a month he had enough money to finally get to Amador's fields of gold.

But Morse did not have much luck in mining. In fact, he saw few men become wealthy. And he quickly realized why. Foremost, he was too late; the gold rush was over. Even so, he knew very little about mining. He had readily accepted as fact the notion of everyone becoming rich quickly and easily. Everything he had heard was greatly exaggerated. And even when he managed to scrape together a little money, prices for simple goods, such as flour and potatoes, were so exorbitant that he was soon flat broke again. It was not much of a way to get rich.

He returned to San Francisco, lucky to have at least a little savings in his pocket. The first day back in the city, he decided he needed a decent suit if he were to find a job. When he walked into a clothing store, he glanced in the dressing mirror and thought someone else was staring back at him. He had grown a foot since leaving New York. He was lean and strong, although he still had a boyish face. Instead of a suit, he bought laborer's clothes, a blue flannel shirt, wool trousers and heavy black boots. The next day he got a job ferrying passengers from arriving steamers to the city's shore.

A year later, now sixteen, he had saved enough money to buy a few of his own boats and start his own business. He branched out from carrying passengers to the wharf to carrying coal and bricks out to the steamers.

He did that until 1854, when he grew tired of the job and went to work for an uncle who was a butcher in Oakland. When the uncle died, Morse took over the business. He expanded the enterprise, delivering meat products up to forty-five miles away, to San Jose and Livermore. One day, he discovered his partner had stolen nearly all the money from the business and was never to be seen again. That was the end of Morse as a meat vendor.

When Harry turned twenty-four, the Civil War broke out in the East and he organized the Oakland militia in the West. The Oakland Guard, as they were called, would be called into action if the violence spread to California. That never happened, but Captain Morse nevertheless worked his way up the ranks by keeping busy watching for any signs of an anti-Union rebellion. The young, muscular captain would sometimes have to deliver a quick jab into a Copperhead's nose to shut him up and send a message to other Confederate sympathizers. These scraps provided Morse with a few moments of thrill, but did not exactly fill his cup of adventure.

So at twenty-six, Morse was bored like he hadn't been bored in years. Sitting at his office desk on that autumn day in 1863, he tried to think of the last really exciting event in his life. Was it really more than a decade ago? He could recall the episode precisely. He was working as an express man on the sloop in San Francisco Bay and saved a drowning boy. By the time Morse heard the passengers yelling for help, it almost was too late. The boy was so exhausted from treading water in the cold bay that he had begun to sink. Morse plunged off the upper rail into the icy water and swam past a small rowboat that was fighting a strong current to get to the boy. Morse reached the youngster and held the boy's head above the water with one arm while treading water with the other until the rowboat arrived.

After the rescue, however, came the monotonous stint as a butcher, then as a grocery store owner. A year ago, he had sold the latter business. Then he was exclusively involved in the Guard, participation in which certainly benefited the twenty-six-year-old man politically but definitely not in any adventurous way. So when the Republican Party asked if Harry N. Morse would be interested in running for public office, he shrugged his shoulders and said, "Sure, why not?" He was quickly elected Republican nominee for sheriff. As a volunteer candidate, he made little effort to get votes. The only issue he campaigned on at all was the need to keep all Union traitors out of Alameda County.

And that is where Morse, an unenthusiastic candidate pondering his future on a tedious election night, found himself when his good friend, Peter Borein, barged into his downtown Oakland office without knocking (he was the only one who could get away with that) to announce the news that would change his life.

"You've won, Harry!"

Borein was a mustachioed man with a high forehead, brown hair parted to the right and kind eyes.

"You didn't lift a God-damned finger and you beat Beazell hands down. You got one thousand three hundred and nine votes to his eight hundred and twenty."

"That's great," Morse replied matter-of-factly to his friend, a fellow Mason.

"You don't sound very excited, Sheriff."

"Yeah, well, nobody thinks the job's worth much."

"It's what you make of the office, Harry," Borein replied. "Your predecessor conducted business very poorly. He was careless and lax. And because he didn't give a damn, we have bands of desperadoes overrunning our hills, attacking our towns. Did you know that? A good sheriff needs to deal swiftly with a threat like that."

Morse looked up, his interest suddenly sparked.

"You know something," he recalled, "Just last week, a visiting merchant, who I used to do business with at the general store, told me he was too frightened to bring his shipment across them hills. He said the few merchants who do take the chance are charging exorbitant prices. So, we're either paying too much for goods or lacking them altogether."

"See, Harry. That is an important issue. That is an issue for the sheriff of Oakland to deal with. Now that you've been elected, you have to take the job seriously."

"Well, ridding the county of Mexican cutthroats is a far tougher challenge than ridding the county of traitors. The latter is what I promised my supporters I would do if I got elected."

"I'm sure there are quite a few friends in the Union party who will be expecting to be rewarded for their unflinching support of you. That's OK. Without the Republican Party, Harry, you don't win anything in Alameda County. But you're the sheriff. And you're everybody's sheriff. This city isn't going to remain overwhelmingly Union forever. And if those Mexican bandits cause too much trouble, and those merchants pack up and leave, you will pay for it. You're responsible for conduct of the office."

"You think those brigands are the biggest issue facing this county, Peter? Bigger than keeping the Copperheads in line?"

"Yes I do."

"Bigger than dealing with squatters?"

"Yes."

"Then we'll have to figure out a good campaign against these murderous outlaws."

"Did you say, 'we?' "

"Yes. When I take the oath in six months, Peter, I want you to be my undersheriff. You know, do the bookkeeping, run the jail. I need someone I can trust to maintain the civil duties of the office."

"I'd be honored. You know I don't know any more about fighting armed Mexican vaqueros than you do."

"Being a good pugilist and knocking sense into Confederate sympathizers is one thing, Peter, but dealing with thieves and killers is something completely different."

Morse sat back with his hands on the back of his head and thought about the time he had outmaneuvered those bandits on that treacherous mountain road in the butcher wagon. Oh, the sweet exhilaration of adventure. He smiled at the thought.

Chapter 2: Embarrassed
Alameda County,
Fourth of July 1865

Harry Morse loved a Fourth of July celebration. His young country had given him so much for which to be proud. Only in his twenties, he had already been a butcher, an Argonaut, an expressman, a grocer, a husband, a father, a military captain and a sheriff. All because he lived in a free country. He and every American from his hometown, New York City, to his new home of Oakland were free to pursue happiness and strive for progress. He could not understand a secessionist or any other rebel no matter how hard he tried.

With a magnanimous feeling on a sun-rich day, Morse hopped into his buggy. He wore a wide-brimmed hat perched on the back of his head, high leather boots over his cavalry pants and held a whip in his hand. His horses high-stepped down the streets of Oakland, where he stopped at storefronts to share cigars with merchants, attended meetings of the Guard and rallied supporters in the Republican Party.

"Happy Fourth!" he cried from his buggy each time he came across a group of people.

Two years into his reign as sheriff, his spirits were especially high today. He was in the midst of a re-election campaign for a second term, and his opponent, Ed Niehaus, had been hammering him on his lack of arrests of unlawful Mexicans roaming the hillsides of Alameda County.

"The Mexican thieves in the backcountry of Alameda continue to prey on easy victims. Our sheriff has been helpless to curb this menace," Niehaus fumed just three days ago on the streets of San Leandro where the two opponents happened to have crossed paths. "These devils plunder at will and escape into the night as if by magic!"

Morse defended his job performance by pointing out that over the course of the past two years he had maintained the peace in a burgeoning city, settled scores of land disputes and kept Copperheads in line.

But on this beautiful July 4th holiday, Morse wished he would run into Niehaus again. Because locked up in his jail were two notorious horse thieves and highwaymen, Agustin Avila and Jose Ramon Peralta. Furthermore, he had caged a dangerous pair of anglo rustlers, William Ward and John Haley. As for the fifth and sixth jailbirds, they were a pair of Chinese men, collared for illegally operating a business.

All six prisoners, Morse thought with glee, can stew inside the dank quarters of the jail, assessing what it means to be free in America. Let's see Niehaus argue against that. With everything in order on the streets of Oakland, Morse decided to continue his jovial holiday celebration in neighboring San Francisco. With great buoyancy and enthusiasm, he insisted that his undersheriff go spend a carefree day in San Leandro with his family. They had earned it, he concluded.

Morse returned home to Oakland around midnight. He did not bother to check the jail, and went straight up to bed. Around 2:00 a.m., he was startled awake by a drunken visitor banging on his front door. Holding a candle in one hand, he quickly pulled his butterscotch pants over his nightshirt and stuck a revolver into his waistband. Morse tossed the door open, ready to verbally accost the interloper. He found himself staring at a brown-skinned man with long black hair yelling at him in a strange language and pointing down the street with great zeal. The man's face was puffy and bloody and his clothes dirty.

"Get away you drunken Chinaman!" Morse warned. "And no more fighting on my streets! Or I will toss you in jail!"

The man looked puzzled and turned away. Morse watched him stagger away, shouting to other residences of sleepy citizens before heading down Twelfth Street in the direction of the jail.

The next morning, Morse went directly to the courthouse. Realizing that Borein might still be in San Leandro, he decided to check on the inmates at the jail himself before going to his office. As he passed in front of the cell window, he stopped dead in his tracks. A saw and two jaggedly cut iron bars were lying on the ground. He hurried inside and instantly recognized the Chinese prisoner, his face battered. It was the same man who had tried to arouse him last night at his door. The other Chinese prisoner was still in custody, too.

"So you snuck back into jail after trying to alert me, eh?" Morse said to the prisoner. "I'm a damned fool."

The man pointed at a note left on the floor in the middle of the main cell. He picked it up and began to read it. The note mocked the sheriff: "We didn't like the Fourth of July dinner you served, so we decided to leave. Sincerely, Avila, Peralto, Ward and Haley."

Back in his office Morse counted on his calendar how many days were left until the election. As soon as his undersheriff arrived, he called an emergency meeting of the Alameda Republican Party to try to minimize the damage from the embarrassing jailbreak.

"Somebody's got to take the fall for this," the party chairman declared.

"How about Borein?" the secretary suggested. "It was his duty to make sure the jail was secure."

"I will not use my friend and undersheriff as a scapegoat," Morse declared.

"It's OK, Harry. You can put me on leave for a while and dock my wages. This whole episode will pass," Borein said.

In the end, it didn't matter what they did. There were just too many Republicans and too strong of a post-Civil War sentiment against Democrats for Morse to lose a second term. Borein remained his right-hand man, and they coasted to victory.

TIBURCIO!

Even if Morse had wanted to commemorate his coronation, the bandits roaming the hills made sure any celebration was short-lived. A month into his new term, two bold raids convinced him that the band of thieves were daring him to act. Narciso Bojorques and Joaquin Olivera drove five-hundred sheep off William Knox's rancho in the middle of the night, moved them into the southern Alameda County hills and sold them to an unsuspecting rancher. Knox brushed off the sheriff's attempts to help track down the missing animals and said he would handle it himself. He eventually recovered most of the flock.

Next, Juan Soto struck. Flanked by his fellow San Quentin convicts Manuel Rojas and Alfonso M. Burnham, Soto rode to the ranch and trading post of Charles Garthwaite near Pleasanton. The bandits kicked at the door of the house. As they entered, Garthwaite's wife, who was alone, fired a revolver and wounded Burnham. Soto and Rojas grabbed the woman before she could shoot again, bound and gagged her and ransacked the house. They left a half-hour later with money, jewelry and weapons. Morse caught up with Burnham in San Francisco, but the bandit refused to snitch on the others. Burnham got eighteen months at San Quentin while Soto remained free and bolder than ever.

These violent escapades, for which Morse was lambasted in the *San Francisco Chronicle* and the *Alameda Gazette*, as well as the jail escape just before the election, did not discourage the plucky, young sheriff. They made him more determined than ever to be a proficient lawman.

"Where did these desperadoes come from?" he asked Borein. "There are suddenly so many."

"They've been in San Quentin, fomenting hatred and forming plots. Now, one by one, their sentences have ended. They're free, angry and feel they have nothing to lose. They're fast on horses, quick and deadly with guns. And they're fearless."

Morse knew little about investigating, pursuing and apprehending criminals, especially hardened ones like these Mexicans. It would take great ambition on his part to change the course. He tirelessly turned to this newest occupation as he had done with all the others. Boredom would never enter his mind again.

Morse began his new campaign by getting to know his enemies and their territory. To do this right, he needed to solidly grasp their language and meticulously study their habits. What type of horses did they prefer? Did they smoke? Did they drink whiskey? What places did they frequent? Who were their friends, their supporters? What kind of boots did they wear? What kind of guns did they favor? What type of tracks did they leave?

As for their territory, he started to learn to navigate the rough mountains and the remote backcountry of the eastern county as well as the thieves did themselves, as well as he, himself, knew every street, house and business of Oakland and San Leandro. He would visit sheriffs in other counties and their jails and even the prison on the hill to find out every detail about the outlaws.

He taught himself how to read the signs of the land and follow tracks. He memorized every natural marker from every direction, because a tree or a rock looks much different from a southern vantage point than it does when approaching it from an eastbound trail. He observed the trails and bushes and plants in every season, because when the leaves fall in autumn and winter more landscape is revealed and your eyes can play tricks on you; when the grasses grow high in late spring, a boulder that was visible in winter is seemingly gone; a deep lagoon in February could be a dry ravine in July.

He became as expert at horsemanship and marksmanship as the great vaqueros. He practiced shooting until he could hit a target one hundred yards away with his Winchester, and draw, cock and fire his six-shooter as rapidly and steadily as a woodpecker knocking on bark. He was soon able to ride for days on a hard saddle and shoot a bullseye from a swift stallion.

It took time. Lots of time. But he didn't have a moment to spare.

Chapter 3: Hills
Alameda County
May 1866

"What do you want these for?" Borein asked his boss, dropping a stack of Wanted posters, sketches and prison photographs on his desk.

"I need to be able to recall each of these outlaws' faces and memorize the descriptions. The better I know them, and can associate faces with names and nicknames, the easier it will be to sort out the mess of desperadoes in those hills. I may even be able to find some informants among their brood."

"And I got the rest of the stuff you ordered out in the wagon."

"Including the ammunition?"

"Both for the .44 and the Winchester. Sixty boxes of each. Why so many?"

Morse looked at his fists and held them up.

"Because I only know how to fight with these. I need to dead shoot. What else do you have?"

"There are mats, blankets, tins, cavalry pants and coats. … Oh, and some phony whiskers! Harry?"

"Yes. Very good," Morse said with a smile. "Peter, there's something else I will need."

"Anything, Harry."

"I need you to be in charge here for a while."

"Again? Where are you going this time?"

"Back into the mountains. Alone"

"What do you do up there, Harry?"

"Learn the ways of the bandidos. I study the topography around their strongholds. This time, I'll need that disguise. I am going to get right under the noses of the actual outlaws you see in these pictures."

Borein shook his head disapprovingly as Morse began to thumb through the pictures.

"Last time, you were gone for an entire fortnight, Harry, scouring them hills, dressed like a vagabond."

"I can't very well wear my daily uniform out there, can I? Nothing else matters anymore, Peter. To be a successful sheriff, I need to hunt down the mountain bandits, kill 'em or clear 'em out."

He continued studying the photographs. Suddenly, Morse stopped on one particular picture, tapping it with his index finger.

"I have seen this man before. It says 'Tiburcio Basquez.' Basquez? With a 'B'? The prison clerk must have gotten the name spelled wrong. It must be Vasquez."

"I know the name, but I don't recall ever coming face to face with him," the undersheriff said.

"Wait. I remember," Morse declared. "It was years ago, perhaps a decade. I was running a butcher wagon through the hills and mountain bandits tried to waylay me. As my wagon careened down the narrow trail I glanced back and caught his eye. We were about the same age, I recall - that's why it stuck in my mind. We were just teenagers, maybe seventeen. Anyway, I looked back and he was letting fly his riata. I am sure he could have lassoed me but something made him deliberately miss. He missed for a reason. I saw it in his eyes. Why do you suppose he did that, Peter?"

"It was a long time ago. Perhaps your memory isn't clear on the details. Or maybe he was just too inexperienced and it was an unintended error. If he is in that stack of pictures, he won't miss again. He's a ruthless son of a bitch."

"They all are, Peter. They all are."

"Why don't you let me go up there with you, Harry? You could use some backup."

Morse shook his head.

"Are you telling me everything?"

"Yes, Peter. Like I said when I hired you as my undersheriff, I need someone to run the office on a daily basis. Don't worry, I'll be fine."

What Morse didn't tell his undersheriff was that he had received word that a small group of desperadoes, led by Eduardo Gallego, was preparing for some action in the hills of Sunol Valley. The sheriff felt he needed to be fleet and have the element of surprise at his disposal in order to apprehend these bad men. So he decided to go into the wilderness alone, dressed like an old, gray-bearded, homeless wanderer.

On his second day in the hills, Alameda Creek was gushing so strong and loud that Morse couldn't hear anything but the rushing water from one hundred yards away. He had on his tattered coat, bushy false hair, a shaggy, gray fake beard and slouch hat. He was making notes in a sketchpad from his perch on a rock, logging the information while it was fresh in his head. He always wrote directly from what he observed rather than relying later on memory of what he thought he saw. He didn't wait until he was in his office to finalize his reports. He sometimes took in a scene for hours, testing himself to find and name as many geological features in the surroundings as he could: a horn there, a sheer ridge over a V-shaped valley there, a hanging valley behind him, a feeder creek to his left. When he felt that he could recreate this site from memory, all the way down to the seasonal weather cracks exposing hard veins of quartz in the granite under his boots - all so he might someday be able to relocate it - he stood up.

He felt the cool breeze on his face. He had worked up a sweat getting up the hill, but the wind had cooled him off quickly, and he pulled the tattered coat tighter around him, sticking the sketch pad in a large inside pocket. He walked over to the edge of the precipice on which he had been observing the scenery and, to his surprise, spied six Mexican vaqueros down by the crashing creek. If they were outlaws, they weren't very smart, he thought, for he could easily see them but they could not hear him even if he shouted at the top of his lungs.

Morse needed a closer look. He pulled his old horse by the reins behind him and started confidently down a trail that he knew, based on his studious observations from several trips to this area. He eventually ended up at the creek right where the bandits were. Near the water's edge, he hid so he could reconnoiter the group. He quickly discovered by the branding that at least two of their horses had been stolen from San Leandro. He also learned that he had encountered this group before, when he had been out on his own and disguised as an old man. He remembered the outlaws mocked him for being too senile not to know any better than to venture into the hideout of such hardened criminals.

Morse decided not to encounter these men yet. Further up the creek, but still down in the canyon, the outlaws set up camp. He looked closely at their setup. Their mustangs were staked on the grass and they soon had a campfire going. When the moon came up high and the campfire went low, Morse shuffled down a deer trail, cracking leaves and whistling until he was at the edge of the camp, looking straight at two of the Mexicans who were on watch by the fire. Both had their revolvers drawn on the old man emerging from the shadows and bushes.

"*Qué quieres, viejo?*" one of them asked.

"*Una taza de café, por favor.*"

The other outlaw tossed some small branches on the embers and then stoked the fire again to get the coffee warm. Morse took a seat on a stump, keeping his face under his brim, out of the direct moonlight.

"I remember you vaqueros," Morse said in Spanish. "I remember a man named Gallegos, but I don't see his horse."

"He keeps his mustang next to his bed. It's over there."

"Where are you going, my friends?"

"Don't ask so many questions, old man. This is the second time we've seen you in these hills. That means you've been lucky twice not to be killed."

"I reckon so. But I cannot help that our paths keep crossing. I have seen you in nearly this same spot both times, eh?"

That's when Morse's plan really paid off, for Gallegos walked up to the campfire at that moment. Morse studied the thief's face.

"Old man," Gallegos said, striding up to Morse with a hand on his holstered revolver. "I was amused the first time I saw you. This second time, I am extremely annoyed. The third time we meet up in these hills, I will slit your throat - before you get a chance to ask for a cup of coffee."

Morse groaned as he slowly rose. Then he thanked them for their kindness and shuffled off with a hand on his back as if he was in pain. The next time he encountered the group, he wouldn't be wearing a disguise, he thought.

When he returned to Oakland, Morse found a warrant issued from San Joaquin County for Eduardo Gallegos sitting on his desk. Gallegos was charged with stealing a large herd of cattle near Mountain House, just outside Alameda County. Morse solicited the help of an old friend from the Oakland Guard, Police Officer Dick Richardson, and another close companion, George Swain, undersheriff of Contra Costa County, just to the north. Richardson was powerfully built and fearless; Swain was brave, reliable and a bit impetuous.

They set off after Gallegos in a speedy wagon and trailed him from Mission San Jose into the San Joaquin Valley, nearly one hundred miles. Gallegos got far ahead of them when their wagon wheel broke, but the three-man posse switched to saddle horses and rode hard for three days and another one hundred miles before losing his tracks.

Morse was forced to return home, but did not give up. He soon got word that the vaquero could be found in a *jacale* at the foot of Mount Diablo, in Swain's part of the country. He telegraphed the two pals, asking them to meet him in Dublin. From there, they headed straight for the rugged black hills.

"Who is with the greaser?" Swain asked Morse while saddling new horses at a Dublin ranch.

"I got reports of at least two dozen armed bandits riding with him."

Swain peered dubiously at Richardson over his horse's back.

"Did I hear you correctly, Harry? In case you forgot how to count, there are just three of us in this little posse you've organized."

"It's all about the element of surprise, George," Morse said encouragingly. "Gallegos would never suspect that one or two lawmen would have the audacity to venture that far into the black hills. He figures they would bring so many men that their movements would be discovered. We'll catch him off guard."

"Harry," Swain continued, "I have been in law enforcement a while longer than you, so just let me say that catching a murderous bandit 'off guard' is not a strategy."

"George, I've studied these vaqueros up close on two separate occasions. They are not the smartest bunch of thieves. They are downright stupid. They never cover their tracks. They leave the original brands on their horses. Besides, when you telegraph me about some manhunt *you're* organizing, *you* can make all the plans. Be as elaborate as you want. But this is my posse. We are using the element of surprise."

On the ride Morse did shed light on a few more details of his strategy. He had thought them up on the way.

"We'll raid the hideout at first light," he explained. "But we are only after Gallegos. That's all we can handle right now. We will extract him from the herd, so to speak."

With the sun breaking at their backs, the three men reconnoitered the *jacale* on the canyon floor from atop a knoll. Their eyes grew big when they saw what looked like a small cavalry unit saddling their horses. Thirty mounts were hitched outside the small adobe hut, prepared to take their riders into town to pillage.

"Do you see Gallegos?" Richardson asked.

"Yes, I recognize him from the campfire. There he is, in the saddle trying to cut the hobbles from his horse. We'll have to act quickly. Ready? Let's go."

Morse and Swain mounted their horses while Richardson set his rifle at his side; he would provide his companions with cover. The two riders galloped down straight toward Gallegos, who looked up to see them approaching from thirty yards away. Gallegos, completely astounded at the sight, froze first, and then tried to draw his revolver.

"Put up your hands!" the sheriff shouted.

Swain put a six-shooter to the bandit's head. Morse deftly clicked the handcuffs on Gallegos and swept away his horse. Richardson took a few cracks with his rifle to unsettle the other outlaws as the lawmen and their prisoner fled. Gallegos was captured and whisked away before the other outlaws could react. Not one had drawn a weapon.

"That was the most foolhardy raid I have ever witnessed, Harry," Swain said afterward, as they waited in Morse's office for Borein to finish locking Gallegos up in the Oakland jail.

"It's not as foolish as you think, George," Morse responded. "If you know your enemy, you know their weaknesses. Those other men would not even piss without Gallegos holding it for them. So they didn't know what to do once we deprived them of their leader."

A little over a month later, Morse and a constable from Amador County took to the saddle again to seize three cattle thieves. They trapped the outlaws before they could get to their fortified hideout. One was shot dead and the other two jailed.

Word spread quickly. Morse rode into town triumphant after his latest successful manhunt. A boisterous crowd of landowners and business people, feeling that finally something was being done about the brazen thievery, led the sheriff to a downtown watering hole. Morse would not have been able to walk home had everybody who wished to buy him a drink that night had done so. Morse was not a heavy drinker, but he did swallow a good amount of the town folks' acclaim.

"How'd you do it, sheriff?" someone shouted.

"Tell us how you shot that bandit and collared the other two bastards!"

"Yeah! And how did just three of you take on them thirty desperadoes up near El Diablo, like the paper said, without firing a shot?"

Morse's eyes fell on his undersheriff across the room.

"Go ahead, sheriff," Borein shouted. "You deserve to tell it. These town folk deserve to hear the good news from their top elected law officer."

Morse gave plenty of credit to Amador Constable Orlo B. Wood, who had actually pulled the trigger that felled one of the three cattle thieves. As for the other escapade, he claimed he could not have captured Gallegos without the help and swift actions of Swain and Richardson.

"And now, my friends, I must go. Please continue the revelry in my absence. Deputy Borein and I have a busy day tomorrow."

The lawmen stepped out into the brisk Oakland air, cold and moist from off the bay. Morse turned up his collar. Borein blew into his cupped hands, and they walked briskly down Broadway toward the courthouse so they could check the prisoners once again and see if the guard needed to be relieved.

After about a block, Morse couldn't contain himself. He told his friend that at last, after more than three years on the job, and many years of toiling in other ventures, he felt there was a purpose his life.

"I have such a sense of accomplishment, Peter. Perhaps this is what I have been called upon to do with my life."

Borein congratulated him, but after another block he remembered to play the role of a partner as well as a good friend, which meant lending perspective.

"Harry, you know there are many more highwaymen scattered throughout Sunol, Livermore and Amador valleys.

They are still terrorizing trading posts and wagons and ranches. I don't think we have put a dent in their operations. You are absolutely correct calling this a lifetime endeavor."

"Well put, Peter. I will call it my 'labor of love.'"

"You may call it anything you want, boss. You deserve it."

"Thank you. The county deserves it."

"One other thing, sheriff," Borein continued sternly.

Morse tilted up an eyebrow. "Yes?"

"You know that you have been extremely lucky so far, don't you?"

"How do you mean?"

"There is no questioning your courage, boss. Without it, you would not have arrested any of those villains. But you are indifferent when it comes to your safety."

"What are you saying, Peter?" Morse asked, affecting surprise at his partner's words.

"Just that next time you are outnumbered and go charging into a regiment of bad guys, give it some forethought."

Morse laughed and patted Borein on the back. He knew exactly what he was saying, but wasn't sure if he would or could abide by those words of wisdom.

Chapter 4: Narciso
San Juan Bautista
September 19, 1866

Borein handed Morse a letter containing a warrant from a neighboring county seeking the arrest of Narciso Bojorques for grand larceny.

"It's for Bojorques," Morse told him. "Do you recall a Narciso Bojorques?"

"Yes. Last month, that butcher in Alisal reported that Bojorques robbed him of one hundred and twenty dollars and shot him in the arm. Remember? You found no evidence in your investigation, except for the butcher's word, so you filed the report away."

Morse rose from his chair behind his desk and walked over to his shelf of files, which had become so numerous over the past two years that they took up a full office wall from floor to ceiling and spilled over into several boxes against the other walls. Miraculously to Borein, his boss quickly located the Bojorques file in the piles of paperwork on the shelves. The sheriff carried it over to his desk, sat down, opened it. After a few seconds, Morse let out a long whistle.

"I've talked face to face with this man. I was out on an excursion in the hills above Livermore. He's a terror, all right. Reckless as hell, carousing and spending all his money at cantinas and whore houses in Alisal. He's sworn never to be taken alive - that's in my notes right here. And certainly not by a white man. Ah, yes. This son of a bitch needs to be captured. Do you remember the murder of that family in Corral Hollow?"

"Yes, some men hacked them up with knives and burned down the house," Borein recalled. "It was one of the most atrocious killings ever. It was the Golding family. I believe the wife was Mexican."

"That's right. Narciso was the leader of that gang. He's friends with Procopio."

"Red-handed Dick?"

"Yes. Here's a picture and my description of Narciso - fair skin, large nose and face, about five-feet-ten inches, stout, graceful, strong like a lion and one of the best vaqueros around."

"Sounds like one the worst we've encountered so far."

Morse studied the picture a little longer. Vengeance coursed through him. He then asked what time it was.

"10:00 a.m."

"I need to be gone by 11:00. I'll change out of my uniform while you saddle up my mustang at the stable."

"What about a posse?"

"No time, Peter, no time."

• • •

Morse rode south for three hours into the early afternoon and came upon a broad stream that emptied into Alameda Creek. He knew by this landmark that he was near old Mission San Jose. After making inquiries at the mission, he learned that he just missed Bojorques. The town folk said the outlaw had left that morning. He was last seen taking the Stockton Pass toward Sunol Valley. Morse followed this lead.

Step by step, dread seeped into the sheriff. The farther he rode down the highway known for its lawlessness the more anxiety gripped him and the less he enjoyed what was typically a beautiful, deep valley shaded with sycamores and live oaks, with geese and ducks soaring overhead and elk, longhorns and deer grazing in the high land. He did not hear the soothing rumble of the Cajon River that rushed out of the mountains to the north, cutting westward toward San Francisco Bay. Toward the east, the direction he was steadfastly moving, he kept his eyes on the road as it rose over the large hills. On the other side, the passage dropped into Livermore Valley; but that wasn't where he was going. Morse turned south onto another, even lonelier road that took travelers to Alisal.

When he arrived at Scott's Corner, about thirty or forty men, mostly Mexicans, were milling about the trading post, speaking in Spanish. He stayed in his saddle as he tried to pick up as much of the conversation as his knowledge of the language would allow. He vowed to double his efforts to master Spanish when he returned to Oakland.

He felt a tug at his sleeve. A stable boy had come out to ask if he could take care of his horse.

"Yes, yes. Of course," Morse said, dropping from the saddle. He walked with the boy over to the stable.

"What is everybody talking about?" he asked. "They seem fairly excited about something."

"Who wants to know?" asked the boy, who spoke English well. Morse was taken aback at his cheekiness.

"I'm the sheriff."

The boy looked dubiously at Morse's faded cavalry pants, slouch hat and old military coat.

"Well then, sheriff, you're timing is not too swell. You should have arrived a little earlier. Narciso Bojorques was here."

Morse pretended not to know the bandit in order to get more information.

"Who is he?"

"What kind of sheriff are you?" the stable boy asked in disbelief. "He's a son-of-a-bitch, that's who he is. He left about an hour ago for Vallecitos, which is on that road leading over the hill, in Livermore Valley."

"Do you think he will return today?"

"Oh, yes. It's the only road for him to get back to his camp."

They were at the stable now, when the boy smirked.

"Are you going to try to arrest him? Alone?"

"He's just one man," Morse answered assuredly.

The boy laughed derisively.

"I need to bring him to justice," Morse said, adding, "I will bring him to justice. And, I could use your help."

The boy stopped his mocking laugh and Morse could see his chest stick out with pride. So he continued, feeling intuitively he could count on this stable boy.

"When he returns, can you entice him into the saloon for me? I will pay you handsomely."

"Sure. That's easy money. He loves to drink."

"I will wait for him around the corner of the store. When he enters the saloon, I will follow. Your job will be done by then."

Morse waited a long time. He sat for a while on an old barrel, then stood and leaned against the wall. He walked around the property for a bit. Then he drank a soda, ate some jerky in the saloon, walked around some more and leaned against the wall again. More than four hours later, in the dark gray evening, the sheriff heard a swift galloping and jingling of spurs. He looked around the corner and up the road to Vallecitos. He was suddenly alarmed at the thought that he hadn't brought a single, trusty lawman with him. What was he thinking? The outlaw looked a stout six-foot-two - much taller than Morse's notes had said - and he facilely commanded with one hand an enormous white mustang.

The stable boy emerged from the shadows.

"Is that him?" Morse asked, his heart beating rapidly.

"I don't even have to look," the boy said. "He arrives like thunder."

"Just get him inside, off his horse and into the lighted cantina," Morse commanded as he drew back out of sight.

Narciso halted his stallion in a heap of dust directly in front of the stable boy..

"The owner would like to buy you a drink inside, sir," the boy said.

"I don't want to drink," the outlaw stated. "Get me some jerky for the rest of my ride."

"I do not have time," the stable boy said. "I must prepare some horses for departing guests. Please, go inside and have a drink."

"I don't want a God-damned drink, boy!"

Morse panicked. He feared the bandit would either harm the boy or ride away. He had no choice but to rush out. He quickly plotted: Grab the horse's reins and yank them upward, sending the horse down on its haunches, then seize Narciso by the throat and pull him off the mount.

The sheriff took five or six long strides toward Narciso. The outlaw drew his revolver, cocked and aimed it at Morse's face before Morse could get anywhere close to the horse's reins.

"No intente!"

Morse felt beyond foolish; his actions were downright stupid and incompetent. He deserved to be shot right on the spot for getting caught in such a ridiculous predicament, looking down the barrel of a gun while his own pistol remained ineffectually holstered at his side and no lawmen standing behind him. In a flash of a second, Morse figured it would be better to be killed right then and there. Death would be preferable to living with the memory of Narciso escaping from his clutches. Death would be preferable to forever hearing how utterly incapable he was as sheriff. His tenure would be over. He would become the laughing stock of Alameda County and any lowly thief would be willing to pick a fight with him, knowing the chances of escape are better than any saloon game. Yes, he thought, it would be better to be shot between the eyes. Right now.

Why is he hesitating? Morse wondered to himself. The pause gave him a small chance and he wasn't about to let it get away. He didn't care where his shot landed, he just needed to get the shot off quickly, for no other reason than to cause some kind of alarm. So he pulled the revolver's trigger, without drawing, and blew the bullet right through the holster into the ground inches from the white horse's massive front legs.

Narciso struck the horse hard with his spurs and darted around the corner of the building.

"You fool," Morse called out to the fleeing bandit, not believing his luck.

While he had been waiting for Narciso, Morse had had a lot of time to observe the surrounding area and he knew that Narciso was heading for trouble. The bandit would either have to leap a four-board fence into a corral, somehow bust out of there and escape into the uninhabited southern mountains, or turn around and duel the sheriff.

Narciso kept galloping toward the mountains and cleared the fence with no problem. Morse leveled his gun at him and rapidly fired twice before his weapon jammed. He thought he saw the bandit throw his body over the side of the horse, Comanche-style, to avoid the shots. But it was too dark to see that far into the distance. Morse waited for the red glow and pop of return fire. When none came, he charged into the darkness and decided he would club the fugitive on the head with his gun's handle if he had to - anything to prevent him from getting away.

Morse got to the fence and saw the rider and his horse. They were trapped inside the large corral. The fence on the other side was too high to get over even for Narciso's strong horse. Narciso abandoned the animal, which continued to gallop at incredible speed along the perimeter of the corral, and headed into the hills alone.

Emboldened by the desperation of the outlaw, Morse quickened his pursuit, following the jingle of spurs as far past the corral as he could. When he couldn't hear them anymore he stopped, fearing he might get ambushed.

Back at the trading post, the crowd had spilled out of the store. Acknowledging that the bandit had either gotten away, or at least could no longer be safely pursued, Morse reluctantly turned back. He walked past an old white man, whom Morse had not seen in the frenzy of his chase, sitting on the fence of the corral. The old cowboy was watching Narciso's horse begin to settle down.

"Nice shot, sir," the old man remarked insouciantly.

"I missed."

"I don't think so. I was quite near and heard the ball from your second shot hit him. He groaned."

"That's why he didn't return fire," Morse said excitedly and he hurried over to where Narciso would have been standing when he fired. "He dropped his gun right here."

Sure enough, the pistol was on the ground, cocked, and the ivory handle was wet. Morse smelled the fresh blood. He ran back to the store and procured a shotgun. Shadowed all the way back to the corral by the stable boy, despite the sheriff's insistence that the boy immediately return to the trading post, Morse followed the blood track several hundred yards to a deep ravine. At an old dead tree trunk, they discovered a pool of blood.

"He must have rested here," Morse observed.

He examined the grounds around the trunk and further discovered cut strands of cloth, apparently from Narciso trying to bandage his wound. He searched the brush slowly and thoroughly for two hours and did not find any more signs of Narciso's flight.

"Come on," Morse said to the boy, knowing he couldn't shake the kid loose. "We'll wait by the corral until daybreak in case he comes back for his horse. In the light, we'll start off again."

"I'll go make some coffee and come back with a pot," the boy said. Morse smiled and thought of his own children back in a warm bed in Oakland. "That's a great idea."

Chapter 5: *Bastante!*
San Juan Bautista
December 1866

The young vaquero spurred his horse steadily north into the cold breeze along the muddy El Camino Real toward the small pueblo of San Juan Bautista. He had been recruited by a band of Mexican outlaws while working at the quicksilver mines. Not yet twenty years old, the rider felt proud that he had been chosen to deliver a very important message to Tiburcio Vasquez, the newly famous revolutionary leader. But finding Vasquez somewhere between San Jose and Monterey was a difficult task.

The rider began his search at the New Almaden Mine near San Jose, where everybody pretended never to have heard of Tiburcio Vasquez. He rode south, stopping at the Twenty-One Mile House, where gringos were suspicious of his questions and native laborers and travelers were grimly silent at the mention of the bandit's name. So he swung up into the eastern Panoche hills and rode out to some of the most remote caves and *jacales*, where Tiburcio's name was praised and any information about *El Capitan's* burgeoning revolution was craved. Still, nobody had actually laid eyes on Tiburcio Vasquez for months.

In Monterey, the young messenger heard whispers from Mexican workers that Tiburcio often visited old friends in town, but he never let anyone know when, where or how long he was staying. By the time the sheriff knew he was in town, Tiburcio would slip away, they said. The young man inquired about Tiburcio's mother, but she no longer lived in the bayside city.

Guadalupe lived and worked twenty miles away in Hollister, selling her tamales and *tortas* to the teamsters. If the messenger could find her there, perhaps he could finally locate Tiburcio. On the road outside Hollister, an old sheepherder suggested he try San Juan Bautista because it was nearly the only town still completely friendly to Mexicans and not yet overrun by gringos. Tiburcio spent a lot of time in San Juan, the sheepherder said, because there he was undeniably safe from the constant stream of posses looking for him and the other outlaws.

The young man, Clodoveo Chavez, was nervous as he approached San Juan. The outlaws had severely questioned and tested him to make sure he knew every detail of the information that he was to relay to *El Capitan*. He was repeatedly reminded not to forget a single point, that lives depended on it. Chavez had memorized their message, but he mostly worried about how he would approach the bold, fearless leader, and how he might receive a young stranger who had been trusted with such an important mission.

When he reached San Juan Bautista, he pulled his longcoat collar up against the cold on his neck and turned off the old mission trail, guiding his horse over the slippery rocks and through the adobe mud to the city plaza. At the top of a hill, he rode past the mission church and monastery and up to the glorious two-story Plaza Hotel overlooking the square.

The hotel was white with its name painted in black and red letters across the front and on the side wall. Outside stood a gorgeous cream-colored horse, well blanketed from the cold. Its mane and tail were pure white and it was stoically hitched to the post next to two light wagons. It was the only horse standing outside. He knew it was El Capitan's famous palomino.

Clodoveo Chavez tethered his horse and tossed a thin canvas saddle bag over his shoulder. He entered the hotel barroom through the narrow doorway and walked into a loud din of voices. The dimly lit room was large with a long, polished, mahogany bar against the back wall that was framed by a shiny brass foot rail. Several card tables were set about the room, where cowboys, railroad workers, miners and soldiers were trying their luck. Along the wall to his right was a billiards table and a few languorous women sitting in revealing dresses on long, soft sofas against the wall.

Nobody seemed to notice the messenger's entry, giving him time to survey the scene. His eyes quickly fell on one group of especially well-dressed gentlemen, who were sharing the company of two women, at the last table next to the bar. Tiburcio Vasquez looked up from his cards and his gaze fixed the young man. Amazing, he thought. The likeness was incredible. Clodoveo stood just a little taller than Tiburcio, about five-foot-eleven, and was a little more stout, perhaps two hundred pounds, with a thick neck. But his skin was of the same light complexion, his eyes almost identically gray and his hair thick, long and black. He wore a goatee around his rather thin lips.

The outlaw was facing the doorway, wearing a gray sack suit, with matching pants, vest and coat. The top button of his coat was fastened but the rest were undone and he wore a black and white silk string bow tie and no hat. His black hair was thick, parted to the right, his eyes gray and intelligent and a wide and long goatee framed a wide, friendly, fixed smile.

The other men, also dressed nattily, looked at the leader and followed his eyes to the new guest. Clodoveo sighed heavily under their gaze and walked straight to the table. Tiburcio spoke first.

"What can I do for you, young man?"

"I have an important message to deliver to Tiburcio Vasquez from Lieutenant Burnham."

"Come over here, next to me, where I can hear you without us needing to shout."

He walked around the table and stood next to Tiburcio.

"What is your name?" Tiburcio asked, warmly smiling.

"Clodoveo."

"Clodoveo, let me introduce you to my good friends and associates. This is Angelo Zanetta, the owner of this renowned hotel and restaurant. This is my first lieutenant, Juan Soto. These folks are Tomas Redondo, Gen. Jose Castro, Bartolo Sepulveda, Abelardo Salazar and his gorgeous wife, Señora Margarita Salazar. And that beautiful woman in front of you is Señora Salazar's best friend, Rita Miranda."

Tiburcio paused, then added, "Rita has a husband, but we've never met him."

The table laughed knowingly.

Clodoveo stared an instant too long at Margarita because she was young and bewitching with blue eyes, black hair and copper-colored skin. But he also stared too long pondering the thought that a woman of supposedly good reputation was hardly ever seen inside a saloon, let alone one in a town so dominated by the Catholic Church, which was, he guessed, precisely the reason she was in the bar. He also thought he had noticed her hand on Mr. Vasquez's leg, and that made him quickly look away again.

"What is the nature of this information you wish to share," Tiburcio asked. "Should we be discreet and talk in private?"

"I ... I ... I think we should," Clodoveo answered.

"OK. Juan, let's take the boy to our room upstairs. Gentlemen, ladies - let's meet for dinner tonight around 7:00. My treat. And if you don't mind, I'd like to bring my mother. And perhaps this young man will join us. Don't forget to save my winnings behind the bar."

Tiburcio, Soto and the boy ascended the stairs, their boots and spurs loudly echoing on the wood steps and down the upstairs hall. Inside the room, Tiburcio flung open the shutters of a window that overlooked the mission. He looked down at his white horse, which was directly below.

The three men sat at a round table at the window. A cool breeze drifted in. Tiburcio set his large Colt cap-and-ball revolver in front of him. Clodoveo looked tensely at the weapon.

"What exactly does Alfonso Burnham wish to tell me?" Tiburcio inquired.

The boy placed the shoulder bag on the table, and said, "I have news regarding Harry Morse, the sheriff up in Alameda County."

Tiburcio and Soto glanced at each other and laughed heartily.

"*El Muchacho?*" Tiburcio blurted out. "What is the concern over a man who cannot shoot straight and gets saddle sores from a twenty minute ride?"

"He cannot even grow hair on his face," Soto added. "Harry Morse's cheeks are smoother than my sister's!"

"*Es la verdad. Es la verdad!*" Tiburcio agreed, still chuckling. He wagged a finger at Clodoveo. "He's more of a boy than you!"

Clodoveo respectfully waited for their laughter to die down. The massive frame of Soto shook with each roar, then became still and disconcerting again.

"Burnham," he started, "told me you might respond in this fashion. Therefore, he wanted me to tell you that a lot has changed since you have been up north. The sheriff is a serious threat to the regiment and the revolution. Burnham thought you might not believe me so he gave me these newspaper articles to show you."

The boy tapped the shoulder bag on the table.

"But before you read what the papers say about Sheriff Morse, Burnham wanted you to know that the northern band of outlaws has become depleted, mostly at the hand of, uh, Sheriff Morse."

The two outlaws weren't joking anymore. The boy continued.

"Morse captured Gallegos with just three men. Three men against thirty outlaws, up in the black hills. Then he marched directly into New Almaden Mine and snatched Joaquin Olivera …"

"Who allowed him in New Almaden Mine to make the arrest?" shouted Tiburcio, pounding his fist on the table. The gun jumped. "That superintendent must die."

"And," Clodoveo continued, "he paralyzed Narciso Bojorques with a gunshot wound to his arm. Narciso managed to get away, but Morse took his horse and gun and paraded them through the hills and into Oakland for everyone to see. Then he tracked Bojorques for a month with a posse."

"Where was Narciso shot by the sheriff?" Tiburcio asked.

"At Alisal."

"At Alisal! There is nothing but Californios around Alisal. Soto! We need to pay the Mexicans there a visit, and remind them of the price of being traitors to their country and abetting the enemy."

"So, Bojorques escaped?" Soto asked.

"Yes. But he's dead now. He was killed in Copperopolis in a dispute over a card game. Apparently, he could not draw very quickly after Morse shot him," the boy said. "It cost him his life."

"Are there any liberators left up north? Or have they conceded everything to this God-damned sheriff?"

"There are enough bandits to keep the sheriff busy. Burnham wanted to make sure I told you that. But undoubtedly Morse's actions have emboldened other lawmen, as well as the citizens. The tide, he fears, has turned."

"What about Narato Ponce?" Soto inquired.

"Three pistol balls and thirteen buckshot. In Pinole."

"Morse?"

"Yes."

Tiburcio did not expect news this bad. If this trend continued, the lawmen would take control of Alameda, then Contra Costa, Santa Clara and finally Monterey, compressing the outlaws into one small territory in Northern California. They would be forced farther and farther south and Tiburcio's recruitment for the revolution would be greatly constricted. He wondered if he had done wrong to let loosely affiliated gangs of outlaws operate independently up north, meddling very little in their affairs, while he, Soto and Procopio stayed exclusively in the Coast Range counties of Monterey and San Joaquin.

Tiburcio, Soto and Procopio had worked hard to secure the Coast Range territory. They recruited as many Mexicans as were needed to get a job done - sometimes six or seven at a time - then split the profits among them. After the heist, the recruits were allowed to return to their legitimate jobs - as vaqueros or farm laborers - with their pockets heavier, their lips sealed and their hearts loyal. The Coast Range anglos, so rich in cattle and living lives like princes, had been easy pickings. But what the hell were they doing up north?

"What do you think of Sheriff Morse?" Tiburcio asked Clodoveo.

The question took the young man by surprise.

"I don't want to know what Burnham thinks," Tiburcio clarified. "I want to know what you think."

Clodoveo took a moment to compose his answer.

"I have never seen a lawman so thoroughly research the criminals he is pursuing and the places they hide out. He is obsessed. The newspapers say he has enough information to fill a book on every outlaw in Northern California, complete with photographs and notes on their habits, appearances and misdeeds down to the finest detail."

"But can he fight?"

"He has a bold streak and ..."

"And what?"

"Uncanny luck."

"Hmmm. Luck. Let me see the newspapers," Tiburcio commanded. "Are there pictures of this Sheriff Morse?"

"Yes."

"Good. We'll need to spread his photograph from the cities to the most remote huts so *bandidos* and our supporters everywhere will know of his whereabouts and be ready for him."

The boy handed Tiburcio three newspapers folded to articles on Morse. They were from the *San Francisco*

Chronicle, Oakland Tribune and *Alameda County Gazette.*
Tiburcio read aloud the *Chronicle*'s first.

"Morse exhibited his eminent fitness for the responsible position from the very onset of his official career, and the 'beardless boy,' as he was first contemptuously denominated by the outlaws who were overrunning the eastern portion of the county, soon rendered himself notorious, alike for the exhibition of shrewdness, energy and high qualities of courage, coolness, and readiness in face of peril."

"Jesus Christ himself did not get such praise when I was in missionary school," Tiburcio wailed.

He silently read the story in the *Tribune* next, sharing these lines with Soto, who was illiterate:

"It appears to be just as feasible for a thief to escape Morse as for a camel to get through the eye of a needle."

"*Bastante!*" Soto grunted. "I've heard enough."

"So, our beardless boy is suddenly a cunning, sure-shot, invincible gringo hero? This one man is capable of bringing down an army of outlaws all by himself, eh?" Tiburcio asked sarcastically. "And what does Burnham want to accomplish by sending you down here to give me this information?"

"He needs your help. He needs you to come back. If you can strike hard at several ranches and businesses under Morse's nose, then maybe it will embolden the remaining outlaws and turn the sentiment of townsfolk against the sheriff - once again."

"Soto, we need to set out in the morning for the East Bay. Tonight, before dinner, let us check out of our hotel room so we don't, in any way, involve Zanetta and his business. I'll stay at Salazar's house while you and the boy find a nearby ranch."

"There is one more thing, if you please," the young man said. "You see, Fred Welch," Clodoveo stopped in mid-sentence and quickly corrected himself - "uh, that is, Alfonso Burnham, would like to discuss matters with you face to face at Mission San Jose. I promised I would return with a confirmation on the time and place."

"You will stay with Soto and me until I say you can leave. We'll send you back to Burnham when we're ready," Tiburcio said austerely. Then he softened, "There's something I like about you kid. It's almost as if I've met you before."

Later that evening, everybody was gathered at the table in Zanetta's restaurant inside the Plaza Hotel. Zanetta had already established his reputation as an extraordinary hotel operator and restaurateur in New Orleans and Monterey. But those previous businesses paled in comparison to the profits Zanetta was making in San Juan Bautista, mostly because of the town's location at the crossroads of several roads. In San Juan, teamsters brought precious metal north from the quicksilver mines and took back supplies for the miners. Dozens of ranchers out west in Santa Cruz, Monterey, Hollister and Watsonville sold and traded cattle and sheep here. Travelers came west out of Stockton and Los Banos in need of stables, food and rooms for the night before pushing on to the coastal cities. Zanetta had a hand in every one of the travelers' needs.

Abelardo Salazar, Margarita, Zanetta, Sepulveda, Gen. Castro, the heedless Rita Miranda, Clodoveo, Soto and Tiburcio Vasquez waited for the arrival of one more guest.

"Has anyone seen my mother?" Tiburcio asked.

"I have not seen her today," Zanetta said. "In fact, A couple of her regular customers came into the hotel to get a meal because she was not anywhere to be found."

No longer feeling that Monterey welcomed her, Guadalupe Vasquez had packed up and moved her home and culinary business to San Juan Bautista several years ago. This city's friendliness to Mexicans and the influence of the mission on its citizens reminded her of earlier days in Monterey. Business was not as lucrative as her patio cantina, but she survived comfortably, selling meals to the dozens of teamsters crisscrossing through San Juan Bautista every day, dropping off ore and picking up provisions.

"Well, if you'll excuse me," Tiburcio said. "I'll ride over to her house and make sure everything is fine."

TIBURCIO!

"Tell Mr. Comfort at the stable to lend you a horse that's ready, Tiburcio," Zanetta said. "No need to saddle your palomino. Let him rest for your trip tomorrow. In fact, take one of my buggies over to your mother's house."

Tiburcio arrived at his mother's house just west of the city to find not a flicker of light in the place. The property appeared as if undisturbed for some time. He entered without knocking. A dog whimpered up to his leg.

"*Donde es la Doña?*" Tiburcio asked the canine.

As if he could answer, the dog led Tiburcio to his mother's bedroom and then curled up outside the closed door. Tiburcio knocked. Then again. No answer. Finally, he opened the door. Guadalupe was lying on her back, staring at the ceiling. She was not blinking. Dread overcame Tiburcio. He walked to her bedside, looked down at her and saw her slowly close and open her eyes. Relieved, he touched her forehead. Her skin was hot to the touch and her lips were cracked and dry.

"Mother! How long have you been lying here. Let me get you some water and a wet towel."

"No, Tiburcio. Bring me some whiskey."

"Water first," her son said.

After Tiburcio applied a cool towel to her forehead and helped her sip the alcohol and water. Guadalupe sat up with her back against the bed board.

"I was going to leave town tomorrow, but I will stay and make sure you are better. I am going to fetch the doctor."

"No, Tiburcio. It's just a bit of the bug. I will send for Maria in the morning. She lives so close. You go ahead and go on your trip. I will be fine."

Tiburcio insisted on the doctor seeing her tonight and sent the buggy driver to get him. After examining her, the physician left a bottle of anti-dysenteric mixture, some ointment and sarsaparilla pills on her bedside table. He assured Tiburcio that Guadalupe, with these medicines and plenty of water and rest, would feel much better in the morning.

Before he left his mother, Tiburcio stepped into her spare bedroom where he had saved his money in a locked strong box. He nearly emptied it. He would dispense the coins among the poor, landless Mexicans between here and Alameda. In exchange, they would listen to his tales of the evil sheriff who wants an all-Anglo countryside. He would tell them of the brewing revolution that will gain back their stolen land and lifestyle. Then he'd terrorize Morse.

After dinner Tiburcio, Soto and Clodoveo stayed to play three-card monte in the saloon. Margarita stayed with them as her husband retired. Rita stayed too. Margarita sat close to Tiburcio while Rita put her arm around Clodoveo and leaned close to him, peering over his shoulder at the card table. She smelled faintly of sweet fennel, he thought. Margarita began telling the newcomer about the woes of living in San Juan Bautista.

"Don't stay long here, Señor Chavez. The quiet of the streets will drive you mad. The silence is smothering. And if that's not suffocating enough, the church, with its Aves and vespers and Hail Marys after confessions, will drive you to be a heathen."

Tiburcio smiled, because he had heard it all before from Margarita.

"She only speaks like this when her husband has retired to home. He loves it here."

"You can make fun of me all you want Tiburcio," Margarita said, lovingly stroking Tiburcio's beard. "You have chosen a better life, a more daring occupation. You have decided to fight against conquest. You have dared to take on a higher cause so there is nothing for you to be bitter about, unlike me. ... And besides, you can leave this town when you feel like it and take to the highway."

"Perhaps you would like to try the highway life?"

"Oh, if only you really could take me," Margarita sighed. "If only."

Around 11:00 p.m., they all stepped outside the hotel. Soto lit a cigarette and listened to Tiburcio explain their excursion.

Margarita rested on a bench with Rita, knowing when to stay out of earshot.

"I have some unsettled business from a long time ago," Tiburcio explained to Soto. "A group of gringos stole some cattle from my brothers and took my mother's land. If they are still up there in Marin, I am going to pay them a visit. With a couple more men we can pick off three hundred head of cattle and move it right through the territory under Morse's nose. We will sell them down here. Along the way, we will pay our sympathizers whatever they need, whether it's a meal, a horse, a cow, a sheep, a gun or a lawyer, for their loyalty. Talk of revolution is strong, and I have two thousand dollars in my purse."

Tiburcio looked over at Clodoveo, who was lost in quiet conversation with Rita.

"Let's see Morse keep up with us when we melt into the mountains before he can even mount his pinto!"

Then, Tiburcio interrupted Clodoveo.

"Are you any good on a horse, son?" he asked.

"Me? Yes, I'm all right."

"We need a good vaquero. Have you ever run cattle? No? Jesus, what did they recruit you for? We will cut you loose, then, before the raid so you can alert Burnham that we are coming. Burnham can help get us through southern Alameda. Go find some shelter for the night, you two, while I walk Señora Salazar home."

Tiburcio tossed a bag of coins to Clodoveo.

Chapter 6: Informant
Oakland, Calif.
January 1867

Alfonso Burnham's name told much about how he was born and raised. Entering this world in Massachusetts, his father brought the family to California in 1849, bought a large rancho and became very wealthy. He later served as a district judge, but died only ten years after arriving on the West Coast. Alfonso spent his youth around Californio boys, learned to speak fluent Spanish and ride like a vaquero.

After his father's death, Alfonso started to run with bad company and ended up in San Quentin on a grand theft charge. In prison, he met Tiburcio and Soto. After his discharge in 1865, he adopted a more anglicized alias, Fred Welch, and fell back in with rough company. For a while, he ran with Soto during a violent streak of robberies. Soto split from Burnham after Tiburcio's release and another spell of bad luck came Burnham's way - in the form of Sheriff Morse. Morse tossed him back in prison for one year for stealing a prized mare.

Morse, as he did with all the felons he captured, checked up on Burnham whenever he could. Burnham would duck around corners or pull his hat down over his eyes to avoid the sheriff on the street. One day, Morse saw Burnham in San Leandro and forced the ex-convict to look at him. The sheriff grabbed the rangy man, dragged him into the alley and stood him up against the wall with a strong hand on his throat.

"What are you doing, Alfonso?"

"I am looking for work."

"Here? You sure you aren't here to cause trouble? In my town?"

"No, I rent a room down at the train station with my wife," Burnham said, and for the first time Morse noticed tears in his eyes.

"What's wrong?"

"I am trying to stay on the good road, sheriff. But I am so damn hungry. My wife and I have eaten only soda crackers for the past week, and only have water to drink. I am afraid we'll die of starvation on the street."

Morse let go of his throat.

"Is this true? If it is true you are trying to be a law-abiding, honest man, I will try to help. In the morning, come to my office. I have some work for you."

• • •

Three horsemen came crashing out of the hills on a moonless night and drove their ill-gotten cattle hard through ravines and along creeks where there was good tree cover until they had no choice but to rest the herd. The beeves were getting thinner under the rigorous pace so Tiburcio hid them in a grassy glen and let them fatten up. The land was tended to by a Mexican *burrogurerra* who was paid handsomely for the risk he was taking giving the rustlers protection. With nowhere to go for several days, Tiburcio ordered Clodoveo to summon Burnham to their temporary grazing spot in four days' time. He and Soto waited.

On the fourth day, they had not seen a sign of either Clodoveo or Burnham. So they waited in the shade of the willows.

"How much longer do we give them?" Soto asked.

"Another two hours."

Around midmorning, they spotted two men on horseback on the horizon.

"It's them. Let's get ready to move."

Unnoticed by the two fugitives, a group of officers had discarded their horses near a creek bed and were creeping through chaparral at the lip of a ridge overlooking the pilfered cows. The lawmen found good cover and watched Alfonso Burnham and his young companion approach the willows where Tiburcio and Soto were camped.

Burnham, tall and slender, with a full beard, walked his horse across the meadow and through their grazing cattle with an unmistakable high gait. The officers spoke in low tones of how Burnham had chosen a very unsafe profession, that of a double-crosser, and took bets on whether he would live much past his thirtieth birthday. As for the young man next to Burnham - if he didn't watch the company he kept, he would be lucky to live to be twenty-five. For now, however, Burnham and his young companion had proved to be quite useful to the lawmen. They had put perhaps the two most notorious outlaws at their fingertips.

The posse waited for a sign that the outlaws were breaking camp below. Through his field glasses, Sheriff John Adams saw movement around the willows. He held up two fingers and two deputies mounted their horses and rode in opposite directions to notify the other posses waiting to the north and south.

Adams turned to Richardson.

"We need to flush 'em out. You cover us from that rock on the crest. Start raking the trees with shots. They'll have to run into the clear or surrender. I'll be ready to gun them down when they make a move. If we don't kill 'em or capture 'em, and they escape, Morse's posse up the road will finish the job."

From behind the rock, Richardson aimed his Winchester and began taking cracks into the cluster of trees. He loaded and unloaded a pair of rifles several times at quick intervals. Suddenly, a riderless horse shot out of the willows. But this was something different. Gunshots were spraying back at Richardson seemingly out of nowhere. Adams peered hard at the black puffs of smoke coming from the madly galloping horse and saw a hand gripping the horn and a spurred boot locked on the cantle.

"One of them outlaws is on that horse!" Richardson shouted to Adams.

The guns went silent, and only the sound of beating hooves could be heard. The pause gave the officers a moment to stand up to take better aim. If this unseen rider chose to turn and come riding back it would only take him a fraction of a second to flip to the other side of the stallion. The sheriff figured he had one good shot is all.

Adams aimed his rifle and pulled the trigger. He thought he had gotten off a good shot, but the horse and rider didn't slow. The massive palomino made a swift turn and was racing madly back to the willows. Adams watched the horse speed past the willows and up a deer trail on the other side of the gorge. Two other horses and riders dashed away from the cluster of trees, too, also heading up the hill.

"They're on the run!"

In a flash, the lawmen swept down on the camp. Eight men from two posses followed the outlaw's horses while Morse, Adams and Richardson took a look around the camp. They found Burnham whimpering from behind a rock, physically unharmed and lucky to be alive.

"You did fine, Alfonso. It will be all right. We're close on their trail. Thanks to you."

"Only if you capture him, sir. Only if you kill him. Otherwise, I am a marked man. I'm good as dead! Tiburcio knows I betrayed him"

One of the deputies found a trail of blood, and soon all eight were riding hard in the same direction. A half mile ahead of them, Tiburcio's stomach gurgled warm, sticky blood from a puncture. He stopped and tied his serape tight around the wound. Clodoveo rode up next to him.

"Tiburcio," the young man called. "You must stop that bleeding. I will divert them so you can escape."

"You turned out to be some rider, kid," Tiburcio said, breathing laboriously. "When did you … discover … Burnham had … set the trap?"

"As soon as I delivered your message, the sheriff came out of a back room and never let Burnham or me out of his sight. So from then on I had to pretend like I was in on the ruse."

"OK. We need to act fast. I wish I could do something for you in return for your courage," Tiburcio said. "Here, take this saddle bag. There's money for you in there."

He tossed the bag to Clodoveo, then unhooked his lariat and tied himself unflinchingly into his saddle.

"No," said Clodoveo.

Clodoveo put his hand into his pocket and pulled out twenty-five dollars in old, wrinkled and faded notes.

"I've been waiting for permission to spend this money, sir. Do you remember? I've been carrying it a long time."

Despite his pain, Tiburcio nodded his head and smiled.

"Yes. Back at New Idria. You may spend it. We are even."

They heard branches cracking a short distance behind. Tiburcio guided his horse off the trail and through the thicket, while Clodoveo made sure the posse saw him. The young man spurred his horse up onto its back legs and began trampling the shrubs to disguise where Tiburcio had gone off the trail. Then he kicked the stallion's sides and galloped off, the lawmen in pursuit.

Every once in a while Tiburcio would awake from unconsciousness and look around in a haze, straining to keep his neck up. Some inner compass still working in his mad mind, even though his physical and mental powers barely functioned, would give him an idea of where he was and he would redirect his horse. Two days and seventy miles later, a cataleptic rider and spent horse showed up near Monterey.

The next thing Tiburcio became cognizant of was that he was alive and lying on a soft bed in familiar surroundings. The bandit rubbed his eyes and tried to shake off the frightening image he had seen in a dream. It was a head in a jar of alcohol in a room engulfed by flames. The face was familiar but frozen in horror. Fire swirled around the head, and red-glowing and smoking timber from a roof fell all around. All Tiburcio could do in the dream was stare at this frightening face - it looked so much like himself. Suddenly the dream images were gone and he was looking up into the wizened, leathered face of someone from his youth.

"Don Cervantes?"

"Tiburcio!"

"I cannot stay here, Don Cervantes! It's not safe for you. I'm a wanted man. I must leave right away."

"Your generosity once saved us, so we are glad to repay you."

"You didn't have to give up your ranch?"

"No, with your money we were able to afford an American lawyer. He entered our property in the county books and called off the land officials. Then he forced the sheriff to evict the squatters. We've been thriving ever since. I have wanted to thank you for so long."

"But this is unsafe, Don Cervantes. I am wounded and cannot get away if they come. I have no idea how I got here, and I may have left a trail."

"Rest, Tiburcio, rest. I will give you some more news when you are fully recovered."

Three weeks later, Tiburcio leaned against a post on Cervantes' patio watching scores of workers doing chores around the ranch. The ranch had indeed grown and prospered, with a blacksmith's shop in the distance and rows of crops stretching to the pines. Tiburcio felt Cervantes come up from behind him.

"Tiburcio, it is time I tell you some news."

"Yes, sir?"

"Sit down. It is bad news."

Tiburcio obeyed.

"Your mother is dead."

"No! When?"

"They tell me it was soon after you left San Juan Bautista."

"But the doctor saw her. She was fine. He told me she would be fine."

"Apparently, she came down with a very high fever and died within three days. Your sister and brothers searched for you, but they had to hold services and bury the body."

"I must go and visit her graveside!"

"It's too soon. It's only been a month."

"My strength is back."

"I mean, the vigilantes have not called off their search for you. They are crawling all over the place"

But as hard as Don Cervantes tried to convince Tiburcio that his life was in danger, he could not stop him. The outlaw was strong enough now to physically resist. So Tiburcio thanked Cervantes for his kindness and hastily took the main road to Monterey, where his mother had been laid to rest.

For four weeks, Morse, Richardson, Adams and their lawmen combed the countryside in search of Tiburcio Vasquez, knowing he was gravely injured. Some conjectured that he had dropped dead off his horse and had been eaten by wolves or mountain lions. But the lawmen kept searching until they were hungry, homesick, sore, and tired. The time had come to call off the search. Then, they saw a lone figure coming up the hill.

"Holy shit!" one of them exclaimed.

Tiburcio Vasquez stopped fifty yards away from the eight armed and mounted men. They drew weapons and slowly approached.

When they were halfway to him, Tiburcio called out.

"I know the way you do justice I'll see a rope before I see jail. If that is the way you want it, I will put up a gunfight that will make your unborn children shudder! But if you can guarantee I won't hang, I will drop this gun belt to the ground and go harmlessly with you."

The men quickly discussed their options.

"You have our word," Morse shouted back.

"There's just one more thing."

"Don't push it, bandit!"

"Take me to my mother's grave before you lock me away."

TIBURCIO!

Everybody kept their word. Tiburcio was returned to the high, gray walls of San Quentin. He whiled away his second prison term laboring in the brickyard and huddling at night in his bunk with just a shabby blanket to protect himself against the San Francisco Bay's chill and fog.

He showed no inclination to attempt an escape this time. Even if he had wanted to, the guards watched him much more closely now. His reputation as a hero in the eyes of many of the Mexican prisoners and his role as instigator of two prison breaks during his previous term kept the attention of his captors unflaggingly fixed on him. He knew the slightest provocation would get him shot and killed. But mostly Tiburcio behaved like a model convict because he felt blessed that he had only been sentenced to four years. And if he were good, he'd be out in three. There was no sense in pressing his luck.

One day, as he often did, Tiburcio walked up to the upper balcony of the stone cellblock and looked across the white-flashing water at Mount Diablo in the distance. Somewhere out there there was the cunning sheriff responsible for putting him back in prison. It may have been your worst mistake, Tiburcio thought. When I get out of here, I'll have fifty more hardened ex-convicts as recruits. I'll be wiser. I will be more methodical. I will trust no one. I will close ranks and lead the rebellion forward. And, unlike before, I will no longer try to avoid bloodshed! I will be ruthless."

Suddenly, in the middle of these self-declarations, he felt the earth move. Though he was standing on stone, the ground was trembling. It didn't shake the stone prison much, but he could faintly feel the swaying nonetheless, and he could hear the vibrations roll across the bay, where he watched buildings here and there topple in a puff of smoke. From the cellblock, the distant buildings looked as if they were wooden dollhouses being pounded by an invisible hammer.

Tiburcio wondered from his safe perch, as he looked across the bay at the silent chaos and fire and smoke, whether the sheriff's great luck had run out.

At that very same moment, Harry Morse stood among the ruins of his flour mill and looked up at the heavens for patience and guidance and answers. Morse had invested heavily in the mill. It would devastate him financially.

Soon after, more trouble visited the sheriff. His wife threatened to leave him because she was so upset at her husband's lengthy absences from home, away from their growing family as he relentlessly pursued criminals all over Northern California. In no little way, their marital acrimony affected their son, too. George had become rebellious and prone to violent outbursts. The sheriff suddenly had more problems than just Mexican bandits.

The earthquake of 1868 had struck quickly, ferociously, but the real, lasting great changes in the landscape were happening more slowly and indelibly. Gringo squatters were erecting cabins and fences, carving up the countryside where groves of oaks grew uninterrupted right up to vast carpets of grass. Once-sparsely settled towns now teemed with people, many of them gringos who had swarmed out of the foothills to the city streets to drink and gamble and, bitter at never striking it rich in gold, take out their frustrations on native Californians. Towns of three or four buildings along one main street grew into cities with several streets lined with bakeries, furniture stores, banks, saloons and groceries.

Up in the gold country, away from the towns and ranches, entire gold-mining towns had completely emptied. Hundreds of abandoned, crumbling wood buildings, rusting pickaxes and rotting sluice machines littered the rivers. Entire gold-mining towns had completely emptied. There was almost no chance any longer for an individual to get rich off minerals in the Sacramento or American rivers.

And, Tiburcio quickly noticed, it was the Mexicans who were being squeezed out of the equation, becoming poorer and poorer.

TIBURCIO!

"When the flames of resentment leap this high, they can't be stopped," Tiburcio whispered to himself. "It is time. *Fuerza de la revolución*! There is nothing more to lose."

PART III: TIBURCIO
Chapter 1: Peddler
Panoche Range
June 1870

Tiburcio Vasquez walked out of the shadow of the prison wall into the yellow-gray light of dawn with purpose in his step. The sun was just rising over the eastern hills, coloring and sharpening the soft edges of morning. Everything in his life, he told himself, now must move with intention toward one goal. First and foremost, he needed to put distance between himself and San Quentin. He had wasted far too much time behind bars.

He needed a wide-brimmed hat, spurs for his boots, a horse and, of course, a gun. He took a ferry across the bay and then hopped on a train, his first time ever riding the railroads. The train felt too confining and too noisy for his liking, but he appreciated its purposefulness, chugging onward without stopping or changing direction.

He thought about the men he had met in prison who had attempted to rob trains. Railroads were increasingly moving enormous amounts of commerce and people all over the state so robbing one or two trains sounded much more lucrative than raiding stage after stage and much less work than cattle rustling. He thought about the men he had met in prison who had attempted train robberies. He couldn't paint an exact picture in his head of how to carry out such a heist, so he asked the robbers: How do you stop a fast-moving train in the open range? You tear up the track and cause a tremendous wreck.

TIBURCIO!

That was the best way, they claimed. It was not easy to accomplish but the payoff was extraordinary, they told him.

He exited the train in Gilroy and found that life outside the prison moved much faster now. There were more people, more horses, more wagons, more stores, more saloons. Tiburcio threaded his way through the main thoroughfare and kept walking south, clear out of town. He would sleep under the stars, if he slept at all.

He scraped together a few hours of shut eye under some thicket, but hunger forced him to rise. He followed the Pajaro River course and watched scores of trout jumping in a calm section of the waterway. He was debating how he might go about catching, filleting and cooking one when he saw a single rider approaching in the distance, likely on his way to Gilroy. The rider's horse was heavy with sacks containing knives, belts, ropes, skins and smoked meat.

Tiburcio scrambled up into the brush to hide. When the traveler arrived at the river, he stepped out and confronted him. The man instantly drew a pistol.

"Wait. Don't shoot! You are mistaken. I only want to buy some of your goods. I need a rope, a good knife and something to eat. I don't even have a gun. Look, I have money," Tiburcio said, producing a leather pouch containing only a few coins and some rocks. "I have no intention to rob you."

"What are you doing out here without a horse or a weapon?" the peddler asked suspiciously.

"I lost heavily at the card tables in Gilroy. I lost my horse, gun and spurs, but in the end I managed to win back a small amount of money. They cast me out of the saloon and ran me out of town, believing I was trying to pull a fast one, before I could buy any of my possessions back. They don't take kindly to Mexicans once they start winning."

"OK," the peddler said, sympathizing with the man who appeared to pose no threat since he was unarmed. "I will unpack this horse to show you my wares if you promise you will purchase something."

He untied his saddle bags and began laying knives, belts, spurs and sizable chunks of wrapped jerky on a blanket on the soft ground at the river's edge. Tiburcio kept an eye on the peddler's pistol, stuck down in his waistband at his back.

"There," the peddler said, standing straight up and gesturing to his display. "That's probably all you're interested in, if that small sack is all the money you have."

Tiburcio pretended to look over the merchandise.

"I've decided I don't want to buy any knives right now. Perhaps just some jerky. Cut me off two dollars worth, please."

The peddler bent down to pick up the wrapped meat and Tiburcio sprung like a cat, grabbing the gun from his waistband.

"You are just a lying Mexican thief?" the peddler yelled, gnashing his teeth.

"I changed my mind," Tiburcio said, aiming the barrel at the man's chest. "I will take a knife. And your horse. And your money."

"You cock-sucking greaser!"

"You are lucky I don't take your life, too," Tiburcio calmly said.

He stepped back and shot the peddler right through his boot. With his pouch full, Tiburcio rode straight away to Cantua Canyon.

Chapter 2: Looting
Coast Range
Summer 1870 to Winter 1871

The two vaqueros spied Tiburcio Vasquez approaching and raced down upon him from the rocky outcrops. Tiburcio knew the lookouts had seen him many miles ago, and he was impressed with their vigilance. They escorted him through the narrow mouth of Cantua Canyon. The passageway opened into a lush glen of abundant sycamores, spotted with oak trees and carpeted with luxuriant grass and wildflowers. The hiding place felt as much like home as anywhere else Tiburcio could have gone.

Yet, Cantua had changed. Since Tiburcio's last visit several years ago, scores more of native Californians had taken refuge there. His escorts told him nearly fifteen hundred inhabited the basin now. He looked around at dozens of huts that had been built as he was led to one of them. He tilted his head to enter the low doorway and was greeted by the large and wild figure of Juan Soto. Francisco Barcenas stood and Procopio stepped forward.

"Welcome home, *El Capitan!*"

"It is good to be here."

"Nice to see you again, Tiburcio," said a voice from behind him. He turned and saw Clodoveo Chavez smiling. The boy still closely resembled him. The two embraced.

"You saved my life," Tiburcio told him.

"No, I got you locked up. I will never forgive myself for not keeping that posse occupied longer. Or killing all of them."

"Hell, my friend, the posse stayed in the saddle for over a month. Whoever heard such a thing? What could you possibly do? No, Clodoveo, I was stupid. And that's how I got caught. No more being stupid."

Tiburcio looked each one of his compatriots in the eyes and added, "The time has come for us all to be smart. Not only smart, but ruthless and unyielding, too."

"No lawman has yet to get near this stronghold," Procopio said. "From San Juan to here, it is absolutely safe - at least for now."

"For now?" Tiburcio asked.

"We have pushed our activity closer and closer to Monterey and up the coast into Alameda and Contra Costa counties," Chavez said. "That's where the herds are and the money is."

"It's also where the law draws the line and makes its stand," added Barcenas.

"We will continue the progress I heard so much about while in San Quentin," Tiburcio said. "But for now, I am broke. I need a sombrero, a good horse, fine *botas,* a decent handgun and a modern rifle."

"We are taking one hundred cattle to re-brand and sell down in San Juan," Soto explained. "You can take a share of that profit and buy what you need from our people in San Juan."

"Thank you. All of you made me feel at home again," Tiburcio said. "But what's next?"

"Next? After San Juan?"

The fugitives looked at each other.

"Yes, we must always be thinking about the revolution, moving toward our liberation," Tiburcio continued. "We must always go forward, just like that train I rode to Gilroy. We must bring this fight to fruition. It is time. We need large amounts of cash to buy the necessary weapons and ammunition. I've had a lot of time to think about this and plan our course. I will tell you more as the days go on. But I met a man in San Quentin who claims he has access to two hundred men and hundreds of stored weapons and ammunition smuggled west from Civil War battlefields. They are hunkered down near the border. I told him when we get the cash, I will find him. We will join forces."

"We go to market in about a week with that herd we're fattening up," Clodoveo said. "That will be a start."

"That's fine. It *is* a start. But does anybody know how to rob a train?"

The bandits laughed.

"Do not laugh. I know a way, and we will do so."

Six days later, Vasquez, Bartolo Sepulveda, Barcenas, Procopio, Chavez, Soto, Carabajal, Molino and a newcomer named Rodriguez led the herd into San Juan, where a buyer awaited. Tiburcio told Soto and Procopio to take care of the transaction and to meet him afterward at the Plaza Hotel.

"Clodoveo, come with me," he ordered.

It was the first time since his capture that Tiburcio had set foot inside the Plaza Hotel, or any public establishment like it. The hotel was even more elegant now, with its polished mahogany bar, cherry-wood poker tables and framed artwork along the walls, including some modern, risqué nudes. Tiburcio and Clodoveo went straight up to the long bar, stomped a boot on the shiny foot rail and demanded two beers. The beverage was warm and foamy and the first sip sent bubbles straight to Tiburcio's head.

"I am afraid beer is too strong for me after all these years," he said to his loyal companion.

"You never were much of a drinker, Tiburcio."

Tiburcio heard his name shrieked. He turned to see the penetrating blue eyes, copper-toned skin and black hair of Margarita Salazar. She tried hard not to show her affection in public but she walked up and stood close enough to Tiburcio that he could feel her warm, sweet breath. Rita Miranda, her companion, was quickly at Clodoveo's side.

"How do you keep getting more and more handsome through the years, Tiburcio?"

"It's not easy. But it is necessary in order to keep up with these younger vaqueros," he joked, slapping Clodoveo on the back.

"Are you in town for very long?"

"We are selling a herd and then we have some business up in the Bay Area. We will be gone for quite a while afterward ... maybe forever."

"Sleeping on the hard ground all that time?" Margarita asked, her breasts pushed up against Tiburcio's chest. "With only vaqueros and outlaws for companionship? Ah, that is no way to live."

"That is why Clodoveo and I snuck up here to the Plaza for a little pleasure while the rest of the men are working."

"Why don't you stay at our ranch tonight? Abelardo would insist."

"How is Señor Salazar?'"

Rita let out a scornful laugh.

"Oh, he's fine," she answered for her friend in a sarcastic tone. "He is very content to have his wife spend the rest of her days on this earth serving his estate. Tell Tiburcio how much you enjoy drawing water, tending to a large and ever-growing family, including dogs, and pulling husks from corn at harvest time like a common Indian. Yes, Abelardo is fine, Tiburcio, but why don't you ask how Margarita is? She and I are not so content."

Rita looked closely into Clodoveo's eyes as if searching for his response.

"Tiburcio!" boomed a voice from across the room. Antonio Zanetta had just descended the stairs with Abelardo. They had been discussing business in his upstairs office. He strode over and threw his big arms around the bandit.

"Your timing is perfect," Zanetta informed Tiburcio. "Our saloon orchestra begins tonight. Their very first night. Have you played quadrilles? It's very popular. Very energetic. You could take up your guitar for the dance!"

"It's been a long time," Tiburcio reminded Zanetta.

"Why make it any longer? Start up again tonight."

TIBURCIO!

When the rest of the vaqueros in Tiburcio's gang entered the hotel saloon later in the evening, they found their leader strumming quickly along with the brass band. Several foursomes were dancing in the middle of the floor. The room was loud and crowded. The saloon stayed boisterous until past midnight, when Tiburcio excused himself and left the bar to walk Margarita Salazar home.

Tiburcio looked forward to resting his weary body on a soft bed for the first time in four years. Abelardo had left the Plaza much earlier, and now Margarita and Tiburcio walked home arm in arm. As they approached the house, Margarita suddenly stopped.

"Take me with you, Tiburcio," she demanded. "I cannot stay here any longer. I am dying day by day."

Tiburcio was astonished at her request.

"It would be too dangerous. There are always posses, sheriffs, gunfights."

"I am not afraid."

"It's too difficult. Day after day of riding for miles on end only to sleep every night on the cold, hard ground."

"If I were with you, I would love every second of life," she said, digging her fingers into his arms. "It's been a long time, Tiburcio. It is time for you to love again."

She began kissing him on the cheeks and then the mouth and desire filled Tiburcio, too. He quickly saw the advantages to having Margarita with him night after night. But the plan was too crazy.

"What about Rita?" he asked. "You would not want to leave your best friend alone!"

Margarita blurted out a chuckle and then covered her mouth.

"She is already with Clodoveo," she whispered. "Waiting for us!"

"You must be out of your mind."

"Come on. They are waiting for us in a cave in the hills. I cannot stay here without you or Rita or anyone I care about."

"What about Abelardo?" Tiburcio snapped. "He is a friend!"

Margarita dropped her hands from his neck and took two steps back.

"A bandit with scruples," she said with a short, sarcastic laugh. "Imagine!"

She ran ahead of Tiburcio to the house.

Despite their disagreement, Tiburcio slept soundly in Salazar's home. In the morning, he pulled his boots on quietly, trying not to wake anybody in the household. He slowly turned the bedroom door handle and was relieved to not find Margarita waiting on the other side.

But she had other plans. Earlier in the morning, she had snuck out of the house and ran straight to where Clodoveo and Rita were waiting. She had felt Tiburcio's passion when she kissed and held him close; he would quickly come around and be happy that she was accompanying him. Clodoveo and Rita agreed with her and assured her that would be the case.

A few hours later, a madman was seen ranting through the streets of San Juan Bautista, threatening to kill that monster Tiburcio Vasquez. It was Abelardo.

■ ■ ■

In the saddle they rode hard, the nine vaqueros and their two female companions. At Tiburcio's command, they held up a fish peddler near Monterey, a sheepherder north of Gilroy and the Twelve-Mile House stage station on the main highway to San Jose.

The spree that started the day they left San Juan went on and on, one crime after another, all through the rest of summer and into fall. With the loot, Tiburcio and Chavez made excursions to small adobes and gave poor countrymen sheep and money and words of encouragement to help them hang on to their livelihoods. The bandits were hidden and sheltered and fed by impoverished laborers and prominent ranchers and landowners alike, all of whom could be trusted to lie to the law officers about their whereabouts.

By wintertime, the bandits' crime spree compelled Harry Morse to send several posses two hundred miles down to the Coast Range and one hundred miles up into the remote Pacheco Pass mountains in search of the outlaws, but the rough, fragmented, roadless terrain forced even his most rugged trackers to turn back without their reward. Tiburcio's band carried on as if they were untouchable.

One day, as they were again moving campsites in Sunol Valley, the bandits came upon a road that led to a trading post. Tiburcio's memory was jogged.

"Soto, did you ever avenge Narciso's shooting at Scott's Corner?" he called out from the saddle.

"No. That was about the time you went to prison and I had to lay low in the area. We never made it back there."

"How much farther?" groaned Margarita, who was riding on her own little horse with her legs dangling to one side above the soft, muddy ground.

She had been a faithful, happy companion for the first three months but for the past two weeks the life of a highwayman had begun to make her weary. She was cold, tired and hungry for real food like they served at the Plaza Hotel. She wanted a cozy room with a warm fire and a soft bed like at home.

"I told you not to ask that question ever again!" Tiburcio shot back. Then, in a lower tone, he said to Soto: "This is getting annoying."

"It's been annoying for a long time," Soto said, his right eye darting toward his nose as his left eye fixed on Tiburcio. "I've gotten used to it, though, like a big blister."

"Tiburcio!" shrieked Margarita.

"*Silencio! Quiero silencio!,*" the ringleader shouted back.

Then, he whispered to Soto: "I better take Margarita and Rita to that abandoned adobe in the black hills. At least they can rest there under some shelter. While we are there, you, Sepulveda and Barcenas pay a visit to the trading post. It could be a lucrative haul at Scott's Corner. Our countrymen told me that Morse and his posse are riding back from the southern mountains, so right now, there is no sheriff in these parts. It's easy pickings. And it will be a reminder that our band never forgets the past and never runs."

As the sun's rays disappeared behind the western slopes, the three outlaws descended onto the Sunol Valley trading post. The town had changed since Morse's standoff with Bojorques. Thomas Scott, the mayor of Alisal, had bought the land from George Foscalina and built a new, two-story store that could easily be seen in the distance. Small houses circled the post, along with vineyards and the old large corral and stable.

But it was dark and the post looked abandoned when Soto, Sepulveda and Barcenas dismounted and tied their horses to some scrub oak about two hundred yards from the new store. Each stuck a large canvas bag in their belts. As they walked forward in the mud from recent rains, they watched the storekeeper look around outside, checking left and right for any last-second customers. Then he shut the heavy wood door and the bandits heard the bolt drop. Soto nodded to Barcenas, who walked up to the entrance and knocked loudly for a long time until finally the clerk unlocked the door.

"I wish to purchase a bottle of whiskey," Barcenas said. "It will only take a moment."

The owner, Thomas Scott, was listening from an apartment at the rear of the store and called to the clerk, a man named Otto Ludovici, to make a concession and let the customer in.

The door closed behind Barcenas. Outside, Soto drew his Colt Army .44 from his sash and approached the store with Sepulveda. The other two masked bandits let themselves in.

"No, no, no. No more customers! He is the last one. We are closed," Ludovici cried out.

Soto saw light coming from the back room behind the counter, where Thomas Scott, his wife, two sons, eight and twelve years old, and some friends were sitting by the fire in the attached living quarters. They were reading and playing checkers. Soto had not expected this many people inside but did not hesitate. He pointed the barrel under Ludovici's nose.

"Don't say anything!" Soto ordered.

The sight of the monstrously large thief, his thick, long, black, matted hair and his cross-eyed gaze shocked the clerk.

"Get out!" Ludovici yelled in a terrified voice to the family. "Bandits! Bandits!"

Loud scuffling could be heard in the back room. Soto raised his revolver and leveled it at the clerk. One blast struck Ludovici in the chest and he fell dead. Sepulveda and Barcenas emptied their guns into the living quarters. Somebody yelled out in pain as if shot. The two outlaws were about to run after the fleeing family and dispatch any witnesses, but Soto summoned them back.

"Take what will fill your pockets and pouches!"

They looted the store of seventy dollars, various clothing, flour, whiskey bottles and coffee beans and quickly sprinted out to their mounts. They spurred the horses north toward the black hills and rode furiously out of sight.

Thomas Scott immediately telegraphed Harry Morse in Oakland, but it wasn't until morning when Morse received the message, gathered his men for a manhunt and reached the trading post.

Unwilling to wait until sunrise for the sheriff, Scott and several cowboys from the area lit torches and began their own investigation. The muddy tracks easily pointed to the direction of the bandit's retreat. They debated whether to pursue the outlaws, but decided they would be at a huge disadvantage heading into the wild terrain and black night without a clear idea of where they were going.

At daybreak, Morse and Nick Harris, sheriff of Santa Clara County, joined Deputy Sheriff Faville of Pleasanton and an expert tracker named A.J. McDavid in front of Scott's store. Scott and several irate citizens were badgering the officers about the brashness of the bandits.

"I lost a clerk. Yet, these thugs run free. As if that's not enough of a tragedy, customers will be scared away from here forever. I am mayor here, and there will political hell to pay for every one of you elected officers if these criminals are not tracked down and a noose dropped on their shoulders. These Mexicans have been terrorizing us for a decade."

"Thomas, I understand your frustration," Morse told the mayor. "I understand the hardship. I understand the pain of losing a fine young employee and friend like Otto. But I need a little cooperation. What did the murderer look like, from what you could see?"

"The leader, the gunman, was unmistakable. He was a huge, cross-eyed ogre with thick, wild, black hair."

"Soto," Morse instantly concluded.

After getting more details, Morse told the group: "Looks like we're going to pay a visit to the black hills. These greasers didn't care enough to cover their tracks. By the look of those sets of boot prints leading over to the corral, there's no doubt who these vaqueros are."

Several of the town's citizens shouted for a vigilante committee.

"All of you may join the manhunt, if you wish, but you will be under my supervision as long as we are in Alameda County," Morse said. "Is that clear?"

Hours before Morse's arrival, Vasquez was smoking a cigarillo in the doorway of the decrepit hut when he saw Soto and his men galloping toward them. By the way they rode, he knew something was wrong.

"What loot did you get?"

"Paltry, Tiburcio," Sepulveda answered, grabbing a whiskey bottle out of his bag and taking a long slug. "Paltry."

"Did anyone get hurt?"

"The clerk is dead," Soto said matter-of-factly.

"Did anyone see you?"

"Scott. Maybe some of his family."

"They will be coming after us."

TIBURCIO!

Tiburcio slipped inside to prepare for their next move. With six men and two women, the *jacale* was crowded even though it was furnished with just a table and two chairs. Rita was laughing and playing cards with Clodoveo at the table and Margarita was lying on a blanket, her head on a bedroll, solemnly staring at the rotting wall.

"We have to leave quickly," Tiburcio said. "In these conditions, our tracks will be obvious, so we need to get to the main road, where our marks will blend with all the other travelers. We will need to split up. Clodoveo, Sepulveda, Barcenas, Rita and Margarita will ride with me south until we reach San Jose. We will take refuge at the New Almaden Mine. Juan, take the rest and continue to the Lopez adobe. You'll be safe there. *Comprende?* Good. Let's go. *Andale!*"

"No!" shouted Margarita, rolling over to face Tiburcio. "I am tired of riding here, fleeing there, sleeping on the rocky ground, being cold. We have lots of money, Tiburcio. Why can't we go to San Francisco and get a hotel room."

"There is no time to argue. Get up!"

"No!"

"Rita - do something about your stubborn friend."

With her usual gayety, Rita tried to roust Margarita. She wouldn't budge, however, and instead began a new tirade about life with a bunch of stinky bandits and how she could not care less if they were caught. She wished she was back in San Juan.

"Soto!" Tiburcio called. "Help Señora Salazar onto my horse and tie her hard and fast in the saddle. We need to get out of here."

With Margarita kicking and screaming in his Herculean arms, Soto did as he was told. The riders galloped away, Margarita's shrieking carrying through the hills.

Harry Morse's well-armed posse took the main Stockton Pass route. When they turned south on the road that followed the twisting path of Calaveras Creek, the sheriff's eyes spotted a lone figure in the distance sitting in some low brush on the side of the road. He could see the body heaving as if heavily sobbing.

"What is that?" he asked.

"It looks like a woman. Alone."

"Careful. It might be an ambush."

The posse approached with caution, their guns drawn. The black-haired woman wore a man's old broad-brimmed Peruvian hat, leather boots, a loose, dirty white shirt and a short, red petticoat made from a coarse material. Her blue eyes were pools of tears, which made clear streaks as they ran down her dirty cheeks.

"*Señora?*" Morse said to her, speaking Spanish, a language he had finally come close to mastering. "Why are you sitting on the roadside, unaccompanied?"

"Why?" she shrieked. "Why? I'll tell you why! That son-of-a-bitch Tiburcio Vasquez kidnapped me from San Juan Bautista, forced me to ride with his gang of bandits for months and then abandoned me in the mountains to be mauled by a mountain lion or raped by highwaymen. He's a son-of-a-bitch and deserves to die!"

Morse dropped from the saddle and stuck his rifle back in the riding holster. He walked over to the woman.

"What is your name?"

"Margarita Salazar."

"I am Harry Morse, sheriff of Alameda County. I am hunting down Tiburcio Vasquez and Juan Soto."

The woman laughed, which Morse didn't like much better than her crying.

"They are not afraid of you, Mr. Morse. They are not afraid of anybody."

"Nonetheless, I will find them. I would like to help you get home safely and comfortably. Perhaps in return you could tell me about this group with whom you have been traveling. Since they kidnapped you, I am sure you will want them brought to justice."

"I don't care what happens to them, except for Tiburcio Vasquez, who ordered them to abandon me on the roadside. I hope you hang him."

"Where is Tiburcio Vasquez?" Morse asked.

"He is going to the mine. New Almaden."

"I see. And the others?"

"They split up."

"Where did the others go?"

"Somewhere south of here. I don't know."

"Is Soto with Tiburcio?"

"No, Soto and Procopio are together."

Morse walked back over to his mounted posse.

"Why would Vasquez leave this woman here? He must have known she would reveal their location."

"Maybe it's a decoy," Harris suggested.

"I don't know. She is pretty distraught. She is very convincing."

Morse looked over at Margarita.

"Two men will take the woman back to San Juan. They need to question her until she gets tired of talking. And then keep questioning her until we get the truth. She will be a treasure trove of information about these bandits. The rest of us ride to New Almaden."

New Almaden Mine was nestled ten miles south of San Jose, between the Pueblo Hills and the edge of the Santa Cruz Mountains on Jose Reyes Berryessa's rancho. Thirty years ago, Antonio Sunol, a Mexican landowner, discovered the quicksilver deposits. After 1845, the mine and the village along the Alamitas Creek boomed as demand for the mercury ore soared with its use in the reduction of gold and silver. No other mine under operation by the Quicksilver Mining Company held such worldwide prominence. And there might not have been a safer place for Tiburcio Vasquez.

Tiburcio and his three men rode down a tree-lined street past the company-owned homes of the miners and past a church, a small school and a cemetery enclosed by a white picket fence. Many people - Chileno, Californio and Mexican - congregated along the street. Their eyes fell on the bandits but nobody seemed terribly interested even though they knew the famous visitor. Tiburcio thought of the heads of these households, young, strong men of great physical endurance. They would make wonderful recruits for his holdups and his war.

The riders halted in front of a grand two-story hacienda. The grounds around the house were immaculately landscaped and fish were leaping in a pond in the front yard. It was the home of the mine's superintendent, Sam Butterworth.

The outlaws hitched their horses and walked up the broad porch to the front door. A servant answered and invited them inside. They waited for the superintendent among several scattered trunks that appeared ready to be shipped out. Butterworth summoned them to his office. He appeared nervous and out-of-sorts. He had bad news for Tiburcio.

"I am being replaced," he said. "There's a fellow coming in named James Randol. He's very authoritarian. I hear he is impressed with techniques of the miners from Cornwall, and has already begun bringing many of them in here. I am not sure how that will sit with the Mexicans who built New Almaden."

Tiburcio contemplated Butterworth's words while he walked over to the upstairs window and looked out at the village that people called "Spanishtown." After a moment he turned back to Butterworth.

"Tell me how it is that Harry Morse walked right in here and arrested Joaquin Olivera?"

"That was a long time ago, Tiburcio. Besides, I had nothing to do with that. One of Olivera's men, a Frenchman named Jean, becomes very talkative when he is intoxicated. Nobody mentions a word of your gang around here. But that French hunchback spilled the beans on Olivera."

"I know *Joroba*. I will tell him to keep his mouth shut," Tiburcio said. "Ah, but we will miss you, Sam. It sounds like things are changing around here. Perhaps some of your workers would like to come with me. I will gladly pay you for them."

"Do as you please, Tiburcio. You have my protection as long as I still reside at this hacienda, which isn't long. Still, I am sure they would be honored to serve your cause. They don't have much choice in the matter any way you look at it."

The next night at a saloon just outside of the mining company's land, employees were wildly spending their hard-earned dollars. They were offended, or at least pretended to be, by Tiburcio's insistence on paying for their drinks.

"But I don't drink alcohol," Tiburcio told them. "So let me buy you all a round to make up for my peculiarities."

The band was a set of five men, two on fiddles, a guitarist, one playing a bass and one more with an accordion. Occasionally, the whooping and yelling of the miners drowned out the music. With hats tilted back on their heads, revolvers flapping up and down at their sides and red eyes wide and aglow with liquor and excitement, miners, cowboys and outlaws high-stepped with a swarm of prostitutes.

Tiburcio leaned his back against the bar and took in the fandango. One of the few gringos in the entire camp was standing next to him. John Young was the camp's bookkeeper, telegraph operator and Wells Fargo representative.

"Did Mr. Butterworth tell you he is retiring?" Young shouted, leaning closer to Tiburcio, who nodded. "The new superintendent is bringing in Cornish miners, from Nevada City mostly. I reckon there will be some unrest here at Almaden. I suppose some wouldn't mind following you right out of here."

Peering through the vortex of revelers, Tiburcio saw one of his watchmen enter and look around the room. The lookout caught Tiburcio's eye and started rapidly weaving his way through the crowd.

"Excuse me," Tiburcio told the bookkeeper and met the watchman halfway.

"Morse just entered the main road down where the creek splits," said the watchman, a Mexican miner. "He's got four officers with him and will be here in about ten minutes."

Tiburcio quickly heeded the warning.

"We can make it over to the hacienda before he arrives. Warn the men and tell them to meet at Butterworth's immediately. We'll wait there until the posse leaves. Then, ask Mr. Young if he would be kind enough to release our horses out of the stable and run them up over the ridge to the far gulch. Morse won't think about looking out there. And make sure this fandango continues at a high pitch. Here's fifty dollars. Keep buying rounds of drinks - for both the men and the women. And here's some more to keep the band playing."

From one of Butterworth's upstairs bedrooms, Tiburcio watched the posse stop at the saloon outside the mine. Morse and another lawman waited as the rest of the men searched the building. Scores of Mexicans came out of their homes and began milling about in the street. A quarter of an hour later, Morse got word that Tiburcio was not in the saloon and he and the lawman trotted up the road toward Butterworth's hacienda. Groups of Mexicans stood in the way of the two riders until Morse shouted at them to step aside.

Morse and his deputy stopped in front of Butterworth's, walked up the porch and rapped their knuckles on the door. Tiburcio and his men froze and listened. Tiburcio could not hear what the servant was saying, but he saw Morse walk back down to his horse. The riders turned around and proceeded back toward the saloon. Morse glanced back at the house. He thought he saw someone peering out from behind the curtain in the corner of the window.

He thought about turning back, pushing through Butterworth's doors and grabbing the bandit - if it were the bandit - and dragging him onto the street. Then he would avenge all the robberies and deaths in front of hundreds of his countrymen. The hanging would send a message of law and justice - that is, if he wasn't first killed by the mob. Tiburcio, for his part, held back the urge to run out and gun down Morse on the streets right in front of the entire Mexican community, a lesson to all gringo lawmen. Or he could haul Morse away and burn the lawman's body in the incinerator, and nobody would ever know what had become of the legendary sheriff. Instead, Morse rode away into the darkness and Tiburcio let the curtain fall back. Morse would find no sign of the bandits and there would be no showdown at New Almaden.

Chapter 3: Shootouts
Saucelito Valley
Spring-Summer 1872

Morse knew his way around every mile of the Coast Range from Gilroy to Monterey. But the rugged inland mountains around Saucelito Valley? He was unfamiliar with its terrain. Yet, when he received the Western Union telegram from Deputy Nick Harris that a posse was being formed to hunt down the region's three most notorious bandits - Vasquez, Soto and Procopio - into the Saucelito Valley if necessary, he did not hesitate and hopped on the next train out of town carrying just his Winchester 1866 repeating rifle.

"We're going in deep, Harry," Harris told him. "We are going right up to their hideout."

"How far can you get us?" Morse asked.

"Without a guide? Not far enough. To the northern edge of Cantua Canyon. I don't know what's beyond that."

"Probably a whole lot of bandits."

In the spring of 1872, the mountain valley was beautifully carpeted with green meadow grass after heavy winter rains. The heat had not yet arrived and Los Banos Creek was a powerful rush of muddy water barely contained within its banks. Alders and oaks fringed the creek's edge and dark green foliage dotted the numerous streams that fed out of the north and south forks. Here, Cantua Canyon, the gorgeous gorge where hundreds of native Californians had taken refuge, stretched north to south from its narrow, well-guarded opening, past the huts and field crops of the exiles, and up and over a half-mile of foothills to where three weather-beaten cabins stood in a row. The top officers in Tiburcio Vasquez's small army occupied the hovels. Tiburcio preferred to stay in the smallest, northernmost cabin, often sharing the space with only a señorita.

On this spectacular spring day, the gang leaders met up in the southernmost dwelling, known as the Lopez adobe. The largest of the three, the Lopez house had a covered porch that ran around most of the building. Three large oaks shaded the house. The men - Vasquez, Chavez, Soto, Sepulveda, Barcenas, Procopio, Carabajal, Molino, Rodriguez, Gonzales and Pio Ochoa - were preparing to barbecue a large side of beef they had just butchered. Tonight they planned on formalizing the ranks of their regiment, estimating how many true soldiers they had recruited, evaluating the worth of those men, where they were residing, taking stock of weapons and ammunition and counting their money in notes, coins and gold. They had a lot of work ahead. But that didn't stop most of them from drinking heavily.

As the men waited for Tiburcio and Chavez to return from the leader's adobe, a longstanding feud between Soto and Procopio began to boil over.

"Sometimes I think this revolution is like the fog," Procopio carelessly lamented, swallowing another swig of the aguardiente. "Once you try to touch it or hold it, it's gone. It's a mist. The chance for revolution passed with Murrieta's death. He was a leader."

The crash of glass against the wall startled everyone. Soto's eyes were fiery red.

"I will not stand for this kind of talk! You lost your nerves when Murrieta vanished and you grew feathers when you were in prison. You are a shell of a man, Procopio. You are lucky Tiburcio lets you live among us!"

"Don't talk like you knew Murrieta. Your looks were so revolting to him he didn't want you close to him!"

"Is that so, *cobarde*?" Soto seethed as he approached Procopio. "Your cowardliness is revolting to me. You think you can speak ill of Tiburcio and his plans to change our people's way of life. You think you can speak that way when he is not present? Then, let's see what's left in you. Grab your revolver and let's go outside to duel!"

They heard Tiburcio's boots as he entered the room. Procopio looked around for intercession. His pleading eyes fell on the stern face of Tiburcio.

"Now is a good time to let us know how you feel, Procopio," Tiburcio said. "We are here to decide who leads, who follows - and who is left behind."

"I didn't mean you are not capable of leading our people, Tiburcio," Procopio stammered apologetically.

Soto strode over to Procopio holding the barrel of a gun in each hand and presented both weapons to Procopio.

"Choose!"

"I don't want to fight you, Soto."

"No? You have no spine left, do you, Procopio?"

Procopio, subjugated, bent his neck and slowly shook his head.

Tiburcio walked over to him and put his arm around his shoulder. He nodded to Chavez to follow them as he escorted Procopio out of the adobe. They had talked a lot about what to do with Procopio, whether he was a liability or an asset. It was clear now, and Tiburcio decided to simply send him away.

"I want you to go north, Procopio, to San Francisco, and lie low in the bordellos on Morton Street," Tiburcio counseled. "Get your thoughts together and decide what you are going to do with the rest of your life. No ill feelings, my friend. It has been a long road, and you are simply weary."

Procopio waited outside as Tiburcio told the others to carry on with the barbecue. He then collected Procopio's belongings, his bedroll and gun.

"I will return tomorrow evening to discuss business," Tiburcio said. "Chavez and I will escort Procopio to San Juan Bautista. Soto - you are in charge!"

As the three bandits descended into the gulch, Tiburcio looked back and could see Soto's massive frame watching them from the porch. He was yelling for Procopio to never return or he would die.

TIBURCIO!

Tiburcio shook his head in disgust.

"He knows better than to shout all over the canyons," Tiburcio told Chavez and Procopio. "It could get us killed."

Chavez suggested they take one of the deer trails to avoid the main road.

"We are probably safe," Tiburcio said. "But it can't hurt."

Wandering in the severe backcountry, Harris, Morse, Winchell and the rest of the posse heard Soto's shouting echo against the canyon walls.

"We must be close, boys," Morse said. "Maybe another mile."

The lawmen were weary. Their journey to Cantua had been arduous. Three days earlier, the posse had reached Hollister, and dropped into an old restaurant and bar. A group of about a dozen Mexicans were playing cards and didn't notice the gringos quietly take their seats. Morse and the others bided their time, smoking cigars and drinking beers, listening to the hum of conversation. Morse was picking up quite a bit of the Spanish in the room, then his ears fell on some English spoken with a peculiar accent, French if he wasn't mistaken. This voice was becoming increasingly excited. Morse turned around to see a man of rough but fair-colored skin who was hunched over and craning his neck to look at his audience. A tremendous lump protruded from his back.

"How many of them outlaws did you see there?" someone asked the hunchback.

"All of them that counts," he hollered. "Soto, Procopio, Tiburcio, Sepulveda … Tiburcio told me never to return to New Almaden again. Next thing I know, they are in these parts, like they was tracking me down or something."

"Where were they going?"

"They were all headed up to the Saucelito hideout. They got some adobes up there at Cantua that they like to hunker down in."

Morse listened some more, then interrupted. The patrons' eyes fell on his shining badge.

"Hey, what's your name?"" Morse asked the hunchback.

"Jean."

"Come have a drink with us. I'll buy."

Jean agreed and Morse asked him what a cripple did to make a living.

"I run with the bandits when I need to, sheriff. Loot falls from their hands like leaves in autumn, so I try to keep my palms open. But when the entire tree - trunk and limbs and everything - falls, I am not going to be around to get crushed, if you know what I mean?"

"Can you get me to Cantua?"

"A deformed man like myself? Hell no, sheriff. An able-bodied man would have trouble navigating that territory."

A half-hour later, Morse left the restaurant and quickly retreated to his hotel room. He jotted down everything he had heard. Then, he smoked another cigar so he could calm down. Before turning in, he removed his badge and put it in a sack.

The posse struck out into Pacheco Pass without a precise understanding of where Saucelito Valley began and how far they would have to travel to get to the gang. They rode for two days across mountain ridges and into canyons. The only life they saw were hawks and deer and white-tailed antelope until at last Morse spotted a lone rider in his field glasses.

"There's our guide!" he proclaimed.

They galloped hard after the traveler and quickly caught him. He was a sheepherder on a donkey and couldn't move very fast. As the lawmen approached, he quickly jumped off the burro and hid behind it, fearing the men were bandits. Morse convinced the sheepherder that they would not harm him.

"Do you know this valley well?" Morse asked.

"Nearly as well as them desperadoes - which I thought you was."

"We are looking for their hideaway, in Cantua. I will pay you handsomely if you would guide us until we find their adobes."

"You better pay me a lot more than the bandits pay me to keep my mouth shut."

"Five hundred dollars."

The sheepherder's eyes grew and his mouth fell open.

"I know exactly where they are. They are less than three miles from here."

"Good. Then let's go," Morse declared and excitedly tapped his horse's side with his boot, stirring the animal.

But the sheepherder did not move.

"What's wrong?"

"I said they are less than three miles from here. But we can't go that way," the sheepherder said. "Are you crazy? It would be suicide. There's a small opening at the mouth of the gorge and it is guarded by day and night by Mexican desperadoes. Just one bandit with a rifle could keep twenty men at bay. No, you don't want to go that way, mister. Besides, if you did, they would know you were coming two miles before you get there."

"Then how do we get into the canyon?"

"That way," the sheepherder said, pointing in the opposite direction. "It will take two days, at least."

"What?" Morse asked indignantly. "Two days? To go three miles?"

"We must go to the southernmost part of the canyon. That is where the men you are looking for will be found. They never guard the south, because they believe no gringo posse could ever get there, even if they did know where it was. There's a peak where you can look right down onto the bandits' adobe. I've seen it. The last adobe is where Soto and his companions stay."

After a treacherously long trek over the next forty-eight hours, the officers were finally lying on their stomachs atop the ridge looking down on their prey. Each took a turn with the field glasses, getting a good look at the back of the Lopez adobe and its rock corral. Morse could feel the nervousness of the sheepherder.

"What you do now is your business," the sheepherder told the lawmen. "I do not want to be recognized. I've done all I can or want to do."

So Morse paid the guide in gold and relieved him of his duty.

As much as he ever did, the sheriff came up with a plan of action. The posse would divide into three groups, each designated a house. Morse gave only one order: If the bandits retreat back into Cantua Canyon, do not pursue them.

"We are only six lawmen," he said. "There may be hundreds of outlaws down there."

Morse and Winchell rode off together and dismounted near the rock corral about fifty yards from the cabin. They spotted one of the desperadoes out gathering wood. Pio Ochoa had been obscured by oak trees, and now Morse had to think fast before the bandit saw them. He signaled to Winchell to stay back as he pulled his wide-brimmed hat over his eyes and approached Ochoa. Morse asked for a drink of water in his now flawless Spanish. The outlaw did not suspect the law could have penetrated so deep into the stronghold, and he guessed that the intruder was just one of the hundreds of refugees from Cantua, so he showed the sheriff through the corral gate. They passed along the west side of the cabin.

Morse looked to his left and took note of one of the bandit's horses hitched in a grassy area. In his surprise at seeing Ochoa, he had left his saddle rifle slung on his horse back in the corral. He would have to enter the outlaws' lair with only a single revolver. They stepped onto the porch and turned the north corner of the building. Winchell, carrying a shotgun, crept along behind Morse and Ochoa, his heart slamming against his ribs.

Ochoa entered the room first, followed by Morse. Two men were standing at the table cutting up meat and a large third man was staring into a glass of whiskey. Morse instantly recognized the gargantuan fellow seated at the table facing the entrance. Soto was wearing a soldier's blue overcoat and was likely to have at least one gun concealed in one of those large pockets.

At first, the devil of an outlaw did not acknowledge that a stranger had entered the room. Then Winchell noisily entered and Soto looked up thunderstruck. Morse did not hesitate. He drew his revolver and ordered Soto and the others to put up their hands.

"Everyone! *Todos*!"

Soto didn't move a muscle or show any fear. He merely gazed with deadly hatred right into the eyes of the sheriff. Morse repeated the order.

"*Manos arriba*!"

He repeated the command a third time, reaching into his waistband with his free hand and grabbing a set of handcuffs. He tossed the cuffs on the end of the table and told Winchell to place them on Soto's wrists.

But Winchell was frozen in fright.

"Jesus Christ!" Morse cursed. "Then cover me with your shotgun while I cuff the monster."

Instead, Winchell spun and fled out the front door.

"Shit!" Morse cried in disbelief. He was alone in the den of killers.

Ochoa seized Morse's gun hand and Sepulveda grabbed the sheriff's left arm. Soto sprung from his chair, producing a pistol seemingly out of thin air. He leaped behind Gonzales, who had been cutting meat, and held him for a shield as he took aim at Morse.

Morse swiftly swiveled his hips and kicked Ochoa hard in the groin and jabbed Sepulveda in the nose with his fist. He hastily fired a shot at Soto. Gonzales' hat flew off but the shot missed Soto. Morse didn't wait for the desperado to return fire. He bounded out the door and off the porch. Morse didn't look back until he was clear around the west side, halfway to his horse and rifle. He would not get there in time. Faced with horrible odds, the sheriff wheeled around just as Soto turned the corner and came into sight. They were no more than seventy-five feet apart.

Morse's first shot missed. He was too anxious, and now he stood vulnerable, knowing Soto was a dead shot. Soto, as he was accustomed, raised the gun above his head and brought it down quickly into the line of fire. Somehow in that furious fraction of a second, the copious notes Morse had compiled on the bandit and committed to memory rapidly coursed through his brain. Morse instinctively fell flat to the ground as Soto's arm dropped and the first shot rang out. Unharmed, Morse sprang back to his feet and got off another errant shot at the bandit. Soto bounded forward, re-cocked, raised the gun above his head, brought it down level and fired again. Morse sprinted a few more feet, then dropped to his stomach again, timing his duck perfectly as the shot whistled three feet over his head. Soto fired two more times in quick succession. Morse dived and popped up, dived and popped up. He was astonished to still be alive.

Finally, Morse was able to return fire. The first ball struck Soto's revolver under the barrel and jammed the firing hinge. Soto for a moment stood shocked, examining his useless gun. Then he turned on the toe of his boot and retreated on a dead run for his own horse. But the horse, spooked by the gunfire, had broken away, and was no longer hitched in the distant grass.

Winchell, who had recovered his composure, ran around the east end of the corral, both barrels of his shotgun loaded. He unloaded one barrel just as Soto disappeared around the corner. Buckshot pelted the wall and sprayed into the yard.

Soto vaulted into the house, tossed his coat to one of the other bandits, yelling for him to throw it on quickly. Then, he grabbed two revolvers hanging on the wall and spun for the exit.

At the sound of the first shots, Sheriff Harris and the other three lawmen spurred their horses down the ridge. Harris rode toward the front of the adobe and caught sight of Soto dashing into the house, tailcoats flying behind him, long black hair tossing. Harris halted his horse and pulled out the Spencer rifle that was attached to the saddle horn. Spotting the first blue-coated brigand running from the adobe, he lined up the sights. The rifle shot killed the man, but it was Ochoa, not Soto.

Soto emerged from another door, racing for a second horse, which was ready, saddled and hitched some thirty-five yards to the north. He was making great strides when, within twenty-five yards of the horse, Morse, re-armed with his Winchester, drew a bead on him and pulled the rifle trigger.

The bullet struck Soto in the right shoulder. The wounded bandit staggered and fell to one knee. The lead ball had passed clean through the shoulder blade and lodged into his breast. He let out a demoniacal yell, turned and faced his enemies head-on.

Soto, eyes ablaze with wild, desperate courage and devilish hatred, strode determinedly toward Morse, a five-shot pistol in each hand. Morse moved forward a few paces, knowing the Amazon half-breed was out of pistol range, to get a better shot. The sheriff slowly, purposefully raised his rifle to his eye. To his amazement, Soto continued advancing. Morse fired again.

The rifle-ball raced through the air and crashed into the center of Soto's upper forehead, ripping off the top of his skull. Soto dropped flat backward, arms out to the side, hands still grasping the revolvers. The notorious bandit was dead.

● ● ●

Tiburcio halted his horse and listened into the breeze. He gave Chavez an inquisitive look.

"Did you hear gunfire?"

"It was probably just the men taking a few shots at rabbits or birds."

He listened again.

"I guess so."

By evening, they had reached San Juan Bautista. They rode slowly past the jail, the blacksmith shop and the stable. Tiburcio perceived residents stealing glances at him and diverting their looks whenever his gray-eyed stare caught theirs. He looked inquisitively at Chavez and Procopio, who shrugged.

At the Plaza Hotel they jumped off their horses and walked inside. Upon first blush, Tiburcio was glad that not much had changed at this establishment. It was one of few public places in the entire region where he felt comfortable. He saw that his good friend, Jose Castro, was there, but his attention fell on a loud, short man with his belly to the bar. This deformed character expectorated after every other sentence into the spittoon at his foot. It was the hunchback Jean.

"I told those posse men to tread lightly up in those hills," Jean said, expelling a good wad of spittle. "Every one of Tiburcio's gang has his ear to the ground, all the time, I told them. The leader asked if I could get them into the valley, and I said my obligation to the law ends at Cantua Canyon. And that will be fifty dollars, thank you!"

The Frenchman laughed so hard he got a large gob of tobacco and mucous stuck in his throat and had to hack and let sail a thick mass of phlegm into the spittoon.

"*Jorbado!*" Tiburcio exclaimed when he was directly behind the hunchback. "If the Plaza Hotel is relying on you for entertainment, it's a good thing I have returned to San Juan Bautista and my guitar is still in the corner."

"T-T-Tiburcio," Juan greeted. "I didn't think you would ever come back here."

"Why would you think that? Tell me, where is this posse you were so kind to have struck up a conversation with?"

"Hell, Tiburcio. I don't even know if they were a real posse. You know how men talk these days. Everybody wants to be a hero."

"Yes, I do know. But I have an inclination that you are telling strangers more than I care to have you tell."

"You can trust me, Tiburcio."

"I trust that you will turn tail and get the hell out of San Juan Bautista and never return. And don't go to Cantua

Canyon, *Jorbado* . You are not welcome there. And don't ever let me see you at the mine. You are not welcome there, either. "

"That forbids me from just about everywhere, Tiburcio!"

"But it spares your life."

The Frenchman paid for his drinks and sheepishly departed, stammering the entire way out. Tiburcio whispered something in Chavez's ear and the lieutenant followed after the hunchback. Tiburcio and Procopio stayed and ordered a sarsaparilla and a whiskey, respectively.

A few minutes after being served their drinks, the hotel bar grew quiet. Behind Tiburcio, there was a shuffling of seats, and a few gasps. All heads turned to the door. Procopio looked, too, but Tiburcio remained staring ahead.

"I could shoot you right in the back," Abelardo Salazar called out from the door.

Now Tiburcio slowly turned.

"Why would you do that, Abelardo?"

"I wouldn't shoot you without warning, because I am not a coward. But kidnapping a man's wife? That is very low."

"I didn't kidnap Margarita. On the night before I departed, she declared her intention to follow me and my band to the end's of the earth. By morning, she was already at the camp, unwilling to stay behind. I let her return when she was ready. I am sorry it took her so long."

"You left her on the road to die!"

"Do you wish to settle something with me?"

"Yes. But not in Mr. Zanetta's establishment," Abelardo said. "Outside."

Tiburcio tossed back the whiskey that Procopio had ordered and slammed the glass on the counter. Procopio followed him into the cool darkness. Hotel patrons spilled out onto the wood walkway. A dozen more townsfolk on the streets stopped to witness the showdown they had been expecting the moment Tiburcio returned to San Juan Bautista.

"Let's not settle the feud in this fashion, gentlemen. Let's talk this thing through," Castro pleaded, but was ignored.

Abelardo and Tiburcio agreed quickly on how they would duel and stood back to back. They took twenty steps in opposite directions and turned to face each other. Abelardo's gun was in his sash; Tiburcio's in the open holster at his side.

"We need a volunteer to tell us when to draw," Abelardo called out.

Nobody answered.

"Jose," Tiburcio said. "You count down from three. We draw on one."

Castro looked to Abelardo for approval. He nodded. So Castro reluctantly took up the solemn duty and counted down. Three. Two. One.

Tiburcio drew quickest while Abelardo was slower but luckier. With the barrel of Tiburcio's gun pointed directly at Abelardo's chest, the cylinder jammed. Abelardo then fired and Tiburcio let out a groan and fell to his knees on the wood planks.

Procopio and Castro drew their revolvers and ordered everybody to step away.

"I don't want to see a weapon. If I see anyone draw weapon, I shoot to kill!" Procopio yelled.

Abelardo looked stunned.

"Is he dead?" he asked, more frightened than boastful. "Is Tiburcio dead?"

"Go on home," Castro told him. "You proved your point. You may end up famous yet."

Castro turned and kneeled to examine the bandit leader. There was a hole in Tiburcio's shoulder where the ball had entered and another one in his neck where it had exited.

"I think the ball went clear through," Castro said, his fingers red with the bandit's blood.

Zanetta approached the pair of bandits.

"I summoned a wagon," he told Castro.

"I will take him to my house," Castro said. "Procopio, get the doctor."

As news of the duel spread, Castro and Procopio knew they had to get the wounded bandit out of San Juan to a quieter location. The next day Procopio drove Zanetta's wagon to New Idria over thirty-five miles of rough, narrow passageways. At times along the way, he would look up at the three-hundred-foot-high sandstone pillars of rock and bow his head. He felt insignificant. And his final deed for the gang seemed futile - he believed Tiburcio was going to die.

At New Idria, he summoned the mining camp's physician and made sure Tiburcio was safe among friends and supporters. Then, he slipped away unnoticed. Procopio had decided he had had enough gun battles and had seen enough people shot dead. He remembered that he had never been happier than when he was in the sinful dens and liquor bars of San Francisco. Tiburcio was right. That's where he would return, perhaps for good.

Chapter 4: Tidings
New Idria Mine
Spring 1873

As he had done five years ago, Clodoveo Chavez again was racing on horseback to bring Tiburcio Vasquez vital news. This time, he was not the nervous kid on his way to meet a hero of the people; he was the bandit leader's first lieutenant and was considered his most trusted warrior. This time around, he was not being duped in an attempt to ensnare the outlaw. This time, his message could influence the direction of the revolution.

He kept off the main trail to avoid lingering posses and roaming bands of vigilantes. He spurred his mount up hills of tall, whispering grasses, golden mustard and dark buckeye and down through valleys shadowed by rocky spurs. He dashed alongside willowy waterways and toiled up steep ridges of reddish-brown and into copses of green pines. Often, he had to climb out of his saddle and pull his horse along to get over massive jagged stones blocking deer trails or to traverse deep crevices.

On what he guessed would be his last day of travel before reaching far-flung New Idria, where Tiburcio had been recovering for several months from his gunshot wound, the fog hung thick over the San Carlos River and he had to pay extra attention to his direction so he did not become disoriented and lost. The fog transformed the landscape, hiding Mother Nature's elements and muffling her voice. He heard but could not see the rushing river, and then everything became very still and quiet, and Clodoveo stopped and peered hard and listened sharply to make sure he was still following the watercourse. He hearkened the call of seagulls and made out the crisp sound of salmon jumping and then he knew he was on track.

He emerged out of the narrow fog-filled gorge and looked down at a valley ensconced in thick mist which nearly concealed the series of sweeping low hills and the flat, bare road leading to the mining community. Squirrels darted across rocks and into the brush. He spotted a bobcat sitting at the edge of the tree line. Swainson hawks floated above him and jays streamed from one bush to another. Chavez put this all behind him and descended into New Idria.

Tiburcio had been invited to stay at a small ranch in nearby Chilaro while he recuperated and laid low from the law. It was owned by a Chilean blacksmith named Abdon Leiva. Leiva was a handsome man with sad-looking eyes. He was exceedingly pleasant to his customers, even though he lacked social graces outside of his blacksmith shop. He enjoyed working long hours at the forge and felt satisfied when he locked up at the end of the day, fatigue weighing heavy on his bones. He was not well-educated, but was literate and found great pleasure in sitting at the warm hearth after work and reading English books until he fell asleep. He was so satisfied with his hard-working life that he hardly noticed his wife's boredom.

It seemed a lifetime ago when they met and married in Santa Clara County. Rosaria was only seventeen. Although she had lived in a fairly remote mountain region not far from New Idria, Rosaria had been widely known as one of the best dancers in the county and enjoyed many fandangos in Hollister and Gilroy. But with her family's land grant swiped away by the government, her father soon preferred her to be married, and why not Abdon Leiva? Abdon had acquired a good, reliable skill that would keep him employed for a long time. And he was kind and good-looking. However, even with a husband and two children to occupy her, Rosaria never lost her love for dancing or the fandangos.

One day, Abdon, although tired from a long day at the forge, succumbed to Rosaria's whims and accompanied her to the restaurant and saloon in New Idria. Tiburcio was there, sitting in a chair, strumming chords and tapping the body of the guitar with his palm in a fairly mellow manner. It was his first outing after being shot. He stood out from the crowd of Mexican and Peruvian miners in his clean black coat with a beaver-fur collar, dark trousers, black velvet vest decorated with floral patterns and his sharply combed hair and trimmed beard.

He paused a moment to look up at the door when Abdon and Rosaria walked in. He was not particularly drawn to her appearance. Rosaria was plump, about five-foot-three inches and her face was faintly pock-marked. But when she moved in her graceful and confident way and her deep chocolate-hued hair bounced, she penetrated your soul with her bright, tantalizing, light brown eyes and filled the room with delight from her charming smile. Her attractiveness was undeniable. Tiburcio smiled and kept strumming.

The couple sat at a table next to Tiburcio. She spoke first.

"If you played something livelier, Mr. Vasquez, I might be interested in dancing."

"I am recovering from a wound in my shoulder and neck. I am trying to take it easy. But I will try."

He started slowly and sped up. Rosaria began moving her feet. Tiburcio instantly saw that she was a skilled dancer. He picked up the beat and she added finger-snapping and spins. His shoulder throbbed with pain, but he didn't care. He stood to play with more vigor. Soon, his forearm was a blur and Rosaria was swiftly moving between the tables. She approached him and he went down on one knee as her skirt brushed against his cheek. When the song ended, she genuflected and he stood and bowed his head. They laughed heartily and took their seats.

"Where did you learn to dance like that?"

"I was one of the best dancers in Santa Clara County about a decade ago. The *jarabe* was my favorite."

"Mine, too," Tiburcio replied, leaning over the guitar on his lap. "I once owned a fandango in Monterey."

"Monterey! Did you grow up there?"

"Yes. My grandfather came to California with the DeAnza expedition."

"Oh, my! My grandfather, Ignacio Alviso, was a member of that expedition."

"Incredible," Tiburcio exclaimed. He turned and introduced himself to Abdon. "You are the blacksmith, yes?"

"And you are the famous bandit," Abdon returned.

Tiburcio stood and pulled a chair out for himself at their table. Upon Abdon's inquiries, he told them the astonishing tale of how he ended up wounded and strumming a guitar at a New Idria saloon. Tiburcio offered to buy dinner, and they talked and sang late into the evening.

Abdon had to work in the morning, but Rosaria hadn't enjoyed herself this much - listening to the guitar, making melody and flirting with a rich, handsome man - since moving to Chilaro. Not wanting the night to draw to a close, she suggested they continue their merriment at Leiva's ranch.

"I would love to," Tiburcio agreed.

Soon after, Tiburcio became the Leivas' permanent guest. Abdon's house was suddenly much more lively, and his quiet reading fell to the wayside.

Chavez entered the town a few weeks after Tiburcio had moved in with the Leivas. He found Tiburcio at a saloon table playing faro with four other men. One of them was Abdon Leiva. More than a dozen other patrons watched, drank, smoked and commented on the direction of the game. Clodoveo was surprised at how many workers were in the bar since it was fairly early in the afternoon.

Tiburcio saw Chavez the moment he walked in and waved him over. He gave his chips to Leiva and told him to keep any money he won.

"Let me have a private word with you, Clodoveo, at the bar. It's been a long time."

"Amazing. The only evidence that you were shot is that small scar on your neck," Chavez said, inspecting his friend as they stepped away from the table. "You are walking and moving fine."

"Well, there's a good doctor in this community," Tiburcio told his friend.

"Why are there so many men in the bar rather than working at the mines?" Chavez asked.

"There are a lot of Mexicans waiting to find work. They came down from New Almaden when that new superintendent took over. The bastard kept his promise and brought in a boatload of Cornish miners. These fellas were all displaced."

"Is there work here for them?"

"No, but I told them I could use them in my noble crusade. They are solid, rugged hombres," Tiburcio explained as the pair stood together at the end of the long bar.

"Where are you staying?"

"Abdon Leiva's house. He's the town blacksmith. That man with the wide lapels is Abdon. It's a bit of a problem, however."

"How is that?"

"I have overspent on gifts for his wife."

Chavez laughed loud.

"*Mi dio*, Clodoveo, restrain yourself," Tiburcio said, chuckling himself. "Satin slippers and shawls from San Francisco can be costly."

"Be careful," Chavez warned. "Do you want another duel with an angry husband?"

"I will be careful. I am working on Leiva to join the regiment. His wife thinks it would be a noble cause. She is wickedly convincing."

"And what does he think?"

"He doesn't give a damn about our revolution. He's from Chile. What does he care what happens in California? However, his wife's mother's land was stolen by gringos. She believes very strongly in the cause."

"I don't understand. If he is unwilling ..."

Tiburcio continued talking but leaned closer to friend.

"Leiva has a small fortune in savings," he whispered, "which we will need since we are broke and have been inactive for so long."

"Very good, captain."

"*Si. Bueno.* But you have some news concerning our crusade?"

"*Si.*"

"And you have been south to Agua Dulce? Did you meet up with my friend Ysidor Padilla?"

"Yes. He recalled meeting you in San Quentin five years ago and discussing the revolution," Chavez said but paused. "First, however, I must share some discouraging news. The newspapers from Alameda and San Francisco are again heaping praise upon Sheriff Harry Morse for his slaying of Juan Soto. They say it was a legendary gun battle."

"I heard about Soto's death. Those were the shots we heard as we were leaving Cantua with Procopio, right?"

Chavez nodded.

"Who was the rat? The Frenchman?"

"Yes. He is not talking anymore. We were the last to see him alive."

"But Morse did not raid Cantua after the gunfight?"

"No. He did not have enough men to go in there and come out alive."

"It won't be long before he returns. We are going to have to move fast."

"I think his strategy is to cut off the head of the serpent. You. You are the last of the famous bandits left in the state."

"Who says?"

"The newspapers. They have enumerated everyone who Morse has brought down in the course of five years as sheriff."

Tiburcio thought about this statement for a moment.

"What about Procopio?"

"The newspapers said Morse simply walked into a San Francisco bordello, marched up to the bandit, pointed a gun at his head and said, 'Procopio, you're my man.' "

"No fight?" Tiburcio asked. "No weapon drawn?"

"Nothing. And Procopio was sentenced to fourteen years in San Quentin."

"That is a long time. They want to make sure no more of us get out of prison alive."

"I have better news, though, Tiburcio," Chavez continued.

"Yes? About Agua Dulce?"

"Yes. It is better than you could have imagined. They have an incredibly well-prepared and organized battalion. There are two hundred men down there, real soldiers from the Mexican Army. Soldiers who have dedicated the rest of their lives to winning back all or most of California. Some of these soldiers are nearly fifty years old. The bulk of them are survivors from the war in 1846, when most of them were not yet twenty. They have waited nearly thirty years for the right time to free their people."

"Who is leading these men?"

"Padilla took me to their leader, Gen. Carlos Soriano. He showed me their entire hideout. I saw with my own eyes and spoke to men who are living on this earth for only one reason: to win back every inch of land stolen by the white invaders."

"What about the arms?"

"They have some, but Gen. Soriano is awaiting an enormous underground shipment of weapons and ammunition from Civil War battlefields. Guns, bayonets, even cannons. These are some of the most modern, high-powered weapons available. When these arms arrive no militia will have more firepower."

"You said they were well-prepared?"

"Yes."

"How so?"

"As you would expect from a general, they have thought about things that we have not. They have begun to store barrels of grain, salted fish and pork. They have stocked bandages and alcohol. And there are not only infantrymen and officers. There are doctors and surgeons and scouts among them. And they keep getting new recruits, too, and many are from the same families as these old timers."

"Well, then, what does the general need us for?"

"Money, more loyal fighters and the support of the people. First, he wants a payment of thirty thousand dollars to secure the weapons when they arrive. Second, he needs thirty thousand dollars to feed and compensate his men. They may be storing away provisions but the men are going hungry. He needs the money before winter sets in."

"He needs sixty thousand dollars to liberate the state?"

"And he needs our people, our followers. He knows we have the unflagging support of the native Californians. He knows that is our greatest resource."

"*We* need sixty thousand dollars."

"And we need another two hundred and fifty fighters armed to the teeth - which he can supply. And the weapons."

"Why doesn't he go steal the money himself? Two hundred men could hold up a lot of stages."

"They are trained soldiers, not highwaymen. That is our expertise, if you will."

"Our band of fighters will meet strong resistance," Tiburcio said, thinking aloud. "We would likely prevail. But with twice as many men at our command, and weapons of such destruction as will be arriving at Agua Dulce, we will be unstoppable."

"The general agrees. I agree."

"And who will lead the revolution? Soriano is a general. And the Padilla I met in San Quentin seemed a bit too ambitious to sit and take orders from a mere outlaw."

"Soriano said if you can't lead the liberation, Tiburcio, it cannot be won. There is not another man in the state who could secure sixty thousand dollars and embolden thousands of people with the will to overthrow the state. There is not another man in all of California who could even think about starting a revolution of the people. That's what he told me. He knows the people will follow you. He knows the foundation of trust you have built among the native Californians. You have helped them survive this long. You will be the one to show them to freedom."

"Well, then, Clodoveo, the time has come!"

Chapter 5: Plundering New Idria Summer 1873

Tiburcio looked at the rugged men who he had gathered in Abdon Leiva's parlor. He had lost many of his trusted inner circle to Morse - Soto, Carabajal, Barcenas, Procopio, Molino, to name just a few - but he believed in these seven men more than anybody else. They would be the ones upon whom he could rely in carrying out the violent precursor to the insurrection. They would be the ones he could count on in his plundering of as many stage coaches and stores and trains as they needed to get Soriano his money in exchange for the destructive weapons and battle-hardened troops.

Closest to his heart were his cousin Teodoro Moreno, a hardened and proven Frenchman named August de Bert, his young top lieutenant, Clodoveo Chavez, and longtime friend and former general Jose Castro.

There was also Ramon Romero, a fellow with sharp whiskers on his cheeks, a full mustache and catlike eyes. He was a former San Quentin inmate who had stabbed to death an American in a quarrel over a woman outside an Oakland fandango and had fatally knifed another man in Sacramento. Romero had drifted in and out of Tiburcio's gang over the years. Next to Romero sat Romulo Gonzales, a former miner from New Almaden, who had joined Tiburcio because he had nothing to lose, no family, no work, no possessions, and therefore little to fear. Gonzales had been at the Saucelito hideout when Soto took a fatal bullet from Morse but got away. Then there was the short-tempered and intrepid Blas Bicuna.

These last three desperadoes - Romero, Gonzales and Bicuna - would do anything Tiburcio asked of them. Their only flaw, as far as he was concerned, was that they were more mercenaries than revolutionaries. To them, the revolution meant money, so Tiburcio would make sure he lined their pockets well.

"There is much urgency," Tiburcio told them. "We must strike fast and move south. The law will be right behind us every step of the way, and the mood of our people will not remain hopeful forever. Our focus now is only on the most lucrative targets. First, there are some local stages to strike, good money that will keep our bellies full and all of our thirsts quenched. But this will not provide us with what we need to finance the revolution. Next, we hold up a train full of gold and then raid stores that have wages piled up high in safes. Up and down the Coast and Diablo ranges we will hit in rapid succession. When we have achieved our financial goal, I want you to join me in declaring a full-fledged war on the government of California. Our army will be nearly five hundred strong. I will send some of you up to Cantua to lead two hundred and fifty able-bodied men to war, and some of you will relocate with me in Southern California where another two hundred and fifty fighters await near the border. They are trained soldiers with weapons that no sheriff and no posse possesses. We will have bought enough ammunition to last us two years and our brothers at Agua Dulce have stocked up on food and the crops are plentiful at Cantua so we can wait out any unseen trouble.

"There is much in our favor," he continued. "There is no state military to speak of, and the federal government's zeal, let alone preparation, for another protracted battle is nonexistent. That means any opposition we meet will come from small local militias. Any defiant effort to stop us will be fractured, at best."

Tiburcio looked at each man.

"Any questions so far?"

His eyes drifted to an inside doorway, where Rosaria was listening. Her husband was sitting with the other men and she was trying to gauge her husband's inclination.

"Abdon? You have not told me your decision. The work pays well. Are you interested?"

"I will provide you a safe house, Tiburcio. That is all. I am not interested in a life of crime."

Out of the corner of his eye, Tiburcio saw Rosaria storm away.

"*Hombres, escucha!* I want your loyalty. By the end of summer, there will be no turning back. Everybody must pull up their roots. If you own land, sell it. If you own cattle, find a way to move your herd. If you have a lover, it's time for them to decide whether to stay or go.

"And one more thing. As long as I am in charge, we will treat all innocent victims, if they do not put our lives at risk, with kindness and respect. And we will be particularly chivalrous to the gentler sex. Any of their needs, whims and requests, within reason, will be carried out. This is not only proper, but it will sway the general populations' opinion favorably to our side."

Everybody nodded.

• • •

Jose Castro was the lookout. He spurred his mount ahead of the San Juan-Visalia stage as it pulled out of San Juan Bautista and rambled east toward Hollister. The former general raced to sound the alarm for the bandits. He had seen not just one or two, but three wagons preparing to depart San Juan. The first carried several well-to-do passengers and a strongbox of money on its way from San Francisco to Hollister. Another would soon leave in the opposite direction with a family migrating from Utah who, Castro said, appeared to have money because he saw them spending lots of it in the pharmacy. A third stage was scheduled to hit the road in about two hours, taking an important Hollister hotel proprietor to San

Francisco for business purposes. The gang had only counted on the first stage.

About twelve miles north of Hollister, the first wagon approached Soap Lake. It was full of passengers and guarded by an armed man sitting up front with the driver. A loaded treasure box was at their feet. The stage started down a shallow ravine when three highwaymen emerged from out of nowhere on the road ahead as if coming straight up out of the ground. Their long, dark jackets were cut away at the waist and skirted down to the backs of their knees. With rifles pointed down at their side, they stood shoulder to shoulder in the middle of the road and waited. The three desperadoes could see the driver and the shotgun messenger exchange words. The wagon slowed as it came to the flat part of the road. The driver ducked forward against the front boot, but the guard remained upright. The outlaws saw a weapon in his hand that gave them pause. The sawed-off shotgun had a pair of barrels easily two-thirds shorter than normal, allowing the gun to be quickly raised. The shooter could spray enough heavy lead from both barrels to take all three of their lives at once. And he was just coming into his gun's range.

"Damn!" cursed the driver, crouching but keeping an eye on the road. "We are in for it now."

"Shut up," the messenger said. "We ain't done for. Not by a long ways."

"You ain't gonna fight all three, are you? That's asking too much."

"I am."

At about forty yards distance, the outlaws separated. Bicuna stayed in the middle and Romero and Gonzales stood twenty feet to either side of him.

"Well, they ain't stupid," the armed guard said.

He unhitched his holster and tapped the revolver, then explained to his nervous driver: "I'll take the one on the right with the first barrel, and save the rest of the buckshot for the one on your side. That will leave us with the pistol to finish off the bastard standing straight ahead. The minute they holler for us to stop, you drop down, jam on that brake and hold them lines tight. Them horses are gonna be itchin' to run."

The wagon stood twenty-five yards from the outlaws and the shotgun messenger was ready to pull the trigger when he heard a loud "Halt!" yelled from the back side of the wagon. Four more desperadoes swooped down on the stage with their guns drawn.

"God damn it!" the messenger relented, telling the driver there was a new plan.

"What the hell is it?"

"Do whatever they say, that's the plan. Let them have what they want. Sooner or later someone will catch the cocksuckers and hang 'em."

The bandits robbed every passenger in that first stage, tied them all up and laid them on their backs out in a field in the sun well away from the road. Three bandits drove the stage around the bend and out of sight of other passing wagons.

When the brigands returned after ditching the stage, the other outlaws were standing around recounting the swiftness and ease of the holdup as they drank water from canteens and chewed jerky. Their horses were resting and eating. The single robbery had netted a pile of money. Tiburcio stood on a large boulder vaguely listening to their chatter.

"*Silencio!*" He ordered. "We are far from done."

He dispatched de Bert up the road and ordered Castro and Gonzales to guard the passengers of the first stage. He then told Chavez, Moreno and Romero to follow him.

Another wagon was creaking along the trail. The horses were moving at a very slow gait as they carefully maneuvered the wagon around big craters in the road. The wagon driver was unarmed and kept glancing back into the canvas-covered carriage. He seemed to not care at all about anything else on the road. Tiburcio felt that something was different about the approach of this wagon. He told Chavez, Moreno and Romero to stay back as he raced up to de Bert and told him to abort the plan. The bandits looked at their leader quizzically.

"Halt!" he called to the driver, who immediately pulled the team of horses to a standstill. The animals looked thin and weakened. The driver's face was pale and sullen and he fidgeted nervously.

"What do you got inside?"

"My family. Take what you want, but please do it quickly. Please, mister, my daughter has consumption and we need to get her help in the city! There was little anyone could do to help in Hollister."

"I will have you on your way in an instant - if you cooperate," Tiburcio said. "Let me look inside. Should I have anything to fear?"

The father shook his head as Tiburcio leaped to the ground and pulled out his Colt.

"Cover me," he said to Clodoveo, and swung onto the back of the coach to look inside.

He was astonished at what he saw. A nine-year-old girl was lying on the floorboards with her head in her mother's lap. She appeared sallow, coughing weakly, shaking and sweating. She was too weak to lift her head up or even open her eyes to see who was interrupting their progress. She weighed about as much as a medium-sized dog and her clothes hung loosely on her. Her throat was swollen past the point of her bony jaw line. A bloody towel was in the mother's hands.

"I am Tiburcio Vasquez, leader of the rebel regiment in this area. Our only cause is to liberate my native Californians. We will not harm you."

He looked closely at the girl.

"It must be in her lungs."

"Yes, sir. She needs a doctor, but we have little money - and time. Is there a doctor in Gilroy?"

"There is. I can get you a wagon with a swift team of horses. If your husband would not mind letting one of my men steer the wagon and another man to ride along as an escort. He could then help you care for and comfort your daughter back here."

"That would be kind. What would we owe you for your time and kindness?"

"Nothing. Just spread some kind words about us," Tiburcio explained with a comely smile. "Because of the propaganda from newspapers and this state's lawmen, people don't understand that we do not want to harm innocent people. We only want to free our countrymen. Please, when you get to Gilroy, use this money to send for the best medical help from San Francisco. There is a couple hundred dollars in there. That will get you a nice room and pay for the doctor's trip and the proper medicine."

The husband tried to protest and attempted to decline the offer, because he perceived it involved tainted money. He tried to refuse as obstinately as possible without drawing the ire of the outlaws. But his wife was adamant - if someone was willing to help her daughter it did not matter who it was as long as his intentions and the outcome - her survival - matched her own desires. There was no time for higher principles, she told her husband.

Tiburcio watched the wagon briskly go west in the company of two of his best men, Moreno and de Bert. He made sure they gave the family clear instructions that when their daughter was healthy again they were to go the nearest newspaper office and retell the story of their encounter with Tiburcio's men.

When the wagon was out of sight, the remaining outlaws immediately rode across the rugged hills to San Juan Grade to catch the third stage. Tiburcio descended onto the main road while the others followed from the trail above.

As he neared an approaching stage, Tiburcio recognized a familiar face sitting guard next to the coach driver. He gave a warning sign for the bandits to stay where they were. This was not merely a businessman traveling to the city. It was Sheriff Wasson of Monterey County. Wasson was running for re-election and had been stumping in Hollister. At the back of the wagon, two deputies were keeping a close eye on the hills, shotguns across their laps. As he crossed paths with Wasson's stage, Tiburcio nodded from under his wide-brimmed hat and passed without suspicion.

Tiburcio was sure the authorities would soon suspect something was wrong when the first wagon didn't arrive at its destination. Wasson's deputies would begin to put it all together and double back.

Another stage came rambling down the grade after Wasson was out of sight. This one Tiburcio also recognized. It was the wagon owned by Thomas McMahon, operator of a hostelry and a general store in Hollister on San Benito Street, near the home of one of Tiburcio's paramours. Tiburcio halted the wagon. McMahon's driver stopped and the merchant quickly exited to find out what was wrong.

"Thomas McMahon!" Tiburcio exclaimed.

"Tiburcio? It's been a long time. I haven't heard or seen you since your run-in with Mr. Salazar in San Juan."

"Ah, news travels fast."

"Where are you staying these days, Tiburcio?"

Tiburcio laughed, because McMahon knew the bandit wasn't going to tell him where he was lying low. McMahon smiled knowingly and continued:

"But you are on the road to San Juan. Have you patched things up with Salazar?"

"I know Salazar is in jail on fraud charges pertaining to his business," Tiburcio replied. "Do you think I don't keep up on the news, Thomas?"

"You're wise, Tiburcio. Folks thought he got the better of you, but look who's locked up and who is well and free now! "

"Thank you," Tiburcio said, and drew his gun. He pointed it at McMahon's chest. "Are you traveling with any money?"

"Tiburcio! You would rob me? I have let you stay free at my hotel!"

"Perhaps for the last time, then. Empty your purse!"

"I have given you a room when I knew the law was after you!" McMahon protested. "What are you thinking? Where is your respect?"

"Do not make me shoot you, gringo! You are still an invader in my eyes, and will pay the price when we liberate the countryside."

"I have heard rumors of a revolution. I do not believe them. I think you only rob in order to buy expensive clothes, enjoy the company of fine women and eat the best food. Do not pretend to have loftier ambitions!"

Tiburcio pulled back the hammer on the gun.

"OK. OK," McMahon said. "You son of a bitch!"

"Do you have any more?"

"No."

"Do I need to search the wagon?"

"Go ahead, if you would like. But *my* word actually means something!"

Tiburcio decided against taking the extra time and bid McMahon farewell.

Tiburcio handed the sack to Chavez. They sat on the side of the road and counted the money. It added up handsomely to seven-hundred and fifty dollars.

"He will miss this money," Clodoveo said.

Romero looked in the direction of Gilroy and saw dust flying. He alerted Tiburcio.

"It's probably Sheriff Wasson. Wouldn't he like to make a highly publicized arrest just before the election?"

"We better get off the main road," Chavez said.

"Let's go back to New Idria."

The desperadoes split up at Chilaro. Tiburcio stopped at Leiva's ranch and Chavez, Bicuna, Gonzales and Romero continued into the mining town.

Rosaria greeted him at the door.

"Is Abdon here?"

"No. He is working late at his shop."

"Then come dancing with me."

It wasn't the first time, Tiburcio and Rosaria visited the fandangos together without Leiva. When they did, Tiburcio never left her side. Off the dance floor, he was attentive to her every word and need. On the floor, they flowed like water in the same river, his front to her back, hips moving together, the palm of his hand lightly touching just under her navel. When they separated, the air between them was like a taut wire, straining to pull them close again.

"Why are you so considerate of me, Tiburcio?" she asked that evening as they took a break from dancing. "You could be in the company of much prettier women."

"They don't make me feel like you do. Only one other woman has ever made me feel this way. She is gone. That is why I prefer to drink in every moment with you. In this moment, I know I am happy. Every day I do not know whether I will be gazing into your eyes while we dance, or staring out prison bars, or hanging from a tree ..."

"You talk of such peril."

"And I see such beauty in front of me."

"The words come off your lips so easily, Tiburcio, as if they have been repeated many times, into many soft, willing ears."

"Nonsense. It is merely springtime. Time to appreciate the beauty of the world. Tomorrow, let's go enjoy the colorful warmth of the hills. Soon, it will be too barren and hot. Don't let this moment slip away, Rosaria!"

The next day they rode up into the distant mountains and crossed a plain of golden mustard and orange poppies before journeying higher into the foothills. After two hours, they stopped among some pines. He helped Rosaria off the horse and they sat down on a log.

"I am a fool to have come," she said.

"No. Don't say that. Let me enjoy this happy day with you, alone."

"Why, Tiburcio?" Rosaria asked solemnly. "Because you will leave Chilaro as quickly as you arrived? Or because you might die tonight, or tomorrow? And where would that leave me, Tiburcio?"

He was silent.

"I will tell you," she added. "It will leave me with many unhappy days to come."

"You can come with me, wherever I go."

"You have abandoned women who have followed you, Tiburcio."

"That was different. Our hearts beat together, our feet move in unison in dance, we laugh on the same word, sing to the same tune …"

"I cannot leave Abdon. But I cannot lose you!"

"Then get him to join our fight."

Later that evening, Rosaria walked into her humble house and Abdon was sitting morosely by the hearth. He had been waiting many hours for her return. When she entered he looked up with his sad but kind eyes.

"Where have you been?" he asked, his voice tired

"With Tiburcio."

"Why?"

"He wants me to get you to join his regiment."

"Tiburcio is a bandit and a cattle rustler. I am a laborer, not a criminal."

"How is it a crime to take back what was stolen from you in the first place?"

"I am Chilean. I do not care what happens in California."

Rosaria knocked a glass to the floor in rage and guilt, frustration and confusion.

"But *I* am a *Californio*. And I would be rich if it weren't for the gringos stealing my mother's land! So pardon the revenge festering in my soul. Even if you cannot understand the need for reprisal on my behalf, can you honestly say that you are satisfied with coming home tired after working all the day at the forge with nothing to show for it? Poor. Forever poor! Tiburcio and his men are not poor!"

"That bandit is making you crazy!"

"Seeing you sitting silently by the hearth night after night with a book up to your face is making me crazy! I may be married and a mother of two children, but I am not dead. I like to go out and dance. Tiburcio dances with me - something you will not do."

Leiva leaped up, strode over to the door, grabbed his coat off the rack and flung the door open.

"Fine. You want to go out. Let's go!"

"You don't understand!"

"What is going on between you and Tiburcio?" he demanded.

"Nothing. We are friends. We share many interests. And he wants you to enlist in his regiment."

"Are you coming?" Leiva grunted.

"No!"

"Then, I am going out alone!" Leiva said and slammed the door behind him.

Tiburcio was strumming his guitar at the saloon. There were few people in the room. He looked up and saw Chavez enter and charge over to him.

"A posse is asking questions around here about you. Nobody claimed to know anything of our whereabouts. But they are camped outside New Idria for the night."

"A posse? From where?"

"Morse sent them."

Tiburcio took a swig of ale and pondered the news.

"Morse? Is he with them?"

"No. There are only four. Sheriff Adams, a deputy and two citizens."

"Camped for the night?"

"Yes."

Tiburcio thought about this for a minute.

"Get de Bert and Moreno. Let's steal their horses and send them home - on foot. I will meet you at the stable."

"You are serious?"

"Yes, I am."

Tiburcio and Chavez met Moreno and de Bert outside the mining camp and devised the plan to steal the deputies' horses.

"I will buy the drinks if this goes off without a hitch," Tiburcio declared.

De Bert, being unknown to the law authorities and light skinned as to not arouse suspicion, struck up a conversation with the posse members as they were resting by the campfire by asking them general directions to Hollister. Then, he asked for a cup of coffee.

"What are you doing this far south?" Harris asked him suspiciously, staring deeply into de Bert's eyes.

"I was inquiring about getting a job at the mine, but it's all greasers working there."

"How is it that we didn't hear or see you approach?"

"Only you can answer that, sheriff."

While they were talking, Moreno snuck downstream along the bank, crossed the river on rocks where it was shallow and doubled back on the other side to where the posse's horses were tethered. He cut the lariats holding the horses to within a couple strands of breaking and returned back across the river.

De Bert thanked the law men for the directions and cup of coffee, mounted his horse and rode away. When Moreno saw de Bert ride past, he fired a rifle shot that spooked the posse's horses and broke them loose from the ropes. Tiburcio and Chavez used their vaquero skills to lasso the stampeding horses and ride them off. The sheriff and his men scattered in every direction in search of the shooter.

"To the horses," Harris called.

When they got to the gulch, they knew they had been fooled - stranded on foot, in rugged country a hundred miles from home.

The bandits rode back into town, four horses in tow.

After celebrating with his men, Tiburcio headed for Leiva's house.

Rosaria invited him inside. She was red-faced, agitated.

Her husband was seated at their block kitchen table, his head in his folded arms. His body was slightly convulsing as if he were weeping.

"What is wrong?"

"Abdon left here in a fury and got drunk at the saloon. He was taunted into a fight with a patron and ended up shooting an innocent bystander."

"Th … th … they are coming to lynch me, Tiburcio!"

"Nonsense. Let's go back to the mine and set the record straight."

"No! It's not that simple. These men have resented me for a long time. Th … th.. they cannot be appeased."

"Get up, Abdon!" Tiburcio ordered. "I have the last word in this camp and anywhere else within two hundred miles!"

Not far from the house, Tiburcio and Leiva met up with three men coming down the road. One of them was the man with whom Leiva had quarreled in the saloon, another was the slain bystander's business partner and the third was a physician from the camp. They were intent on apprehending Leiva and taking him to New Idria to face quick justice.

"Do you have a quarrel with one of my men?" Tiburcio asked.

Everybody remained in their saddle.

"Leiva rides with your gang?"

"Indeed."

The three men looked at each other apprehensively as if the answer wasn't what they expected.

"We don't want to disturb you or your men," the doctor said. "But ..."

"But what?" Tiburcio asked. "Neither do we want to disturb anybody or the camp in general."

"But the blacksmith killed an innocent man." the dead man's partner said incredulously.

"Who among us is truly innocent?" Tiburcio asked.

"He killed him in cold blood."

"And who are you?"

"I worked with the deceased. We own the cooperage."

"Does the deceased have family?"

"No."

"That makes it tidy, then. I will pay all of his outstanding debts, including what he owes for his half of the business. Any questions?"

The men uttered some words amongst themselves, then addressed Tiburcio.

"You are fair, Tiburcio. If we had known the blacksmith was part of your band, we would not have come so boldly down the road."

When the three men left, Leiva thankfully shook Tiburcio's hand, then abruptly let go of the grip, as if a horrible thought had just occurred to him.

"Does this mean I must enlist?"

"There is a lot to consider regarding that," Tiburcio said cryptically. "You see, in a few weeks my men and I can no longer headquarter here. We are going south. The revolution is at hand. If you are indeed one of my soldiers that means relocating Rosaria and the children. It means selling your ranch and the animals."

Leiva's sad eyes vaguely showed comprehension of his predicament.

"But if I stay," he ventured, glancing up the road, "those men will exact their punishment."

"Maybe. Maybe not. I will not be here to know. But you have little time to decide. Perhaps you should ask Rosaria what she thinks."

At home, Rosaria did not hide what she truly desired.

"But you must go with Vasquez and his men," she said impatiently.

"We will have to sell our possessions at a loss."

"If you stay, and that man's death is later avenged, I will truly have nothing left."

"I don't know what to do!"

Rosaria gritted her teeth in silent frustration. If Tiburcio rode off and she was separated from his life, she would be forced to swallow the twin poisons of never seeing her lover again and of suffering the monotony of her old domestic existence. Life would seep out of her day after day, the only ray of sunshine coming from the memory of Tiburcio and their time together, a blissful insanity but an insanity nevertheless.

"Perhaps I will ride with him on one excursion, just to see ..."

"That would be a good idea," Rosaria smiled.

Chapter 6: Unexpected
Near Hollister
Summer 1873

Rangy Henry Morrison, owner of seven-hundred thousand acres of land in the San Joaquin Valley, came riding down from his ranch with a sack of gold on his saddle and ran straight into Tiburcio's gang. The outlaw pondered the moral predicament. He knew that Morrison and his partner Charles Knox employed and conducted business with dozens of descendants from the state's earliest Mexican families. Therefore, much of the western side of the valley had retained its Mexican lifestyle with little gringo influence. Tiburcio valued this rare expanse where his culture remained unblemished. He also did not want to harm any of the Mexican population for which he was fighting. On the other hand, Tiburcio knew how Morrison came to own much of his land. He would buy out one heir of a large rancho, raise cattle on his portion of the land, then eventually buy the other heirs out with his profits; or, he would loan money to struggling cattle ranchers and when profits did not meet his expectations he would foreclose on them, many of whom were Californios.

Tiburcio's men waited in the hills for his signal as the cattle baron approached. Morrison sat in the saddle with the confidence of knowing that all the highwaymen in Northern California could not steal enough from him to make a dent in his fortune. That in itself was enough to make Tiburcio strike. So he did. At gunpoint, the cattle king handed over his sack of gold, wished Tiburcio a good day and started to lope away.

After a few steps, Morrison stopped and called back to Tiburcio.

"Mr. Vasquez," he said, looking as sheepish as a very rich man could. "Seeing how you took all my money, and I still need to go into town, would you mind letting me borrow twenty dollars?"

Tiburcio chuckled and obliged. His men enjoyed the rest of the day and most of the evening carousing in Hollister. The tale of the holdup and the twenty-dollar loan spread quickly. Even Morrison enjoyed telling and re-telling the story.

At daybreak the next morning, the bandits went back to work. From atop a hill, they furtively watched an olive green, oval-shaped Concord coach swaying side to side as its six-horse team loped down a flat part of the trail. They could make out two pine trunks strapped to the top of the coach and the hand-painted landscape on the side-door panels. The Concord didn't stir up much dust because of the morning dew.

A reins man and another traveler sat up in the box in front and inside a small group of six passengers were doing their best to endure the trip. A beautiful Spanish mother, well-dressed and wearing a veil to keep dust out of her face, her nine-year-old son and their nurse were sitting on the leather-covered hardwood seats, shoulder to shoulder, facing ahead. The boy sat in the middle. Their knees nearly touched the knees of the three passengers facing them, an elderly couple sitting side-by-side and a young man of about twenty-five on his way to San Francisco. The leather curtains were rolled down and fastened tight.

The bandits drew bandanas over their faces as they approached. The pair of men outside the coach quickly knew what was coming. The reins man pulled on the lines and halted the horses.

"Go to the coach," he told his companion, "and tell them we're about to get robbed, and if anyone has arms, take them out and put them in their laps and put their arms up."

The man got down from the driver's box, cracked open the finely painted door and conveyed the information to the passengers, then shut it tight. The passengers peered through the curtain slits as the highwaymen approached, guns drawn. The young, single man put his small pistol on his lap. They watched and waited in tense silence and stillness. The elderly male passenger next to the window reported to the others that one bandit did not have his face covered. He was holding back and watching from a distance, nearly out of view. He was dressed in a fine frock coat with satin lapels that opened near the top of his stomach. He was light skinned, handsome and sported a goatee.

"I think I've heard of that man," he commented. "I have seen his picture and read about him in the papers. Oh, what is his name?"

The refined woman became curious and tried to sneak a look past the roll-up curtain but sat back as a commotion arose outside the carriage.

"Get your hands up," shouted one of the bandits in a French accent to the driver who was still in the box holding onto the reins.

"You are a fool if you think I will drop these ribbons and get down. Do you want the team to fly away!"

"Put the reins around the break jam and get your fat ass down or I will shoot you right in the forehead!" de Bert said, leveling his pistol at the driver.

Another bandit, in broken English, told the man who had been up in the box with the driver to slowly get off the step.

"Are you armed? No? Then, get back up there. You are going to disarm the other travelers. If you miss a gun, you will be the first to die."

The man obeyed. He entered the coach and came out with one pistol. He closed the hinged door again so the ladies and the little boy could be spared if any violence should occur.

"OK. You passengers in the coach," de Bert shouted, "we have you surrounded, four guns pointed right at this stage. Get out! And know that I'll shoot every man, woman or child who doesn't keep his hands up and in sight!"

Nobody emerged from the coach.

"I will give you five seconds to walk out of that coach!" de Bert demanded. "One ... Two ... Three ..."

The door opened and the elderly couple, the young man and the nurse stepped out. De Bert turned around and glanced at Tiburcio, who wore an amused smile.

"The woman and her boy refuse to leave the stage," the young man fearfully informed the desperadoes. "She says she is tired, dusty and homesick and doesn't want to be delayed any longer."

"A woman? Making demands?" Tiburcio asked, dismounting with a light leap. "This is a woman I must meet."

He could feel every eye watching him - his own men as well as the travelers. He smiled at everyone, enjoying the attention and a little diversion.

Spurs jangling, Tiburcio walked over to the stage. He straightened his coat and stepped on the boot rail, the weight from his heavy foot slightly tilting the coach. He cracked open the door and crouched to peer inside. He gasped and thought he saw a ghost.

Tiburcio's gray eyes grew large and his face turned pale and he was suddenly dizzy. In an instant, he came to realize this was no apparition - because a hand of real flesh reached up and cuffed him across his cheek with such force it left half his face stinging and red.

He eased all the way inside, shut the door and sat across from the mother and child. His eyes teared up, but not from the strike of her hand.

"You are alive!" Tiburcio cried in Spanish.

Anita, sitting there across from him, was dressed in a pale lavender silk and wool faille bustle dress. She was adorned with a pearl necklace, gold chain on her wrist and a jeweled ring. She had removed her veil and he could see her beautiful, dark eyes.

"To hell with you. You deserted me! You left me to die!"

"No!"

"Don't lie to me again, Tiburcio! Don't start with lies again!"

"How can you believe that?"

"I believe it because my father told me so. I was steadfast in my desire to spend the rest of my life with you - no matter what the consequences. I convinced myself that our love was stronger than my own blood family who loved and cared for me and gave me comfort. We spent the most beautiful night together under the stars, and then the next thing I knew the man to whom I had bestowed my heart was gone, a mere memory. I woke back in my own bed, my head and body sore and bandaged from being pushed off the horse, but that pain was nothing compared to my ripped-apart heart. The man I loved deserted me and destroyed my dreams and left my life in shambles."

"Pushed?"

"Ah, you don't remember anything either, no?" she asked cynically in her native tongue. "My father filled in the missing details. He told me how indecent you are, how you pushed me off the side of my horse to save your own neck. I was slowing you down and you wanted ride faster to get away. I hit my head on a rock and lost consciousness. A few days later my father explained to me what had happened. He preferred to say, at least publicly, that you had abducted me, although I earnestly tried to tell him I had chosen to elope with you. Either way, it didn't matter, because I came to know your true nature. After a night of riding after us, my father and his posse began to close in on us, and you panicked and abandoned me with no regard for my life, only to save your own skin. All you could think about was fleeing from your captors as fast as possible. And you did so at my expense."

"I did not! Your father is just trying to protect your - and his - reputation. He and his men were shooting dangerously, wantonly, at us, Anita. A ball from one of their guns struck you in the temple. You fell to the ground. Although they were drawing near, I jumped off my horse and risked my own life -

without hesitation - in the middle of a hail of gunfire to return to you and tend to your wounds. You were badly bleeding and were as still and cold as a statue. I felt your pulse and listened to your breathing and prayed for any sign of life, but I felt nothing. Nothing. I thought you were dead, so only at the last moment, in great anguish, I decided to ride away to safety. I have gone over every detail of that day in my head to see if I could have or should have done anything different. Sometimes I wished I would have just stayed with your body and suffered the consequences. I have mourned every night since ..."

"And I, too. I had no choice, after that but to marry a suitor of whom my parents approved and return to the life I thought I was leaving! A foolish girl!"

Anita told her son in English to step outside. She assured him everything would be all right.

"Go to Mary," she directed. "Tell her I am fine. I will be there in a moment."

As the boy got up, he looked directly at Tiburcio. Tiburcio did not see the boy's polite-as-can-be, half-smile. He was mesmerized by the child's handsome, light gray eyes.

The boy opened the door and stepped out. De Bert asked Tiburcio if anything was wrong.

"N, n, no!" Tiburcio stammered, then gained composure. "Give me one minute more."

"We are risking being caught, *El Capitan*!"

"*Uno momento* ! Tell the other passengers we will do them no harm. Do not steal anything from them! They will all be free to go in a minute."

He jerked the stage door shut and leaned closer to Anita.

"Your father was trying to protect you. He fabricated the story that I tossed you from that horse only to save my own skin. And he made up the story, for the public to hear, that I abducted you. He did not want to taint your social standing so you could still marry into wealth."

For a moment both looked down at the floor and neither spoke. Then Tiburcio reached out and caressed Anita's small, soft hands. They looked up at the same time and their lips met gently at first, then their kisses grew stronger and more passionate. Anita's fingers moved through Tiburcio's hair and his hands softly squeezed the back of her dress and pressed her toward his chest. A minute later they parted, breathing heavily, their faces an inch from each other's and flush with excitement, eyes dancing, hearts wildly thrashing.

"Oh, my God! You are alive!" he poured out.

"What do we do now?" she asked in a desperate whisper.

Tears welled in their eyes.

"I must see you again!" he confirmed.

"It is not possible! Our lives are not the same anymore."

"Yes, it is. Just think, Anita - when did you discover love? Was it not forever defined, chiseled in stone, when we were together, singing poetry and riding in the hills and laughing? Is this not how you still see pure love in your head and your heart? We cannot escape our early knowledge of what perfect love is, now that we have felt it so deeply. It is still there, is it not?"

"But you will leave again. I have heard whispers of the rebellion. And I know how it is to follow you, Tiburcio. I tried, but I ended up alone. And that was before all of this."

"I have one last duty to my old country, Anita, the country you and I knew when we fell in love. Before the liberation begins, I will return for you and we will reunite forever."

"What if you die?"

Tiburcio did not answer. But he asked another question.

"Why are you traveling alone? Where is you husband?"

"He is dead. It is only my son, my Indian servants and me. Since I lay claim to six hundred square miles and thousands of cattle, I must travel to do business. I am not a traditional wife, Tiburcio."

"You should not dress so richly when you travel," he advised her, looking at her jewelry.

"You should see me at home doing chores in my brimmed straw hat, old leather boots and loose shirt," Anita said, allowing a small grin.

"How did he die?" Tiburcio asked, but he knew he did not have much time left.

"In an accident on his horse."

Tears fell from the pools in her eyes onto her fine clothes.

"You miss him."

"No, Tiburcio," she cried out, "I miss you."

"I remember when I last saw you," Tiburcio said, wiping the tears from her eyes. "It's been nearly ten years. But give me one more chance. Everything is new again."

Somebody called his name from outside the stage.

She smiled and kissed his cheeks, his lips and the lids of his closed eyes.

"What is your boy's name?" he asked.

"Rodolfo."

"How old is he?"

"Nine."

After a moment, he exclaimed: "I must see you again, Anita!"

"You will," she whispered. "But I must sort this all out before the next time I see you."

Her hand trembled as she searched her handbag for something. She pulled out a gold heart charm laid into green satin on a necklace.

"Take this, my love. Until we see each other again!"

"Soon! I will write before ..."

He opened the carriage door. They looked upon each other for what seemed like several minutes. Then he finally exited, his heart racing, mind swirling, throat constricted. She leaned back, closed her eyes and felt the same disbelief and inability to act that one experiences after surviving an earthquake.

She heard him bark orders and soon the passengers were boarding again, much concerned about her tremulous condition. Tiburcio watched the wagon hurl away, the driver intent on getting to the next stop to alert authorities. Anita peered out the back window until Tiburcio faded from view.

Clodoveo stood next to him.

338

"It looks as if you've seen a ghost," he said, and asked if he was all right.

"Everything has changed," Tiburcio said softly. "Fifteen minutes ago, nothing mattered except the revolution. It is still our greatest concern ... but now there is ..."

"There is what?"

"Love, Clodoveo. Of all things. Love, and the discovery that the power it wields still exists in my newly impassioned soul. This must sound terribly strange to you."

"Listen to me, Tiburcio!" Clodoveo said. "Nothing has changed! Nothing about the revolution has changed. Your life depends on it. You cannot survive without the revolution! Just like this air you are breathing ...   And no, it does not sound strange. I always knew it would take some special, deep love - somewhere, somehow, of yourself, of others - to rebuild after the revolution. That is where love plays a role."

"Everything is in place then," Tiburcio whispered.

"Almost everything. It is time to leave New Idria on our march to Agua Dulce."

Chapter 7: Raid
Firebaugh's Ferry
Summer 1873

The eight bandits descended on Firebaugh's Ferry seemingly out of nowhere. With gusto and bravado, they galloped into the town along the San Joaquin River only to discover Firebaugh's Ferry was nothing more than a store, a livery and a few houses.

"I don't even see a saloon," Romero deadpanned.

But the town wasn't dead. Two dozen men lingered around the store, many of them Morrison's vaqueros waiting to be paid. Inside, the storekeeper anticipated great business.

"Draw your pistols," Tiburcio told his men as they approached the center of town. "Ten grand awaits us."

They picked up the gait and arrived in a display of exhilaration that took the placid gathering by surprise.

"Get down. Anybody standing will get shot!" Tiburcio screamed in Spanish and then English.

As planned, Moreno, Leiva and Romero hogtied every single man outside and searched their pockets. Gonzales and de Bert did the same to everybody inside the store, leaving only the storekeeper untied. After everyone was searched, Tiburcio dropped from his golden palomino and strode into the store.

He pointed a pistol in each hand at the storekeeper.

"Give me the combination to the safe or I'll shoot out both your eyes."

The storekeeper obliged.

"Now tie him up," Tiburcio ordered Gonzales.

Tiburcio concentrated on setting the numbers and gears correctly and, with great zest, flung open the safe's door. His face fell in disappointment. A mere two hundred dollars in bank notes sat there for the taking. And a gold watch. He tossed the timepiece to Gonzales.

Then, they heard a commotion outside, the arrival of a stage. When Tiburcio stepped outdoors, the other robbers were holding the driver and his passengers at gunpoint. Tiburcio ordered the stage box to be searched, but only a few hundred more dollars and some worthless bank papers and mining shares were inside. The passengers carried little money and jewelry themselves. The Firebaugh robbery was quickly turning into a farce.

Tiburcio barged into the store again.

"Where is the ten thousand dollar deposit?" he demanded of the storekeeper.

"What? Was it not on that Kingston stage that just arrived? I expected to do great business today. I am staying open late to provide these vaqueros with provisions, so I am disappointed too!"

"I don't give a damn about you! I think you are lying! I will search every inch of your house for the money."

Tiburcio walked past his men and stepped over several bound victims on his way to the house adjacent to the store. The minute he walked through the door, he was accosted by the shrill of a woman.

"Where is my husband, you thief?" she demanded, disregarding the two Navy Colts in the intruder's hand. She began slapping Tiburcio on his vest.

"In the store, you mad woman. In the store!"

Ignoring Tiburcio's demands to stay put, she started out the door. Tiburcio thought for a moment and decided this one ardent woman could do more damage than he might imagine. He sprinted after her. Tiburcio found the wife weeping on top of her prostrate husband, whose hands and feet were roped behind him.

"Where is the watch?" she asked, looking up into the empty safe then turning to the leading bandido. "You are Tiburcio Vasquez, no?"

"I am."

"Then I know you are not so bad as to take the watch I gave my husband when he was courting me."

Tiburcio smiled.

"No, I am not so bad," he said, turning to Gonzales. "Give her back the love token."

"But this watch is worth three hundred dollars. It's worth more than we got from the safe!"

"*Silencio*! Give it back."

After Gonzales handed the watch to the wife, she asked Tiburcio to follow her. They went back to the house and she fetched another timepiece.

"Here, take this one," the wife said. "It's worth even more - to you. You haven't got such a bad heart after all."

The bandits mounted their horses and formed a semicircle in the street in front of the store. Everyone was looking accusingly at Castro.

"What?" he asked defensively. "The money must be on another stage from Kingston. You saw! The vaqueros were waiting for it, too!"

"This raid is going to get the law all up in a frenzy," de Bert said angrily. "And for what? Nothing. We'll be caught and hung for a few hundred dollars and some jewelry, because of your fucking mistake!"

Tiburcio knew what to do next.

"We've had enough robbing and riding for the day. I have on good word that a number of gorgeous *señoritas* will be at a hotel in Hollister for most of the week. Tonight is the last night of a big, three-day fandango. Let's go there and forget about this."

The men looked dubiously at one another.

"Hollister? But we will be within striking distance of the sheriff."

"We have nine sets of eyes to watch the doors and the crowd. We must not let our spirits dry up. Are we not alive and richer than we were a few hours ago? To Hollister!"

TIBURCIO!

It was nearly midnight when Tiburcio's gang arrived at the hotel but they found the fandango nowhere near ready to close down.

"Drink up, men!" Tiburcio called out as they entered building.

The floor was busy with dancers gliding across it. Several dozen men mingled about the place, and Tiburcio remembered his old fandango, so many years ago. He caught the eye of someone he knew, a vibrant girl with gleaming eyes and the blackest hair. Tiburcio sat at a table in a dark corner of the room and she walked over and took a seat next to him. She looked deeply into his eyes. She sang softly in his ear and kissed his neck. Her attentiveness allowed his body to relax, but thoughts of Anita never left his mind. What had she done for all those years? Who had loved her? What had made her laugh? Cry? How long had the memory of him stayed with her? Did she ever believe they would meet again? How did she keep the secret that she was alive from him all these years? And would she really give up her life and property to come to him?

The crowd thinned considerably around 3:00 a.m. Tiburcio took note of his gang's whereabouts. Romero had slipped away a few hours ago, back to his shadowy, solitary existence outside the band of outlaws. Moreno and Leiva had quickly become too edgy watching the door and soon departed back to New Idria. An hour ago, Bicuna, Castro and de Bert had walked over to another hotel/saloon with some prostitutes. And Chavez and Romulo Gonzales were still playing cards in a chamber off the fandango ballroom. Then, he noticed a man who he had seen when they had first entered. He had been hanging around most of the night.

"Who is the solemn fellow near the door?" he asked his companion.

"I thought you knew him. When I danced with him earlier, all he did was ask questions about you."

"What kind of questions?"

343

"When did you arrive in town, with who, from where?"

"OK. I must alert Chavez. You keep an eye on him."

Chavez and Gonzales set out to find the Bicuna, Castro and de Bert, but they quickly returned.

"A posse is coming down the street right now," Chavez warned Tiburcio. "Somebody overheard them talking about surrounding the hotel!"

"You and Gonzales find the others and get out of town," Tiburcio said. "It will be easier for me to escape alone."

"We can't leave you here. How will you get out of here without being noticed?"

"I'll think of something."

"Go upstairs to my room," Tiburcio's paramour told him. "My friends and I will distract the snitch."

"And then what?" Tiburcio asked.

"What else? Dress like a whore! You'll blend in."

Inside the woman's room, Tiburcio undressed, tossing his clothes into a large lady's handbag. Then, he slipped into a woman's skirt and full blouse and crammed his feet into some heeled boots. He found a scarf and put it around his head. The black-haired beauty knocked and entered the room. She and her friends laughed at the sight of Tiburcio.

"OK. Have your fun," he told them, unable to keep from smiling as well. "Now what?"

"Hunch over like an old mother hen and the three of us will help you down the hall and out the side door," she said. "If anyone asks, you are Mother Whore!"

The group shuffled unhurriedly in a tight circle as if they were a coterie of giggling friends into the alleyway and past an armed deputy guarding the side of the building. They emerged onto the main street in the dim dawn light and kept walking to where Tiburcio had left his horse, concealed among some olive trees by the livery. He quickly pulled off the tight women's footwear and slipped on his own boots that were in the bag. He kissed his lady friend, leaped into the saddle and casually trotted out of town.

TIBURCIO!

At daylight, Tiburcio was coming out of the hills between San Juan Bautista and the small town of Tres Pinos where he would get back on the main road. He easily recognized the figure coming his way. Henry Morrison - big, strong, long-legged, eccentric - made his horse look too short, as if he were on a low barstool. Tiburcio drew his gun.

"Tiburcio!" Morrison called from up the road. "Put away your revolver. This is becoming droll. I have a debt I want to repay you."

Tiburcio's palomino sidestepped next to the rancher's horse. Morrison held out something in his hand.

"It's the twenty dollars I borrowed from you."

Tiburcio laughed as he scooped the gold out of Morrison's hand.

"Where's the interest?" he asked.

"Nonsense. We never discussed interest. But I can share some valuable information that's worth much more. May I speak as we ride together a ways?"

"Certainly. But you'll have to ride in my direction. I cannot backtrack."

"I understand," Morrison said as they started up the road on horseback. "I heard you tied up a bunch of my ranch hands back at Firebaugh's Ferry."

"All for nothing," Tiburcio answered matter-of-factly. "Where was the ten thousand dollars?"

"I knew you planned to ransack the place so I delayed the deposit. Put it on the first train the next morning."

Tiburcio stopped his horse, not believing what he was hearing.

"I was betrayed?"

"You know you shouldn't steal from your own countrymen, Tiburcio. It's terrible business."

"I have a war to fight," Tiburcio answered astringently. "I cannot always be accommodating. And besides, those Mexicans who you employ are traitors. They've taken the easy way out - working for a gringo."

"The fact is I cannot have you stealing from my workers. They must get paid or they are very unhappy. And unhappy workers are a liability. On the other hand, content workers will be loyal. Even to a yanqui landowner."

"I was betrayed," Tiburcio repeated.

"Perhaps you had a disloyal follower. Someone who is not happy and content."

"Is this the information you wanted to share with me?"

"No," Morrison said, turning frank, "something more important. I want you to know that I have earmarked a twenty thousand dollar deposit for each of two stores in this valley. Snyder's in Tres Pinos and Jacob and Epstein's in Kingston."

"Why are you telling me?"

"The money is for you. For your revolution. If you can get away with it."

Tiburcio's gray eyes bore into Morrison's. There was no evidence that he was lying.

"You are asking me to steal your money? Explain."

"I cannot just hand the money over to you. I must be discreet or I will be hung as quickly as they'll hang you. But if you can pull off the robberies, the money is yours. And I will simply look like a victim."

"Why do you want to help us?"

Morrison thought for a while about how to explain this.

"That's a good question. To me, it's money well spent. I am not altruistic. I've never been very enthusiastic over a strong central government in the first place. I don't trust governments. The men in power see my vast land holdings as an easy opportunity to steal, like a sack of gold left open. They have no qualms about seizing property under the name of progress, as you well know. One way or another they will take my land and my money. They will force me to split up my holdings. They might want to lay a railroad right through it. Or give a big piece to the Indians to placate them. You see, Tiburcio, I like my lifestyle. I like the old ranch way of life. The way it is now. There's plenty of cheap labor, no unrest among the workers. I have lots of open space for hunting. I am very wealthy. Why would I want any of that to change? So I decided, let's see what Tiburcio can do with his little rebellion. Maybe he will succeed and, in doing so, save my way of life. At the very least, maybe an armed insurrection, however small, will delay the inevitable, put a gate up in front of the authorities.

"In fact, my partner Knox and I have a wager going. He says your movement will be snuffed out before you have a chance to fight one good battle. I say, on the other hand, you will keep the state government busy for years trying to quell the revolution. I think you can disrupt most of the south state and move into the north before the federal government can get around to sending in the Army."

"What if you've miscalculated?"

"Then I lose a mere forty thousand dollars."

"If you win, who says I won't take your holdings faster than the government?"

"Because you will need me."

"So why those two stores?"

"Both are in quiet little towns, Tiburcio. It shouldn't be a problem for you to swoop in and out. The papers say you like to avoid bloodshed. I like that - I won't feel guilty. You go in, tie up the storekeeper, take the money and leave. It's almost as easy as if I handed it to you."

"It's a trap ..."

"Tiburcio! Why would I care to ensnare you? The odds are stacked high enough against you as it is."

"Perhaps. But if it is a trap, we will come and kill you, your family and your workers and burn your property to ash."

"Ah, I would expect so."

Chapter 8: Thunderheads
21-Mile House, near San Jose
Summer 1873

Personally. Politically. Professionally. Harry Morse knew the good times couldn't last forever. He just hoped the three pillars didn't all collapse at once.

The first sign of trouble came in his personal life when his unruly son, George, was expelled from military school. Morse saw the academy as the last option in dealing with George's errant behavior. He had concluded that he, as a father, simply didn't have the answers, the knowledge, or the skill to rear a maverick son, and therefore enrolled him in officer training. If that couldn't straighten him out, what could? Now, Morse would have to find the answers himself. George's problems weighed heavily on his mind and drained his energy away from his work.

If it were only George's personal problems distracting him, life would not be difficult. But the political landscape was changing drastically and the sheriff was trying to figure out why and how to maneuver. Politically, the Democrats were gaining in numbers all over the region, forcing strange alliances. An ally's loyalty could be fleeting in any given election and backing a losing candidate could come back to sting you. Republican nominees handpicked for high civic positions held by party incumbents was not a sure thing anymore. Citizens were listening more closely to what politicians said and what they did rather than sticking to one party line. There was more open discussion on the streets and more diverse opinions being shared. Scores of new residents without long ties to the area, or its leaders, were arriving every day. These newcomers switched allegiances quickly. Despite it all, Morse still believed he had the experience and charisma to survive this new political climate. But it would take a lot of work - if he had the energy for it.

The most solid pillar of them all - the professional side of his life - was teetering the most. He had been riding high after the capture of Bartolo Sepulveda and Procopio and, most of all, the killing of Juan Soto. Newspapers up and down the state detailed his prowess and everyone from mayors to the governor of California heaped praise on him. His unflinching efforts galvanized law enforcement officials and bred success from county to county. Wasson in Monterey and Adams in Santa Clara had had nearly as much success going after and weeding out evildoers in their bailiwicks as he had in his own.

Then the Vasquez band ratcheted up their campaign against the citizens of California. Their raids grew bolder and more frequent. And the newspapers started painting a much too flattering picture of the outlaws. Morse cursed as he read newspaper articles about Tiburcio Vasquez's kindness. It made him sick. First, a Utah couple credited the bandit with saving their ill daughter's life. Then, a female passenger emoted to a reporter how the desperado allowed her stage to pass through the most dangerous stretch of road with a mere smile and a kind word. Another victim of Tiburcio's evil banditry, whose life could have been snuffed out in an instant, merrily laughed while telling a reporter how Vasquez returned a love token at her simple request. A *San Francisco Chronicle* reporter took it upon himself to roam the hills to find Mexican ranchers, sheepherders and laborers willing to talk about Vasquez. They extolled Vasquez and his outlaw gang for helping them get through financially tough times and for protecting their property from the government and squatters and other thieves. Morse read about how handsome and chivalrous this violent criminal was. How well he dressed and spoke. How he could melt hearts with a stroke of a guitar string.

Morse was not jealous. He was vexed and alarmed. In the past few months, news of some of the most audacious attacks ever carried out in the state was being widely disseminated but not at all scrutinized; all people wanted to hear was the romantic version of the crimes. Perhaps it made them feel safer. Morse was shocked that there weren't more cries for a prompt lynching after the Visalia stage robbery, where Vasquez and his men left passengers tied up and roasting in the sun for hours; or after Firebaugh's Ferry, where thirty people were hogtied and robbed at gunpoint. What did Morse hear on the street instead of cries for Tiburcio Vasquez's head in a noose? He heard mocking conversation about how his own deputies - his best men - had been left stranded in the backcountry on foot after Tiburcio and his followers snuck into their campsite and stole their horses right out from under them.

Morse chose to sit back and wait as Adams and Wasson put together a twenty-man posse to scour the hills and mining towns in search of Tiburcio and his army. They came back frustrated at every point, unable to get near the gang. They railed against the Mexican community in the mining towns, native ranchers in the hills and scared white settlers staking remote claims who, out of fear or admiration, protected the desperado's hiding places and movements throughout the region. Morse decided he was not going to sit back any longer.

It was late in the evening, about 9:00 p.m., and he needed to get out of the office. He wanted to take a walk in the fresh air before going home. He plucked his hat off the rack, opened his office door and took two steps into the antechamber before he was stopped by his undersheriff.

"Telegraph, sir," Borein said without looking up from the message he was reading at his desk. "21-Mile House in the Divide has been robbed. Six or seven Mexicans."

"Vasquez?"

Morse was ashamed he had asked the question when he discerned the obvious answer in his undersheriff's expression. The cool night air was still on his mind. It would have cleared his head before walking into his house to face his wife's disappointment that he had spent another fifteen hours at work today and hear her stories about their son's latest outburst in a store, on the street or in a saloon.

Borein watched his boss's mind churning.

"Wire Adams and tell him to meet me at the 21-Mile House. I'll sleep on the train down."

"That's not all, sir.

The sheriff looked at Borein.

"Yes?"

"There are reports of a train robbery earlier in the day."

"This is war," Morse said.

■ ■ ■

Just after sunrise - about the time Morse was arriving for his long day at the office that would end with the telegraph - Vasquez was in the back room of a saloon at New Idria detailing his next strike. The bandits' jaws dropped.

"Nobody here has ever pulled a train robbery," Gonzales reminded Vasquez. "In fact, I've only heard of one train robbery ever done anywhere."

"Well, there is a pay car with sixty-five thousand dollars in gold sitting in it. And we're going to take it," Tiburcio declared. "And here's how. There is a place in the Divide between San Jose and Gilroy where the train slows down to a crawl as it climbs a hill. Romero and Moreno will jump on board at that time and secure the engineer and fireman. Romero, Gonzales and de Bert will be with them and go to the coach and make sure no passengers put up resistance. Chavez and I will cut away the baggage cars and find the safe. We will have to act fast. Leiva, Castro and Bicuna will dismantle the track at the bottom of the hill so the train won't get past the Divide. We must jump off the train before it descends. When it derails, we clean up what we need and go. Easy."

The train was scheduled to come down the tracks between San Jose and Gilroy at 3:10 p.m. so they had to get moving. The notorious band had a hard ride ahead. They changed horses midway at a ranch and reached the Divide at 2:00 p.m.

Leiva, Bicuna and Castro carried their heavy leather bags with crow bars and hammers and picks inside from the tethered horses down to the side of the track. As they started trying to dismantle the iron, the others rode over the hill and waited for the train. Chavez was the first to spot the pitch-black steam from the Southern Pacific train billowing into the sky as the locomotive clattered toward the hump.

"Damn! It's running early," Tiburcio shouted. "We aren't going to be able to get on that thing. We will have to get the safe when it crashes below. Romero! Ride ahead and tell Leiva, Bicuna and Castro the train is here and they need to tie the rope and pull up the timbers now! We are right behind you!"

At the top of the hill, the engineer saw the horsemen riding along the tracks and quickly guessed their motive. Below he saw the three men working to tear up the track.

"More coal! More coal!" he yelled back to the fireman. "Get us a strong head of steam! Bandits!"

The fireman heaved coal into the firebox in a frenzy, while down the track the robbers frantically shoved their crowbars into the ground under the rails and sledgehammered the ends, desperately trying to dismantle the track. They could hear the train now. Engine groaning, cars shaking and wheels clattering, it chugged over the top of the hill and raced down with great speed. Knowing they could not keep pace with the train, Tiburcio halted his group of men. The train's crew hung on tight to steel levers and handrails as the engine hit full speed toward Leiva, Bicuna and Castro. Everybody watched in horror.

As the first cab thundered past, the three bandits dived away from the track, and the throbbing rush of the cars streaked by them. Leiva, Bicuna and Castro lay sprawled on their backs. As they watched the last of the cars fade out of sight down the track and the black steam lighten and dissipate into the sky, the others rode up on their horses. It was several minutes before anyone spoke.

"OK, to hell with train robberies," Tiburcio said. "Let's get to the 21-Mile House saloon. We are not going home empty-handed, my friends."

Vasquez and the others rode up to the hotel and saloon as the sun was beginning to set. He ordered Chavez to stand guard out on the porch as the others entered the bar. Their disappointment from the botched train heist grew heavier as they looked around the near empty room.

"Let's take a table and have a drink," Tiburcio sighed.

Tiburcio observed the room. A man named Newton Finley was standing behind the bar talking to Archie Tennant, the brother-in-law of the hotel proprietor, who happened to be out of town. Seated at a table to their right was an area rancher named John Horne and two of his farmhands, and at another table was a traveling sewing machine salesman named Perkins, who had stopped for the night.

"Five," Tiburcio said, and the men knew what he was thinking.

Vasquez was the first to draw a weapon. To the surprise of most of his men, he pulled out a large Bowie knife instead of a gun.

"Everybody stay quiet and don't resist," he threatened.

The salesman began laughing, believing it was a joke, until Tiburcio took three bounding steps toward him and thrust the sharp blade against his throat.

"I want you all to lie down exactly where you are - except for you, barkeep. You stay standing up so you can show me where the money is."

The rest of the bandits pulled out their guns. Rope and blankets were found in a supply room off the kitchen and used to tie and cover the victims. The bandits took about two hundred dollars and four watches from the victims and placed them on the bar.

"I know it has been a disappointing trip so far, men," Tiburcio said to his gang. "Why don't you all help yourself to some whiskey from behind the bar before we set out again. I'm sure these five fellas won't mind."

But really there were six people at the 21-Mile House that evening. The bandits did not see the Chinese cook in his quarters at the back.

After drinking a few bottles, the party rode away and the cook emerged from the back and untied all the men. Not long after that, Morse received the telegraph from Santa Clara County Sheriff Adams and wired back that he would meet him at the 21-Mile House.

Chapter 8: Arms
Agua Dulce
September 1873

At a secluded camp hidden among the jagged rocks of Agua Dulce, twelve large wagons arrived with a deadly freight. Two dozen solemn men unloaded the wooden boxes of expensive Colt Army and heavy Starr revolvers, powerful Springfield and accurate Enfield muskets, short-barreled carbines, rapid-fire Spencers and other rifles with telescopic lenses, .44 caliber bullets and minie balls and bayonets.

In silence, two-by-two, the men carried the boxes over to a wide-mouthed cave and set them inside in orderly fashion. When the arms and ammunition were unloaded, they unhitched two howitzers and a mortar from the back of wagons and rolled them over to the cave. When they were done with this last task, the delivery men wanted their money. They hadn't expected to arrive alive, at least not all of them. Now, after their dangerous, illicit journey across the country against all odds, they were very determined to get paid, get the hell out of California and disappear.

Ysidor Padilla took their demand to the general.

"Is the entire shipment accounted for?"

"Yes, sir."

"The agreement was thirty thousand dollars upon delivery, yes?"

"That's correct."

"Do we have the thirty thousand dollars?"

"No. I must go north and find Vasquez. He has promised the money. I will leave tomorrow."

"It's summer now, but winter will come fast. If our men do not have food and warm clothing, they will grow restless. Will he have the entire sixty thousand dollars for the weaponry and the troops?"

"I believe he will. But the men who are here want to be paid now."

"Our guests will have to be reasonable and wait for your return. Go tell them they are welcome at our camp and they are safe here. They are our guests until you return with the money."

"What if they do not want to wait?"

"We will throw them off the top of the mountain. They have no choice."

It took Padilla several weeks to find Tiburcio at New Idria. He had expected the rebel leader to pay the cash, accompany him back to Agua Dulce at once and sound the bugle heralding the revolution.

He was badly mistaken. In fact, he could not believe what he was hearing as he stared blankly at Tiburcio Vasquez and Clodoveo Chavez across a table in the corner of the saloon.

"You do not have the money?" he repeated incredulously.

"We've had some setbacks."

"You've had nearly a year to obtain the amount. The men waiting back at Agua Dulce have made a long, perilous journey and have held up their end of the bargain. Now we must honor our end of the deal. You are putting us in a very bad situation. Perhaps if your men did less drinking and shared less time in the company of prostitutes, you would have the money."

"I must keep my soldiers happy," Tiburcio said blankly.

"General Soriano does not care about the pleasure of your men," Padilla continued. "If I do not leave here with the money, he will sever ties with you. And when he does, you won't survive two months before a posse catches up to you."

"I always stay ahead of the posse."

"Not if they know where to find you. *I* had no trouble finding you."

"Shut up, Padilla. Don't threaten me or you'll end up with the pigs down at the slaughter yard! If you want your money, I will get it. But I need a little more time."

Padilla sighed and shook his head.

"How much do you have? And how much more time," he asked.

"I have none of it. But I can get it by the end of the year. No longer."

"None?" Padilla asked rising from his chair. "Zero?"

"Sit down, Ysidor!"

"Tell me something," Padilla asked, still standing. "I do not see the same urgency in your mission. Are you still willing to risk your life for the cause?"

"I have risked my life a hundred times over."

"Perhaps. There is something different, however. I don't see in your eyes the sharp edge of the desperate and lonely man I remember in prison. You felt you had lost too much time being irresponsible and locked behind bars. You said when you left San Quentin nothing would stand in your way."

"Nothing but the revolution has consumed my thoughts day and night."

"What about your followers? Are they ready, as ready as you are?"

"In mining camps, in the backcountry, at Cantua, my countrymen are simmering. We are sitting on a tinderbox, Padilla. It is ready to explode. Just like we talked about when we were in San Quentin."

Padilla sat down again.

"Let's hope so, Tiburcio," he said. "Let's hope so. Now, how are you going to get the money? I am risking my own hide giving you this much latitude. I cannot walk away with empty promises!"

Tiburcio smiled. The gesture distressed Chavez so much that he could not remain silent. After all, it was he who first visited Agua Dulce and promised Soriano that they could get the entire sum to pay for the men and weapons.

"Yes, Tiburcio, where are we going to get sixty thousand dollars? We have rebels to the north and to the south ready to fight to the death and we have been unable to steal enough money to finance the war."

"I must apologize to my young lieutenant," Tiburcio said. "He is fiercely loyal but I have not had time to explain to him."

Chavez leaned back in his chair, exasperated.

"Do you remember when you left me at that hotel in Hollister, after we botched the train derailment and came up empty at Firebaugh's Ferry?" he asked Chavez.

"Yes. And you had to conceal yourself in women's clothes!"

Chavez could not contain a laugh.

"Yes. Well, I never told you whose path I crossed on the way back to New Idria."

"Whose?"

"Morrison."

"And?"

"You won't believe. I didn't believe it at first. But let me explain."

After he told Padilla and Chavez the story of his encounter with Morrison and the offer, the young rebel shook his head.

"The white cattle baron is going to give us forty thousand dollars?"

"In a sense, yes. And this must remain a secret between only us!"

"I will believe it when I see it," Chavez said.

"But even if you take Morrison's money, you are short of the total," Padilla reminded the bandit.

"I know. Why do you think I so desperately want Leiva to ride with us?" Tiburcio asked Chavez.

"I thought you were just fond of Rosaria."

"I am. I was. Nevertheless, her husband has ten thousand dollars stashed. I think I can get it, if I play my cards right."

"Well, that still leaves us short."

"There is one other person who has that kind of money," Tiburcio said reluctantly.

Chavez thought about who it might be for a minute, then nodded.

"Anita?"

"Yes."

"Oh!" Padilla exclaimed. "So Anita is back in the picture. I should have suspected as much."

Chapter 9: Tragedy
Tres Pinos
October 1873

Tiburcio Vasquez roused his men and told them to immediately begin preparing to move south. There was urgency in his voice.

"The time has come. There is no looking back, no turning back. By now, you should have sold everything except what you can haul away on horseback because you are either in with us all the way, or you are not at all. We have started to howl, and like a vicious windstorm, we cannot be controlled and we certainly cannot be stopped."

Tiburcio again laid out the final, grand plan. After taking the haul at Snyder's and then at Kingston, Soriano will be paid and Tiburcio will have command of his weapons and men. Events will move lightning fast after that. Well-armed, well-trained, experienced soldiers will swarm out of the Agua Dulce mountains and march through southern California, laying claim to vast tracts of land and cities. Hordes of desperadoes will empty out of New Idria and Cantua Canyon. Hundreds of sympathizers will feel the pull of glorious change for which they have waited so patiently and descend out of the northern hills, uniting with the southern flank. Up and down the state chaos and riots will erupt. Rogue fighters will jump into the fray. When the spirits of the invaders break, there will come concessions from the state government in Sacramento. At the very least, the rebels will have achieved a split state. The ultimate success, however, is conquering all of Alta California and having their land returned to them. Tiburcio shared this vision with his eager men.

The only exception was Leiva. The blacksmith was downhearted and reluctant to push on with the life of an outlaw. But his wife would be damned if she were going to remain in an empty mining camp and grow old in solitude and tedium.

"If I stay with this band I will not be able to make a living anywhere," she heard her husband tell the men at the table as she stood in the kitchen. "I have already sold my ranch and my cows at a great loss. I will have to move out of California."

"Leiva," Tiburcio reasoned, "if you remain resolute and don't lose your nerve you will be able to do anything you want and live anywhere you wish."

"Except here in Chilaro where I want to."

"Not now. But perhaps later. You squandered that chance when you killed a man. You are not Mexican, therefore I do not expect you to stay with us to liberate the state. But after the Tres Pinos and Kingston raids, you will have enough money to buy land in Arizona or Colorado. I will pay my debts to Soriano and the rest is ours. We are all going to be very comfortable."

"I am finished. *No mas* ," Leiva concluded and walked out to tend to his animals.

Rosaria started after him, pausing for a moment at the door.

"His 'no' is not very strong," she told Tiburcio. "He will go. He really has no choice."

Tiburcio turned his attention to the remaining core of bandits.

"This is it, my friends. I plan on taking quite a bit of money out of Tres Pinos and Kingston. Afterward, we will divvy up the spoils and split up as we are being trailed. Chavez and I will hide out at Jim Heffner's ranch, near Lake Elizabeth in Los Angeles. Moreno and Gonzales will go up to Cantua and prepare to break camp. You will gather all the men, women and children there, and move those forces into action when you get the word. The rest of you will go south through Tejon and wait in Rock Creek Canyon in the San Gabriel Mountains until we will meet up with you with Soriano's deadly, modern weapons and hundreds of battle-ready men."

Then, the door opened and Leiva entered the quiet room.

"I will come," he said.

The men cheered. Behind Leiva, his wife stole a shrewd glance at Tiburcio. There was no way she was going to let Tiburcio ride away, leaving her in Chilaro. Once Tiburcio rode away with the rest of the bandits, the mining town's soul would be gone. She was much too young to wither away in a soulless New Idria - she had decided that from the moment she first danced with Tiburcio.

Tiburcio nodded and continued in the same somber tone.

"Therefore, Leiva and Gonzales will go into Tres Pinos first, reconnoiter and make necessary adjustments. Nobody knows their appearance from that of any other stranger, so they will not attract attention. They will buy some cigars at the store, look around. Buy some drinks at the saloon, acquaint yourselves with the place. We must, as accurately as possible, ascertain the number of citizens we might encounter. Next, I will send Moreno and Bicuna into town to do the same thing. None of you will do anything else until my arrival. Chavez, Castro, Romero, de Bert and I will scout the outlying area for sheriff's deputies and then join you in the evening, around 5:30 p.m.

"One last thing," Tiburcio said. "We will try to pull these heists off without unnecessary violence. It will make our retreat easier. If we can get out of Tres Pinos without bloodshed, we can get a jump on our pursuers. And this will aid the rebellion."

■ ■ ■

Tiburcio and his men set up camp in a secluded spot in the hilly area outside Tres Pinos. The following afternoon, Leiva and Gonzales left for town. Then Moreno and Bicuna departed. It was nearly 5:30 when Tiburcio and Chavez started down the main road to Tres Pinos, the last of the gang to arrive.

TIBURCIO!

About two hundred yards outside the town, the bandits came across a Hollister resident named McPhail. Tiburcio recognized McPhail as a grain hauler who had been under contract with New Idria Mining Co. Tiburcio asked in spotless English for McPhail to stop his horse and wagon.

"Pardon me, traveler, do you know what time it is?" he requested.

McPhail took an expensive open-faced golden watch on a silver chain out of his pocket to check. Chavez lifted in his stirrups, ready to vault off his horse and seize the timepiece, but Vasquez shook his head. He settled back into the saddle and Tiburcio wished McPhail a good evening with a tip of his hat.

As planned, the bandits rendezvoused at the south end of the Main Street in late afternoon.

"How much do you know?" Tiburcio asked Leiva.

"It's a quiet town," Leiva said. "It will be even more quiet with dinner time approaching."

"What else?"

Leiva said Snyder, the owner of the general mercantile store, also ran the hotel next to it but was leasing it to a man named Davidson. Snyder, who reserved two rooms at the hotel for his own family, had just returned from a branch store in the Panoche Valley with his wife, three-year-old son and a nanny. Snyder had unhitched the horses from his buggy and was putting them in the stable at this very moment, Leiva said.

"Now, that's something we can use. We must strike now," Tiburcio said.

He sent Gonzales and Leiva into the store and hotel. Snyder entered his business from the rear, where the stable was located, and found the two Mexicans standing in the center of the store with rifles in their hands and several revolvers in their belts. His clerk was behind the counter apprehensively watching the pair. Four more Mexicans rode up to the front of the store, dismounted, tied their horses outside and entered. They also carried guns.

Tiburcio walked up to Snyder and placed a hand on his shoulder.

"Mr. Snyder," he said. "I was wondering if a letter I have been expecting has arrived."

Snyder walked behind a high desk in the post office section of the store and suspiciously looked through the incoming mail.

"You, lie down!" Chavez shouted at the clerk.

Snyder turned around and saw his clerk drop to the ground.

Tiburcio had walked over to the front door and was standing in front of it with a rifle in his hands.

"You too, Mr. Snyder," he said. "I no longer need that letter but I appreciate you checking."

Snyder looked around the room at men with revolvers and rifles cocked and pointed at him. Still, he didn't comply.

"This is the last time we will tell you, sir," Tiburcio shouted. "If you don't get down on the ground with your hands out to the side we will shoot the top of your head off!"

Shielded by the high counter, Snyder reached his hand back and could just barely feel the cold steel of the shotgun he kept behind the Post Office desk. It was loaded with buckshot. Certainly, he could gun down two or three of the bandits with two blasts. But he thought of his family in the adjoining hotel and envisioned how his actions would play out, and in all probability lead to the killing of his wife, child and Mrs. Moore, the nanny. He came around the desk and dropped to his knees with his arms outstretched.

Vasquez took a quick look outside, then returned and ordered his men to tie up the store owner.

"That is unnecessary," Snyder claimed.

"Look. I have but one way of doing business and that is to be safe. If I were you I would submit to the command. Unless you wish to get shot."

"I will obey," Snyder answered. "Under one condition."

Tiburcio raised his eyebrows, disbelieving a man with three rifles and several revolvers trained on him was negotiating. Snyder continued.

"I will allow you to tie me without resistance if you promise me that the women in my family will not be molested in any way whatsoever."

"I'm insulted," Tiburcio replied. "I am a gentleman, Snyder."

He walked over and tied Snyder's hands behind his back, pushed him over onto his face and covered him with a blanket. His clerk was then tied with his heels bound to his hands.

"OK, now ..." Tiburcio started, but stopped speaking.

A man had entered the store to buy some goods. He was quickly apprehended and tied up.

"Listen up," Tiburcio started again, but stopped abruptly as a wagon pulled up to the store.

As the man and his wife approached the front door, Bicuna and Gonzales leaped outside and put revolvers to their heads and ordered them to lie down inside the store. As they were tying up the husband, the wife began screaming ceaselessly.

"No! No! Let my husband go! He has a bad heart!" she hollered. "He is a good man. Don't shoot him! We have six children!"

"Shut up or we will shoot you," Tiburcio shouted above her shrill.

"No! Who will take care of the kids? Please let him go," she tearfully lamented. "We have six children. Young ones."

"We will shoot you dead, missus, if you don't stop hollering," Tiburcio shouted again.

The commotion now drew Mrs. Snyder out of her hotel room. She entered the store through a side door and instantly understood the danger. She walked straight over to the overwrought woman and took her arm.

"Quiet, ma'am. Quiet. They will not harm anyone if you are quiet," she told her.

In Mrs. Snyder's arms, the woman began to calm down, her sobs subsiding. Snyder's wife led her back into her hotel room.

"Bicuna!" Tiburcio called. "Guard the window outside that room and make sure nobody tries to escape."

Then they heard a four-horse team arrive outside the front of the store. Tiburcio gave Leiva a cold stare.

"Jesus Christ, Abdon! I thought you said it was quiet around here!" Tiburcio cursed.

"Moreno, Romero, take care of our next guests, *por favor*? Perhaps then we can get on with what we came for. Snyder, you must have a hell of a lot of money in that till, if you are always this busy."

Tiburcio heard Moreno order the man off his wagon. He refused. They told him they were robbing the store and everybody better obey orders or they will get killed. The man, John Haley, kept calling for Mr. Snyder.

"Mr. Snyder! Are you in there? Is everything all right."

Snyder didn't answer and then there was silence outside. Moreno and Romero dragged Haley in through the entrance. He was unconscious and bleeding profusely from a split on his forehead where de Bert had hit him with his revolver.

Vasquez was still standing near the front entrance, trying to continue the robbery. Across the store and through the back door he saw some activity at the barn. He glared at Leiva, who avoided his gaze.

"Everybody stay put. I'll take care of this," he declared, striding across the room and out the back. "Gonzales, follow me."

George Redford - a young boy when he first encountered Tiburcio Vasquez, Juan Soto and Anastacio Garcia on that San Juan Bautista street many years ago and was knocked to the ground - had driven his teamster's wagon up to the barn. Redford jumped down from the seat and walked to the head of the horses to begin unhitching them.

"Taste that dirt!" Tiburcio shouted, not recognizing the boy-turned-man.

Deaf, Redford did not move. Gonzales was fed up with the pluck of all these Tres Pinos residents resisting orders, even at gunpoint.

"Get down on your knees in the fucking dirt!" Gonzales yelled.

Redford, in his silent world, slowly turned his head and saw the red-fierce rage on the Gonzales' face. Frightened, he bolted around the team of horses toward the livery stable. Tiburcio took a shot at him and missed on purpose.

From the store, Chavez heard the shot and sensed trouble outside. Standing at the back door, he saw Redford running toward the stables. Chavez raised his rifle and shot the teamster in the back just as he reached the stable door. The bullet sailed straight through Redford's body, through the barn wall and struck a horse. The horse bucked wild and the stable erupted with scared animals. Redford stumbled and fell face first into a horse stall, dead.

"It's falling apart," Tiburcio said to himself, and wondered if Morrison had deceived him. This was anything but a quiet, little town.

He marched back inside the store and told Romero, Moreno and de Bert to get outside and keep everybody inside their homes or businesses.

"Get on the street and keep everyone inside. Nobody comes to a door or a window."

The three bandits ran into the middle of the street just when Davidson, the hotel owner, opened the front door a crack to see what was going on. They aimed their revolvers at the door. Mrs. Davidson, who had been back in the Snyders' room and already heard what was happening, came racing toward the hotel entrance to warn her husband. She reached over Davidson's shoulder to shut the door, but a bullet ripped through the wood and pierced Davidson's heart. He fell dead into his wife's arms.

A Portuguese sheepherder who was coming down the street in hopes of getting a room for the night saw Davidson get shot and bolted for Snyder's store, believing it was safer anywhere inside than on the street after what he just witnessed. The first shot from Moreno's revolver struck him in the teeth but he kept running for the store, blood spouting all around him. Staggering onto the porch of the store, he surprised the bandits inside and paid for it with lead from three guns that ripped apart his breast. He fell just inside the door.

Inside Snyder's, Tiburcio paced up and down in his black suit, holding two revolvers and rambling loudly and frantically.

"I am sorry to trouble everyone this way. I would rather work hard each and every day of my life in an honest way, but the minute people found out who I am I would be hanged. I didn't start out this way, but I only have one way to make a living in the state and as long as other people have money I intend to rob them for it. And sometimes, God damn it, that means killing a man to get it. Now everybody stay still and we will take what we came for and get the hell out of your lives once and for all."

The bandits began plundering the pockets of the bound victims and the shelves of the store. They started loading Redford's wagon with merchandise from Snyder's business to take with them. They took clothes and food and rope.

"We need everything we can get on that wagon for the war!" Tiburcio cried. "We will divvy it up later."

When they finished stocking up, they pulled down boxes of crackers, rounds of cheese, tins of oysters and sardines and rolled a ten-gallon keg out of the storeroom and tapped it.

"Do you think you could hurry?" Snyder asked from his position on the ground next to the post office desk.

"Well, we are hungry," Chavez answered. "All of your antics have made us hungry. We will leave when we are finished eating."

The gulping and slurping stopped for an instant when a boy of about seven years old skulked through the door and asked innocently: "Where is my father?"

He was the son of the clerk.

"I have come to tell him supper is ready," the boy said.

A couple of the bandits lay him down next to his father and told him to stay quiet but did not tie him up.

"Tiburcio!" Snyder called. "Good God, could you loosen this rope a bit."

The bandit leader looked over at the storekeeper. His arms were swollen and blue up to this shoulders.

Tiburcio bent over Snyder and whispered in his ear: "Where have you stashed Morrison's deposit?"

"Loosen these ties, bandit!"

"If you do not tell me where that money is, the whole deal is off, and I will show you that even a gentleman must compromise his values for a greater cause."

"It's in the iron chest, behind the counter."

"The key?"

Snyder moved his hips.

Tiburcio reached into his trouser pocket and grabbed the key. Then he obliged and eased the storekeeper's discomfort.

On his way to the safe, Tiburcio told his men to stop eating and get as many horses as they could take from the stable.

"It's going to be a long haul out of here."

As the bandits rode south into the night with more than twenty thousand dollars in cash, a wagon full of store loot and ten horses, the clerk's son untied everybody in the store. Snyder was overjoyed that his wife was alive but then the town folk took an accounting of the bandit's raid. A deaf man lay dead in a horse's stall, a widow cried in tremendous agony as she held her lifeless husband, and a sheepherder's bloody corpse was discarded on the store porch, his pockets split and their contents gone.

Chapter 10: Pursued
Tres Pinos to Elizabeth Lake
(near Los Angeles)
Morning after Tres Pinos

Santa Clara County Sheriff John Adams slowly, reluctantly descended from his hotel room a little after 9:30 a.m. to meet up with a group of local Republican candidates to do some electioneering in the town of Gilroy. The sheriff was disinclined to do even the minimum campaigning necessary to hold onto his elected office. He preferred serving his constituents from the saddle, on the trail of a bandit, not listening to and giving speeches in a large hall or from the back of a caboose. Campaigning generally bored him and he felt restless as he walked through the hotel lobby toward the group of politicians waiting in front of the hotel.

He heard his named called. The telegraph operator was waving his arm, urging Adams into his office. The worker was grim and spoke with great concern. Adams glanced at politicians and turned to enter the telegraph office.

"Sheriff! Terrible, terrible news has come over the wire. It's from Hollister. People are frantic. Last night Vasquez and his bandits raided Tres Pinos, and shot three men dead. They fear he will return."

Adams quickly checked the tall clock in the lobby.

"When's the next train scheduled to come through?"

"There is a freight train scheduled to arrive in about fifteen minutes, at 10:00 a.m., on its way to Hollister."

"Will it stop here?"

"Yes."

"I will ride the caboose to Hollister. Let them know in Hollister I will be coming into town and will need men and provisions for a posse and a string of horses shod and ready. Also, telegraph Sheriff Wasson in Monterey and tell him to meet me in Hollister as soon as he can. Tell him to bring some men along. We are going to hunt that bandit down."

Outside, Adams told the other politicians about the Tres Pinos tragedy.

"Jesus. What are we going to do?" asked J. C. Black, the district attorney.

"I am catching the next train to Hollister. I must leave as soon as possible - every minute is valuable. I may be gone a long spell hunting these murderers. You will need to keep the citizens calm."

"If you can arrest these outlaws that will be the best bit of electioneering anyone can do," county treasurer D.C. Bailey said. "John, we'll tell the crowds and reporters that you are on the tails of the men who have carried out the boldest raid this state has ever witnessed and coldheartedly took the lives of innocent people, and that it's elected officials like us who are not afraid to pursue Tiburcio Vasquez, or any of his gang, and we will not rest until he and every one of his followers is tried and hung."

"That's a good speech, Bailey," Adams said perfunctorily. "That's a real fine speech. I gotta get to the station. Farewell!"

Dozens of men greeted Adams when he stepped off the train in Hollister. They were armed and determined to guard the town day and night in case Vasquez and his gang decided to raid their city next. The city's mayor shoved his way to the front of the vigilantes, greeted the sheriff and introduced one of two residents who were standing with him.

"Sheriff, this is Johnnie Zumalt. He managed to sneak away when the shooting started in Tres Pinos and walked thirteen miles back here to inform us about the raid. He had to avoid the main roads. It took him several hours."

371

Adams nodded once and then looked at the other man whom the mayor introduced as Joseph Cochrane.

"Mr. Cochrane encountered Vasquez and one of his men on the road as they were leaving town. When he got to Tres Pinos he saw the bodies of the innkeeper and two other fellows laid out in the blacksmith's shop down there."

Adams listened to Cochrane and other Tres Pinos residents excitedly recount the holdup. Then, he asked who would join his posse to search the entire countryside for the murderers. Nobody volunteered.

"We are going to protect our town, sheriff," the mayor said. "We need everybody to stay home and defend their families and property."

"I admire that stance, boys, I really do," the sheriff responded. "But I need men with some pluck, who are veterans in the saddle, to ride with me until we track the bandits down."

"I heard Tiburcio Vasquez has five hundred men at the border just waiting for his command to take over the state. What's your posse going to do against an army like that?" one resident asked.

"Tiburcio Vasquez is a coward, and he sells that horse shit to other cowards so he can continue to intimidate the citizens of our great state," Adams shouted back.

He stared into their faces. Still, nobody stepped forward. Adams turned on his heel. He had work to do.

Striding up and down Hollister's streets, the sheriff barged into saloons and stores and stables trying to get a posse. By noon, only two men had volunteered for the posse. It was 2:00 p.m. when Adams began to lose all patience. He regretted not starting out immediately, even with just three men. Now he was nearly twenty-four hours behind the outlaws. Perhaps he shouldn't wait for any more vigilante volunteers, or for Wasson, and set out on his pursuit, he thought. But he didn't. Instead, he gathered more information and descriptions about what the bandits had hauled off from the store and the stable, tried to get a definitive count of how many men were in on the raid and what they looked like and how they acted.

An hour later, Wasson rode into town with his undersheriff. With the provocation of the Monterey sheriff, the lawmen succeeded in getting three more citizens to join. They persuaded a blacksmith to shod their horses, took out an IOU at the general store for food and blankets and around 5 p.m. eight posse men finally galloped and whooped and hollered out of town in a wild flurry, uncertain how long their journey might be or where it would take them.

Starting out along the banks of Tres Pinos creek, they quickly picked up Vasquez's trail and rode hard into the warm night. Along the way, they deputized seven more determined riders. Now, the posse was formidable, comprised of fifteen well-seasoned horsemen who were familiar with the rugged countryside within one hundred square miles. They found hoof prints and broken brush and remnants from a campfire. By 7:00 p.m., they had traced Vasquez's trail more than sixty miles. Entering Hernandez Valley, the trail suddenly disappeared.

"Let's keep quartering these parts and work our way toward Cantua Canyon. I am gambling he struck out toward his old hideout," Adams said. "At least, some of his bandits did."

Crossing over the mountains toward the canyon just as daylight was ending, the posse picked up another trail. This time, signs pointed that the gang had turned south, nearly all of them who had raided Tres Pinos. Adams counted seven or eight men, ten horses and a wagon. A rancher happened to be out riding on his land and invited the posse to supper. Over the dinner table, he informed Adams that the bandit Tiburcio Vasquez and several men had been seen riding earlier in the day, but nobody knew about the deadly raid. The rancher said the bandits had a wagon full of boxes and barrels and extra horses but had not gone into the canyon.

"They kept riding in the direction of Pleasant Valley," the rancher said.

As the posse gathered their rested horses, Adams had doubts. He looked at Wasson and shook his head.

"It's not like the bandit to let anyone see him or know his whereabouts."

"Not if he knows he is being trailed," Wasson said.

"Yet, we've been following these tracks and with the rancher's information, it looks like he's taking the straight way."

"He may be trying to make good time on the main trails and not concerned about covering up his tracks," interjected George Chick, one of the riders they had picked up outside Tres Pinos.

"A mad dash," Adams conjectured.

It was late but Adams decided they should start out again. The posse traveled as fast as they could in the black of night, riding into the next morning. They saw conflicting signs of which way the bandits were headed, and twice had to double back. Stopping to check an abandoned camp site at the top of a ridge, Adams looked down at a valley.

"The bandits have scattered," Adams said, peering down at the canyon's thick brush. "It looks like they finally split and went in three different directions."

"Which way do we go?" Wasson asked.

"South."

They continued again until they caught sight of a Mexican sheepherder in the distance. Two posse members rode after the sheepherder, who was frightened by the sight of armed riders approaching in full gallop. But he did not flee. When they reached him, he claimed he had not seen anyone riding in these parts for days.

Another hot day riding at a fast clip was taking its toll. The riders and the horses were fatigued, thirsty, hungry. Most of the men were napping in the saddle. They stopped at Baker's ranch in mid-morning, ten days since the raid at Tres Pinos, to feed and water their horses. Five of the horses were so broken they would not eat. Nearly half of the posse members decided to halt their journey, physically unable to continue. Three more hadn't planned to be away more than a week and returned home. While Adams acquired some fresh horses for the remaining men, he cursed the ones who dropped off.

At Baker's Ranch, the remaining riders found tracks leading to Tulare Lake. Adams was again inspired. He, Wasson and four others rode hard along the plain that was blazing in the sun like a furnace. They passed several deserted houses along Carey Creek and scoured the countryside until they were several miles northwest of Tulare Lake, hundreds of miles from Hollister. Again, the trail disappeared.

Adams, sitting erect in the saddle as the others slumped in fatigue, knew he had come to a turning point. None of the men had knowledge of this southern terrain. They had tried to obtain fresh horses along the way, but were unsuccessful. Wasson, meanwhile, had not expected to still be traveling and urgent business called him back to Monterey. A murder trial needed his testimony or the defendant would walk out of court a free man. He couldn't ignore the telegraph message. Adams decided it was time to break up the posse.

He insisted that his fellow lawman from Monterey take a train from Fresno back home.

"I am sorry," Wasson said, firmly grasping Adams' hand in his. "I will send McKenzie and another man down on the next train to help you, John. Nobody is better than old McKenzie. Your hunt will not be in vain. I'll tell you what, when the trial is over I will stay up there and resume hunting the bandits who split off near Cantua."

"That's a fine idea, Jim," Adams said.

As Wasson rode away, the Santa Clara County sheriff turned to Chick.

"Chick, take the rest back to Hollister with this note so they can collect their fee. They're free to make their way back up the state. I appreciate their help."

"You can't continue alone, sheriff. And you're way out of your jurisdiction. What are you going to do?"

"Keep riding."

Adams was relentless. Now alone, he had hardly spent a half hour off his horse in more than a week. He ate while riding and finally reached Bakersfield on September 1. He felt his persistence was about to pay off. He paid a guide for information on Vasquez's Southern California habits and haunts. The guide recommended Adams ride to Panama, a Mexican community about fifteen miles from Bakersfield. There, they picked up the recognizable wagon tracks that he had seen off and on all the way down the state.

"Vasquez is running out of land," Adams told the guide, who silently nodded.

Adams left the stage road and took a trail that passed around Buena Vista Lake, where he came upon an old Mexican steering two thin, weary horses and a mule around the body of water.

"Where did you get those animals?" Adams asked. "It looks like somebody has been driving them hard."

The man spoke fair English and said he found them wandering around the west side of Tulare Lake.

"What else did you see there?"

"Some remains of a calf and some tracks. Big horse tracks."

The lawman rode strong and confidently along the base of the Tehachapi Mountains toward Tejon Pass, which would drop him into the Los Angeles area. Along the way, they surprised a man lying in the grass with his horse tied to a willow. He was catching a nap and using a sack of clothes for a pillow. The clothes he wore were old and dirty.

"What is your business here?" Adams asked the man, who bolted upright to see who was interrupting his rest.

"I am traveling from Livermore. My horse has finally given out. So I am resting."

The sheriff was trying to match this man's light complexion, black hair, high cheek bones and small stature to any descriptions in his memory of the Tres Pinos bandits. He knew it was not Vasquez, Chavez or Moreno. He decided to get off his horse and examine the man's pillow sack.

"New clothes, eh?" the sheriff inquired, looking up from the sack. "A coat, vest, pair of pants."

"They are my Sunday clothes."

The descriptions of some of the bandits who were part of the Snyder store robbery were pretty vague so Adams didn't know for certain if this traveler was one of them. But the clothes in the sack were new, and clothing had been stolen from Snyder's.

He drew his gun and told the man to not move.

"If you arrest him, you'll have to backtrack twenty miles to Bakersfield, the nearest jail," the guide said in a low tone to Adams. "That will delay your pursuit of Vasquez."

"I feel we are very close to the bandit. We are crowding him with each mile we ride," Adams said. "You're right. This greaser is a small fish compared to Vasquez and Chavez."

He turned to the traveler.

"Take your Sunday clothes and get out of here," Adams called out to the man. "You may want to go to Mexico. Because if I come across you again, in other circumstances, I will haul you off to prison."

Adams swung around the south end of the lake and arrived at San Emedio at midnight. A rancher, John Funk, agreed to furnish fresh horses in the morning so the men could continue their trip. Even though it was late, he called on the blacksmith to get the horses ready. When Funk returned to the ranch house, he startled Adams with some news from the town's blacksmith.

"Vasquez and Chavez brought in two horses yesterday to get shod - a large sorrel and a large palomino. They were then spotted making their way through Tejon Pass."

Adams was now certain the bandits were in the vicinity. It was time to bring in Los Angeles Sheriff Billy Rowland. Not only could he use Rowland's men and expertise, but he was about to tread heavily on Rowland's jurisdiction.

Adams set out for Fort Tejon right away, not waiting for Funk to gather the fresh horses. That would take too much time. At the fort, Adams had a telegraph message waiting for him. It said to expect the arrival soon of David McKenzie - a man known for his intrepid tracking and hard riding despite his sixty years of age - and a one-legged vaquero named Young, whose skills at riding, rifle shooting and lassoing were not to be underestimated despite his disability.

Adams took the opportunity to rest at the fort. He ate a large supper at the house of telegraph operator Newton Ewing and walked back to Ewing's office afterward to send a message to Rowland. He urged the sheriff to meet him at 11:00 a.m. the next day at Delano's, the last station on the pass at Elizabeth Lake.

McKenzie and Young arrived at the telegraph station on the next train. They were an odd sight, one gray and wrinkled with age, the other missing a limb. But with great alacrity, the three of them left in the morning for Elizabeth Lake.

Outside Elizabeth Lake, the three stopped and decided it was time to play it safe. To attract as little attention as possible, they would ride into town one at a time. Their destination was Jim Heffner's ranch, where Heffner ran a large general store and a bunkhouse for poor laborers and travelers, mostly Mexicans. Adams was the first to take off. He tethered his horse and stepped into Heffner's store.

He was beginning to realize the residents down in these parts were a bit looser in the mouth when it came to information regarding Tiburcio Vasquez. He struck up a conversation with the store clerk, who was fascinated that he had come all the way from up north.

"No kidding! Monterey County? You sure must want your man, sheriff," the clerk said, then he snapped his fingers trying to remember something about a customer who was from those same parts.

"Yes, yes, I remember," the clerk said. "A wagon came into town about a week ago with a Mexican woman and her two children. And her husband arrived just the other day in another wagon."

"Where do you supposed they are staying?"

"I believe at Chico Lopez's place, about fifteen miles from here. Lopez provides rooms for traveling families or workers," the clerk answered, then slapped the counter in astonishment. "In fact, two other vaqueros came in right after that man. They are all together I believe. Imagine, all of you from the same area."

Adams was momentarily speechless.

When David McKenzie and Young arrived fifteen minutes apart, Adams quickly told them to follow him. They rode off the main road, dismounted near a creek side and talked over their plan. Adams wanted to raid the Lopez house immediately.

"What if Vasquez isn't there?" McKenzie asked. "Coming down here from Santa Clara and raiding innocent residents' homes without informing the sheriff? That's trouble a brewing. Rowland will run us out of town, if he doesn't arrest us first. This is his bailiwick."

"Or what if Vasquez is there and he has an entire platoon of bandits. There's rumor that he keeps two dozen men around him armed and ready to kill. Our little army of three wouldn't stand up to that," Young added.

"I am certain only Chavez and Vasquez are there. Perhaps Leiva, too. The store clerk would have mentioned it if there were more. Besides, signs all the way from Pleasant Valley have shown there are just two or three of them together," Adams argued.

"I'm just saying, nobody really knows how many men might be holed up at Lopez's ranch," McKenzie concluded. "His whole gang could be there."

"OK," Adams said, wondering if his hard traveling hadn't made him a little crazy. "We'll go back to Heffner's and wait for Rowland's stage. Then, we'll attack."

When the time came for Rowland's stage to arrive, the Los Angeles County sheriff and his posse were not on it. Adams was irate.

"Vasquez is going to slip away!" he lamented to his two companions. "With or without Rowland, we need to act. If you don't want to return to Lopez's and fight, I'll go alone!"

"All right," McKenzie conceded. "We're in this together."

The three men scoured the place with Young's field glasses as they hid in the chaparral. Lopez's house was L-shaped, with a short line of one-story rooms facing the road and a long line of rooms extending back farther onto the property. A common square existed in the back along with a well, stables, outhouses and storage buildings with stairs that descended twenty feet into the cool earth.

Adams dropped the glasses to his side.

"McKenzie and I will go around to the right. Young, you go around the long way to the back. Whoever we flush out will run straight into you. I'll take the shotgun and four revolvers, McKenzie, you and Young take the rifles and a couple six-shooters. Ready?"

Adams stood up, but McKenzie and Young just looked questioningly at each other.

"What is it?"

"There are a lot of families, lots of women and children. I don't know if we should raid the ranch as if only a bunch of outlaws were holed up there. There are a lot of innocent people."

"OK," Adams sighed. He was done talking.

He got up and with large strides walked straight toward the ranch. McKenzie cursed as he and Young, hopping alongside, started following about twenty yards behind Adams.

"Shit. We're coming. We're coming," McKenzie said.

Adams, shotgun held across his chest, hurried into the square. Women doing washing stopped to look, children playing tag paused, men playing cards or combing their horses or chopping wood all froze. He ignored them and threw open door after door only to find more startled, innocent residents. Disappointed, he walked back around Chico Lopez's hacienda to his horse, mounted and rode off to Heffner's, leaving behind a quiet and stunned crowd of onlookers. McKenzie and Young scrambled to catch up to him and followed in silence.

The trio was again standing and waiting outside Heffner's store the next morning when a full stage pulled up. Off the stage, one after another, stepped the most excellent horsemen and gunfighters in Los Angeles. First, W.W. Jenkins, a tall, robust fellow; second, Major H.M. Mitchell, wearing full military regalia from the civil war; third, Pete Gabriel, a thin, wiry, intelligent-looking rod; fourth, "Babe" Crowell, a mighty, six-foot-five hunter strapped with several arms and a bandolier; fifth, an Indian guide named Jose Redowna who at one time had a choice whether to follow a fellow halfbreed named Juan Soto into a life of crime or live straight; sixth, Eduardo Sanchez, a veteran of the Mexican War who the United States was happy to have convinced to come to their side; seventh, a man going by the single name of Benites, short but lively with a deadly look in his eyes. Lastly, the portly and confident Sheriff Billy Rowland stepped down. The sheriff was dressed nattily in a jacket and vest and bow tie with his revolvers at his side. His hair was slicked back, parted sharply to the right. His mustache was a full, dark, upside-down V that blended with a thick goatee, which was slightly graying at the tip. Despite his ample stomach, the sheriff was fleet in his movements.

Many passersby stopped to admire the lawmen. The lawmen waited patiently for Rowland's command. The L.A. sheriff peered ahead and caught sight of what he somehow believed to be the party who had summoned him. But they looked so motley and un-dangerous that he wasn't completely sure.

Rowland's posse followed their leader's eyes first to a man whose clothes hung loosely on him. His face was dirty, beard uncombed and uncleaned for weeks, eyes wild as a trapped bear. This was Adams. Next Rowland's gaze took in a man who looked so ancient he must have first fought in the War of 1812. This man's hair was all white and his beard grew coarse and patchy around his face. He was slightly shaking. It was

McKenzie. And on the other side of Adams they all looked at the one-legged man leaning on a crutch.

Rowland approached the trio.

"Are you Adams?"

"Yes."

"Ya'll look like you've been through hell."

"And you are late!" Adams admonished.

"Late? Good lord, sir. Do you think I can just leave Los Angeles any time I feel like it? At the drop of a hat? My absence in town would spread like wildfire. The bandits we are hunting would know I was coming. They might even flank me and sack my town. Sheriff, I had to set up a decoy to get up here to you. So do not chide me - not on my territory! "

"Nevertheless, as a result of your tardiness, we missed Vasquez and his men. We could have arrested them at Chico Lopez's."

"That's bullshit," Rowland said. "We know Tiburcio Vasquez is not there. In fact, we have a damn good idea that Vasquez is over in Little Rock."

"That's twenty-five miles from here. Where did you get that information?"

Rowland turned around and called to the stage driver to get their prisoner out and bring him over. The driver had tied the reins down and had a shotgun pointed at the coach. He set the shotgun down on the box, drew a Dragoon pistol and leaped off his seat. He opened the door for the prisoner and ordered him over to where the sheriffs stood.

The prisoner looked at Adams through his sad, Chilean eyes.

"You don't get better information than this," Rowland bragged. "We don't only know where Vasquez is, we have hooked the bait that will bring him in, too."

Chapter 11: Leiva
Los Angeles
Fall-winter 1873

In Southern California, Tiburcio Vasquez could not move about as freely as up north. He could not rob as compulsively and he had to be as much a stealthy fugitive as a gunslinger. His identity and whereabouts were not so easily kept secret down here. He was heavily armed at all times and always prepared to go down with his finger on the trigger. He planned his movements more wisely than, say, impulsively deciding to rob a train. He relied on a smaller, ironclad, trustworthy circle of friends rather than a countryside of acolytes. And he needed extra sets of eyes, so he sent spies into Los Angeles in shifts to keep watch over Rowland and his officers. He was always in search of a hideout where he could see all that approached him.

At about the time Adams was circling Buena Vista Lake, Tiburcio was plotting his next move.

"The Tres Pinos raid has unleashed every officer of the law in the state," Tiburcio said to Chavez as they rode toward the Lopez ranch. "I think we've paralyzed the state. It's time to rob Kingston, get the money to Padilla and start the war!"

Chavez nodded.

"When we get to Chico's, we need to get Rosaria, Leiva and the kids out of there," he said. "It lies too flat to be a good hideout.

"Where will we go?"

"Up to Rock Creek, for now. Camp out while the weather is good," Tiburcio told his lieutenant. "Then we'll go to Sonora, and see if we can't find a more permanent settling spot."

They rode for a while before Tiburcio spoke again.

"I will get my hands on Leiva's ten thousand dollars soon."

"Have you thought about how you will approach Anita?"

"No."

The bandits loped up to Lopez's property and halted their horses outside. Vasquez looked around and Chavez followed his eyes.

"We are vulnerable here. Let's take the horses around the back."

As they swung wide around the house, Leiva came running up, two Dragoon pistols drawn. Instinctively, the mounted bandits drew their weapons.

"Mi Dio! Leiva. What are you doing?" Tiburcio shouted as they all stood with guns pointed at one another.

Leiva stuck the guns back in his sash.

"I am going crazy here, Tiburcio. Ever since Firebaugh's Ferry and Tres Pinos I think every noise is a posse," Leiva cried.

"If you keep acting crazy like that it won't be a posse that kills you. It will be one of us. Take these horses to the stable for food and water. We're pulling out of here. Meet us inside."

Rosaria had been watching for the arrival of Tiburcio with a strongly beating heart. Well perfumed and dressed in silk and jewels, she rushed to the bandit leader and threw her arms around him the moment he walked through the door.

"Tiburcio, I've missed you so much!"

Her head rested on his chest. She felt supple and nice and her hair soft as he stroked it.

Rosaria looked up into his gray eyes.

"He is driving me crazy, Tiburcio! He is so nervous. He hasn't slept for two nights. He's going to get us all captured or killed. Look at these," she said, pointing to several newspapers on a table. "He keeps reading about Tres Pinos and all the posses crisscrossing the state trying to capture him."

"And how about you? Are you sleeping well?" he asked Rosaria.

"No, but you know why I am not sleeping," she said in an urgent whisper. "My whole body aches for you, Tiburcio."

Chavez busied himself in the kitchen looking for something to eat or drink. There was nothing.

"We need some provisions!" he called, just as Leiva entered the house again. Rosaria quickly pulled away from Tiburcio but not before her husband's eye fell on them. But he said nothing.

"We will need to make do with what we got," Tiburcio said. "We'll get out of here and go back to Heffner's when we can."

"We were just there, captain," Chavez reminded him. "We have to lie low."

"That's why Abdon is going to go."

"I am not leaving the house," he said.

"Why not?" Rosaria blurted out.

"Yes, why not?" Chavez added.

"I am nervous enough waiting here, where nobody knows where I am. I can't go out in the open."

"We're all leaving here," Tiburcio said. "You need to get the children packed and on that wagon."

"Where are we going now?" Leiva asked.

"Little Rock Canyon."

"Why?"

"This place is no good for hiding out."

"That would have been nice to know," Leiva sighed. "We've been here for two days. Anything else you need to inform me about?"

His sarcasm made Rosaria and Chavez laugh, which only angered Leiva.

"Look, I am getting pretty sick of this whole enterprise," Leiva ranted. "I am not prone to acts of violence. I am not used to this. Why did I get involved? I am Chilean. I was not wronged by the gringos. I was perfectly happy at home at New Idria, before all this wildness and plundering and murdering and miles and miles of riding and hiding. It's all dissatisfying -

and I have yet to see it pay off. Where is all the money, Tiburcio? Rosaria what happened to our peaceful life, a home for you, for our children?"

"You were hunted in the camp, just the same as you are being hunted now," Tiburcio hissed. "Those boys you upset at New Idria would have slit your throat at the first chance that I turned my back. So stop talking about New Idria being so idyllic. At least now you have a fighting chance."

Leiva turned and stormed toward the door. As he flung it open and it crashed into the inner wall, he shouted: "Some fucking ranch, this is. Not even a chicken or a goose for some eggs!"

With that, he went out to prepare the wagon.

At Little Rock Canyon, they set up camp among the sandstone rocks, above the orange, purple and yellow wildflowers, up where the creosote shrub and mesquite trees precariously gripped onto life in the hard ground. The evening was warm but would quickly cool. They could sleep well in the crisp outdoors under the stars but needed warm blankets.

It was mid-afternoon, pleasantness all around him. Still, Leiva sulked and ruminated.

"We need provisions now, Leiva," Tiburcio barked once they had set up camp. "You can get to Heffner's by 7:00 p.m., load up and return before midnight."

"Why am I going?"

"Nobody has your description," Tiburcio reminded him. "You won't be conspicuous. You have never been arrested, and I doubt anybody in Tres Pinos got a good look at you."

"We can't starve to death," Chavez quipped. "Somebody needs to go."

"It will do you some good to get out and about," Tiburcio said. "It will free the mind. Take the wagon and load up."

Leiva continued to protest.

"Look, Abdon," Tiburcio finally said, with a tone of annoyed finality. "Chavez and I need some sleep. Go get the provisions so we can trade off some shut eye."

"I am the one who needs sleep!" Leiva insisted.

Tiburcio kept his calm.

"Do it for your children, Abdon. They need to eat. We'll see you back about midnight."

"I just don't ..." Leiva tried to add, but his wife cut him off.

"I am hungry, Abdon! The children will need breakfast in the morning, and we have nothing. Please, just somebody go to the store!"

When he left, it was agreed that Chavez would sleep while Tiburcio remained awake in case any unwanted company dropped by.

Chavez was a light sleeper. Nonetheless, he curled up under some blankets near a thick oak tree trunk and began to breathe heavily. Rosaria, barely able to wait for Chavez to drift off, came up to Tiburcio and held him tightly. They kissed tenderly at first, but the wonderful familiarity of each other's body, physical after so many days of abstruse memory, quickly fueled their passion. Tiburcio tried not to let visions and thoughts of Anita cloud his mind. He grabbed a blanket and led her behind some bushes. He laid it out and holding onto each other they fell madly to the ground. Rosaria pulled another blanket over them, just in case the children awoke from their sleeping spot.

Meanwhile, Leiva's mind continued to reflect on his predicament as he journeyed down the mountain. He had traveled about an hour when his thoughts grew terrible, jealous. Had he seen Rosaria and Tiburcio holding each other intimately? Had they spoken to each other in tender whispers on the way up the mountain? Rosaria had chosen to ride behind Tiburcio on horseback rather than with him in the wagon. And they both were quick to dispatch him to get provisions.

Perhaps his nerves were just too raw. He kept on his way - at least for a little longer.

To be certain of Rosaria's fidelity, he told himself, he could turn around, ask his wife to join him on his trip to Heffner's. It would be under the guise that he wanted to talk to her, make peace and reconcile. But it was a rugged ride for a woman to make. She had just endured the ride out to the camp. And it would soon be dark.

It would be dark and Tiburcio and Rosaria would be alone, he thought. The children would be in bed and Chavez away, perched on a rock watching the trails. He could not go farther. Leiva turned the horses and wagon around and rode faster than was prudent back to the camp.

Leiva stopped the wagon down the trail a ways and walked up to the campsite. Chavez never saw or heard Leiva return. He had fallen heavily asleep. Leiva stepped over him as he searched the campsite. Then, he saw two bodies moving under one blanket and his stomach rose into his chest and throat and he drew his Dragoon pistol.

"Get up, Tiburcio, you son of a bitch," Leiva shouted, pointing his gun at his leader.

Rosaria rolled off her lover, taking the blankets to cover up. Tiburcio, shirtless and unarmed, raised his hands.

Chavez snapped awake at that moment, leaped up and covered Leiva with his Colt.

"Shoot and I'll blow your fucking brains out!" he warned.

Rosaria started to wail.

Leiva put the gun back in his belt. Pointing his finger at Tiburcio, then at Chavez, he declared:

"You have wronged me, Tiburcio. Now, I want a duel."

Tiburcio stood, tightening his pants.

"I do not wish to take your life, Leiva," he said. "I will not deprive your children and wife of their provider."

"Then I will kill you when I next get the chance, Tiburcio! Chavez cannot protect you forever. You remember, I will exact my revenge on you."

"And I will be forced to defend myself," Tiburcio answered.

Leiva next addressed his wife.

"You will come with me," he ordered.

"Where are we going?" Rosaria asked.

"Back to Chilaro."

"Don't be foolish!" Chavez said.

Leiva did not care to listen to his advice. In the warm, dark night, Leiva and his family rocked down the mountain in their wagon. Tiburcio and Chavez listened to Rosaria's wails trail away in the distance. Somewhere between there and the foot of the mountain, surrounded by blackness and silence, Leiva decided to surrender and become a traitor to Tiburcio. He would serve his time and return to his family and Chilaro and blacksmithing.

The next morning Tiburcio told Chavez he was going to go get Rosaria and bring her back.

"We have bigger plans, Tiburcio. Leave her alone."

"Nothing is bigger right now. I will not be outdone by Leiva. He must pay the price for his actions. What if he begins to brag about holding me at gunpoint and riding off unmolested? You should have shot him, Chavez."

"Well, you're still alive. But we are left here without food. Or Leiva's money."

"I was working on that."

"What should we do?"

"Are you not listening, Clodoveo? We must go after Leiva, if not for my pride, then to get that money."

"Yes, for the money."

Two days later, the bandits, stuck without food provisions, killed a deer and hung the meat to dry for a supply of jerky. They snuffed out the campfire, and Tiburcio prepared to ride down to Heffner's while Chavez remained at Little Rock Creek. They did not know that two posses, a large one led by the cocksure Sheriff Rowland and the smaller following the exhausted but unremitting Sheriff Adams, were slowly moving in their direction.

Shortly after leaving the campsite, Tiburcio caught sight of the lawmen through the thicket as they rode on a lower, parallel ridge. He followed their movements as they closed in on the campsite but was unable to outflank them and get back to warn Chavez. They came across the fresh ashes of the campfire and the hanging meat. After examining the site, they drew their weapons.

Suddenly, one of the posse members called out, "There's a man!"

Tiburcio dismounted and fell flat. But when he glimpsed over the outcrop he discovered that they had spotted Chavez, not him. Chavez heard the cry and pointed his steed up the dry, steep, craggy canyon wall. The horse's hoofs kicked down rocks as it struggled to gain ground. The posse fired at the bandit but their horses would not remain steady and the shots scattered wildly. Some of the manhunters dismounted and steadied their rifles. But before they could shoot, Chavez and his steed went up over the ridge and disappeared.

"There's nothing but thick brush on the other side. He won't make it far," Adams shouted. "Let's track him."

The sheriff, joined by old man McKenzie, started working his way up the rocky wall on foot. They hadn't gone more than a third of the way up when two rifle shots whistled over their head from another location on the ridge. They looked up at the huge boulders atop the canyon and saw puffs of gray smoke. Adams and McKenzie scrambled for cover among some rocks.

"Those shots are coming from over there," Adams said. "Somebody else has seen us."

Vasquez loaded and fired a half dozen more shots at them. When the bandit's shooting stopped, Adams and McKenzie popped up from their hiding spots and fired.

"Rowland, let's charge that shooter and take care of him," Adams shouted after two more exchanges with the bandit.

"That's suicide," Rowland declared. "They have the vantage point."

Adams cursed. Then, he signaled to McKenzie. The old man hurried over, crouching as he ran. McKenzie got to the sheriff and sat with his back against a rock.

"You cover me while I try to get up this hillside," Adams said. "There are several boulders I can hide behind on my way up."

Rowland, relenting to Adams' crazy plan, ordered his posse to fire on the other bandit when he revealed himself. Two minutes passed before Vasquez pointed his gun's barrel over the ledge and fired. As soon as he did a heavy salvo of lead cracked and hissed all around him. He found it too hot to stay around and as soon as the barrage subsided, he abandoned his vantage point, jumped on his horse and galloped after Chavez, who wasn't far because he had stopped at the sound of shooting.

Rowland ordered a charge up the mountain. The posse, half on foot and half mounted, whooped and hollered as they dashed upward. In their exhilaration, it took them only a few minutes to scale the steep side. Once over the rim, they ran or galloped over the thick sage brush and through the manzanita shrubs.

"Those outlaws can't get far in this stuff," Rowland yelled out.

The posse's energetic pursuit had taken the bandits by surprise and Chavez and Tiburcio were unable to carefully pick their path. Crashing pell-mell through the thicket, they abruptly stopped their horses. The ground ahead had disappeared before them and they peered down a sheer drop. Vasquez pulled his horse back for fear that it would slip and plunge into the abyss. He looked back. Rowland and Adams' men were charging into sight.

"I've been down this canyon before," Vasquez remembered, heaving for breath. "On the other side of this deep ravine is Rancho La Brea. It was once owned by my cousin. There's a creek below that runs right through La Brea. If we survive the descent, we can follow the creek all the way to the Los Angeles mesa. From there we can quickly vanish into Sonora among our people. Before Rowland even gets out of the high country."

"How far down is it?" Chavez asked, moving his horse sideways to get a look at the descent.

"Far. A mile."

"A mile straight down?"

"Nearly. And it's dense thicket. But it's our only way out."

Chavez smiled.

"Well, what are we waiting for?"

Down the chasm they started. All went well at first. They leaned far back in the saddle and lurched and slid and hung on for nearly an eighth-mile down the canyon. Then, Chavez felt his horse lose its footing. Its hooves violently uprooted small bushes and dislodged the earth as it fought for a grip until suddenly rider and mount fell and somersaulted several yards. Chavez rolled hard into a jumble of manzanita and his horse tumbled and slid several more yards until its saddle caught a small outcrop of loose rock. The animal turned to face the mountain and tried to stand on all four legs. Tiburcio, holding his own reins tightly, could only watch as the saddle snapped. With a monstrous grunt that echoed in the canyon, the horse spiraled to its death far below. Tiburcio dismounted for his own safety and both bandits knew they would have to pick their way down on foot.

The posse above them galloped to the cliff and peered into a void where they could hear grunts and curses and rustling in the overgrowth, but it was too dense to see anything to shoot. That didn't stop them. Three rifles, a shot gun and eight revolvers unloaded a fusillade that ripped into the thicket.

The bandits held their breath, but none of the shots came close and the shooting soon ceased. They slid, crawled and toppled from one rocky foothold to the next for another quarter of a mile down. They were cut, bruised and bloodied all over their faces and legs.

Above, a few of the lawmen tried to descend on foot but quickly crawled back after only a few yards, shaking their heads.

"They're goners," one said.

The Indian guide, Jose Redowna, saw where the bandits had entered the abyss.

"I will go after them," he said and coaxed his valiant horse over the ledge.

A moment later his horse slipped, flung off its rider and hurtled to its own mangled death. Redowna crawled back up, sure that nobody could make it down alive, alone or on a beast.

The bandits reached a point nearly three-fourths of the way down where they could see the twisting waterway at the bottom of the cliff. They each had a hand gripping the thick trunk of a mesquite bush and a boot precariously lodged between stones under thicket.

Chavez peered down and blinked hard when he saw no piece of earth between his foot and the bluish-green ribbon winding its way through a narrow pasture.

"There is no more shrub, just slick stone from here on down to the water," Chavez alerted his friend. "How far down do you think it is?"

"I don't know. Hundred, two-hundred feet," Tiburcio answered. "I have a better question."

"Yeah?"

"How deep do you think that river is?"

"If you're thinking of plunging, you better shove off good and hard," Chavez advised.

"I think we can slide down to that foothold right there. That would put us another twenty-five feet closer. And maybe save our lives."

Chavez positioned himself on course for the small ledge that was his target and let loose. He gained more speed than he had hoped to, but his boot heel dug into the gravel and he rolled and somehow popped up in one motion. But now he was upright, and after a moment's defiance of gravity, unable to stop his momentum. He had no choice but to thrust off the mountainside on one foot. He sailed toward the water with his arms straight down at his side. He hit the water hard and his body twisted and rolled downstream until he was soon floating in a relatively calm spot. Choking and spitting and scared, he flapped and kicked toward the bank.

Tiburcio, having the advantage of being a little bit north of Chavez, was able to continue his sliding nearly to the bottom, where he fell bruised and scraped and bloodied into the water.

Chavez thought Tiburcio was dead when he saw him drifting downstream. He dove into the river and paddled toward his companion. He grasped Tiburcio's collar and yanked him toward the bank. Both fugitives struggled to the shallow shore, rolling over onto their backs in the wet sand. They lay there for several minutes.

"I narrowly escaped my horse's fate," Chavez groaned, leaning on his elbows.

"But we made it."

"We lost our saddles, bed rolls, rifles …"

Despite his wounds, Tiburcio sat straight up.

"The money?"

Chavez laughed and then groaned from pain.

"Don't worry. I stashed it in the mountains. It's safe. But we'll have to return for it."

At the top of the ridge, Adams sat on a large rock. He looked haggard and depressed and uncertain if he could continue his hunt for the bandits. Rowland told him he didn't have to.

"Sheriff," Rowland said, standing over his disappointed, worn, wary and gaunt peer, "you go on back to San Jose. You've been in the saddle nearly two weeks. You've tracked Vasquez across the countryside for seven hundred miles. I can see a deep line on your forehead for every one of those miles. But the greaser is in my territory now. Let me deal with him. If he's still alive."

Adams slept nearly the entire train ride back to San Jose. McKenzie and Young rode north on horses, frequenting many saloons along the way.

• • •

TIBURCIO!

After resting and cleaning their wounds by the river, Vasquez and Chavez stumbled their way onto the Los Angeles mesa and caught a ride on a mule wagon to Sonora. By the time they arrived the sun had set and an aching, groggy fatigue gripped both of them. At a well-known saloon, some Mexican patrons recognized the bandits and deferentially told them about what they had heard around town and read in the papers since the Tres Pinos raid.

"All of Alta California is in an excited state of mind," one of the patrons said.

"Bounty hunters are crisscrossing the state looking for you," another added.

"What else have you heard?" Tiburcio probed.

The patrons weren't sure how much to tell the ferocious outlaw.

"There is something else, no?" Tiburcio asked.

The first patron who had spoken cleared his throat.

"The blacksmith, Abdon Leiva, has turned himself in," he said, waiting a moment to let that settle in before continuing. "He's sitting in a Los Angeles jail, waiting to go up and testify against Teodore Moreno."

Tiburcio grabbed the man's collar and shook him.

"Are you lying to me, *cholo*?"

"No, sir."

"Moreno has been captured? And Leiva surrendered?"

"Yes."

"Where is Leiva's family?"

"They were left at Jim Heffner's in Elizabeth Lake."

"Tell him everything," prodded another patron.

Tiburcio's eyes darted between the two men until one spoke again.

"They say Leiva has turned on you. He told Rowland's posse exactly where you were."

Tiburcio looked at Chavez, whose expression was blank.

"Thanks for sharing what you know," Tiburcio said and, although still seething underneath, pulled out a wet bag of coins. "Please, I am buying the food and drinks tonight. I will also need a couple horses. We have some business up in Elizabeth Lake. Who can get me some strong stallions?"

"Henry Morrison just came through with a herd of mustangs," another of the local Mexicans suggested.

"Morrison?"

"Yes. In fact, he said he was looking for you. He said he wished you were in town, because you are always interested in new steeds."

Tiburcio laughed.

"If somebody could get to Morrison and let him know I need two, no three, horses immediately, saddles and all, I would be obliged. Tell him I will pay handsomely for the mounts. We also need a pair of rifles. "

Two men volunteered.

"Do not give away my whereabouts to anybody except Morrison," Tiburcio warned.

Tiburcio and Chavez ordered a second ale and conjectured upon on how Moreno got caught.

"I think he will be more tight-lipped than Leiva," Tiburcio stated.

"A blacksmith and a sheepherder," Chavez said with a strong loathing. "You can only trust true mountain vaqueros."

It was the last word spoken between them for a long time until the barkeeper walked back over to them.

"*Señors*, you look very tired. Perhaps, you should get a room at the hotel and sleep before you ride off. It is safe and friendly."

The next morning Tiburcio set out north for Elizabeth Lake on a fresh mustang provided by Morrison, and Chavez backtracked to get the stashed money. Tiburcio pulled another horse with saddlebags alongside. In the thicket around the lake, he set up camp and slept most of the day and into the evening. At dusk, he changed into some old, ragged breeches, a tattered shawl and a straw sombrero to look like a poor native. He wore a wig and false beard and walked around the plaza unrecognized until it was dark.

TIBURCIO!

At 9:00 p.m. Tiburcio slipped into Rosaria's room and heard heavy breathing. He recognized it was she under the blankets. As he approached the bed, Rosaria's children woke and looked up in awe at the stranger. Tiburcio hushed them with a finger to his lips and held out his palms to tell them to hold their tongues. Then, he uncloaked himself. They giggled.

"Why are you dressed like that, Tiburcio?" they whispered, suppressing their laughs.

"Ssshhh."

He walked over to their sleeping mother and gently shook her shoulder until she awakened. She let out a gasp.

"Tiburcio!"

"Sssshhhh. I am taking you to our camp."

"No, Tiburcio," Rosaria protested. "I am feeling sick. I cannot ride."

"You must. I don't know when I will be back."

"I have felt awful since this morning, Tiburcio. Please."

"God damn it! I will take you by gunpoint if I have to!"

Rosaria was stunned at his insistence and quickly obeyed. They gathered up their belongings. Outside, Tiburcio lifted Rosaria onto his saddle and then placed the children on the other horse.

"Do you remember how to ride?" he asked them, smiling. They nodded.

As Rosaria groaned in discomfort, he climbed up behind her and they galloped back into the mountains.

Two days later the newspapers blared massive headlines:

"WIFE OF VASQUEZ TRAITOR ABDUCTED. BANDIT LEADER SUSPECTED."

Leiva might have been the last man in Southern California to hear the news. His decision to turn state's evidence was not going as he had planned. From the moment he approached Undersheriff Jenkins he was whisked away from Rosaria and the children and asked a thousand questions, many of them over and over again, about Firebaugh and the Tres Pinos tragedy.

397

"Who shot Davidson, the innkeeper?"

"Vasquez."

Hours later into the interrogation, again: "Who shot Davidson?"

"I don't know. Gonzales, maybe?"

"Not Vasquez?"

"I don't know."

"You said it was Vasquez, not Gonzales."

"I didn't see it. I just wanted to get out of the gang!"

Leiva repeatedly asked his captors if he could see his wife and children.

"Yes," Jenkins said. "Before we ship you up to San Jose, we will allow you to visit them. In shackles and with a guard on hand."

"When will that be?"

"Real soon."

"Where are they?"

"At the ranch."

"How long may I visit them?"

"Not long. Moreno has been captured and is going to trial any day now. We'll need to get you up there soon to testify against him. It will help your cause, Mr. Leiva."

On the morning it was arranged for him to see Rosaria and the children, Leiva washed up, combed his hair and put on fresh clothes that the jailer had cleaned for him. He heard Jenkins' footsteps coming and became happy for the first time in weeks. But Jenkins looked sullen.

"Your wife has been abducted by Tiburcio Vasquez," Jenkins told him. "We believe he sent your children to Mexico to stay with relatives."

Leiva broke down in tears and Jenkins left him sobbing on the floor. When he was done heaving and moaning, Leiva vowed to fiercely carry out two goals until his dying breath: Make sure Vasquez went to the gallows and reunite with his wife and children.

After all, he knew a lot that the authorities would love to learn. The first step would be showing the prosecutors he was serious about turning state's evidence by helping lock up Moreno for a long time.

"Then I am coming after you, Tiburcio!" he cried.

• • •

Rosaria was mostly happy the first few days with Tiburcio even though they needed to keep moving to stay a step ahead of the sheriff. Rosaria didn't complain about packing up from camp to camp at a moment's notice, nor did the hard, long mountain rides bother her.

But then her initial sickness returned and worsened. Cramps buckled her knees and one morning she discovered that she was bleeding from the vagina, at first lightly and later significantly. She suffered silently, even though she was scared and felt all alone. She could not risk the capture of Tiburcio and Chavez so she forced herself to rise and mount her horse despite the nausea and blood. Sometimes she would conceal her vomiting as she rode.

Rosaria minded her own business but one day she overheard Chavez talking to Tiburcio and it was worse than the sickness she was fighting.

"Tiburcio, we must abandon Rosaria! It is dangerous enough in these hills without her dragging us down. This is the last place Rowland has left to search. And you can bet he will come soon. The only reason he hasn't found us is he thinks it would be crazy for us to return here. When he does, we are sitting targets."

Tiburcio nodded.

"With her, we will never get to Kingston. We will never make our way to Agua Dulce to inspect the weapons and pay off Soriano. You have Leiva's money, right?"

"Yes."

"Listen, I am talking to you as your faithful lieutenant with only one motive in mind - keeping you and the rebellion alive. She must go."

"Give me some time to think about this. I will tell her when we are alone."

Tiburcio told Chavez to go into Sonora to get updates from their spies on the whereabouts of the law and see what was being written in the newspapers.

"And while you're there," he said, "find us a secluded spot, some place where we can keep a watch on anyone approaching. Be sure you have found the perfect place. I will see you in three days. And then we go to Kingston and pay Soriano."

As Chavez rode down the trail, Rosaria felt a debilitating fear come over her. Her dreams of spending her life with Tiburcio were gone. But she had clung to one more hope. With she and Tiburcio alone, she couldn't keep it secret anymore. She told Tiburcio she was pregnant.

"Everything will be fine," he finally muttered after several silent minutes, then smiled awkwardly.

The next day, Rosaria could not get out of her bed of blankets and the red gush from between her legs gave her great foreboding. On the last day before Chavez's return she confided to Tiburcio that she believed something had caused her to have a miscarriage. Tiburcio comforted her in his arms but did not speak. When she awoke from a long, restless, dream-filled afternoon slumber, he was sitting on the ground near her bed of blankets with his back against his large Spanish saddle, whittling a branch with his large knife.

"It is time for you to depart," he said. "I will get you as close to Heffner's as I can."

"No!" she wailed. "You cannot abandon me, Tiburcio. Not now!"

"I will give you money. You can tell the authorities anything you wish about your abduction, so as to protect yourself and your children. It is out of my hands, Rosaria. It's in God's hands."

"I know you stole Abdon's money but I don't want the money. I want to be with you."

"You must go back to your children."

She did not have time to argue. Chavez came riding into camp in a gust of exhilaration. Charging on his heels were five other vaqueros, two of them - August de Bert and Blas Bicuna - shared a saddle with women. Rosaria skulked away.

"Tiburcio!" Chavez announced, off his horse in excitement. "I have news!"

"So it appears! Tiburcio said. "Where have you been? And who have you brought?"

"First of all, meet the daughter of George Allen - come here, darling!"

She was a dark Greek beauty with large eyes and a chasm of a smile that seemed to invite and welcome only good times. Her smile had gotten Chavez's attention at a fandango in Sonora. Out of the saddle the girl vaulted, impressing the bandit leader with her flair. The forest trees seemed to sway with her every movement as she walked toward the leader of the revolution.

"Yesterday morning we rode out to her father's house. It's about eight miles out of Los Angeles. *Su padre es muy, muy loco,*" Chavez laughed. "He is called Greek George and he used to raise camels. Camels, Tiburcio! And once upon a time he convinced the U.S. Army to buy a bunch of them for transport. He claimed they would be better than burros."

"Do not mention the camels to my father," warned the girl, pretending to be stern. "Never bring up the camels in conversation. It is the reason father was forced to go into traditional ranching, which he despises due to the fact that it involves hard work."

Everybody laughed and then Chavez continued, formally introducing them.

"So you now know Georgina!"

Tiburcio kissed her hand.

"It turns out that her father's adobe in the mountains is a perfect safe house for us," Chavez explained. "There is only one trail up to the property. From the house, which sits on the flat at the top of a hill, you can see for miles around."

Tiburcio turned his light gray eyes on the girl.

"What will it cost us to stay there?"

She stepped closer to the bandit.

"If it were up to me, *el Capitan*, your presence would be enough," Georgina said in a soft voice so only Tiburcio could hear, then added louder: "On the other hand, my father will want to be paid handsomely."

"On account of the camel deal not working out so well?"

"I told you not to mention the camels!" Georgina laughed.

"Does anybody live or work on or around your father's land?"

"There are no neighbors. Just a few Mexican workers travel on the road that takes you by the house. The road ends in a forest area beyond the property. Every day they collect firewood in a wagon from beyond papa's house and sell it in town. But they can be watched all the way up and down the road. The same workers, every day."

Tiburcio turned back to his lieutenant.

"Do you feel this is safe?"

"For the time we will be there, we cannot do any better, *el Capitan*."

"What else did you learn?"

"Information is harder to come by these days in Sonora," Chavez answered. "Rowland has taken action - mostly bribery - to gain standing among many natives. I had to kill a man just because I did not know if he was an informant or not."

"*Was* he an informant?"

"I never found out. But he never led me to believe otherwise. So I took ninety dollars and this gold watch from him."

Tiburcio nodded and walked up to the others. He greeted Bicuna and de Bert.

"And who are these others you bring into our camp?" he asked Chavez.

First Chavez introduced the other woman, a prostitute that gave Tiburcio pause.

"She will be back in Sonora by sunrise," Chavez assured, and continued the introductions. These two are a couple of fierce fugitives from the law - Gomez and Monteres. And this third man is named Lebrado Corona. He is a distant cousin of yours, *El Capitan*."

"Is that so? Have we ever met?" Tiburcio asked.

"No, sir," Corona answered.

"Men," Chavez shouted zealously. "this is your new leader! You obey him and you die for him as you would your country!"

Tiburcio welcomed each of them with a handshake. Over a dinner of cooked deer and rabbit meat, he apprised them of the great fame and riches to come their way, if they were loyal. After the meal, he quickly ended the formalities and urgently took Chavez into the shadows of the camp.

"You are right. We need to get rid of Rosaria," Tiburcio whispered.

"I understand."

"On our way to Greek George's house, we will get as close to Heffner's as we can and leave her there."

Chavez looked surprised.

"I thought you meant, kill her!"

"No. Of course not."

"She knows too much, Tiburcio. It is foolish. Look at what her cowardly husband did."

"We will not kill women, Clodoveo!"

Chavez nodded and changed the subject. He told Tiburcio more of what he had learned in town.

"If the papers are to be believed, then the bounty hunters who flooded the hills and valleys after Tres Pinos have mostly disappeared, except for Rowland. The hunt to find us has died down. There are also reports that the state is seeing a surge of settlers from the east coast but many of them have stopped in Sacramento and are refusing to move until they get assurances for their safety. The time to start the liberation is upon us. If we can keep this next wave of gringos too scared to settle, we are half way to victory."

Tiburcio heard Rosaria softly moaning in the dark distance and peered over at the figures sitting in the glow of the campfire. The long ago image of the snake in the dark cave flashed into his mind. It had been a while since he had recalled the snake, since he had been enfeebled by fears. He knew terror instinctively and how it manifested in the body and felt in the pores of his skin. Debilitating fear touched him now. He took a breath and let the dread fill his lungs, and then another breath and another, until calm slowly washed over him.

"Are you all right, Tiburcio?" Chavez asked.

"Yes. Grab a bottle of aguardiente," he told his faithful servant, "and let's go over to the fire. We should get to know our visitors."

Chapter 12: Raid (2)
Kingston, Calif.
December 1873

The Mexican gang arrived on the cold north banks of the Kings River at 7:00 p.m. It was pitch dark, frigid and still. They obediently followed their leader's directions, tying their horses in a thicket of mesquite and tossing several hemp ropes over their shoulders or latching them onto their belts. The robbers drew their Dragoon and Colt pistols, cocked their Henry rifles, clattered south across the toll bridge and marched into town. Their destination was the center of Kingston's main street where a hotel, blacksmith shop, two general stores and four saloons stood. On the way there, three men stepped out of a livery stable near the bridge and stopped directly in front of the bandits.

"Get down on the ground!" Tiburcio immediately ordered them.

Peter Bozeman and John Potts dropped quickly and, stealing glances upward, noticed their third companion was still standing.

"Get your ass down here before we all get shot!" Bozeman shouted to the recalcitrant man

"No!" Martin Woods objected. "I will not lie down in the dirt in my new suit. I bought this suit for Christmas and it took six months and three alterations to get it right."

"Get down!" Chavez demanded.

"I would rather take my suit off and lie in my bare skin than dirty these clothes!"

"Fine!" Tiburcio relented. "Take the suit off. But it's damn cold out here!"

Woods shed his coat, unstrapped his suspenders and dropped his pants. He folded the attire neatly, kicked off his boots and laid the clothes on top of them. Then he lay in his long underwear on the cold ground next to his friends.

The bandits chuckled.

"Tie them up and leave them in the middle of the road!" Tiburcio commanded.

The gang continued down the main road until they came to the cluster of buildings on main street. Tiburcio placed Romero, Corona, Monteres and de Bert in front of each of the stores and Gomez in front of the hotel with orders to tie up and rob every person who crossed their path.

"Chavez, Bicuna and I will start with the hotel," Tiburcio ordered. "Wait for us to come out before entering any of the other places."

As he, Chavez and Bicuna were about to enter the hotel, they came face to face with the owner of the establishment, O.H. Bliss. Chavez and Bicuna quickly thrust guns under his chin. His legs and hands were tied and he was ordered to get down and be quiet.

"Please, the ground is too hard," Bliss pleaded. "I have a problem with my head. My doctor says it's some neurology problem."

"Toss him the blanket off that horse," Tiburcio said.

"Must we mollycoddle every man in this town?" Chavez asked.

Tiburcio laughed.

"Tie him up and give him the blanket for a pillow," he repeated.

"Now may we go in?" Chavez asked sarcastically.

Vasquez, Chavez and Bicuna entered the saloon through the hotel entrance and forced a dozen men to the floor. Several drinking glasses broke as the patrons scrambled nervously to the ground. The bandits leaped from one patron to another -

thirty in all - tying them up with the hemp rope and emptying their pockets and purses of anything valuable.

The gang swiftly moved to the adjacent dining room. In the sitting area outside the restaurant, an out-of-town visitor, two canvas travel bags with leather straps at his feet, refused to drop to the ground. Chavez looked at Tiburcio, who shook his head in disbelief. The leader promptly knocked the uncooperative victim unconscious with the handle of his .45 caliber Colt.

As Tiburcio was taking the patron's money and watch, the boorish Blas Bicuna barged into the dining room, where two dozen people were enjoying their meals.

"Get down or die!" Bicuna shouted in his thick, Spanish accent.

A woman screamed and the din of conversation halted. The man dining next to her heard the shrill but had not understood Bicuna's order.

"You drunkard! What did you say to the lady?" the man, Lance Gilroy, demanded. "You will apologize!"

Bicuna stepped toward Gilroy, who quickly seized a chair by the legs and bashed it against the bandit's midsection. Chavez leaped across several prostrate diners and slammed the butt of his rifle into Gilroy's nose, spraying blood across a row of tables with white cloths. Gilroy's knees buckled and he collapsed at Bicuna's feet. Bicuna kicked him hard a half dozen times.

"The next person to move from the floor gets their brains blown out!" Tiburcio bellowed.

The room fell silent again. Outside, Tiburcio heard shouting.

"Finish up in here!" he told the others and ran outside.

Tiburcio nearly collided with a store clerk who was trying to alert the town that robbers were everywhere. He collared the clerk, Ed Ellinger, and dragged him back to the Jacob & Epstein general store, where he found Monteres and the proprietor, Epstein, arguing.

"I will torture you if you don't find me that iron chest and key!" Monteres threatened.

"It's not here! Ellinger, have you taken it?"

Ellinger shrugged his shoulders.

"You have thirty seconds to get me the deposits," Tiburcio warned Epstein.

"What deposits?"

"You now have twenty seconds to get the money, all twenty thousand dollars of it," Tiburcio declared, pulling his gun's hammer back and thrusting the barrel into Epstein's mouth. "They had the money up in Tres Pinos so I know you have it here!"

Epstein nervously led the bandit into a small back room and clicked open a large iron chest. He handed Tiburcio a bag. Tiburcio examined its contents while Monteres tied up the clerk and storekeeper. Tiburcio emptied the money drawer into the same sack and the bandits walked out into the cold air.

Romero and Corona were guarding the S. Sweet Mercantile across the street. Monteres and Tiburcio rushed past them and began emptying that store's money drawers.

In the commotion of the ransacking, John Sutherland, a prominent Kingston rancher, slipped unseen out the back door of the hotel with his Henry rifle and rounded up two other residents. They snuck around the building and spotted Romero on the street outside the S. Sweet store. Sunderland raised his rifle and fired.

"Aaaaahhhhh," Romero cried out. "I'm shot!"

Tiburcio and Monteres dashed out with a gun in each of their hands.

"*Vamonos! Vamonos*!" Tiburcio yelled. "We have the loot! To the bridge!"

Chavez, Bicuna and Gomez fled the hotel and joined Tiburcio, Monteres, Corona and de Bert in a sprint toward their waiting horses. Sutherland and his men followed, shooting on the run.

"Oh, shit!" Chavez yelled, pulling up straight out of his sprint just as the bandits were bounding across the bridge. A ball had struck him an inch above the back of his knee.

Tiburcio stopped. He thrust his shoulder under Chavez's arm and pulled him along, hopping, skipping and running. Midway across the bridge, they both looked back. The armed town folk were within two hundred feet.

"No, Tiburcio. It's too slow. You have to go. Leave me!"

As they shuffled across the bridge, Tiburcio encouraged his lieutenant.

"Come on. I will not leave you. We have get to the horses. Try!"

Tiburcio paused for just an instant.

"Listen," he said. "They are out of bullets. Keep moving."

Sutherland stopped to reload his Henry rifle and caught up to the mob just as it reached the foot of the bridge and the bandits were leaping onto their saddles. Tiburcio and Chavez were the last to reach the end of the span. Sutherland, standing at the other end, took one last aim at the gang. The bullet grazed Corona's neck but that didn't slow the marauders' retreat. In an instant, all Sutherland could see was silent darkness ahead.

Sullen and disappointed, Sutherland returned to town, where he found no less than thirty scared and revengeful people tied up. Tiburcio's gang rode fast to a nearby adobe owned by a friendly Mexican family, dressed their wounds and divided up the booty. They had galloped away with eight thousand dollars in hard coin and jewelry in addition to the twenty thousand dollars that Morrison had deposited as promised. But they had left Romero in the clutches of the Kingston citizens.

In the morning, the gang started out in the direction of Tulare Lake, leaving in their wake not only Kingston but most of the state in great agitation. They robbed four more stages and towns before splitting up near Los Angeles.

"The next time we see each other the war will have begun," Tiburcio told the others before departing with Chavez, Bicuna and Corona. "Fight proudly!"

Not even the governor of California could ignore Tiburcio and his gang now.

Chapter 13: Governor
Sacramento, Calif.
January 1874

Gov. Newton Booth gazed out the upstairs window of the State Capitol building. After years of work, the marvelous white replica of the nation's capitol was nearly complete. Still, Booth's office was dusty and cluttered with remnants from the construction. Boards were stacked in a corner, pipes were leaning against the wall, saws and hammers were discarded around the perimeter of the room and saw dust was swept into several large piles on the floor. Workers had tried to tidy up for the governor's move to his new office, but it wasn't close to the pristine statesman's room that it should be. Not that Booth was paying much mind to the disarray of his working quarters. He was looking down at a dozen or more covered wagons hitched across what would soon be a grassy area with trees and a walkway but was currently just a lot of mud. Several men talked in groups around the wagons and children were running around playing tag.

"One God-damned bandit," Booth cursed under his breath.

His private secretary strained to hear from his seat in front of his desk.

"Pardon?"

"I broke up the monopolies within months of taking office. I worked out years of strife among the Asiatics and the white laborers before my second year in office. Now what? One bandit, Tiburcio Vasquez, rears his head and the entire state is frozen with fear."

He waved his arm in front of the window.

"Look at these Easterners, all enthusiastic in their wagons with all their possessions, ready to set out for a new life in

Monterey and Los Angeles and wherever. Suddenly, they won't leave the shadows of the State Capitol for fear they are going to get shanghaied by bandits.

"There are countless men in countless posses in six southern counties who can't hunt down this man," Booth seethed. "In the dead of winter, he is raiding towns and stages unmolested. If he can do this when the roads are muddy and the trees are bare and the valley grasses are brown, what will happen in the spring when he has plenty of cover to hide in and his horses have plenty to eat?

"And the damn newspapers with their dubious accounts of every misdeed Tiburcio Vasquez carries out," the governor raged on. "They sent reporters out for weeks with posses and ended up trying to outdo each other with ridiculous reports of successful pillaging and unsuccessful manhunts. They are stirring up trouble with each overblown story - I mean, has anyone actually seen a shred of evidence that Tiburcio Vasquez has a standing army and legions of followers ready to overrun California?"

His voice was now booming out the office door and down the hall.

"Firebaugh's Ferry, Tres Pinos, Kingston, Coyote Hole - every raid detailed in breathless prose. And when this evil man does one decent act in a thousand evil ones he is described like a saint. He leaves a woman unharmed in a stage robbery. He gives a victim a pillow for his head. Does this make him a good man?"

Booth caught his breath and drummed his fingers on the window ledge. His secretary waited patiently.

"Mr. Hart," Booth said. "Do you know what I need to do? I need to organize a state-sponsored posse led by the bravest and most morally straight man in the state. An irreproachable lawman. A born leader. He needs to be able to assemble experienced, courageous and tireless lawmen and lead them to the ends of the state, whether it takes a week, a month or a year. He needs to be singularly focused on one job - capturing Tiburcio Vasquez - and carry it out until the *bandido* is hung.

He needs to boast a reputation of bringing down the worst of villains, the most evil outlaws, the most notorious, dangerous brigands. The mention of his very name needs to send a tremble through the most hardened criminal."

"And he needs to be a Republican," Hart added.

Booth turned his eyes skyward to think about that remark for a moment. Then he nodded.

"Yes, of course. But who?"

"Two names come to mind, sir. Adams and Morse."

"Adams had his chance," Booth snapped. "But Morse. Yes, Harry N. Morse."

"He'll need full support from the state, governor. Legislative support. Financial support. He'll want all the provisions and funds we can provide. His posse and their mission will need to carry the full weight of the central government of California."

"Yes, Hart. You're right. Telegraph Morse immediately," Booth ordered. "And call the Senate and Assembly to order."

By the time Morse arrived by train in Sacramento to discuss the matter with the governor, the legislature had appropriated five thousand dollars for the posse to use for food, lodging and other expenses. It had also approved a reward of two thousand dollars for Vasquez dead, three thousand dollars alive.

Three men from the governor's staff and four officers of the law escorted Morse from the train depot to the Capitol. They walked by the conflux of wagons, mules, horses and people. Morse, dressed in a heavy tailcoat and leather gloves, stopped and stared up at the new white Capitol. Then, he looked down at his muddy boots and shook his head. They continued up the outside stairs to the statehouse until Morse paused again at the entrance. He took his gloves off and placed them in his large coat pocket and looked down at his footwear crusted with mud.

"Don't worry about tracking mud in here, sheriff. It's still a mess from the construction."

After formalities, Booth wasted little time getting to the point of his call. Morse sat in a leather chair across the walnut desk with a veneer so polished and shiny he could see the governor's reflection in it. Booth gave him a detailed account of all that had happened leading up to the day he telegraphed the sheriff.

"I was very pleased in the Legislature's decision to fund such a police action. In the absence of a state military, we have not had a manhunt like this since a force was assembled to track down Joaquin Murrieta. That was about fifteen or twenty years ago, wasn't it, Hart?"

"1853, sir," the secretary answered from his small side desk. "Twenty-one years."

Booth shook his head at Hart's proficiency.

"Harry, have you had time to think about how you'll go about finding Vasquez?"

"Yes, sir. But, obviously, more preparation will be needed once I leave Sacramento."

"Of course," the governor replied perfunctorily. "You'll want to break up and send smaller posses to search his suspected hideouts. And since we are dealing with several thousand square miles from Alameda to San Bernardino, you'll need sufficient numbers. I think you will need to assemble thirty men."

"I respectfully disagree, sir. I've never traveled with more than four men, sir. A smaller number allows for more swift operations and tends to draw less attention to us and our movements. We can better disguise our purpose and affect that we are surveyors."

"Ah, well, it's your posse, Harry," Booth said, opening the thin desk drawer in front of him. "But I happen to have a list of thirty names right here ..."

"With all due respect, governor, I need to select these men myself."

Booth stole a glance at his secretary, who had suggested before Morse's arrival that the sheriff would want to handpick the posse.

"Yes, I suppose you would. Who do you have in mind?"

"They are all upstanding citizens, sir. You would approve of all of them. However, one of the men I need is sitting in San Quentin, sir."

"A prisoner?"

"Yes. I will need you to furlough him."

"I have no prisoners on my list. Why do you want to ride with a prisoner?"

"He's Ramon Romero. He has ridden with Vasquez, very recently. He was shot and captured in Kingston, and nearly beaten to death I might add. He knows the bandit's intimate hiding places and, up until his capture, knew where Vasquez was going and what he was planning. He was privy to every one of Vasquez's plots. He is a fantastic tracker and would be a great asset among the native Californians as far as trust goes."

"Have you spoken with this inmate?"

"I frequently visit inmates that I have pursued or captured, sir. Romero, in particular, has expressed an interest in helping bring some of his former acquaintances to justice in return for time off his prison sentence and some money to help him get established once he is freed."

"Time off and daily pay?"

Morse let out a big sigh.

"Governor," he said, "there are a lot of good law officers up and down this state, but you chose me to do the job. The Assembly and Senate supported your choice and gave you a small fortune to get the job done. Now, how much are you willing to trust your instinct? How much rein are you willing to give me?"

"OK, sheriff. You can assemble your own posse. And I will consider letting Romero enjoy some fresh air and the wide countryside. But I will not stand for merely four men plodding down the state in search of a murderer who has eluded capture for years. You must have an efficient number of men. I cannot, in good conscience, allow fewer than fifteen men to join you."

"Any more than eight and I cannot do the job. And if this mission is going to be kept secret from the public, the fewer the better."

"Fine, Mr. Morse. As you wish!"

The governor sprung out of his chair and strode to the window. The wagons and travelers, suspended in their journey, below angered him. He turned to face Morse again.

"How much preparation do you need?"

"Two months."

"Two months!" Booth angrily shouted.

"I need to get commitments from posse members, procure well-fed horses and provisions, map out routes, pinpoint locations, develop disguises. Besides, in two months' time, there will be plenty of grasses to feed our horses and the rivers will be passable once again after the winter rains. I have given this plenty of forethought, governor."

A factory horn sounded outside, and the governor was no longer angry.

"Yes, I see," Booth conceded. "You are a prudent man. And that's why I staked my reputation on you when I made the proposal to the chamber. You do as you see fit, sheriff."

Chapter 14: Pursued (2)
Across California
March 1874

In his fusty office with hundreds of files packed onto shelves and littering the floor, Morse cleared some space at his desk and looked at a piece of paper with the names of six men who had agreed to help him hunt down Vasquez and his band. Three of them were easy choices and, had he gotten his way with the governor, he would have stopped there. Tom Cunningham, the wisecracking but fearless San Joaquin sheriff, and two friends from the Oakland Guard days, Ralph Falville and A. J. McDavid, would be his most trusted lieutenants on the ride.

The second tier of posse members he asked to join him were Harry Thomas, the deputy sheriff from Fresno, and Ambrose Calderwood, former Santa Cruz County lawman. These two men were familiar with the bandits, because of raids in their towns. Thomas also had an ulterior motive for helping capture Vasquez - to gain the trust and support of Kingston again in the aftermath of the audacious raid.

The riskiest pick of his posse was Ramon Romero, his expertise being, in addition to horsemanship, the handling of a Bowie knife. He knew all the highland trails from the Coast Range to Cantua Canyon. He was very familiar with all the bandits who lurked there and the spots where they liked to hide. Romero had ridden side by side with Vasquez, even as late as a month ago. Vasquez had taught Romero how to play the guitar while both were doing time in prison and on long nights laying low in the mountains. Romero's shortcoming was his violent nature, but Morse desperately needed a man who knew the territory and haunts of Vasquez as well knowing as the bandit leader himself. The price for Ramon was steep: five dollars a day, plus five hundred dollars if they got the reward.

As Morse set aside the list and picked up a second piece of paper with other names to consider, there was a knock at his door. His son, George, entered.

"What are you doing, Father?"

"I am deciding who the last members of my posse will be. I have six sworn. And I believe the seventh will be a reporter from the *San Francisco Chronicle* whom I have come to know."

"Are you sure you want a reporter coming along?"

"I trust Mr. Henderson. Boyd has been very fair in his reporting of the conflict with the Mexican bandits. These days, son, you need to sell your actions to the public. You need to gain their support, and you do that through the newspapers."

"I thought you didn't want publicity."

"He won't have time to write anything until the noose is around Vasquez's neck. But then our story will be told for the ages, from our side of the fence."

"That leaves one more posse man, right?"

"Yes," Morse confirmed and started scrutinizing the names again.

"Father? Father?"

"Yes?"

"I would like to join you. I would like to be the eighth man in your posse."

Morse looked up and stared at his son. Even though George had matured and calmed his wild ways, Morse was taken aback by the suggestion. He stared not at the boy, but at a man, across the desk. Strong, tall, eager. George was trying to get back into military school. He had shown an interest in law and was currently working for a local judge. It had been nearly two years since he had last had an altercation.

Morse set the paper with the names down.

"You will be under my command. Not as a son, but as a member of the posse. I will treat you the same as the others."

"I understand."

"OK, George," Morse said, standing and extending his hand. "It's a deal."

The preparations were complete. The men would meet up at Firebaugh's Ferry on the thirteenth. A.J. McDavid would bring a four-horse wagon with cooking equipment, tents, bedrolls weapons and ammunition. A dozen horses had been feeding on grain for two weeks at Firebaugh in preparation.

Morse felt fortunate for not having had to pay for the horses, thanks to Charles Knox of the Morrison and Knox Ranch. He had originally asked Knox's partner, Henry Morrison, who owned the greater stake in the ranch, but surprisingly he had acted coy upon the request.

"Ask Knox," Morrison had said indifferently.

Knox, on the other hand, quickly offered a dozen horses free of charge - and with that the last snag in the planning stages was taken care of.

For the first two weeks the nine lawmen scoured the Almaden Mine area and rode down into the Coast Range, leaving not an acre of flat or mountainous land unchecked. They discovered vast herds of stolen cattle and horses, but the vaqueros tending to them quickly fled and hid in their remote hovels in the mountains until the posse passed through. They soon found that the few mountain settlers willing to talk could not be trusted anyway.

"We talked to some Mexicans who said they recently saw Tiburcio in these hills," George Morse excitedly reported back at camp after having split from the rest of the posse to search out information.

"They are probably lying," Romero said. "The majority of the vaqueros and borregueros out here claim to have never heard of him. Vasquez's friends do not betray him so easily."

"You did," George retorted.

"He abandoned me, *pendejo*! He left me for dead with the rabble in Kingston."

In the third week they set out some eighteen miles from where the supply wagon was set up and came upon a small herd of mustangs at the eastern foothills of the Santa Lucia Mountains, south of Monterey. The posse's presence as it came over a hill spooked a vaquero watching over the herd. The lawmen rode hard after the man, through the dry chaparral and up into an oak and pine forest. They didn't catch him but they found his decrepit hut, erected with large branches stuck in the ground and smaller sticks binding them together under a roof plastered over with mud. A crystal-clear stream gurgled nearby and then fell away underground a short distance away. George Morse dismounted and entered the *jacale* while the others took their horses to the stream to slake their thirst.

"Hey, father. Come here," George cried out.

Inside, Harry saw his son holding a photograph and a letter. Morse looked at the photograph first.

"Somebody wanted these Mexicans to know who I was."

"How did they know we were coming?"

Morse shrugged and examined the unsent letter. It was addressed to a post box in Sonora. He ripped it open and stood in amazement at the words.

"Someone was going to alert Vasquez of our whereabouts," Morse told the others. "If this address is correct, Vasquez is no longer in these parts. He's in the south."

"Whose hut is this?" Cunningham asked.

"Let's look around and find out."

As they searched the discarded saddle bags and blankets inside the hut, they found newspaper clippings relating to the slaying of six men by Manuel Lopez and a revolver with the initials M.L. engraved on the ivory handle. Romero was familiar with Lopez.

"That's his gun. He occasionally joins the Vasquez gang for raids in these parts, but mostly he's in it to profit himself," Romero said.

"Let's find his trail and get him," the sheriff decided.

"But Vasquez is in the Los Angeles area," Romero said. "I can find him there."

"Maybe. Maybe not. We've been fooled before. As long as we're picking up clues in these Mexicans' houses, it is not a waste of our time. Just think what a live person can tell us. Besides, it is quite a prize in its own right to catch Lopez."

"What about the chuck wagon? Do we go back for that?" Falville asked.

"We don't have time. We eat what we have in our saddlebags."

"We still have not searched Cantua," McDavid added.

"Cantua will have to wait."

For the next six days they followed Lopez's trail in the Santa Lucia Mountains, crossing over the snow-spotted summit to the soggy western slope that faced the Pacific Ocean. When the tracks went as cold as the mountain air, they rode back again to the arid eastern side. Morse finally gave in to complaints from his shivering, hungry posse and ended the pursuit of Lopez.

"I apologize, men," Morse said at the campsite. "I should not have gotten sidetracked on Lopez. We go to Cantua next, and then to Los Angeles."

They rested in Monterey for a day before setting out for Cantua. On the ride, Romero filled the sheriff in on what he knew about the hideout.

"Tiburcio allowed all native Californians to live freely, eat well and house in comfort there if they proclaimed significant enough zeal for the revolution. Men, women and children are just awaiting word from Vasquez for when they should leave Cantua and set out for the southland and join his army in the quest to free the state.

"So be prepared," Romero warned. "For anything."

As the eight-man posse set out across the plains, the sheriff expected his luck to change. In saloons and ranches along the way, he spread the word that he would reward anyone in the region an extra one thousand dollars, in addition to the state's sum, if they would disclose any information on the whereabouts of Vasquez that would lead to his arrest.

However, by the first week of April, the posse men had already ridden one thousand miles, crossed every known northern haunt of Vasquez's, except Cantua, and talked to dozens of his countrymen, and nobody claimed to have knowledge of the bandit and his gang. At last they approached the jagged rocks leading into Cantua Canyon. The air was warm and still, but not as stifling hot as it would be later in the spring. Nevertheless, the men were thirsty after riding the dusty, barren route to Cantua. They stopped, ate some jerky and drank water.

"They say a dozen or more men passing through the narrow mouth of the gorge can easily be outgunned by just one man," Romero warned. "If we meet resistance that we cannot overcome, our journey ends in a hail of bullets and you, sheriff, will be forever remembered as leading one of the state's most expensive failed attempts at justice ever."

"He's trying to keep us away from Cantua," George Morse said. "He is protecting them."

"Listen, Romero," Morse said impatiently, "if you want to stay out of prison for a little while longer, keep breathing this fresh mountain air and making a little bit of money, I need you to help us seize this camp. You've been inside that canyon, I am counting on you. We can turn the tide on Vasquez. If we capture legions of his defenders, which you said Moreno claims are holed up there, these Mexicans in the hills might not feel so protected and invincible anymore."

"The only way to take Cantua is to attack swiftly and pray earnestly," Romero said. "Even so, they probably know we are here already."

With that, the posse swept down toward the canyon's small entrance. Morse took the lead, giving his horse rein with one hand and holding his Henry rifle with the other. He darted through the gap, waiting to hear the implacable crack of gunfire. Instead, only silence filled the air. Soon he was through the treacherous mouth of the canyon. He halted his horse and looked around at the dramatically transformed climate. There was green grass, a gurgling river, willows and oaks and small wildlife leaping around. The rest of the men galloped behind the sheriff into the clear, armed and ready to shoot. But the canyon was devoid of human life.

• • •

After nearly thirty days in pursuit of Tiburcio, the posse finally turned south. Morse sent a dispatch to Booth explaining his next move and detailing his progress. The report was bleak.

"We're having great trouble getting fresh horses. We are sleeping in our saddles and going for days without eating," he reported to the governor. "Throughout our first month and two thousand miles, we have not found one Mexican settler willing to betray Vasquez. It is going to be hard work finding the bandit leader. He has so many friends among the Mexicans, they hide him and feed him, and lie to the officers. They admire this bandit to a high degree, but I believe there must be someone between here and the border he has double-crossed and who is willing to talk if we make it worth their while. Having swept nearly every mile of northern California, I am now convinced that our prey is somewhere south of the Tehachapi Mountains near Los Angeles, but I fear we need more help. Therefore, as a greater incentive, if it is possible, I would like to increase the reward for Tiburcio's capture to eight thousand dollars alive, six thousand dead.

"Request granted," came the reply from Booth. "I will issue the proclamation."

Next, Morse telegraphed Rowland.

"At the behest of Gov. Booth, I am pursuing Tiburcio Vasquez. Convinced he is in your jurisdiction. Expect our arrival at the San Gabriel Mission one week from today."

Then he reluctantly allowed Boyd Henderson to send a dispatch to his editors. It would be the newspaperman's first since the trip began. The increased reward and the posse's new direction was reported in the next day's *Chronicle*.

• • •

Farther south, Tiburcio read the same news.

"Come get me!" he declared, and Chavez laughed.

They were sitting at a heavy wood table in the kitchen at Greek George's house, near Anastacio Garcia's old La Brea Ranch. The hiding spot, just as Georgina had described it, sat on a high plain about eight miles out of Los Angeles, with a lake below surrounded by thick willows. Seven-foot-tall mustard and fennel plants grew in the fields leading up to the house. The wagon truck used by the firewood gatherers coursed past the house but was visible at all times from the main room, the one in which the friends now sat.

Tiburcio usually slept in one of the beds in the house while the three other gang members flopped on blankets out in the mustard fields or by the lake, providing security in case any unexpected visitors happened to approach. Greek George allowed the bandit leader to sleep and eat in the house as long as he did not show any romantic interest in his daughter. But the air was thick with sexual tension to which the father was either not keen to or chose to ignore.

Georgina carried Tiburcio's breakfast plate over to the table and set the meal in front of him, her small, firm breasts touching his upper arm. Greek George looked up from his seat near the hearth.

"What are you talking about?" she asked.

"Nothing," Tiburcio said tersely, tossing aside the newspaper.

They waited for Georgina to leave the room before continuing their conversation.

"As I was saying," Tiburcio continued, "I have decided not to bring Anita into the makings of our revolution. Entreating money from her is out of the question. It is not appropriate and is ill-mannered on my part."

"I do not disagree," Chavez said. "But we are ten thousand dollars short."

"Lebrado has been scouting the area looking for targets."

"We have been lucky. That is not easy money to stumble across. What if there is nobody to rob?"

"I know where my brother, Fernando, is working. He's our last chance."

"But you still want me to go talk to Anita?"

"Yes, when Lebrado returns. You will tell her that I cannot ask her to join me now as much as it hurts my heart. There is too much to risk for her. But after the glorious revolution begins, if she so desires, we can unite again, never to part."

"You trust my words?"

"Yes. But I will pen a letter for you to deliver."

In the middle of breakfast, Lebrado Corona barged into the house, quickly nodded to the owner and Georgina and marched right up to Tiburcio and Chavez.

"You said one more robbery, one more victim and the war can begin, right? Well, I have found him."

Corona said an Italian sheep herder who lived only six miles away had just sold a large number of his flock.

"What's his name?"

"Alessandro Repetto."

"Do you know that name, George?"

"Yes. He lives too close. Do not attack our neighbors."

Tiburcio ignored his plea. Greek George would be paid handsomely for his burden.

"Let's ride down there and check out the area. First, Clodoveo and I must finish some business. Then, Lebrado, Bicuna and I will go looking for Mr. Repetto."

When they were alone, Tiburcio turned his attention back to Anita. The room was empty and he sat at the table to write her a letter trying to explain his thoughts. He ached to be next to her but did not want to put her in harm's way. He had loved her for so long but knew nothing about her life now. She had once risked her life to be with him but he could not imagine she would again welcome peril. Yet, when he saw her in the Concordia coach that day he thought he understood that she was free and would be willing to embrace him and his life, with all its danger and predicaments, again. But how does one write such a letter?

Chavez walked into the room.

"Words are failing me, Clodoveo," Tiburcio admitted, smiling wryly. "For the first time, I cannot write verse nor prose. Not even to Anita."

"Why don't you start by trying to write to Rodolfo, then? Perhaps it is he who holds the key to her decision."

Tiburcio grinned with pleasure at the suggestion. He had never been told that Rodolfo was his son, but there was no mistake when he looked into those light gray eyes.

"My son?" he asked as much to seek confirmation that he had fathered the boy as to wonder if Rodolfo should be the recipient of his words.

"Yes, your son."

"That's a grand suggestion."

So he began:

"With a sincere love, I worship you
When, beauty by my side, I had you
With a sincere love, I pledge my adoration
I worship you, I adore you, with my soul
Separated from you, alone, lost
Sad and meditating, I pass the time."

When he returned the pen to the ink well, Chavez was gone but he felt a presence in the room. He looked up and saw the dour face of Georgina.

"I know you are going to invite that other woman into my house," she uttered. "I will not stand for that!"

"You should not eavesdrop."

"I cannot tolerate it. It is too much to bear, and I cannot believe you would be so bold, so insensitive, as to even contemplate such a thing!"

"Georgina, I have been honest with you. Whether Anita - "

"Ahhh," Georgina exclaimed. "Don't say her name!"

" - comes or not, it will soon be time for me to leave. Forever."

Tiburcio heard a floorboard squeak and Greek George stepped out from the back bedroom.

"Have you been listening in the shadows, too, like your daughter?"

"No, but with your making plans to leave I'd like to remind you that you haven't yet paid me for my hospitality."

"George, you will get paid. As soon as I settle a longstanding debt I owe, my last obligation, I will compensate you well beyond our agreement."

Giving Tiburcio a warning glance, Georgina stepped outside.

"If you would excuse me, I need to finish my letter and poem," Tiburcio told George.

The poem took a turn and it was unmistakably Anita whom he was now addressing. The well had burst.

" *Alone, remembering an idolized love,*
In my solitude, alone contemplate
I call to you and ask that you help me ... "

Later, Tiburcio told Chavez that he wanted to deliver the note himself. But the lieutenant disagreed.

"I understand that you would like to, but that is foolish," Chavez said. "We must stick with our plan. I will skirt around Morse and ride north to deliver your letter. If Anita insists on coming, I will arrange the train fare for her and Rodolfo and ride back alone. When they arrive, I will meet them at the train station, escort them to your door, and with the last of the money, we will leave immediately to Agua Dulce."

Tiburcio walked over and put his hands on the young man's shoulders.

"I want you to know that I love you like a brother, Clodoveo. No, like a son."

"I know, Tiburcio. I feel the same."

After finishing his task, Tiburcio stepped onto the wood porch and Georgina suddenly appeared at his elbow. Her father was on the other side of the house and they were alone.

"I can't stand it when you leave, Tiburcio. I don't know if you'll ever return. I have nightmares that you are in the arms of other women or that you have been shot and killed. When you come back, I hardly have a moment of peace even then because I cannot have your complete devotion and you don't accept mine. Do you know how I feel, darling?"

"I have no peace either, Georgina. I, too, lie awake in bed plotting ways to be next to you only to wake, starving and unable to reach the fruit."

"Then you do not have any other lovers?" she asked.

"Yes. But that same heart beats for you, my sweetheart. Because you are here, a beautiful, daily presence in my life, how can it not?"

"And she lives far away, no?"

"Too far," he told her honestly. "Now I must go, Georgina."

He held the side of her face with his right hand and pressed it against his cheek. He turned his head and his lips lightly touched her ear, then her cheek and quickly passed over her full lips. He smiled gently and stepped away.

• • •

Tiburcio, Bicuna and Corona rode toward Alessandro Repetto's sheep ranch and camped in the area for a few days so they could observe the land and plan an escape route in case they were pursued. Tiburcio looked northeast at the shadowy San Gabriel mountain range rising in the distance. He was pleased they had very good horses, thanks to Morrison.

"If we must escape in a hurry our line of retreat will be through the Soledad Canyon," he said, pointing out the direction in the waning, orange-blue daylight. "On the way up we will face a precipitous climb over rock spurs and ridges and then drop through manzanita so thick it could stop a grizzly bear. There's a trail part of the way, but we will want to leave it for the lawmen to take. It abruptly stops at a sheer cliff. To get back to Greek George's safely, we'll drop down through the Big Tujunga Canyon and follow the river to the mouth of the Arroyo Seco. Unless they have an expert Indian guide, they won't be able to follow us."

In the morning, they met a traveler who mentioned that Repetto was hiring sheep shearers.

"It would be a satisfactory job for ya'll," the traveler said. "Plenty of work, indeed. I was in town a week ago and they were talking about how Repetto had just made a ten thousand dollar deal on wool."

The bandits approached Repetto's property the next morning and discovered from a sheepherder on his property that he was home.

"I am an expert sheep shearer, sir," Vasquez said to Repetto as they stood outside the door to his house. "These are friends of mine, both very good vaqueros, looking for jobs, as sheepherders."

Repetto welcomed the three men inside to further discuss the work and was immediately surrounded at gunpoint. Repetto cursed loudly and a frightened fourteen-year-old boy ran into the room.

"Calm down, Repetto, and if we can come to some kind of agreement I won't have to kill you," Vasquez said. "You have a lot of money from your sheep sale, and I want it in exchange for your life."

"True, I had a lot of money for a short while, but I bought supplies and paid off debts so I now have very little to show for it. I have only eighty dollars here at the ranch."

"Liar!" Vasquez retorted and ordered his men to keep a gun on Repetto and his young nephew while he began ransacking the house.

He only found eighty dollars.

"Where is the rest, Repetto?"

"Please, I will show you my ledger and bank book."

Tiburcio nodded and Repetto produced the books. He had written down a ten thousand dollar deposit, followed by a trail of withdrawals totaling nine-thousand five-hundred dollars.

"I do not have much credit, but I can write you a check for eight hundred dollars. That's all I have."

Tiburcio laughed.

"I should shoot you for believing I am stupid enough to walk into a bank to cash a check with my name on it. It's a meager amount, but I don't intend to walk away empty-handed. Here's what we'll do. This boy will ride into town with the check made out to cash and bring back the money."

Everyone's eyes fell on the wide-eyed boy. He was trembling.

"I do not want you to cause any alarm in town," Tiburcio said to him. "Do not show any agitation. Just present the check to the clerk in ordinary fashion without raising suspicion."

Repetto signed the check and Tiburcio walked the boy out to the stable to get his horse.

"Remember, your uncle's life - as well as your own - is in your hands. Dare to betray me and I will kill him, then I will kill you. If you think you can bring the sheriff with you, remember you can't hide from me or my men. We are everywhere, and we will find you. So be very calm, son. Hurry back!"

Tiburcio watched him ride off and reentered the house. Corona and Bicuna had Repetto tied up and were fixing breakfast for themselves in the kitchen.

The boy loped into Los Angeles and entered the bank as if everything was in order. He laid the check in front of the clerk, but as the employee examined the signature and began to ask general questions about the boy and his uncle's well-being, his cheeks began to flush and his hands quavered slightly but perceptibly. His shaky voice betrayed his emotion.

"Are you all right?" the clerk asked the teenager.

Fearing that he was about to cost his uncle his life, the boy burst into tears. The clerk asked him to wait and went to get the bank president, who quickly asked the boy to come into his office.

"Explain yourself, lad."

Moments after the boy astonished the bank officials with his story, the clerk sprinted out of the building straight for Rowland's office. Rowland could not believe what he was hearing.

"Tiburcio Vasquez? The boy said it was Tiburcio Vasquez and two other men?" Rowland repeated. "Unbelievable. He's just sitting at a ranch a few miles from here, waiting for the boy's return?"

The sheriff's glee could not be suppressed. Rowland quickly called in two deputies and devised a plan.

"How many men can we mobilize?"

"A dozen or more, sir."

"How long?"

"We need a half hour."

Rowland told the clerk to go back to the bank and detain the boy for a little longer while he organized the posse.

"I need a handful of men to block any escape north or south along the Los Angeles River while I take a half-dozen men with me and follow the boy back to the ranch," Rowland said. "Tell the bank to give the boy the notes. Then, he needs to ride back and deal with those criminals with as much calmness as he can muster."

Back at Repetto's, Corona spotted Repetto's nephew in his spyglass coming up from a ravine and ran back to the house to alert Tiburcio.

"He's alone," Corona said.

"For now," Tiburcio said suspiciously. "Get back out there and make sure he's not being followed."

The instant the boy set foot inside the house Tiburcio snatched the bank notes and began examining them. A few minutes later, Corona burst back in.

"Riders are coming! They just came over the rise and they have rifles!"

"*Vamonos!*"

Vasquez sprinted out the door followed by Bicuna and Corona and the trio spurred their horses toward the mountains to the northeast as planned. Dropping two men at Repetto's house, Rowland and four others stayed on the bandits' tail but their horses were not superior and after winding through wild gorges and angling up rocky paths for several hours they lost sight of the bandits.

Well ahead of the posse, Tiburcio smiled as he got back on the wide main trail. He saw three engineers were returning to the city in a Los Angeles Water Co. wagon after finishing their work in the area.

"Halt!" Tiburcio ordered. "I want your money, now!"

One of the three engineers, Charles Miles, laughed, nodded and shook the reins to get his team moving again. Tiburcio reached behind his saddle, pulled his Henry rifle out of the scabbard and pointed it at Miles.

Miles now understood he was serious and the three water employees were forced off the wagon. Corona and Chavez started rifling through their pockets but not much money appeared.

"What kind of work are you doing up here?" Tiburcio asked.

"We are preparing the land for a large citrus grove."

"Out here? It's too dry."

"We can get the water to the trees by aqueduct."

"You God-damned gringos just keep stealing land, don't you?" Tiburcio said. "So why shouldn't I take what I want from you? Give me that fine gold watch you have."

"Please, it was a gift from my wife."

Tiburcio fired a shot at Miles feet. The engineer quickly tossed the watch to the bandit.

"Look!" cried Corona.

In the distance they could see dust swirling into the air.

"That didn't take them long," Tiburcio said with a smile, impressed. "Let's go."

The bandits rode the wagon trail for a few miles, then dismounted and led their animals down narrow, declivitous trails. Rowland's team mimicked their moves until darkness started quickly falling. Vasquez's men rode into one more canyon, seamed in by high ridges. Nightfall forced both parties to make camp - Vasquez on the crest and Rowland's men below. The sheriff took no chances and ordered two of his men to stay awake and alert to avoid any ambush.

At sunrise, the chase resumed. Rowland's men toiled over the top of the ridge and found themselves looking down a steep canyon above a river. There, they spotted Vasquez, Corona and Bicuna forcing their way, foot by foot, through a wall of vigorous, prickly chaparral just out of rifle range. There was no trail under their feet and they had abandoned their horses elsewhere.

"Our horses will never make it through that chaparral," Rowland reasoned. "We can backtrack and get down the canyon to the mouth of the river and cut them off to the south before they get out of that mess."

"Sheriff, Morse's posse is in the Tehachapis!" one of Rowland's men excitedly reminded the sheriff with a tone of optimism. "If we get a message to him, they could ride down and we would have Vasquez trapped between us."

"Morse is incompetent and unreliable," Rowland retorted. "He hasn't arrested one bandit or even gotten close to Vasquez since he set out with great flourish over a month ago. Hell, Sheriff Adams blazed the same exact trail and he at least arrested a few of Vasquez's men along the way. I am not going put my faith in Morse the way the governor has. He's just throwing money away. Didn't we almost capture Vasquez just now without even trying? We know where he is. We know where he is going. We just need to ambush him at the river."

Only forty-five miles north of Rowland, Morse and his posse had reached Fort Tejon at the foot of the Tehachapi

Mountains. It had been two days since the Repetto robbery, but the lawmen had not heard any news of the crime. They had been traversing the isolated San Gabriel Mountain high country, far removed from any civilization.

"My editor is going to fire me if I don't find a telegraph soon," Henderson complained as they reached the fort. "I need to post a dispatch on our progress."

"That will be a short report," Cunningham said.

Morse heard his wisecrack but knew the sheriff was never malicious in his banter. It was his nature to joke. Morse smiled.

At Fort Tejon, they got the first reliable whisper of Tiburcio's whereabouts in nearly a month when the telegraph operator informed them of the Repetto robbery.

"They say Rowland has pursued Vasquez into the mountains and his posse is waiting for the bandit at the mouth of the Big Tujunga River," the operator said. "But there's been no sign of the bandits coming out of the mountains for two days. The entire south state is in a panic now that they know Vasquez is down here."

"Do I have any messages from Rowland?" Morse asked.

"No."

"Are you certain?"

"Yes."

"Rowland knows our route and timetable. We telegraphed him before we left the Coast Range. Why hasn't he tried to reach us? We can come down and squeeze the bandits right out of the mountains into Rowland's arms. What's the quickest way to the river?"

The telegraph operator spread a map over his desk and showed Morse.

"And where is Rowland?"

The employee pointed to a place on the map called Dark Canyon.

"We don't need Rowland's invitation. Let's ride, men," Morse said, hurrying back out to his horse.

"But I need to report to my editor," Henderson cried out.

"You can do it in San Fernando. After we get Tiburcio!"

"It makes for a better story," Cunningham added with a wink.

They furiously galloped fifteen miles until the trail suddenly stopped in the middle of the canyon. An enormous landslide blocked the route.

"Son of a bitch!" Morse cursed.

"He didn't tell us about the landslide either," Cunningham fumed. "Now we've lost an entire day."

They had no choice but to return to Tejon and take the well-traveled road into Los Angeles County. Morse cursed Rowland all the way back.

Henderson knew he had an intriguing story. Petty jealousies among sheriffs. Murdering thieves slipping away unharmed. He excused himself and roused the Fort Tejon telegraph operator so he could get down to work. The reporter unleashed a dispatch soundly criticizing Rowland. His scathing words went out with the *Chronicle* editions the next day.

"Had Rowland sent us immediate notice and notified us of the impassibility of the canyon, we could probably have taken such steps as would have insured the capture of Tiburcio Vasquez," Henderson concluded in his article.

Riding fresh horses and with decent food in their stomachs, Morse's gang swung wide of the landslide area and headed for Rock Creek Canyon, where Adams had bogged down in his pursuit a few months earlier. For the next week, nobody in the posse was aware that the *Chronicle* reporter among them had touched off a war of words in statewide newspapers. Stuck in their saddle and riding exhaustively through wild landscape from dawn to dusk, they were unable to respond as other sheriffs around the state weighed in on the Rowland-Morse conflict, stating their opinions, proffering advice and taking potshots at each other through their favorite reporters.

Tiburcio, Bicuna and Corona hiked through the interior mountain peaks and valleys, camping in the shelter of megalithic boulders and keeping their fires low at night. They stayed hidden in the rugged terrain and avoided the open river trails. Throats parched and stomachs hollow, they threaded their way down into a valley and found a small Mexican community. The inhabitants welcomed the folk heroes and fed them and patched their torn clothes and boots. Once they were well-rested and had acquired fresh horses, they rode back to Greek George's hideaway, never having to confront Rowland.

Nearly all the pieces were in place and Tiburcio was not going to waste any more time. The law and the public were agitated in the south. In the north, the Cantua camp was on the move. Morse was bogged down. Lawmen were bickering over jurisdictions and ordinary citizens were too frightened to travel anywhere. Tiburcio and his men were safe. His hideout was unassailable, and even if a posse knew how to navigate the numerous crags, fast rivers and lush, gloomy ravines east of Los Angeles, they would be spotted coming from miles away. Chavez would arrive any day now with Anita's word and then they would immediately depart to Agua Dulce to prepare Soriano and his army for his arrival and the start of the revolution.

Just one detail remained. It was not a small one. He had counted on the money from Repetto to pay his final debt to Soriano and sound the revolution. Now ten thousand dollars short, and Los Angeles crawling with lawmen seeking his head, he had only one choice for getting the money. He would pay a visit to his brother.

Fernando was a successful lawyer in the Los Angeles area who helped California natives maneuver through the legal system. Tiburcio had not spoken to Fernando since his decision to become a desperado, but they were of the same blood so it was worth a try. And if Fernando did not give him the money? He would have to plead with Soriano to consider the last ten grand a loan.

Fernando Vasquez's secretary stood in front of the young attorney's desk with a stunned visage.

"Yes?" Fernando asked with raised eyebrows.

"Somebody is here to see you."

436

"That's what I'm here for. To see people. To help people," he said in staccato.

"I believe, Mr. Vasquez, that the visitor is your brother."

"Ah, why didn't you say so? Send Antonio right in, please."

The secretary remained like a statue.

"Mrs. Lopez?"

"It's your other brother."

It took a minute for the words to sink in. Then, Fernando quickly shuffled around the desk and threw open his fogged-glass door. Tiburcio stood there in disguise. He wore a dirty poncho, tattered sombrero, badly scuffed boots, thick whiskers on his cheeks and above his lips, but there was no mistaking that he was standing there in the flesh.

"Get in here!" Fernando barked.

Rushing his secretary out, he told her to not disturb them.

"What the hell are you doing here? What gumption! I ought to go get the sheriff right now, you son-of-a-bitch. I don't see a brother. I see a murderer. A thief. A disgrace to our family!"

"Mother gave me her blessing when I set out to change society. Who gave you a blessing to help the gringos take over our land?"

"Blessing? Did she give you her blessing to miss her last rites and funeral. I know she did not give you a blessing to leave her to die while you went about pillaging innocent people. Could you not have stayed by her side when you saw her dying in bed, Tiburcio?"

Tiburcio flinched in red anger, resentment and shame.

"What? Are you going to draw that gun you have under that despicable poncho and shoot me dead?"

"I came to ask for help."

"To hide? No!"

"I need money."

"I will not fund terror."

"I'm sorry, it was a mistake to come," Tiburcio said quietly.

He turned and walked three steps to the door.

"Wait!"

Tiburcio looked over his shoulder.

"I will give you the money - if you promise to leave this country. I will give you enough money to go to Mexico and spend the rest of your life there. Never return. I will gladly pay for that, something that will save lives, even if one of them is yours."

"I am not leaving my home."

"You are going to be killed here, Tiburcio. There are not that many places left for you to hide. I do not want to see you ever again, but I do not want to see you hung, either. Take the money on this condition!"

"And if you want to survive, Fernando," Tiburcio said as he opened the door, "get the hell out of my way when I come riding into town with an army behind me."

Chapter 15: Captured (2)
April 1874
Los Angeles

The hunt had gone on for sixty days, much longer than anyone had intended. Sheriff Morse's posse was exhausted, frustrated, disappointed. And most of its members had urgent business calling them home. They had falsely chased one last hope. An old mountaineer informed them that Vasquez was staying four miles into Soledad Canyon. The posse left Falville back at the wagon with most of their accoutrements and charged up the long, twisting canyon trails. They spotted the house described by the old man and quickly surrounded it. The occupant gave up much too easily to be the ferocious bandit. It turned out to be an old hunter of Irish descent. The end of the pursuit was near.

When the posse returned to the wagon, Morse informed them that it was time to end their southern expedition. Unfamiliar with the terrain and hampered by false information, they had been unable to locate with any precision the bandit's hideout. Hell, Morse thought to himself, Rowland cannot even find Vasquez on his own territory.

"We will ride slowly back north, checking Vasquez's old haunts one last time," Morse said to the posse. "Perhaps we will come across his trail along the way. If not, I will begin organizing another manhunt. I would like you all to join me again."

The posse left Soledad on April 26 and reached Fort Tejon the next day. Morse estimated it would take two days to prepare for the long journey home. On the day they were going to depart, he was abruptly awakened by his son George at his bunkhouse door.

"Yes, George, what is so urgent?"

"A man and his daughter are here and would like to talk to you. They have been following our progress in the newspapers and have urgent information."

The man, his face leathery, and the woman, dark and exotic, were sitting in the telegraph operator's office. He greeted them perfunctorily. Then the hammer fell.

"We know where Tiburcio Vasquez is holed up," said the man.

Sixty-one days in the saddle from sunrise to sunset and nothing, Morse thought. Now, this odd pair appears out of thin air and breaks the case. He was skeptical.

"Do not lie to me! I am in a foul mood, and if you are wasting my time I will find some charge to pin on you that will have you cooling in a county jail for two years!" Morse burst out.

"My name is George Caralambo, now George Allen, but everyone in Los Angeles knows me as Greek George," he said undauntedly. "I own a small adobe south of Soledad Canyon and northeast of Los Angeles. That is where you'll find Tiburcio Vasquez."

"And you live there?"

"Yes. My daughter and I."

Morse rubbed his forehead and pressed his tired eyes with the palms of his hands.

"Why do you want to betray the bandit? So badly that you have come all the way up here to deliver me the news?"

"I heard the reward for his capture, alive, has been raised to eight thousand dollars. The risk seems to be worth it. The bandit owes me one thousand dollars for rent. Even if he tripled what he owes me, I stand to make a much tidier profit by turning him in."

"Who are you?" Morse asked the woman.

"I am Georgina, his daughter."

"I bet I can guess why *you* want to turn in Tiburcio Vasquez?"

"It's not for the money," Georgina agreed.

"He has not always treated women well, despite his reputation," Morse said, then turned back to Greek George: "Why didn't you go to Sheriff Rowland with this information?"

"Vasquez's men are always watching Rowland. I would be killed by them before the bandit was captured."

"How many men are staying with him?"

"Three at my house but he has dozens in the immediate area and I hear he has hundreds near the border waiting for the revolution."

"Just three?"

"One is expected to return soon with his ... Tiburcio's ... lover."

Morse looked at Georgina, who avoided his eyes.

After about an hour of interrogation, Morse watched the father and daughter ride down the pass in their wood wagon. Then he summoned his son, George.

"Do you think the information is reliable?" George asked.

"Yes. But here is my dilemma. If I were sheriff of Los Angeles County, I would not like to have an officer from six hundred miles away snatch the most-wanted bandit in the state from under my nose. Besides, it would be nearly impossible to turn around this entire party and go back down there without our presence being known to everyone."

"What will you do? Telegraph Rowland?"

"What would you do?"

"I would board the evening stage for Los Angeles and arrange to meet Rowland somewhere safe. I would insist on joining the party that will apprehend Vasquez in exchange for the information. If you must let Rowland in on this, you deserve to be there."

"That is exactly what I was thinking."

Morse arranged for his posse to wait at Tejon while he met with Rowland. He decided to only take Henderson along.

"What do you say, Boyd? It will be the story of the century," he told the *Chronicle* reporter.

They arrived at the Los Angeles Real Estate Agency and sent word for Rowland to meet them there. The sheriff, surprised that Morse was still in town, quickly showed up. Morse shared the information with Rowland and suggested they put together a small party of no more than four lawmen - himself included - to ride to Greek George's house and make the arrest.

"I have explicit directions to the house," Morse concluded. "We can pounce on him before he knows what's going on."

A small, condescending smile crept onto Rowland's face. He shook his head in disappointment.

"The information is a sell, sheriff," he said. "You've been duped. I know Greek George very well. He is a cheat and a liar. On top of that, he is crazy. *Muy loco.* He tried to make a fortune in dromedaries, if that tells you anything. I don't know who signed the papers letting him into the United States from Cyprus, but they ought to be hung, because the man is nuts. I am quite confident he knows nothing about Vasquez and I will not waste my time on false leads!"

"Why would he ride one hundred miles to Tejon to tell me lies? And he sounded very convincing. He gave me details nobody could fabricate on his own."

"I don't know, sheriff," Rowland replied sternly. "Probably because he knew I wouldn't listen to him. Maybe he just wants to try to get the reward money. It doesn't matter. Greek George cannot be telling you the truth because I know where Tiburcio Vasquez is hiding and I plan on getting him myself."

"I must join you. I have the authority of the state, the weight of the governor's office, behind me for the capture of Tiburcio Vasquez and for bringing him to justice."

"This is my jurisdiction, Harry. If the governor wants to come down here and tell me how to run my office, then that's one thing. But until he does, you need to get the hell out of Los Angeles before I charge you with obstruction of justice."

"I have authority vested in me by the state! I demand to accompany you to arrest Tiburcio Vasquez! That is, if you even know where he his."

"My patience is being strained," Rowland barked. "I am the authority over every square inch of Los Angeles County, and I have allowed enough northern posses down here for one bandit. Every one of your missteps - and I have calculated many - has made my job of capturing this outlaw more and more difficult. I will not allow any more intrusion from northern lawmen. You can take my words back to the governor. You have acted professionally in bringing me this information, however erroneous. Now, act professionally in letting me conduct business in the way I was elected to do, and go home, Harry. Go home!"

Morse sighed heavily. He was at the end of the road.

"I know you have many friends and contacts in the Californio community," he said, standing up to leave. "If anyone knows which informants are reliable and which are not, it's you. If you think Greek George is lying and you have more reliable information on Vasquez's whereabouts, I trust your judgment. I just didn't want any stones to go unturned."

"And none will be. We know where Tiburcio Vasquez is. I will telegraph you in Oakland when we catch the son of a bitch. Thank you for understanding, Harry."

Morse considered whether to tell Rowland what he knew about his Vasquez's rebellion, but in the end he did not. On April 30, he departed Fort Tejon for home.

Rowland wasted no time in preparing to capture the bandit. He kept the information Morse had shared secret until he could learn more and verify it on his own. He quietly sent for one of his most-trusted friends, a farmer named David Smith.

"I called you in, David, because I know you will be tight-lipped about this," the sheriff explained. "You are familiar with the general area around Greek George's property, right? I need you to locate exactly where his adobe is. There is word that Tiburcio Vasquez might be holed up there. Reconnoiter the premises and find out if he is there and, if so, how many of his soldiers we might have to contend with. I want to know their strength in numbers, what they do up there, their comings and goings and anything else you might see."

Two days later, Smith returned to Rowland's office.

"Once you get through the rough terrain, you can only approach Greek George's house from a single road, but I crept up on a bluff about a half-mile away and got a good look. Three men on fine horses came and went while I was watching. From the pictures I've seen of him, it's Vasquez, and a couple of his gang. Anyway, you won't have to battle any more than three outlaws, if you choose to do so. There are some ranch hands who help Greek George around the stables and such, but I don't think they are a problem or that they even know who is staying at the house. There is a lake and some trees below, near the road leading past the house. It appears the only spot that is hidden from view of the house."

By the second week of May, Rowland was ready to act. Relying mostly on close friends rather than his regular deputies, he spoke to each man separately so no rumors spread through the town. Smith quickly agreed to accompany his pal. They were joined by Detective Emil Harris, Los Angeles Police Chief Billy Hartley, Constable Sam Bryant, saloon owner Walter Rogers, Undersheriff Albert Johnson and attorney and special deputy Henry Mitchell. Finally, he invited George A. Beers, a reporter who had given him and his causes positive press.

On May 13, the eight-man force quietly met at Mitchell's law offices. Rowland explained that he could not go with the group up to Nicholas Canyon, where Greek George's house sat. Continually in the shadow of Vasquez's spies, who seemingly were watching every saloon, store, stable and corral in Los Angeles, the bandit would certainly know if the sheriff left the city, he told them.

"I will be a decoy," he said. "I will make myself visible around town. More than usual."

He told them that Undersheriff Johnson would be in charge of the actual raid.

"Let me be frank," Rowland told the party. "I want the entire gang captured alive."

Rowland next addressed weapons and ammunition.

"I'll have all the Henry rifles, revolvers, shotguns and Bowie knives, whatever your preference of weapon is, boxed up and stashed at Jones' Stable to be picked up en route to the hideout. The arms will be waiting for you when you set out tomorrow evening."

Then Rowland broached the subject of transportation.

"To keep this operation secret, I have assigned each of you different routes, times and stables to pick up your horses. Once you get your horse, meet at the corral near the arms cache. A couple hours after midnight, you will ride out together to Nicholas Canyon. Wait there for daylight before approaching the premise."

"How do we approach the house?"

Rowland gave a droll smile.

"Honestly, I do not know. That is up to Johnson. I fully trust he will devise some great strategy."

The posse waited for dawn at a lake area off the main road to Greek George's house. They were hidden in willow and thicket about a mile and a half from his front door. The morning fog rose so thick that they could not see the rising sun. Johnson, Mitchell and Smith, who knew the area better than anyone in the posse, hiked a half mile up the mountain side, then crawled on their bellies to the bluff where they could get a good view of the house - if it weren't for the heavy brume. Mitchell's field glasses were useless.

Before noon, the fog thinned and in the haze the soft shape of the Greek George's L-shaped adobe could be distinguished in the distance. Mitchell again trained the field glasses on the house. He saw a man step out of the house into his view and throw a saddle over a white horse.

"Is it Vasquez?" Johnson asked.

"There's still too much mist. I cannot tell for sure."

"He's going to ride down the road," Johnson said. "Let's alert the others. Smith, stay here and let us know if any others leave."

Johnson and Mitchell ran and slipped and slid down the mountain. When they reached the bivouac, there was a commotion going on. Two Mexican laborers in a four-horse wagon were being held at gunpoint by Constable Bryant and Police Chief Hartley. The wagon had come around the turn and caught the lawmen by surprise. Bryant and Hartley drew guns first and demanded the driver to stop. That's when Johnson and Mitchell came running up.

"Mitchell, take Rogers and get that rider who will be coming down the road."

As they galloped off, Johnson turned his attention to the men in the wagon.

"Where are you going?" Hartley asked the pair on the wagon, but they just sat in silence on edge of the spring seat in the shade of the canyon. "We are not going to harm you. Simply tell us what your business is and we will let you proceed."

The Mexicans still did not speak.

Bryant, who spoke Spanish fluently, repeated the demand in their language.

"We are going to get a load of firewood," the driver told him, relieved to finally be communicating clearly. "We come up this road every day to get firewood. We never come across a living soul. What do you want?"

"OK, just wait here for a minute," Bryant said.

Rogers came loping back from up the road.

"That was Greek George who left the house," he said, glancing frequently at the men in the wagon. "He said Vasquez, Corona and his daughter are still up there. There's a stable boy and a couple ranch hands, too, but they are not involved with the bandits. He said Vasquez was still sleeping when he departed."

"Where is Mitchell?"

"He's detaining Greek George just a quarter mile up the road, out of sight," Rogers said, again looking curiously at the wagon.

"We know who is up there but it's still too risky to attack," Johnson said. "One glance out the window and they'll see us approaching. But I think I know how we can get up there without being seen."

He walked over to the wagon and ran his hands along the high sideboards, closely examining the cart's boxed bed.

The others looked at him quizzically.

"How long is this wagon? Eight feet?" Johnson asked. "These side panels go up about three feet, eh? And it's empty."

"Yes, it's brilliant," Hartley said, realizing Johnson's plan.

A few minutes later, Johnson, Hartley, Harris, Bryant, Rogers and Beers climbed into the boxed bed of the wagon and lay down. They were packed tightly shoulder to shoulder so no parts of their bodies or any weapons could be seen. Bryant gave the Mexicans the order to drive right up to Greek George's adobe.

"If you give the bandit the slightest signal that something is awry," Bryant hissed, training a sawed-off shotgun at the driver, "I'll riddle you with lead."

Lying on their backs, the wagon took Rowland's men up the mountain road until the house was visible, then veered down a small hill toward the adobe.

Inside the adobe, Tiburcio Vasquez could not believe how well and how long he had slept. Greek George's conversation with the stable boy had awakened him, but he stayed under the covers until he heard the horse's hooves clap away. He stepped out of his bedroom with his Henry rifle in one hand and his belt and revolvers in the other and looked around the house. He stared for a while out the front door, which was open, watching the last of the cool mist drifting away. Bluejays were warbling outside and the sweet smell of fennel and jasmine wafted up to the doorway and into the house. It was going to be another warm day, and he smiled.

Yesterday, he received a letter from Chavez with wonderful news. Anita insisted on giving money to the revolution for the arms and would not hand over the gold until Chavez agreed to allow her to come to Agua Dulce and talk to Tiburcio face to face about how she had come to her decision, and what the future might hold for him and her and Rodolfo.

Chavez included in his letter details about when he would likely reach Agua Dulce and when he would meet Anita at the train station and escort her to the hideout.

"Leave at once!" he pleaded with Tiburcio. "I conclude this letter with Anita's words that when she sees you again 'it will be the happiest day of my life.'"

Georgina broke Tiburcio's pleasant daydream. She called tersely from the kitchen that she had breakfast ready and asked him to come to the table.

"Where is Lebrado?" Tiburcio asked, still looking out the door.

Georgina did not answer. She rarely talked to him anymore. Her manner and speech was curt. He didn't mind, though. It wouldn't be long before he departed.

He saw a wood wagon creaking its way up the road. Nothing unusual, he thought. He recognized the wagon and was familiar with the team of horses. He saw that he knew the driver and his companion from their daily trips to the woods. They would occasionally stop at the house to rest and talk. Tiburcio turned back inside, propped the rifle against the wall and slung his gun belt on a hook. He walked over to the table and sat down with his back to the door. The wagon pulled onto the road leading to the house.

Georgina silently placed the plate of eggs, ham and bread in front of him.

"Thank you. Invite the men in when they get here," he told her.

TIBURCIO!

Vasquez heard Corona's boots bang up the back porch and his companion entered. They nodded to each other as Corona took a seat.

"It shouldn't be long before Chavez returns," Corona said.

"No. The time is near. He is en route to Agua Dulce now."

Outside, the wagon stopped and Johnson cautiously peered over the sideboard. Opposite of the house, he saw fields of mustard and an enormous white horse picketed and feeding. The palomino was saddled and a rifle rested in a scabbard behind the saddle. Then he glanced quickly over at the house and saw the back of a man sitting at a table.

"Beers to the west, back door, Smith to the north, and Hartley up to the stables. Bryant, Rogers, Harris come with me," the undersheriff commanded. "Act quickly and according to your conscience!"

Hartley sprinted for the stables near a small lake while Beers positioned himself at a back door on the west side of the house. Johnson and his three men piled out and crept within ten feet of the open front door when suddenly a woman inside let out an ear-splitting scream. Vasquez leaped to his feet, his chair crashing to the ground.

"Bar the door!" he shouted. He looked desperately at his guns lying out of his reach.

Georgina slammed the door with two hands, but Harris was quick enough to stick the muzzle of his rifle into the opening and pry it back open. The lawmen surged into the house. Bryant caught a flash of Vasquez darting around a corner and fired. The shots missed and the bandit vanished down the hallway.

Corona, uncertain where to run, found himself paralyzed in his seat staring directly into Johnson's Henry rifle. He threw up both hands.

"Don't shoot! Don't shoot!" Corona cried.

Vasquez sped down the hall toward a small, open window ten paces away. He could see his horse and rifle outside. He dived through the small opening, rolled on his shoulder and popped up like a tiger, ready to dash to his horse and gun. Beers came around the corner just as Tiburcio sprang to his feet and discharged both barrels of his shotgun. The buckshot spun the bandit around. Harris, who had followed the agile bandit chief down the hall, stood at the window, rifle ready. When Vasquez whipped around, he unloaded a musket ball into him.

Vasquez crumbled to the ground, bleeding from holes in his left arm, leg and shoulder. The musket ball had sailed clear through near his pelvic bone. Beers dropped his shotgun in the grass and stood over the bandit. Harris awkwardly fell to the ground from the window ledge. Johnson, Rogers and Hartley came around the corner of the house. They bent close to Vasquez and checked his vital signs. His eyes were closed and his breath belabored.

"Grab that sheepskin hanging on the fence," Johnson told Smith.

The lawmen carefully supported Vasquez while he was placed on top of the skin.

"Get some linen so we can dress his wounds," Johnson called to Georgina, who was sobbing hysterically, having set the horrible events in motion. "Hurry!"

She frantically darted around the house but could find none. Beers joined her search and they finally settled on ripping up bed sheets into long strips. When they brought out the torn cloth, Vasquez had his eyes opened. He gave a little grin.

"Oh, yes," he said weakly. "Remember, you boys do a good job dressing my wounds and nurse me real careful and you get eight thousand dollars. If you let me die, you only get six thousand dollars. That's an extra two thousand dollars for being kind."

The lawmen chuckled nervously, the humor melting some of the captors' sternness. Vasquez smiled back.

"It's my fault," he confessed. "I don't blame you boys. I was a damned imbecile to run. And you were damned lucky. Another ten minutes and I'd have had my guns on me."

TIBURCIO!

Beers and Georgina started rolling the ripped sheets into bandages. Johnson tore away Vasquez's blood-soaked shirt from his chest and left side. Vasquez saw their eyes look down at the heart charm on a silk ribbon around his neck.

"Please, don't remove it."

Johnson nodded. He was more concerned with the condition of the prisoner, who he believed wouldn't live. Vasquez was badly bleeding and seemed to be growing weaker.

In the meantime, Rogers and Hartley scoured the house and found a stolen gold watch, some silver and gold coins, four rifles, seven revolvers and four hundred rounds of ammunition. Then they went to Greek George's barn and hooked up two mules and a spring wagon and drove it over to where Tiburcio lay.

"Think you can make it eight miles in that wagon?" Johnson asked the bandit. "We'll put a mattress down in the back and take it slow so it's not such a jarring ride."

"Give me a few minutes," Tiburcio answered.

When he was ready, they carefully lifted Vasquez onto the wagon. Next to him sat Lebrado Corona, whose hands and feet were tied with rope. Johnson took the lines, Smith sat next to him and Bryant, Rogers and Hartley guarded the prisoners. Beers and Harris convoyed on horses. Mitchell soon caught up to the cavalcade and congratulated the rest of the men. The wagon and riders entered Los Angeles, where rumors of Vasquez's capture were already shaking the city with excitement.

Chapter 16: Jailed (3)
Los Angeles County
May 1874

Sheriff Rowland walked up to Tiburcio's cell, picked up a tin cup sitting on the ground and rapped it against the metal bars.

"Get up, Tiburcio," Rowland said. "You got more visitors."

"I'm talked out, sheriff," the prisoner said without stirring. "Maybe tomorrow."

"You might be gone tomorrow. Once Dr. Widney says you are healthy enough to travel by ship, you're going up north to face trial for the Tres Pinos murders."

Rowland didn't wait for the prisoner's response.

"This visitor isn't a reporter or an editor or a doctor," Rowland said.

Tiburcio sat upright. He saw a tall stranger in a fine suit waiting at the bars.

"My name is Tully," the visitor said. "I am going to be your lawyer."

Rowland left Deputy Schilling with the prisoner and his counsel and departed to soak in the attention outside.

"Rowland made me wait a long time, but finally he has allowed me to see my client," Tully explained. "I'm sorry for the delay."

"Mr. Tully, I have no money for a private attorney."

"I'm not just another lawyer trying to get a finger in the pie, Mr. Vasquez," Tully said. "My services are fully paid for. Knox and Morrison put an advertisement in the newspapers soliciting representation. I answered, and out of a dozen lawyers interviewed - most of them charlatans - I got the job."

Tiburcio smiled but shook his head in disbelief.

"You think I got a chance, then?"

"Yeah. You got a chance," Tully said.

The attorney glanced at Schilling with raised eyebrows.

"May we have a little privacy?" he asked.

Schilling shrugged his shoulders and walked over to his chair where he was out of the range of a whisper. He picked up a newspaper to read.

Tully held through the bars a small poster card celebrating Tiburcio's capture in words and images.

"This has been circulating among the throngs outside the jailhouse," Tully explained.

Tiburcio slowly walked over to examine the card. Rowland's picture was at the top and photographs of the rest of the posse were placed in a circle around an image of the house where Tiburcio was captured. The bandit's photo was seen at the bottom of the poster.

"I wanted you to see it," Tully said. "Everybody is trying to make a buck off you. They are selling this postcard for two bits. It's a circus out there, Mr. Vasquez. Anything can happen when there's a circus."

They heard two sets of footsteps coming down the corridor and Rowland reappeared with a delivery boy holding two bouquets of flowers.

"Delivery for Tiburcio Vasquez," Rowland announced, drawing his revolver. "Schilling, open the cell door."

The delivery boy looked for a place to set the flowers. Around the cell were a dozen other bouquets, scores of handwritten notes and stacks of photographs of women.

"The public must be pleased you are treating your prisoner so well," Tully mordantly remarked to Rowland, as the delivery boy set the flowers next to Tiburcio's bed.

"We are not barbarians, Mr. Tully. We understand the great interest and curiosity surrounding our colorful convict. If the public wishes to send the prisoner flowers and notions, I will not stand in the way. However, we did confiscate the gifts of wine. Gotta draw the line somewhere."

The deputy shut the cell door with a loud, echoing clang and they listened to Rowland's boot steps fade away down the hall as he showed the boy out. Tully motioned to Tiburcio to lean in closer to the bars and began where he had left off.

"As I was saying, anything can happen. I don't think Rowland will give us much time, so let me make clear what you need to be telling these lawmen, the reporters and anyone else you talk to. Our stories must match. In short, what I am telling you, Tiburcio, amounts to our defense. First, nobody can place you at Tres Pinos at the time of the murders. Nobody with any certainty, that is. That's a fact. The only ones who can with any confidence are Snyder and his wife - and they refuse to testify and have left the state. We cannot find them. And if we can't, the prosecutors can't. Second, by all accounts, you told your men not to use any violence at Tres Pinos. Unfortunately, they did not heed your words, and since you did not show up on the streets of that town until after the killings, you did not commit murder and are therefore innocent. Any citizen in Tres Pinos who has even a hunch that they saw you carry out the robbery and the murders cannot identify, with conviction, that you fired the shots. That's a fact. Besides, Leiva, Corona and Moreno have all sworn that you ordered your gang not to shed any blood. So that makes you merely the leader of a gang of outlaws that was caught in a situation that spun desperately out of control.

"When you finally reached Tres Pinos to provide leadership to your men you were told that three people were dead. Three people who were murdered before you got there. Who shot these unfortunate citizens? Leiva and Gonzales and Romero. That is a major point in our argument and we will not back away from it.

"Lastly, we plan to go for the juror's sympathy. After we are finished with our arguments, everybody in the courtroom and beyond will know that your criminal career grew out of certain circumstances that few white people could ever begin to understand. You and thousands of other Californios have been cheated and wronged over the past twenty-five years. More than two decades! Your land stolen, your livelihood crushed, your wives and children abused and denied rights. And because you were burdened with great charisma, you were chosen to lead the fight. But, we will emphasize to the jury that being a hero to your people and a source of inspiration to the downtrodden is not a crime. Not in this country."

"You've been working hard on my behalf," Tiburcio said.

"I am just doing my job. There are many hundreds of followers willing to risk their lives to free you. I know that, Tiburcio. As your lawyer, my first interest is to get you out of jail by any legal means that I have at my disposal. However, in the course of my work, I have become privy to a movement afoot to release you from captivity. Although I cannot professionally condone such actions, I want you to know that I am also knowledgeable of a brewing rebellion. I do not have the details, nor do I necessarily want them. But a man whom you have placed in high regard, and a trusted lieutenant in your, uh, army, has put together a plan to rescue you from jail. He is working to convey that information to you in captivity."

Rowland came striding back to the cell.

"Time is up, Tully!"

"One minute more, please."

Rowland looked at his timepiece and reluctantly nodded. Tully gave him a meddlesome glance until the sheriff took a few steps out of earshot.

"When you are given this information, through some secret visitor or a clandestinely delivered note or whatever, I don't want to know the details. But I do need to know some things. First and foremost, have you spoken to a woman named Anita since you have been jailed?" Tully whispered.

The bandit grabbed the lawyer's lapels through the bars.

"Where is she? Is she here? Is she outside?" he insisted.

Rowland glared at the two men.

"No. Answer me!" Tully said urgently, trying to keep his voice at a whisper. "Did you have a conversation with her about any plans regarding the revolution and what might happen if you are captured or killed?"

"I did not."

"Whoever did, could they be using her as part of those plans?"

"I don't know."

Rowland began walking toward them.

"Let's keep her name out of our conversations so the prosecutors don't get to her. We cannot let anyone get to her."

"Time's up!" Rowland barked.

"Tiburcio," Tully whispered. "The next time I will see you is up in San Francisco after you are transferred there for trial. Don't worry needlessly. We will talk more up there."

Chapter 17: Transferred
Santa Clara County
May 23, 1874

Tiburcio's legs were shackled in iron and he was handcuffed to Undersheriff Johnson. They shuffled down the dim corridor to the exit, where the heavy jailhouse door creaked open and the lawman and bandit squinted into the bright daylight. At the end of the steps leading down from the building, six deputies guarded a six-horse wagon. A crowd of two hundred people stretched in a horseshoe shape down the sides of the steps and behind the wagon. Two dozen deputies kept the bystanders a short distance away.

Tiburcio heard a smattering of applause as he started to walk down the steps, but he was uncertain whether they were cheering his capture or his cause. He scanned their faces, looking for a familiar person. About a third of the people appeared to be of Mexican descent, another third women, some crying, others holding flowers, a few clutching babies in bonnets. He saw nobody he knew, beyond the reporters who had interviewed him in his cell.

From the jailhouse, Tiburcio was taken to the San Pedro dock. Mitchell and Rogers escorted the prisoner from the wharf onto the steamer Senator, and for two nights and a day, they never let him out of their sight or even unshackled him. When the steamer arrived in San Francisco, they saw that the circus had moved up there. Bulging forward against the arms of dozens of deputies, a lionizing crowd frantically tried to see the captured villain. Tiburcio walked with his head held high, appearing to enjoy the attention.

Among those waiting on the dock to get a look at Tiburcio Vasquez was Harry N. Morse. Calm among the sea of eager faces, Morse stood afar quietly watching Rowland's men hand Tiburcio over to Sheriff Adams. Morse interpreted Tiburcio's smug appearance as a sign that he knew his time was not up, that one last, great stratagem had yet to play out. Then, unseen, he turned away. Let them put on their little show.

Morse would never forget the moment he first read the news of Tiburcio's capture. It was well before he reached home from his fruitless twenty-seven-hundred-mile pursuit. Newspaper frozen in hand, he stood stunned as he realized he had been double-crossed by Rowland, cheated out of the reward money, the fame and two months of his life. His first instinct was to ride south again and knock Rowland to the ground with his fists for lying to him. But his days of settling disputes by fisticuffs were over. Besides, he didn't have the time.

Instead, with his son George in the saddle next to him, Morse trotted out the remaining miles contemplating the gravity of the arrest and its aftermath. In the newspapers and in saloons, rumors about a secret rebellion persisted. There were stories about other henchmen in Tiburcio's company who were still at large, most notably Clodoveo Chavez on whose head the governor had now placed a large reward. Hearing these accounts, Morse quickly realized that in his myopic pursuit of Tiburcio he had not taken the time to interrogate the bandit's closest associates. These associates were easily available. Corona, Moreno, Leiva were biding their time in jail. Rosaria and Margarita were home alone, contemplating their own unwise choices. Perhaps it wasn't too late, Morse thought.

"George," he said to his son as he lay wide awake on his hotel bed in Hollister, fewer than one hundred miles from home. "We need to delay our journey home. I want you to leave here on the first train in the morning and return to Los Angeles."

"Sure. Why?"

"First, I need you to be my eyes and ears in that mob outside Tiburcio's jail cell. People will be talking. Next, get in to the jail and speak to Corona. He was placed in a separate cell from Vasquez and has kind of been lost in all the attention swirling around the leader. You should get easy access."

"What are we trying to find out?"

"Anything. Everything. Is there a revolution brewing? How many men does Vasquez actually command? Are there plans to break him out of jail? Where is Chavez?"

"And then what?"

"Go find where Rosaria is living and talk to her. Once you get her started, information about Tiburcio and his gang should come gushing forth. I'll have Borein interrogate Leiva in Salinas and I'll go up to San Quentin and visit Moreno and some others."

Morse stared up at the ceiling as if trying to recall someone or something he was forgetting. Then, he bolted upright.

"Oh, and find Greek George's house and talk one more time to his daughter. She may have learned something between the time we saw her at Tejon and when Vasquez was captured."

After George's train pulled out of the station, Morse returned to his hotel room to complete another task that he had not finished. He penned a cathartic letter to editors throughout the state praising and congratulating Rowland and Gov. Booth for their skilled hand in capturing Vasquez. It was time to put the circumstances of the arrest and his individual feelings behind him.

A few weeks later, a nattily-dressed Morse was on the dock watching the prisoner disembark. Later, he was ushered into Tiburcio's cell in San Jose. Morse was clean-shaven and wore a bowler hat cocked jauntily to one side and a gray suit with a vest and a gold watch chain. Behind bars, Tiburcio, equally as fashionable in clothes Tully had shipped from San Francisco, smiled at the sheriff as if he were a brother coming to visit.

When two ambitious men's lives get tangled in one another's affairs, there simply isn't enough good luck to go around. Something must give way. Someone must come up on the wrong side of luck. Would it be Morse or himself whose good fortune would end? That's what Tiburcio was thinking when the rangy sheriff entered the jailhouse.

"Your visit amuses me, sheriff," Tiburcio said, playfully stroking his goatee as if he were thinking serious thoughts. "Did you come here to get the satisfaction of seeing me locked up? I bet you couldn't rest until you saw for yourself that I was behind solid iron bars. *Si*? Well, here I am! The Great Lover-Bandit at your mercy!"

"Rowland and his gang got to you first," the cocksure Morse answered, taking a few steps closer to the cell. "Surprising, isn't it, how that happened?"

"With all the gringos who wanted me dead or alive, you end up being double-crossed by one of your own," Tiburcio answered. "Rowland ends up with the fame and the eight thousand dollars. My capture surely would have been your crowning accomplishment. After you got to Redondo and Soto, your fame was beginning to rival my own, sheriff. Everything was set up for a showdown between us, good and evil. I guess Rowland got us both on that one. Still, your young life has been legendary enough, even if you lost out on the reward money and the glory. But tell me, how do *you* think Rowland's company apprehended me, and not you?"

"If you believe the newspapers, you knew every one of my movements," Morse replied. "They say you flitted around my camp at night without me so much as suspecting it. I don't care about the money or the legacy, Tiburcio. I want to know the truth. Did you really know my every move?"

"I assure you, sheriff, that's Rowland getting his two cents into the newspapers. I did not say anything to cause you shame in those interviews. These reporters write whatever they want. Some write whatever Rowland wants. The fact is, I thought you and your posse were still lurking in the hills so I stayed put at Greek George's a while longer - a little too long as it turned out. I was just as surprised that Rowland's men showed up at my house as you were. I definitely knew his whereabouts. So I was not expecting visitors when they arrested me – or I assure you the final outcome would have been different."

Morse looked around the jail cell. Once again, the cell was not gray and lifeless. There were flower bouquets, chocolate candies, envelopes both opened and unopened, and many pictures of women, a few of them indecent with notes attached. Morse looked over at three dozen red roses in the corner of the cell, bright against the colorless limestone. Tiburcio's eyes followed.

"An admirer?"

"A genteel lady concerned that I receive humane treatment. I don't know her. I didn't spend much time in those circles."

Morse's eyes then fell on the postcard leaning against a pitcher of water on a table.

"Let me see that card," Morse said.

Tiburcio handed it through the bars. He examined the postcard celebrating Tiburcio's capture with Rowland's picture at the top and photographs of the rest of his posse. He looked at Vasquez's photo at the bottom of the poster. His own picture, of course, was omitted.

"And this postcard?" Morse asked, tapping it in the palm of his hand. "A keepsake?"

"They were being circulated outside my cell in Los Angeles, before I was transferred up here. People kept asking me to sign them. Someone said it was to raise money for my legal fund, but that's not true. I imagine somebody just wanted to make some money."

Silence followed. Then whooping and hollering could be heard from outside the jail where a crowd of several dozen had lingered ever since the capture.

Morse smiled amusedly.

"Even up here, they keep coming, every day hoping to get a glimpse of you. Adams has more deputies out there controlling the crowd than there are law officers in all of

Northern California. Still, it doesn't have the feel of a lynch mob, though."

"What a relief."

"Just some curious folks, I guess. And a couple dozen Mexicans who think you're a hero. Up here, however, close to the friends and family of the murdered, I think the overarching sentiment toward you and your cause is anger."

Morse pulled a low, three-legged stool close to the bars and sat with both feet firmly planted on the ground.

"Let me get down to business, Tiburcio," Morse said, leaning forward in conspiratorial fashion. "I have a witness who can place you near the Tres Pinos scene at the time of the killings."

"Impossible!" Tiburcio exclaimed.

"Tell me, did you ask a traveler for the time just outside Tres Pinos?"

"I'll only tell you this: I am innocent of killing anyone since I was born. Certainly, you don't expect me to answer your questions without my lawyer present."

"We just need one person to put you at the scene to get a conviction and a hanging."

"Even if you could, nobody saw me shoot anyone."

Morse laughed.

He felt no animosity between himself and the bandit. Their backgrounds were different, but Morse felt they were similar in more ways than not.

"You know, we're the same age, Tiburcio. We were born on opposite coasts. Me, a descendant of New England puritans. You, a descendant of great Mexican and Spanish explorers. You could break mustangs and ride with the best vaqueros in the state by the age of ten. I chose the adventures of the sea, and arrived in California on a tall windjammer at age fourteen. I know you used to watch those trading ships come into Monterey, bringing fine clothing in exchange for cowhides. Perhaps you even set eyes on my ship.

"Funny thing is," Morse continued, "the gold invasion changed both our lives. I left a career as a seaman and tried my luck at mining. I had some mediocre success. Then I pursued some business ventures, as you did with your fandango. We were both young businessmen. That's when circumstances sent us in different directions, Tiburcio. I organized the Oakland Guard in support of the Union, then became a sheriff. You shot a constable, and became an outlaw."

"You are saying we are not so different?" Tiburcio replied.

He felt the familiar feeling of hatred for all white anglos surge into his heart but his face and its expression did not change.

Morse nodded.

"So, how the hell did we end up like this?" the sheriff asked. "You, at the end of your rope, and me, a long, free, lucrative life still ahead?"

"The end of my rope, you say sheriff?" Tiburcio stonily answered. "*El revolucion* has not yet even begun. I have entire regiments in the hills from here to Ukiah. They are armed to the teeth and prepared to take back the land. The capture of me, *el capitan* , doesn't extinguish the deadly fire burning in their guts, fueled by over twenty years of oppression. You only bought yourselves a little time by capturing me alive. When the rebels come swarming out of the hills and rip apart the thin foundation of your society, there will be hell and more to pay. You won't know when they will rise up – but the time is approaching. You can be sure."

"Perhaps after you are lynched?" Morse interrupted.

"Then I will not have died in vain!"

Morse stood up as if he were ready to leave.

"Will you stay for a minute more, sheriff?" Tiburcio asked. "I'm enjoying our talk."

"No, I must catch a train. I have to find somebody. It's very important that I talk to her."

Tiburcio bristled.

"Who?"

"Anita Garza."

"What the hell for? She is innocent!"

Morse pulled a folded letter out of his pocket.

"Her words would suggest she is anything but innocent. She appears to be very much involved in your revolution, and perhaps plans for your escape as well."

"Where did you find that?"

"My son returned to the house where you were captured. It had been left behind in the search. Greek George's daughter had it in her possession."

More self-possessed now, Tiburcio looked directly into Morse's eyes.

"You will not find Anita until it's too late!"

Chapter 18: Rebellion
Agua Dulce
July 1874

Clodoveo Chavez looked over the motley band of men shaded from the harsh desert sun by jagged outcrops. In two fists held over his head, he waved wads of paper money. A guttural huzzah rose up and echoed throughout the stony canyons.

"This money is ours to pay for our great liberation!" Chavez roared and was greeted with another throaty cheer. "First, our leader's freedom! Then, our entire homeland!"

Anita peered out of the opening in her tent and heard the yelling. She heard Chavez's voice and thought about Tiburcio. It was supposed to be his voice. He was supposed to be here with her. That was the agreement. She felt an inexplicable emptiness like she had felt after their elopement, when her father told her Tiburcio had abandoned her and would never return. Again, he was gone and she was left confused.

"Do not look upon Tiburcio's capture as defeat," Chavez shouted. "Those waiting outside his jail cell report that he is alive and well and more determined than ever to reverse the course of our stolen country. In a short time, we will send word to our jailed leader about our plan to liberate him from his prison. Do not turn your backs. Never turn your back. We've come this far. Those of you who are true Californios, stay with me, stay on the course of righteousness, free Tiburcio and save your countrymen and progeny!"

Chavez had met Anita at the Los Angeles train station two days ago. She was carrying ten thousand dollars. In his carriage, he took Anita, her son, Rodolfo, and the man servant with whom they traveled to a hotel and bought them dinner and paid for their comfortable room. When Rodolfo and the servant retired to their beds, Chavez and Anita talked alone of freeing Tiburcio and how the revolution might unfold.

But Anita was sick with apprehension. She had little hope left.

"Be patient," Chavez told her. "You and Tiburcio will be reunited soon."

"I'm scared," Anita confided.

"It is not over, Anita," Chavez encouraged her. "He still needs you. We still need you. And you must be strong. Don't worry, we will affect a rescue and free Tiburcio once and for all. You must stay resolute. I will give you all the details. When you visit Tiburcio in jail to impart the information, you must be able to pass on the entire plan down to the most minute aspect so nothing can go wrong."

Chavez did not want her presence at Agua Dulce, but Anita insisted that he escort her to the hidden, mountainous region and show her the enormous, illicit stockpile of weapons and the strong but savage men who believed they were truly fighting for a noble cause and trusted their lives to Tiburcio. She wanted to tell Tiburcio everything exactly the way it was. Chavez rejected her notion.

"No, no, no, Anita. The men do not take kindly to outsiders, particularly a woman. And the trip to Agua Dulce itself is like going into Hades."

"Mr. Chavez, I am a businesswoman," she replied sternly. "I am about to hand a fortune over to you. I want to see what I am paying for. I demand to see my investment!"

"Your investment?"

"Take me to Agua Dulce! Or I will keep every bit of my money."

Chavez agreed.

"Perhaps seeing the men who are willing to put their lives on the line for your Tiburcio will give you hope and encouragement."

TIBURCIO!

In the morning she left her servant and her son at the hotel and rode up front with Chavez in a sturdy two-horse wagon with a floppy leather hat covering her head. Anita absorbed the surroundings. She noticed the sentries Chavez had placed along the route in the cliffs. Nobody could come through the pass unnoticed. When she arrived at the camp whispers that she was the lover of the famous bandit drifted through the ranks, but the men were considerate of the only female among them. Her appearance lifted their spirits.

That evening she witnessed the most brilliant sunset she had ever seen, as if Agua Dulce was closer to the sun than anywhere on Earth. Waking in the morning, she felt surprisingly fresh and alive despite sleeping on the hard ground. She was up before the sunrise and emerged from the tent stretching. A flash of light on the horizon caught her attention and she watched the sun come up just as rich orange and vivid as it had disappeared last night.

Chavez brought her to the caves where the weapons were stored and she was astounded by the firepower before her. She met Soriano and some of the other men. Truer warriors never lived, she thought. Tiburcio will be impressed when she tells him. But her approbation did not last. She listened to Chavez rally the men and felt lonely.

The next morning, Chavez escorted her back to the hotel and took her, Rodolfo and their servant to the train station for their trip back to northern California. Along the way, he explained in detail how they would free Tiburcio and carry out the rebellion.

Chavez watched closely as Anita boarded the steamer dressed in a lavender sheath dress that draped from her thigh down to the floor, her slim figure conspicuous in the form-fitting bodice. She held Rodolfo's hand. He wore a velvet suit with knee pants. Their man servant carried their bags, ten thousand dollars lighter. On first glance, the travelers did not look anything like the conspirators they were. Chavez felt assured.

But on the train, Anita wore a troubled and strained expression. Rodolfo tried to play games with his mother, but she shook him away with a stern look and stared out the window. A rangy man and a younger fellow who boarded at the next stop caught her attention. They slowly made their way down the aisle until they reached the seats where Anita and her son sat across from the servant.

"May we have a seat?" the older man asked.

Anita annoyingly looked around at any number of other empty sections where they could settle instead. However, before she could utter a word the two gentlemen sat down. The wiry man held out a sheriff's badge in the palm of his hand.

"I would like to have a private word with the lady," Morse said, signaling for the servant and the boy to go elsewhere.

Anita, trying to remain unemotional, swallowed hard and told her servant and Rodolfo to sit elsewhere for a few minutes.

"Where are you coming from, ma'am?"

"Los Angeles."

"What were you doing there?"

"That is none of your business."

"Mrs. Garza, my name is Sheriff Harry Morse. It will do you no good to refrain. I have spoken with many acquaintances of your paramour, Tiburcio Vasquez. In these conversations, your name was not seldom mentioned. In fact, everyone seems to believe you might be one of the three or four people closest to Mr. Vasquez, and therefore might know some of the innermost details of his operation."

"I was close to Tiburcio Vasquez a long time ago. I have not seen him for twenty years."

"Did he not stop your wagon down near Hollister two years ago?"

"Briefly. That hardly constitutes a close or a renewed relationship, Mr. Morse. You have locked up Tiburcio Vasquez - what more do you want?"

"Let me tell you something, Mrs. Garza. I have done a little investigating. You are a very wealthy woman. And you have a lot of business savvy. The merchants who have dealings with you are highly impressed with your financial acumen, doubly so because you are a lady. Your father and mother are well-respected. The Constanzas and Garza family reputations are sterling, far-flung. That is why it is quite puzzling that you might be willing to throw away such a comfortable life on some romantic notion involving a very evil man."

"I have never been satisfied with comfort, Mr. Morse!" she dangerously quipped as the train rocked. "And Tiburcio Vasquez is not an evil man. Furthermore, I assure you, I am not stuck on romantic notions."

Morse glanced over at Rodolfo, who was staring back at him through his light-gray eyes.

"I see two possible conclusions to our predicament, that is, our impasse, Mrs. Garza. Two principle lives are at stake here. If I can prove you are abetting Vasquez's gang and helping foment rebellion, I can - and will - send you to prison. As for your son, well, I'm not sure his life would amount to much once his mother is incarcerated, her assets seized by the state and the world discovers that in his veins runs the blood of a murderer who terrorized the state for twenty years and was finally hung in ignominy."

Anita pushed back against the head rest as if a blast of hot air had hit her.

"You have never told Rodolfo that he is Tiburcio's son, have you?"

She gasped for breath.

"Yet, another outcome is possible," Morse continued. "If you cooperate with me - and it has to be only with me - you may return to the family, life, reputation and luxuries that you and your son enjoy. Nobody will know anything about your role in this ugly, deadly plot."

"Not if it costs Tiburcio Vasquez his life."

"He has already lost his life."

"Not yet. And not in vain."

Now Morse leaned in closely.

"Let's face it, Mrs. Garza. California is changing. The charm and simplicity of the past is gone. Blame the gold hunters. Blame the invaders. Blame whoever you want. But it's not my fault, it's not your fault, it's not the newcomers' fault. It's simply progress. The fault of time. I can't stop evolution. Neither can you. And, although he doesn't know it, or chooses to ignore it, Tiburcio Vasquez and three hundred determined men can't stop time, either. Californios all over the state are assimilating into our evolving culture. Hundreds of thousands of people of Mexican descent are contributing to the economy of this state. Great men are bringing water and citrus groves to Los Angeles, industry to San Francisco and railways jutting out in every direction are moving commerce through Sacramento. This is powerful change. Tiburcio Vasquez thinks he can stop innovation, put a halt to this incredible transformation, with just his one single finger in the dyke? His time is over. He played the hero, but there are other heroes now. Heroes of industry, heroes of invention, heroes of arts, heroes of politics. Yes, he is a brave vaquero. A charismatic leader. But he cannot bring back the rural life in which he was raised, riding on open plains from a fiesta to a friend's adobe, from the mountains down to the ocean without seeing a living soul. He says he is fighting on behalf of all the wronged native Californios. But most of those people, thousands who were here long before me, are finding ways to cope and succeed in the new world. They do not need help. And you, Mrs. Garza? You are better off than most of them. You are on top of the hill. You will do just fine. And your son will become an integral piece of this progress, a hero in his own right, as will his sons and their sons. Isn't that really what Tiburcio Vasquez was fighting for? Please, don't ruin your life. And moreover, don't destroy your son's. I think then, Tiburcio's legacy will not have died in vain."

"Where do you get your ideas of conspiracy, Mr. Morse? How could you prove I am - how did you put it? - 'fomenting revolution.' I am simply a widow returning from a trip with her son and manservant. I hardly think I fit your idea of a dangerous conspirator."

Morse waited before he pulled his final card out. Then he leaned toward her.

"I have a letter in your handwriting that spells out exactly how much of your money you have handed over to that bunch of outlaws and how you intend to join Tiburcio in his cause. It's not a small amount, Mrs. Garza. So, I will explain it to you one more time. You either cooperate with me and return to your ranch and your normal life with your son and your servants, or you never see Rodolfo again after we depart this train and you hang for your role in Tiburcio Vasquez's deadly plot."

"What do you want from me?" Anita said fiercely.

"Tell me where his rebel army is hiding. And tell me what they have planned."

Chapter 19: Waiting
Santa Clara County
August 1874

The flower petals had faded and fallen and the crowds were gone. Tiburcio remained alone for long hours in his cell. He saw fewer guests, one a week at the most, and wondered if the revolution would end like the heavy click of an empty gun chamber. No bullets. No smoke. Little noise.

The summer heat cooked the jail during the day. Tiburcio sweltered in his limestone oven until around midnight when the air finally began to cool. Often, he would put his head up against the iron bars of the window to feel the breeze. He fought boredom, bedbugs and hunger. The food was sparse, bland, the same every day. He had lost fifteen pounds. Nobody brought him the guitar he had requested. But perhaps it was just as well. The woeful strumming might be too sad for him and the other prisoners. Dreams of Anita, and how things might have been different, haunted him as it was.

Tully's fortnightly visits tended to hearten and reinvigorate him while they lasted. The lawyer kept steadily working away, scratching off witness after witness who said they were unable to accurately describe the bandit or unwilling to swear they saw him shoot anybody. Sometimes Tully brought in newspapers, but only when there was something positive written about the case or the trial or his exploits. But as time went on public news of the case became less and less frequent.

"I feel like I've been forgotten in here," Tiburcio confided to Tully one day.

"The case is just in a lull right now. It's perfectly natural. We just have to keep on denying you were there at the time of the murders, denying you ever killed anybody at any time in your career. People have established their opinions, and we're all just waiting for the trial to begin."

"What are their opinions?"

"I figure, based on Judge Collins' and my conversations with town folk here in San Jose and down in Monterey, over in Hollister, and even up in San Francisco, that half of them believe you weren't even in Tres Pinos at the time of the Snyder raid. Most of those who do believe you were in Tres Pinos think Leiva did the shooting and is trying to save his hide by cooperating with the state. We may see Leiva hung before our trial even begins."

"And when might that be?"

"Look, it's very hard to convince a man sitting idle in jail that his state of affairs is moving along, let alone looking very positive. But they are, Tiburcio. The state has one credible witness, just one, who claims he can place you just outside of Tres Pinos before the shootings. But I am not so sure his story can hold up under examination. Beyond that, they have a bunch of brutal thieves and jilted lovers with biased grudges against you."

Tiburcio ignored Tully's words and changed the subject.

"What about the state of the revolution? Where is my army? What are the rebels doing?"

"I told you that is not my business, Tiburcio," Tully snapped. "I am here to get you free. The legal way."

"You know what is happening with the revolution, Tully. Don't pretend otherwise. Isn't Morrison still paying you?"

Tully rubbed his forehead and pondered what to tell Tiburcio next.

"Sheriff Adams is banning all visitors from seeing you, Tiburcio. It's as if someone told him about an escape... I don't know what. He is trying to cut off any outside communication with you. I was supposed to arrange Anita's visit but I don't know ... "

Tiburcio swallowed hard. He felt tears were about to gush forth so he quickly spoke.

"Where is she? Where has she been? When will she come?"

"Listen, Tiburcio. I was approached by one of your lieutenants. He asked me to set up a visit between Anita and you. That's all."

"So you talked to her?"

"Yes. But the prosecution may have gotten to her. She knows too much. And they aren't letting her in here."

"What? We must speak! When will I see her?"

"After the trial."

"I could be condemned by then!"

"No. We have a very strong case."

"What has she been doing, Tully?"

"She is biding her time at her ranch. Just going about everyday chores and business."

"Did she ask about me?"

"Of course. She told me to tell you that her heart is aching to see you. None of this is easy for her. She appeared very distraught. That's why I think somebody might have gotten to her."

• • •

The trial loomed on the horizon like a large boulder held at the edge of a precipice by a single pebble. The day after Tully visited Tiburcio, N.C. Briggs kicked the pebble away, and events came hurtling down at blinding speed. He knew time was quickly chiseling away at the memories of witnesses, and the longer the delay the better chance for Tiburcio's followers to plan his escape.

Therefore, the prosecution and county law officers scurried into action. Briggs, accompanied by two other judges and a second attorney, immediately called on Judge Bedlin to see about moving the trial forward as fast as possible. They believed they had a critical and credible witness who could place Tiburcio at the scene - before the murders - and they didn't want him changing his mind.

Sheriff Adams added armed deputies all around the jailhouse and banned all of Tiburcio's visitors except those having official business with the case.

In October, Bedlin opened court for arraignment. Once again, a large crowd gathered outside the jail and along the streets to watch Tiburcio go from the San Jose jail to court. But they only caught a glimpse of Tully, Briggs and their assistants. No common person had seen Tiburcio in public in weeks, and some speculation swirled over whether he had escaped.

Inside the courtroom, the defense counsel stood before the magistrate, seeking to delay the arraignment as long as possible.

"I have filed the necessary affidavits," said Judge Collins of Gilroy, who was working closely with Tully. "We move for a continuance on the grounds that important and material witnesses are absent. In fact, the defense has doubts that they will ever appear."

"Motion granted," Bedlin said. "On Jan. 5, 1875 at 10:00 a.m. I call forth Tiburcio Vasquez and his defense attorneys to appear for arraignment. Jury selection will begin shortly thereafter. Court adjourned."

Tully had bought himself eight weeks. But on that day in January, the jury never was selected. The one witness who the prosecution brought in for arraignment, D.H. McPhail, sat outside the courtroom while his testimony was being heatedly discussed inside, the attorneys sharp words sounding into the hall. The prosecution and defense had been debating a motion for three hours.

"This man cannot positively identify Tiburcio Vasquez," Tully fervently argued, striding back and forth in front of his honor's chair, "and therefore there is no witness, despite nine months to prepare for this trial, who can determine that my client was in Tres Pinos at the time of the murders. The witnesses, whom we have interrogated numerous times, only recall a large man in a gray suit and a man in a broad-brimmed hat as the shooters. Judge, that's a pretty vague description when a man's life hangs in the balance, literally. I believe this is a rather potent issue since Tiburcio Vasquez is on trial not for being the leader of a band of outlaws but for killing an innkeeper, Davidson, and a sheepherder, George Redford, both of whom may have lost their lives at the hands of someone else - that someone else being, in our opinion, Abdon Leiva."

"It's immaterial at this juncture who the prosecution theorizes is the murderer," interjected Briggs.

"Continue," the judge replied indifferently.

"And Leiva, just like our client, sits in a jail a block from this courtroom, with as many witnesses willing to pick him out as a murderer, but, unlike my client, does not fear he will lose his neck to the noose."

"Is witness McPhail present?" the judge asked.

"He is outside."

"Let's seat Vasquez and call McPhail in to see if he can identify the defendant."

Collins leaped out of his seat.

"I object!" he yelled. "With one man sitting in the courtroom, in broad daylight - unlike the conditions in which he actually claims to have seen my client - it would be easy to declare that man as Tiburcio Vasquez."

"What do you suggest?"

"Could McPhail pick out Vasquez in a crowd of fifty other Mexicans?"

The judge looked inquisitively at Briggs.

"This matter can be solved right here in this courtroom, right now," Briggs commented. "My client could be intimidated into silence if he were forced to walk through a yard of criminals to pick out a man who is facing the gallows."

"Would you oppose to bringing Vasquez and several others into the courtroom, Mr. Collins?"

"Again, these are false conditions. And think of the security problems with transferring convicts to the courtroom."

All the while, McPhail sat impatiently in an uncomfortable chair outside the courtroom, constantly checking his watch, the same one Tiburcio had prevented Chavez from stealing on their way to Tres Pinos. It was nearing 5:00 p.m. when the judge finally called McPhail to the witness stand.

McPhail told the attorneys and the judge about meeting the two robbers just minutes before the robbery.

"What time was it when you were allegedly confronted by Mr. Vasquez and Mr. Chavez?" Tully asked, boring his eyes into the witness.

"Around 4:30 or 5:00 in the evening."

"In other words, between sundown and dark?"

"Yes."

Tully and Collins tried not to smile.

"Would you be able to identify Vasquez on sight?"

"Absolutely."

"Even though it's been eighteen months since the robbery?"

"Yes."

"Even in the approaching darkness?"

"Yes. I will never forget his face."

The defense attorneys kept grilling McPhail until finally Briggs asked for adjournment until morning. The sun was setting.

"No!" the judge grumbled. "I am tired. It is late. We are going to go down to the jail yard while there's still a ray of light and see if McPhail can identify Vasquez!"

In the bitter cold but calm evening, they all stepped into the barren dirt yard and looked upon dozens of Mexicans and native Indians. Half of them were criminals, the other half had quickly been paid by the court to fill the yard. McPhail, flanked by his attorneys, peered into one face after another, some light-skinned and some with dark complexions, some with thick beards, some with goatees and some with a several days' growth of whiskers. Collins and Tully waited at the gate as the judge had ordered so they could not alert Tiburcio to the test.

In the darkening gloom, McPhail began to doubt himself. He had been so certain on the stand. Now, he looked at Briggs and shook his head. Briggs encouraged him to look closer, and to take his time. A small breeze stirred in the frigid night and everyone in the yard pulled their jackets in tighter.

McPhail slowly walked the perimeter of the yard, once last time, his chin buried into his shirt. Time was running out, and he knew it. He drew his watch and looked at the time, as he was in the habit of doing.

"Hello," one of the criminals said cordially out of the blue.

Collins and Tully heard something across the yard and looked up in dismay.

"It's you, McPhail," the thin Mexican convict said in good English, chuckling. "That was a fine watch and I've always been sorry I didn't get it!"

"This is Vasquez!" McPhail shouted, thrusting a finger at the prisoner while taking several steps back. "This one is Vasquez! I told you I would recognize his face!"

Judge Bedlin, Tully and Collins came running over to the group.

"Are you Tiburcio Vasquez?" the judge asked.

"Of course," Vasquez answered.

"Good. We will begin jury selection tomorrow," Bedlin said loudly as he walked past the crestfallen Tully and Collins and exited the dim jail yard.

Chapter 19: Trial
San Jose
January 1875

As the courtroom filled with throngs of people, Tiburcio Vasquez appeared proud and unaffected by his surroundings. He smiled gently and looked around. He saw a vast number of ladies in the gallery. This was a marked improvement over sitting in his cold cell. What a sensational display this will be, he thought. They have come to behold a bandit leader's last chance, his final days, and they will end up learning of his acquittal and witnessing the dawn of a revolution. Judge Bedlin's loud voice broke his revery.

"I call to trial the case of Tiburcio Vasquez vs. the people," Bedlin barked. "Note for the record that Attorney General John Lord Love assisted by N.C. Briggs and the Honorable W.E. Lovett of Hollister and District Attorney Bodley of Santa Clara County are present for the prosecution. Judge W. H. Collins and Judge J. A. Moultrie of Santa Clara County and Mr. P.B. Tully of Gilroy are representing the defendant."

Bedlin let his words sink in as he looked around the courtroom, astonished at the number of women in the audience.

"Mr. Vasquez, seated at the table with Tully and his assistants, is placed on trial for the murder of Leandro Davidson and George Redford on Aug. 26, 1873, in Tres Pinos. Let's begin selecting the jury."

By the end of the day, twelve men had been seated and the judge told the courtroom that witness examination would begin the next day at 9:00 a.m. sharp, beginning with Abdon Leiva.

When Leiva walked to the witness stand it was the first time in over a year that Tiburcio Vasquez had seen him. Leiva's sad eyes avoided his stare. He was sworn in and laid out in detail the role that Tiburcio Vasquez played in the murders. The courtroom crowd was stunned at the precise description, and some women began to touch their wet eyes with kerchiefs or the ends of their gloves. Leiva went on, gently encouraged by Briggs, to explain how his wife prompted him to join Tiburcio's gang.

"Yes, sir," he said. "She did persuade me. She told me to go in with these men and rob the store and others."

Upon conclusion of Briggs' questioning, Tully rose and confidently strode over to the stand to question the former blacksmith. His line of questioning focused on Leiva's description of the sorts of clothing the robbers were wearing, and he let this sit with the jurors.

Sheriff Adams was the second witness called by the state and in his testimony corroborated Leiva's story, interconnecting the interviews he had conducted with various witnesses. Then a third witness, presented to the surprise of Tully and Collins, gave a voice to what happened. His name was Johnnie Zumalt, a Hollister resident who happened to be in Tres Pinos at the time of the raid and was the first to arrive at the telegraph station to alert authorities. He had snuck away when the shooting started and walked the thirteen miles to Hollister, taking several hours on the back roads to avoid meeting up with the gang.

Zumalt wasn't the only surprise witness unearthed. An egg buyer and his son, who were unhitching their horses in the stable near Snyder's store when the shooting began, had also slipped away on foot. Then there was Joseph Cochrane, another Hollister resident, who claimed he had seen Vasquez and his men riding horses about three miles outside the city on the afternoon of the robbery.

The prosecutors also questioned Leiva's wife, who knew intimate details about Tiburcio's plan to raid Tres Pinos and explained what he had confided to her afterward.

"I whisper too much into the ears of my sweethearts," Tiburcio said quietly to Tully. "It's one of my weaknesses."

Finally, as a crowning blow, Briggs brought in McPhail, who could place Vasquez at the edge of the town before the shootings.

So by the fifth day, when the state closed their case, even Tully and Collins were overwhelmed at the mountain of evidence they had to surmount. But Tiburcio sat composed, with a peaceful expression on his face, as if someone else's life was at stake.

The defense called back each witness to cross examine, carefully going over the descriptions of the shooters. Their sharp interrogation broke down Rosaria, who confessed she would like to see both her husband, Abdon, and Tiburcio hung. The audience chuckled.

And finally, Tiburcio Vasquez was called to the stand.

A murmur washed through the gallery. It was the first time many of the spectators had ever seen the bandit in person, and most agreed with reports in the newspapers that he did not appear the cutthroat villain they might expect. He walked slowly to the stand, a slender, wiry and quiet figure, dashing in his brand new black satin vest and coattails.

He denied taking part in the murders. Some spectators nodded, others shook their heads as he explained what happened. He had uttered the words so many times they rolled off his tongue with an air of truth. His voice was soft but firm.

"I sent three of my party, Leiva included, to Tres Pinos. I made Leiva the captain. I instructed them to take a drink, get acquainted with the town and wait around until I arrived. I told them to use no violence, and when I came I would be the only one to do any shooting," Tiburcio continued, his voice just slightly rising. "When I arrived with Chavez, however, I found three men dead. My gang told me Leiva shot two of them and

Romano one. I condemned Leiva and the others for acting contrary to my orders and said we could not stay long. That's when we took provisions from Snyder's store and left for Elizabeth Lake."

Although his earnest testimony fell on open ears, Tully was unable to call any witness to fully corroborate Tiburcio's story. Tully thanked his client, turned on his heel and walked back to his chair trying not to show his concern that the chances that the twelve jury members believed him, above all testimony, was very slim, indeed. Yet, Tully still had hope. After all, Judge Collins was on Tiburcio Vasquez's side, and Collins, whose elocution and polemic was unparalleled and legendary, was scheduled to begin closing arguments the next day in front of a throng eager to hear him deliver his oratory.

That morning, Briggs rested his case. He immediately acknowledged Tiburcio's smooth tongue and addressed insinuations that Leiva was guilty. He laid out the evidence that had been presented and detailed how Tiburcio set out to ruin Leiva by forcing him to sell his property and by coveting his wife. The learned prosecutor made references to the historical figures of Aaron Burr and Harman Blennerhassett.

Tully followed.

"Gentlemen of the jury, there is grave doubt about the guilt of my client," Tully concluded after an hour of speaking. "Based on what you heard, justice demands you give him the benefit of the doubt - and mercy calls on you to release him from the shadow of the gallows. There are others in this room more deserving of that fate."

Judge Bedlin then announced to the courtroom that Judge Collins would make the closing arguments for the defendant in the afternoon. Before calling a recess, Bedlin addressed the masses, knowing Collins prodigious gift of making indelible impressions upon an audience.

"There will be no head wagging, no utterances, no whispers and no applause of approbation or disapprobation during the closing arguments or I will hold the guilty parties in contempt and lock them in jail!" Bedlin stated firmly.

In the afternoon session, more people, perhaps two hundred, packed into the courtroom. Every seat was occupied and everyone standing was stuffed shoulder to shoulder, taking up every inch of the floor along the walls.

Collins stood and abruptly began: "May it please your honor, gentlemen of the jury."

The counsel was a handsome, dignified-looking man in his fifties, with blondish hair going gray and a closely shaved beard. Taller than nearly everyone in the courtroom, he moved with such grace and ease that nobody noticed his constant pacing. One moment he'd be in front of the jury and the next you realized he had changed his position in the room and was now leaning with a hand on the balustrade in front of the gallery. Most astonishingly, however, he spoke extemporaneously as well as expressively.

"When I first entered upon my duties as counsel on behalf of this unfortunate man," Collins boomed, "I thought then that the party I was to defend was Tiburcio Vasquez. Yet, I learn today, for the first time, that the scene is moved back along the years that have gone, and instead of standing before you, I stand, as it were, in the old commonwealth at home, and my client is the oily, silvery-tongued Aaron Burr; and Leiva - the swarthy Mexican who stood there on the witness stand - is the mild, honest and outspoken Blennerhassett, and this affair, instead of happening at a place called Tres Pinos, occurred in the beautiful little island that sits out on a lake, separated from us not alone by land but by the rolling waves of two oceans. And I was only recalled back to the reality by the broken English spoken by this Castilian; reminded that I stood here before a jury of my fellow men in the flower-carpeted valley of Santa Clara."

He had engaged his audience, mostly teary-eyed females, but most importantly he was locked onto the twelve men before which he now stood and paused.

"The duties of an advocate in a capital case are at all times solemn - yea, solemn beyond the power of the human tongue to describe - yet, but in this case, they are doubly solemn. We can meet the issues of fact and law that have arisen here, but when called upon to confront a great black cloud of prejudice that forces its way in at every opening and at every crevice; when a great roaring river of passion is one of the things we have to meet, and when through the great black clouds of prejudice there are heard, just as thunder is heard, roaming over the storm clouds, great damnable cries of revenge, coming from a maddened populace; when here, at the very trial, we are met by the law officer of the state, who, not content with asking justice at your hands, holds before you a cup and says: 'Fill it with blood! Fill it with blood!'"

Some members of the audience gasped. He then addressed the circumstances of Tiburcio's upbringing.

"Who is this man, that by a simple yes or no, you can send into at one flash, unprepared, into the realms of eternity? His name is Tiburcio Vasquez."

And then, he bore into Abdon Leiva's credibility.

"This witness, Leiva, does not tell a straight story as to what happened on the way. As to these two men, you and I will agree on one accord, that this defendant, accused here of crime, is a much better man. And yet, Leiva's story does not hang together, either; because, if this statement of facts connected with the tragedy is true, the balance of the people who were there are very much mistaken."

Collins brought in the testimony from Moreno's trial to contradict Leiva's words. He called Sheriff Adams a purchased witness. Then, he challenged the statements of witnesses who claimed to have seen Vasquez do the shooting. He pointed out that their view of the scene was compromised behind shut doors and by the swirl of excitement.

"I don't say that Vasquez may not be guilty of many wrongs. I don't say he may not be a bad man. I don't say, gentlemen, that, in view of all the facts elicited here, that he is a good man. I say to you that when a man simply robs, he does not commit murder; that they are two separate and distinct offenses."

Collins now paused dramatically for his conclusion. He glanced upward, toward heaven. The silent audience saw him take a breath and noticed his eyes were watery. But by the time he looked down and stared at each man in the jury, his eyes were clear and radiating with passion. He described a scene he would like to see:

"The jury has returned. Joy sits upon the countenance of the prisoner; tears of gratitude, mingled with heartfelt smiles, are upon the countenance of his friends. The mother's face, radiant with joy, is turned toward heaven. The verdict of 'not guilty' has been pronounced. I know not, gentlemen, whether you think it your duty to render such a verdict in this case or not. Should you do so you will gladden my heart. Need I say to you, that you will gladden the heart of this defendant. But I do know that you will take into consideration the doubts that hang around and surround this case; that you will seriously take into consideration the uncertainty of the testimony introduced upon the part of the people, and the danger that we all labor under of being led astray by passion or influenced by prejudice. I earnestly hope that your verdict may be one of acquittal. Such a verdict, it seems to me, under the circumstances, is a just one. Gentlemen of the jury, I commit to your keeping, the life and liberty of Tiburcio Vasquez."

There was a short wail from the back of the room, but it was stifled almost as quickly as Bedlin looked up, his admonishing stare directed to the rear of the gallery. When he was satisfied there would not be any other outbursts he summoned Attorney General Love to close the case.

Love argued for a guilty of murder verdict or nothing at all. He concluded with a call to the jury.

"And with that guilty verdict, his crime deserves, aye society demands, the death penalty be affixed to it," Love said, punctuating each word.

After Love took his seat, Bedlin looked upon the overflowing auditorium and, before giving the jury clear and full instructions, again warned that there would be no applause and no jeers whatever the outcome of the deliberations. At 4:45 p.m., the jury retired to their chambers to deliberate. Tiburcio was taken to a guarded room.

At three minutes after 8:00 o'clock the court was notified that the jury had reached a verdict. Tiburcio Vasquez was summoned and moments later he appeared. A solemn hush came over the courtroom. Vasquez said nothing and took his seat. The judge called the names of the jury members and each one responded that they were present.

"Gentlemen of the jury, have you agreed upon a verdict?" Bedlin asked.

"We have," answered the foreman, George Reynolds.

He handed a folded piece of paper to the court clerk, who handed it to the judge in stifling silence. No one seemed to breathe. The judge took the note, sincerely looked at the writing, turned it over and read it silently once again. Then he handed it to the clerk.

"Read it aloud, please."

The clerk stood in the center of the court surrounded by complete silence.

"We, the jury, find the defendant guilty of murder in the first degree and affix the death penalty."

Nobody applauded. Nobody spoke. Several handkerchiefs came out as ladies dabbed their eyes. Tiburcio's expression was unchanged, his face wore an unmistakable pallor.

"Court will reconvene for sentencing on Saturday, January 23, at 10:00 a.m.," Bedlin declared and left the bench.

Reporters dashed out the door. Some men attended to the women who had fainted. But most people slowly ushered themselves away, silent and stunned, as if they had expected something more, something different, something more final. They had heard the verdict, but fears associated with the past twenty years of terror committed at the hands of this defendant, now being led away by deputies in handcuffs, did not dissipate. Nobody felt even a slight breeze of relief in the air. As long as he was alive, trepidation lingered like a single dark storm cloud on a bright spring day.

TIBURCIO!

In the back of the courtroom, Harry N. Morse stole a glance at Tiburcio, who caught his eye and smirked.

"If you only knew," Morse said under his breath and slipped through the crowd.

Chapter 20: Letter
San Jose
January 1875

Ever since Anita, shortly after Tiburcio's arrest, betrayed to him the location of the rebels, the size of their weapons cache and the plan to free the rebel leader, Morse had been tirelessly planning his counterinsurgency. In secret. Nearly alone.

Up until the day of the verdict, Morse was conspicuously absent during most of the court proceedings and the actual trial. He didn't mind; this was Sheriff Adams' town, his jail, his show. And Morse had his own work to do. Anita swore that she did not know the date or time of the jailbreak, only that there was a plan of attack in the works. The sheriff guessed Chavez and the rebels would wait until after a verdict came down, and he was right. But would they come before the sentencing, or perhaps during the execution, if that was what the judge ordered.

Just like he had done a decade ago - when he was hunting the Mexican desperadoes in the mountains throughout Alameda, Santa Cruz and Santa Clara counties - Morse immersed himself in studying firsthand the trails and terrain at Agua Dulce - alone and in disguise. He began his surveillance immediately after confronting Anita. He stepped off the train at the very next stop and didn't leave Southern California until he was satisfied with the information he had gathered. He encountered Chavez's sentinels twice, but to them he was just a surveyor. They never allowed him to get close enough to see the army so he busied himself with getting to know nearly every square foot of the passageway leading to their den, meticulously detailing a map of the area. Every time he carefully read his map and notes, he realized how badly the cards were stacked against him.

"Some of the most jagged, precariously piled blocks of mountain I've ever seen," he wrote in his journal. "Wagons cannot make it over much of the pass. One narrow abyss in this treacherous land links the outside world and the rebel's hideout, but it is too well guarded. I must find another way."

For some time this equation baffled him. So he let those plans simmer and, as soon as he returned to Oakland, turned his attention to finding, enlisting and marshaling as many capable fighting men as he could. No small task, either. The rebels and their hideaway were much more formidable than he had imagined. He chose to go about his work secretively to avoid spreading panic among the citizens, to not risk alerting the rebels and to keep other lawmen out of his way. Morse's force had to be handpicked, loyal and trusted because he would be unable to directly lead them once the time came. They must be able to act on their own, for he would be invited and expected to attend the hanging of Tiburcio Vasquez, and by that time his fighters needed to be in position to quickly respond.

Who else could he turn to other than his longtime brothers in the Oakland Guard?

The first two on his list were Ralph Falville and A. J. McDavid - both of whom still personally felt the sting of failing to capture Vasquez in the first place. At first count, Morse, Falville and McDavid figured they could persuade or conscript twenty-five disciplined, practiced men and obtain most of the weapons, large and small, that they needed from long-unused lookout posts of the Oakland Guard.

By the time that was accomplished, Judge Bedlin had meted out the sentence for Tiburcio Vasquez. Morse got the news by telegraph.

Forty miles away, the judge told Tiburcio to stand up. The guilty bandit stood calm and straight as Bedlin told him:

"The judgment is death. That you be taken hence and securely kept by the sheriff of Santa Clara County until Friday, the 19th day of March 1875; that upon that day between the hours of nine in the morning and four in the afternoon that you be hanged by the neck until dead. And may God have mercy on your soul."

Morse quickly summoned his undersheriff to his office. By the look on Borein's face, he knew something was wrong. Borein offered the newspaper in his hand to his boss, jabbing a finger at a front-page letter to the public. Chavez had raised the stakes. His simple message: You are not safe. His letter, printed in every major newspaper in the state, read:

"I let you know that if Vasquez is hung by his enemies, who through fear, have turned against him, I will show you I know how to avenge the death of my captain. I do not exact of you to set him free, but do not want him hung, because he was not bloody. It was I who was at the head of the affair at Tres Pinos, in which the murders were committed. Mr. Vasquez certainly was our captain; but on account of Abdon Leiva I neglected the orders that Vasquez had imposed upon us. If this is not sufficient, or if by this means Vasquez does not get his sentence appealed, then you will have to suffer as in the times of Joaquin Murrieta - the just with the unjust alike will be reached by my revenge. Let him be punished according to law, then you will never more hear of me in this country or in this State - neither of me or of my company."

Morse was unconcerned about the letter.

"Vasquez is going to the gallows, Peter," Morse explained. "That much is certain. Now we have less than six weeks to assemble twenty-five men and get four wagons of weapons and artillery seven hundred miles away into harsh country against a well-fortified enemy, without raising suspicions. Needless to say, we have no time to lose. And no time to worry about that letter."

"Do you believe the lady?" the undersheriff asked his boss.

"Who? Anita? The widow?"

"Yes."

"What do you mean, do I believe her?"

"Cannons? Enough guns and boxes of ammunition to supply five hundred troops? How would she know? Where would they have gotten such largesse? How?"

"Do I believe her?" Morse repeated. "I don't know. But these desperadoes aren't out to celebrate the Fourth of July, Peter. They plan to take over the state of California. And you don't do that with just pistols."

"But she recollected seeing only about one hundred men? You don't take over a state with one hundred men. And what about the reports of as many as five hundred?"

"You have to trust her, and hope that smaller figure is accurate. Because we don't have close to that many men to fight against them. If there are one hundred men armed and hell bent on a cause, and we have no state militia, then we got ourselves a big problem. That's what we have here, Peter. A huge problem on our hands. And little time to take care of it."

"So if we forget for a moment about encountering an enemy four times larger than us - how do we move the Guard right under Billy Rowland's nose without being detected?"

"That's a good question," Morse said thoughtfully as if working out the details just then in his head. "We can't send in fewer men, or fewer wagons. We need two wagons just to pull the howitzers. We'll just have to conceal ourselves the best we can. And figure out how to get past the sentinels in that hellish pass."

Two days later, Morse asked Borein to sit down in the large leather chair in front of his desk, and smiled. He had been poring over his notes and meticulous maps the night before, burning more than a dozen candles down to the wick, when the thick walls of confusion started to crumble. By freshly looking at his fighting force as the sum of many parts he saw where they could break it up into smaller units to slip through the stony fortress and amass again on both sides of the gulch through which the rebel army would have to move.

"Once we marshal our forces down there, we can ambush them from the canyons above. They gotta move a lot of men and weapons through that narrow flat mountain floor before they reach any main road," Morse explained, concluding with a wry smile: "It's all going to take a little luck."

"A lot of luck," Borein corrected.

Chapter 21: Gallows
San Jose
Six weeks leading up to execution

Tiburcio Vasquez sat in his dimly lit cell listening to Tully explain that Gov. Pacheco had refused to grant a reprieve.

"I suggest you see a spiritual adviser, Tiburcio," Tully said with defeat and sorrow in his voice, as he stood to leave.

Tiburcio smiled.

"So it is time to consider the affairs of my soul, counsel?" he said sarcastically.

"I don't know what else I can do. I am sorry. I'm devastated, Tiburcio."

"It's not over."

"You're a doomed man! I don't know how you can sit in here, reading, smiling, chatting with visitors as if you don't have a care in the world."

"Well, Mr. Tully, you never wanted me to tell you what is afoot with regard to plans to spring me from captivity. I don't suppose you want to hear it now. But I am getting out."

"Now? Now you are going to be saved?"

"Yes, and doesn't it seem wonderfully fitting, considering this dashing life I have led up to now, that my last chance to live may come down to a reckless, last-minute assault never to be forgotten?"

"You are as confident as ever, Tiburcio. Even here. Even now."

"You've done a hell of a job, Tully! I mean that sincerely. I hope Mr. Morrison pays you handsomely. But don't worry about me. I always believed it would come down to my way over your way. They weren't going to let me walk out of here.

There was no way in hell. The only thing left for me to say to you is, 'Thank you and good-bye.' "

Tiburcio watched Tully take a few steps down the corridor, then shouted:

"Tell Morrison he might yet win his bet!"

Tully hesitated. Then he turned around.

"Morrison has already paid all his dues. He hasn't followed your case for months, Tiburcio. He's moved on to other things. He gave up. But I thought we had a good case. Good luck. I hope your friends have better success securing your freedom than I did."

Several hours after Tully exited the San Jose jail, Tiburcio set down the book he had been reading and listened to new footsteps approaching in the shadowy corridor. He figured it was Father Serda. But to his astonishment, Harry N. Morse came walking up.

Morse had never seen a condemned man look so natty, fresh and good-natured. Tiburcio sat tall in a wood chair against the wall. He wore a new flower-patterned black vest, tie, black pants and shined black boots. As for himself, Morse knew he looked like he felt - mentally and physically exhausted, worried, aching and in need of a bath and a bit of a shave. Morse was in an incompatible mood.

"Where the hell were you?" Tiburcio asked. "You missed one hell of a trial, sheriff. But at least you got to see the most dramatic part - the ending. What theater!"

"I'll tell you where I've been. I've been trying to fathom how your boys are going to attempt to free you in these final hours."

"Adams is running the show. Let him figure it out, sheriff. Let him lose the sleep. What concern is it of yours?"

"You are big enough of a problem to occupy two of us, Tiburcio."

Both men chuckled against their wills.

"Nobody is talking, then?"

Morse smiled scornfully.

"Tell me," he replied. "Has Anita visited you?"

"No!" Tiburcio answered sharply.

"Why is that? You expected her to, did you not? Especially, in your time of need."

Tiburcio leaped at him, reaching through the bars to try to grab the lawman.

"What are you telling me, Morse?" he said, gritting. "You got to her?"

"Have you ever abandoned her in *her* time of need?"

"She would never utter a word that might harm me. She would never compromise my cause!"

"Not even under the threat of arrest? The threat of ruin?" the sheriff asked unforgiving. "Not even under the threat of her being incarcerated - or worse, hung - and her son living without a mother or a father, or any guardian for that matter?"

"You would not dare! Not even somebody like you would have the audacity to jail a respected, wealthy member of society on some charge that you viciously invented. Definitely not a woman, not a widow with a child! Just to make me talk!"

"Why would any of that worry me, Tiburcio?"

"Because you risk soiling your standing in the community and your legacy. And what's the only thing that separates you from me? Your reputation among the gringos."

"My standing? My legacy? The only reputation in jeopardy is the reputation of Anita Garza when the gringos, as you call them - the people with whom she does business, invites to dinner and visits at social gatherings - find out who she really is. Lover of a Mexican criminal. Conspirator. Enemy of the state. An accomplice to murder. A killer herself, perhaps? Hell, maybe her husband's death wasn't so accidental, huh? I'm sure we could reopen the inquisition into that. And how about the good standing of young Rodolfo? How might he shake the blood connection to one of the most violent outlaws ever to be known. How might he live down being the son of a man who made women and children shriek in horror? A man who left boys and girls orphaned and wives widowed. You will not be the only one who to pay for your sins, Tiburcio!"

"What the hell do you want?"

"For the life of me I don't know why Anita was willing to risk so much for you. She had everything. But you can see clearly, right Tiburcio? You understand now, right? You won't be seeing Anita. Your rebellion will be crushed. Nobody will come save you. This is how it ends, Tiburcio. This is how it all ends."

Tiburcio examined Morse's face closely and smiled cynically again.

"Don't threaten me, sheriff! I shook off fear a long time ago. I have not let fear rule me since the night before my first stage robbery. I was still a teenager. I was alone, inside a dark cave with a rattle snake stirring its shaker at the side of my bed. I drove that snake away, it slithered off, and with it every ounce of my fear gone. Do I look scared, sheriff? I think you're the one who is afraid. You have more to lose than I do."

"Frankly, I am too prepared, too decisive, too righteous and too lucky to be afraid. Or to lose."

"You may be all that, indeed. But that won't stop one hundred soldiers dead set on liberating me without regard to the consequences. And you certainly cannot stop three hundred, if Chavez decides to send that many. And for that matter, all your virtues stand harmless against the waves of rebel warriors who will follow after that. I have always said, if I had sixty thousand dollars and three hundred men I could liberate Alta California! We are about to see if I was right, aren't we?"

As disheveled as Morse looked, as agitated as he was from lack of sleep, he gazed calmly, patiently at the prisoner .

"And that's why I didn't wait for Chavez to make his move," Morse said. "I have already sent my men down there to dispatch your liberators."

"Is that so? How many men did you send to their certain death?"

"Twenty-five. Well-armed, disciplined, professional, dedicated soldiers."

"A handful of men to confront an army?

"To ambush your army."

Tiburcio laughed loud and hard.

"That is useless. You have false hope, my friend. You will have blood on your hands."

"At the very least, I will delay your liberators. They will be too late to free you."

"Ha! Who cares? The revolution doesn't stop with my death, sheriff. And what if they are already on their way, gone before your men even arrive. What if I told you they are already here?"

"We will find out soon, Tiburcio. Anita told us everything."

"Anita told you where they were hiding?"

"Everything."

"Their numbers?"

"Yes."

"Their weapons?"

"Yes."

"Their plans to rescue me?"

"Yes."

"You are lying. I want to see her."

"You want to see the woman who betrayed you?"

"If what you say is true, let her visit. She holds no more secrets."

"That is Sheriff Adams' decision. I am finished with her."

• • •

It was certain that a more fashionable woman had never entered the San Jose jailhouse. From the diamond comb in her shiny black hair to her high button boots, from her graceful walk to her sweet voice, Anita Garza's entire presence seemed to soften the stone and iron edifice. Tiburcio heard her coming down the corridor, the recognizable footsteps of a woman, two soft shoe taps to every heavy thud of the guard's boot. She wore a soft pink knitted vest and short petticoat over a lilac gown. She was well perfumed.

Tiburcio felt ashamed of himself and his predicament, feeling that in Anita's eyes he appeared to be every bit like a wild, caged animal. So the first words out of his mouth, even before he looked up at the beautiful, dark-haired, black-eyed woman standing outside his dungeon, were: "I'm sorry."

Likewise, Anita felt embarrassed that she had dressed so elegantly, as if she were mocking the prisoners.

"No, dear. *I* am sorry," she said quietly as the guard retreated a few steps down the gloomy hall. "I look so presumptuous. And it has taken me so long to come see you …"

As her voice trailed off, he reached through the bars and held her hand. It reminded him of his mother's visits to San Quentin. The shadows from the iron bars mottled her pretty face. He felt and saw her shiver.

"You are trembling," he said.

"I wanted to be strong," she answered.

"And you are cold."

He longed to hold her tight against him but could not.

"I gave Chavez the money," she blurted out.

"You did well," he said indifferently, looking deeper into her eyes.

"We were so close to being together."

"Here we are!" he smiled.

Anita's eyes grew tearful and she began sobbing.

"I am sorry, Tiburcio!" Anita cried.

He squeezed her hand tightly. She was pale.

"What is wrong?"

She collapsed to the ground, still clutching the cell's bars in her sweaty palms. Tiburcio looked down and saw Anita's skirt encircling her like an eddy. Tiburcio dropped to one knee, and clung to one of her small, cold hands.

"I told him everything," she confessed as he looked at her in bewilderment. "I didn't want to, but I was scared and I didn't know what to do!"

"Who did you tell?"

"That sheriff. Morse. I told him all about Agua Dulce and the men and the weapons. I told him how to get there. He said Moreno and Leiva had already betrayed everything so I had nothing to lose. He threatened me and Rodolfo."

"Did you tell him about my escape?"

"I told him I know there is a plan but I am not privy to the details. I told him all I know is they are supposed to try to free you but no date, or time or anything. I think he believed me, given all that I had told him before. As soon as I found out, I sent Chavez a message that I have gained access to you."

"Then you were very smart and brave. You saved your and Rodolfo's life and you may have saved mine. There is nothing more you could have done. But we are alone. Can you tell me what you know? What did Chavez want you to tell me?"

"You are supposed to prepare two speeches to give as your final statement," Anita began. "This will buy some time. The first speech will begin: 'To My Former Associates.' The second one: 'To Fathers and Mothers of Children.' After finishing the first one, you will pause as if emotion has overcome you, and when you pause, be prepared."

"For what?"

She explained exactly what Chavez had told her as Tiburcio caressed her arms through the iron bars.

"He said the rescue will be flamboyant. There will be only a few armed officers, the executioner, a priest and a half dozen dignitaries on the scaffold. The noose will be placed around your neck before you are asked to speak any final words. A step away from death, you will pause, and a soldier planted in the crowd will yell "Free Tiburcio" - and that is the signal. Twenty-five of our compadres will be commonly dressed and mixed in among the other spectators. They will arise out of nowhere and strike swiftly and violently. With great precision they will gun down every officer they have accounted for. A dozen men will jump onto the hangman's scaffolding, cut you loose and fend off any resistance. An additional two dozen soldiers will gallop out of the shadows with the getaway horses. Like thunder, you will all escape in a furious dash into the hills of Contra Costa County.

"Finally," Anita whispered in reverie. "A relay of messengers on horseback will alert Chavez that you have been freed. It will take three days to get the message delivered but then the rest of the fighters remaining at Agua Dulce and armed to the teeth will roll out of the mountains and sweep northward through town after town toward the middle of the state. Bakersfield, Kingston, Firebaugh, Stockton will all fall. Hundreds of families who had lived for years at Cantua Canyon will pour out of their remote hovels to relocate into these ransacked cities. The rebel army will strike lightning fast, gaining more and more converts, what Chavez calls 'invisible hands everywhere but nowhere at once.'"

When Anita was finished she watched his face to see if Tiburcio had faith that the plan would succeed. If he believed in it, she could find a way, too. But he showed no expression.

"And Morse knows nothing of this?"

"He only knows that upon your escape or death - either one - the entire insurgent army starts rolling."

"Knowing and being able to stop it are two very different things," Tiburcio said but turned away from Anita and began pacing in his cell. "Certainly he will suspect the attack will happen on the day of the execution. Certainly he will be prepared."

"I am sorry, Tiburcio. I only told ...," but her voice trailed off.

"It doesn't matter. I have burdened you too much for one life, my sweetheart!"

"I only did it to protect my ... our son!"

"Rodolfo."

"You know?"

He smiled and kissed her forehead through the cold bars.

"Yes, I know. Even if no crusaders arrive to save me, I will at least face my Creator knowing that you and Rodolfo are safe. The revolution be damned. You are more important, Anita! I should always have known that."

Tiburcio's gray eyes, so much like Rodolfo's, glistened.

"Don't say that, Tiburcio. Chavez is coming. Your followers are coming, and a greater day awaits."

"We will see."

"What do you mean?"

"To achieve their goal, the liberators will have to reach San Jose before the day I am appointed to be executed. Morse will know in a few days whether his men have been outwitted or out-battled by our fighters and are on their way. You must talk to Sheriff Morse."

"Never again!"

"You must tell him that I need to know whether he confronted my troops and what was the outcome."

"He won't tell me."

"You deserve to know. Tell him I need to know before I die. He will grant me one last wish."

"And then what?"

"If the liberators are on their way, you must stay as far away from here as possible. Morse will grab you and arrest you first if I am saved from the gallows … But, if there is no hope for me, you must come to the hanging and show me your sweet, sweet face once more as I stand ready to drop into eternity. I know it is difficult. But you must be the last sight I see before I depart this weary world. Only then can I die in peace, Anita. Swear to it, Anita! Swear to it!"

"I will, my love."

The jailer approached them and barked that it was time to leave.

"I love you, Anita!" Tiburcio called as she was hurried down the hall.

"Be ready, Tiburcio. Be ready to be freed, and we will be together again! They are coming. Rodolfo and I will be waiting!"

501

Chapter 22: Ambush
Agua Dulce
Two weeks before execution

Six-hundred miles away from where their leader awaited death in a meager cell, an army prepared for the unknown, cleaning and loading its guns and moving extra weapons and ammunition onto wagons. No one spoke as they efficiently went about their deadly preparations with grim faces. Evening settled in and they ate a hearty dinner of roasted duck and bread. After the hard work and meal was finished, when it was completely dark except for the vast, vibrating stars in the sky above, Chavez leaped onto a large boulder and simply told them the time had come. No words were left to say, only action, only to do what they had trained for, only what they had dedicated their lives to.

"Silence honors the history we will make," he cried, motioning for them to move out.

The wagons, horses and men rumbled across the mountain floor in a column.

Once the army was on the other side of the range, fifty soldiers - Tiburcio's emancipators - would advance northward while the rest of them camped until they saw the horseback messenger's signal that their leader had been freed and it was time for the war to commence.

Chavez anticipated with great pleasure riding triumphantly into town after town, seeing the apprehension in the white citizens' faces and the joyful disbelief of fellow Californios when they witnessed before their very eyes the secret rebellion that had been whispered about for so long. He hardly had the patience to wait to read breathlessly written stories that he imagined would be printed in the newspapers about the insurrection. The insurgent army was finally on the march. And he, a poor, young man who grew up in the state's remote quicksilver mining camps, was leading the charge.

Those were his thoughts on that pitch-black night as they filed through the long gulch with its high mountain walls.

Suddenly, his reverie was violently interrupted. Stars exploded in the sky in loud percussions. Two detonations behind Chavez lit up the gulch and mountain wall for a brief instance. Then, all was dark again. But there quickly came more dull, chest-thumping blasts and bursts of light. Chavez thought he saw a severed head and body lying on the ground. Several other men around him gasped, groaned and collapsed.

Then came the direct hit. The mortar struck in the middle of the column of wagons. It landed on an ammunition wagon and in a violent white flash Chavez was blinded and unable to hear anything except a loud ringing in his ears. When his eyes adjusted from the fire flash, he saw men scattering and dropping and hiding behind broken wagons and dead horses. Soldiers fired their rifles up into the cliffs where they believed the enemy stood only to get shot in the back from an unseen sniper. Horses broke loose and reared dangerously. Dirt and dust and powder churned in the air and choked any breathing being. More explosions shook the ground at Chavez's feet. He steadied himself despite the bloody confusion all around him. With enormous strength and will, he yanked and pulled the first frantic, kicking horse he could reach to a standstill and leaped into the saddle.

"Onward! Forward!" Chavez yelled, uncertain whether he could be heard or was even making sense. "Follow!"

In the shadowy fire light, he caught the eyes of a few men beginning to comprehend what was happening. Those who were on horseback or could quickly snatch and mount a steed bolted away with their leader, riding at breakneck speed. As they looked back, they saw and felt the mountainside begin to crumble and boom and reverberate like an earthquake until massive granite sheets came crashing down and crushed whatever was left on the floor below. The men who didn't perish under huge piles of rock were the unfortunate ones, hopelessly trapped by the landslide to die a slow, hungry death.

Clodoveo Chavez and twelve other riders bolted to safety before the rockslide buried scores of their compatriots. They galloped toward Mexico, unaware that a handful of Oakland Guard members who also had escaped death in the rocky ravine were relentlessly chasing them.

Chapter 23: 'Pronto'
San Jose, Calif.
March 1875

On the Wednesday before his scheduled execution, Tiburcio heard hammering and sawing in the prison yard as the platform was erected. Sheriff Adams had permitted the public to come examine the pine lumber scaffold, and hundreds had walked through the yard and run their hands along the finely crafted framework of the ten-square-foot structure. It stood twelve feet off the ground, allowing for a nine-foot drop.

But now it was Thursday, the eve of Tiburcio's visit to the gallows, and everything was quiet. He finally agreed to see a spiritual adviser but more for the company than the comfort. He and Father Serda talked into the night.

"I've prepared two speeches, father, to read as my final statements," Tiburcio confided to the priest. "I rather like the way I wrote them."

"I would prefer you not read them. You need to keep your attention on your state of mind and think of a glorious afterlife," Father Serda said. "Tell me, my son, do you believe in a future state, an afterlife of some sort?"

Tiburcio smiled at the priest.

"I would like to believe so, because if it's true I will see all my old sweethearts again!"

Father Serda chuckled. Then, he saw a shadow pass over Tiburcio's face and the prisoner withdrew into his own thoughts.

"I have great peace, father," he said after a few moments. "I have lived surrounded by fear for most of my life, and am quite comfortable and familiar with its presence. Fear is absent now."

"Peace in your heart is needed in times like these. I am glad to hear, with you, that it is so. Then I will leave you in private. May I bring you anything?"

"A cigar, some newspapers from the week and a glass of wine, please."

"Certainly," Father Serda agreed

Tiburcio slept until 2:00 a.m., when he rose, smoked the cigar Serda had brought him and drank the glass of wine. He looked for an article about a battle between Mexican rebels and yankee fighters. When he did not find one he felt a small flicker of hope inside. Then he fell asleep again.

Friday morning, the crowds began gathering at sunrise, even before the prisoner had awakened, swelling with each passing hour. The tension in the air was thick. It was going to be a sunny, warm day.

Father Serda came to his cell early, the only visitor permitted. He promised to stay with Tiburcio until the time of the execution.

At 1:30 p.m., Sheriff Adams, his undersheriff, several deputies and three reporters stepped into his cell to read the warrant of execution. Tiburcio showed no expression and declined Father Serda's request to drop to his knees while the warrant was read. In his hands he clutched the two speeches he had written.

After the warrant was read, Tiburcio said quietly, "I am resigned to die. May God have Mercy upon my soul."

With that, the jailer led them into the corridor and the group walked slowly and steadily toward the rear side door and stepped outside into the spring warmth. A large crowd of about four hundred people murmured loudly when they saw the prisoner emerge. As he followed the jailer up the stairs of the gallows, Tiburcio recognized several figures standing solemnly on the scaffold - Morse, Tully, Collins and a half dozen other judicial officers and lawmen. He exchanged a quick glance with Morse. Both tried to surmise in the other's expression whether either had heard any news, any clue as to what might happen in the next few minutes.

Serda and the jailer led Tiburcio to the center of the trap as the other witnesses took their positions behind the prisoner. As Adams' undersheriff tied Tiburcio's hands behind his back, Serda began administering the last rites. Tiburcio's mouth grew into a half smile and he held the appearance of being calmer than any other man on the platform. The undersheriff slipped a white robe over his shoulders and brought the noose down over his head and around his neck, adjusting the thick, heavy, knotted rope. He then held a black cap over Tiburcio's head.

"Just one moment," Tiburcio said, scanning the pale-faced crowd below. He still grasped in his tied hands the paper on which he had written the speeches. Was it time to request a final word?

He turned and struck a questioning glance at Morse, but the undersheriff pulled Tiburcio's head back to face the crowd. Morse took a step forward on the gallows and whispered from behind to Tiburcio:

"I solemnly promise, so help me God, it is all over, Tiburcio. Be at peace."

"Do you see Anita? Is she here?"

"Look in the very back center of the crowd, and a bit to the left."

Tiburcio looked to where the sheriff had indicated and saw the most lovely sight he had ever seen. She wore a long black veil but her eyes radiated through the thin material and her beauty was inescapable, as it had been his whole life. She brought two fingers to her lips, mouthed "I love you" softly, waved gently and turned to walk away.

"Pronto! Pronto!" Tiburcio instructed the executioner, dropping the papers.

Without delay, the black cap was brought over his head and the trap was sprung.

Made in the USA
San Bernardino, CA
30 January 2015